THE PRIME WAY PROGRAM

Caroline George

"I'm proud to praise God. Fearlessly now, I trust in God."

Psalm 56: 10-11 (MSG)

PROLOGUE

Debris coats the windowpane. Smoke fogs the glass, blurring the desolate landscape into a kaleidoscope of gray and black. Emptiness. Even the sky seems to scream with the horror of war: the blood, the death, the constant fear rippling through the streets below. I watch families duck in and out of the dilapidated buildings, searching for food and supplies. I see terror on fathers' faces as they watch their children cower by their mothers' sides. I was meant to protect them; Legion, the world's victor. But the world has been turned into a horrible place where even the brave cower like children when bombs begin to fall and their loved ones begin to die. I couldn't fight even if I tried.

Somewhere outside in the roads of Cleveland, Ohio, a dog begins to bark. It's the first familiar sound I've heard all week, beside the constant wail of sirens and the quake of distant explosions. Just today I've seen three nuclear clouds rise up from the east. I know I should feel something. but I don't. I'm numb. That's more than I can say about the people suffering from burns and radiation poisoning downstairs. Their sobbing echoes through the dimly lit halls of the hospital day and night. Sometimes I wish I were one of them, but my kind is immune to the effects of the Titan's missiles.

"Don't give up. Keep fighting for me, for our people, and for your family. We'll see each other again one day. I love you, Kyle Chase. I love you so much."

I can't escape the memories. Whether my eyes are closed or not, I'm forced to relive the night of the attack. I see and feel everything as if it's happening all over again. It's my punishment for believing I could do something honorable, worthy of being remembered. Instead I created a holocaust.

"I've missed you so much."

There's another explosion outside my window and immediately I remember the moment when Ave Givens was blown to pieces. It's as if I can still feel the heat on my skin as his body was incinerated by the blast of energy; shards of broken armor slicing through the foul air, gore splattering my face. He fought and died for a victory that didn't come.

"Kiss me."

I see Cora lying on the ground with a hole in her chest. I feel her last breath against my cheek and her weight in my arms as I lifted her from the floor of Deven's satellite. My mind replays what few memories were collected after the platform landed. I see myself carrying her into a medical outpost and laying her on a makeshift table while my soldiers rushed back and forth giving aid to the wounded. Then I hear the words that destroyed my life.

"There's nothing we can do. Either she'll heal herself or die, but the chances of her surviving are close to nothing. You need to prepare for the worst, Legion." It was Deirdre that delivered the news. She cleaned Cora as best as she could, clothed her, and gave her to me as if she were ready for burial.

A nurse rushes down the hospital corridor and drops a bag of food in the doorway, only to accompany the others piling up in the threshold. I haven't eaten in over a week, haven't slept, haven't spoken. All I do is stare out the window at the approaching doom or sit protectively by the girl with the braid. Her heartbeat. It's the only sound that doesn't cause pain in my chest.

I turn from the window and face the interior of Cora's resting place. The room has changed since I was last here. The once yellow walls have been painted starch white and the old couch in the corner has been replaced with an uncomfortable cot. An old heart monitor beeps with the subtle evidence of life pulsing from within her chest.

Cora has been left to die in this sterile crypt.

The bed sits in front of me with Cora's frail body tucked away in its sheets. She's extremely thin and unhealthy with pale skin, brittle hair, and wounds that have yet to heal. Stitches cover her chest and stomach. Her lips are chapped and her breathing is shallow. I'd thought that the doctors here would be able to heal her, as they did me. But I was wrong. Medical supplies are nonexistent and a superhuman girl at death's door isn't priority, even if she is the Blue-Jay.

"The sky was blue this morning, Cora." I collapse in the chair beside her bed and reach for her slender hand. It's cold as ice. "The clouds were white for a short time and even the birds sang." I glance down at her sickly face and feel a paralyzing despair spread through my body. Tears can't even come to my eyes. They've been drained. "You're strong. You've always been strong. I need you to get better. We're a team. I'm the sword and you're the arrow."

"Has no one else stopped by?" Matthew's voice catches me by surprise.

I release Cora's palm and look over my shoulder at the Legionary. He's dressed in gray armor and has a nuclear-powered gun strapped to his side. His skin is cluttered with the bruises and scrapes of war. "Truman visited us a few days ago and some of my soldiers came yesterday to pay their respects."

He nods. "You look pretty rough. I brought a shaving kit, some soap, and a fresh change of clothes. It should get you feeling normal again. Better yet, why don't you take a few days and go back to Prime Way, or what's left of it? I can stay and take care of Cora while you get yourself in order." His Australian accent trails on his words.

"I'm staying with her."

"This isn't healthy, Kyle; not eating or sleeping. You're going to kill yourself before the real war starts." For the first time in days, someone calls me by my original name, not 1026 or Legion, just Kyle. It's the name I've almost forgotten.

"Did you come all this way to lecture me about my health? I'm fine."

"No, actually I came to tell you that your family in Dallas is under protection, as well as Michael Stevens. An outpost was built a mile from their homes so in case of emergency, they'll be the first ones evacuated. I thought that might give you some peace." He sets a bouquet of lavender and orchids on the nightstand.

"Thanks." I glance at the bouquet with bewilderment, wondering where he was able to find orchids and lavender in Ohio.

"The flower-shop downstairs was abandoned. Found them in the fridge. Cora has always liked lavender."

"I know."

"I also came to alert you that the Titan's Regiment is advancing west into Sector 5. I need orders, Legion. The world is getting more anxious as the death-rate continues to rise. One country may be under attack now but as soon as Deven's done here, he'll move on to the next landmass. Prime Way needs their leader to lead them before we're all destroyed. Cora would want you to move on and save what remains of us."

"Don't you even care that she's dying, Matthew? Last time I checked, you claimed to love her as much as I do." The words taste bitter as they slip past my lips.

"Of course. It's killing me, but I'm not going to allow her death to be in vain. I must move on before Deven ruins us."

I caress Cora's cheek and focus on the beeping of the heart monitor. She is still breathing. She is alive for now. That's all that matters. "Why didn't you tell me where she was, Matt? You went after her without alerting me first. You betrayed me and now she's dying." The question is one I've been waiting to ask since the night when the War of the Titan began.

"What was I supposed to do?" he stutters. "Once you found her, I knew I'd never have a chance to win her affections. I knew she'd run back to you. I love her too! I didn't expect anyone to get hurt."

"She is dying because of you." The truth begins to sink in. "If you hadn't lied to me, she'd be okay!" I stand and face him with eyes blazing. "This wasn't my fault; it was yours!"

"Wait a second, Kyle…" He takes a step away from me.

"And what were you doing on Deven's airship when Cora was shot?! How'd you get there?!"

"You need to calm down." He grabs my fist and pins me to the wall. "Breathe. You're not seeing things clearly."

"Oh, I see everything perfectly." One punch sends the soldier flying backwards, across the room and onto the fold out cot. I always underestimate my strength.

Matt cautiously climbs to his feet and stares at me with a mixture of fear and pity. "You think you're the only one in the world good enough for her, don't you? It doesn't matter who has feelings for her; you will always be her *other half*. Well I do love her, Kyle, but I'm strong enough to let her go if it means saving our kind." He leans over her body and touches the hole in her chest. Before I can stop him, he fits his lips to hers.

Fury and anxiety explodes from my numb heart as I watch Matthew kiss the girl I love. I lunge at him and rip his face from Cora's. He lashes back and knees me in the stomach. I roar and throw him to the ground. Like two schoolboys, we wrestle on the floor of the hospital room. Tears stream my face. I cringe when blood begins to drip from my nostrils.

It's at this moment when Cora's heart races. The monitor hooked to her wrist starts beeping out of control, like a time bomb on the verge of detonating. I glance at the machine and release my grip on Matthew's arm. He looks at me and I look at him, both with uncertain excitement. Could her body have healed itself? Could she survive? Or is this what happens before someone dies?

Matt rises to her bedside in a trance. "It's impossible."

I jump from the ground with anxious tears in my eyes, waiting, praying, watching for a miracle. To conquer, one must have something to overcome. I need her to overcome death.

"Cora, don't die on me." I lean over her fragile body and stare at her closed eyes. The beating in her chest continues to grow until I'm afraid it'll burst. That's when the strangest thing happens.

Her hand grabs mine.

Part 1—Cora Kingston

CHAPTER 1

Warmth. It covers my body in radiance. Sunlight. Bright ethereal rays, burst from the cloudless sky and wrap the world in clear, halcyon splendor. I laugh and sink my bare feet in the ashen soil. Green sprigs rise from the scorched dirt, budding and spreading across the once dead earth. Alive. Real. A paean to the hope of a better future.

I lift my face to the sun and twirl with my arms outstretched. The skirt of my blue sundress lifts in a balloon of fabric around my legs, ruffling and rippling with the sway of my hips. I'm clean. My skin looks healthy again and my body is no longer starving. Like the plants growing beneath my toes, I've defied the one thing even life has deemed unconquerable.

Rolling hills surround me, dotted with newly planted orchards and gardens. Flowers fog the air with sweet perfume. The ocean sparkles in the distance, a mirage of diamonds and light. This is my home; a distant, nostalgic memory of what my life should be.

"Cora!" he shouts my name from across the field. His lips lift into a blissful smile and his hazel eyes shine the way they did when we first met. Life pulses through his strong body, consuming my scars and skeletal fears. He's what keeps me from falling to pieces, the rope binding my shattered heart. I'm only alive because he exists and I love him with all that's left of my

1

world.

Again he calls my name, those sugary syllables melting off his tongue like candy. His blonde hair wisps lazily in the breeze. His sculpted arms open to let me in.

I run to him and throw myself around his neck, waiting for his strong embrace to consume my body. He lifts me in his arms and spins me around. The world becomes a kaleidoscope; blue, green, swirls of sunshine and dots of flora. Then without guilt, pity, or fear, I kiss him. And he kisses me back.

Beep…beep…beep…

The repetitive noise stirs my subconscious. I hear my heart, slow and steady inside my body, beating and pulsing and living. Pain. It grinds through my frame, tearing through muscles and vaporizing veins. It's unlike anything I've ever felt before. This discomfort is empty, as if someone has stabbed a tube between my breasts and scraped out what little filled my chest. I've been hollowed, the marrow sucked from the depths of my life source. Is it truly gone? Has the muscle that once defined the line between humanity and creation been converted into nothing more than an unresponsive blood-beater?

Beep…beep…beep…

The sound continues. I taste my own saliva in the back of my mouth. It's dry and tepid from lack of hygiene. My eyes sting as they stir behind their heavy lids.

"Wake up, Cora. Death has spared you. Life has given you a second chance," something screams in the back of my brain. I feel the numbness in my limbs sink away, growing fainter until it becomes nothing more than a slight tingle. *"Get up, Blue-Jay! You are brave. You are hope. You can change the world. Love makes you strong. It gives you purpose."*

I breathe. It's the first gust of air to enter my lungs in what seems like an eternity. My fingers press against the rough fabric binding my torso, feeling for the hole in my sternum.

My eyes snap open.

I'm lying in a rickety hospital bed, in a dark room curtained by silence and the odor of antiseptic. I gasp and sit up, glancing in a panic around the empty space. I'm alone.

There is a vase of flowers on the nightstand—lavender and orchids. The petals have long since faded and the once healthy stalks now slump over like corpses. It's the only thing in the room not reeking with disinfectants and morbid thoughts.

Piles of bagged food lie by the door. I can smell the mold growing inside the tightly sealed packages and the rot of unrefrigerated meat. Where has everyone gone? Have I been forgotten, the derelict Blue-Jay waiting for resurrection? Where's Kyle?

I look down at my chest. It's bandaged. Cringing with discomfort but seeping with curiosity, I peel away the piles of cloth. One by one, the layers fall away to reveal the fatal wound that almost stole Kyle's life, the wound that placed my dying body in this empty hospital.

I bite my tongue as my eyes meet the gaping maw; black with dead skin, oozing with old stitches, grinning with the pink tissue of living flesh. The hole plunges through my core. I can feel the emptiness with every movement. This is what Kyle has been feeling for the past year, hollow and heartless. How could he have seemed so alive with a concave so devoid?

I quickly recover the hole, hiding my imperfection and weakness. My stomach churns. Loneliness gnaws at my bravery. Why have I been left alone? Has the world ended? Is this all that remains of civilization?

"Hello? Is anyone there?!" I call towards the dark hall. Silence.

Blinds have been drawn over the single window, keeping the darkness of the world away from my fragile state. A fly buzzes behind the plastic slats, searching for an escape out of this tomb. I lift my legs off the mattress and slowly press them against the cold, tiled floor. How long has it been since I last walked; a week, a month, a year?

Terrified of my surroundings, I cautiously rise to a standing position. My bare legs quake under my weight. My hands grip the walls of the room for support as I waddle towards the window like a toddler learning to walk for the first time. I trip over a cot and almost lose my balance. I glance at the unmade bed and smile to myself. Kyle was here. I can smell the sandalwood from his body-wash on the sheets. He didn't leave me here to die. He couldn't have. Something must have taken him elsewhere.

I reach the window and raise the blinds.

Fog has settled in the debris littered streets outside the building. Abandoned cars fill the parking lot below like carcasses left after a battle. Dead animals blanket the overgrown courtyard; starlings, pigeons, two crows, a stray dog and cat, and a Blue-Jay. Like everything else I've experienced since my awakening, all is silent and empty. What happened here?

I lift the right sleeve of my nightgown and stare at the numbers inked on my bicep. 237—proof Prime Way existed. It confirms my identity but leaves more questions to be answered.

"Is anyone here?!" I shout again, this time with more anxiety. "Please, help me!"

No answer.

I feel the sting of tears in my eyes but quickly brush them away. I can't cry. I won't cry. I must be brave. I am brave. I'm the Blue-Jay.

The rumble of air in the vents catches me by surprise. I gaze up at the ceiling, feeling a sudden breeze of cool, dry air wash over my face. The hospital still has power.

I shuffle over to a phone bolted into the wall and press the receiver to my ear. When I hear the low hum of machinery, I sigh with relief and dial the one number I know will bring help, even if I despise the person helping me.

"Hello," a man answers. Though the voice sends a chill down my spine, I'm grateful for the sound. "Hello? Who is this?"

I fumble for words. "Truman, this is Cora Kingston." My speech is dry and scratchy, bouncing from my weak vocal cords in a raspy tone. "I'm alive. I need help. I think I'm in the same hospital Kyle was sent to when he was shot."

"Oh my goodness…" Truman trails off, leaving me once again in silence.

"Hello? Please, don't hang up on me. I'm alone and still very weak. I doubt I'll be able to find my troops on my own. Please. Help me."

"My dear girl, I'll be there to pick you up within the next three hours. Stay put. Help is on its way. I'll explain everything when I arrive."

"Where's Kyle?" I ask before he cuts the connection. "What happened?"

"He's alive and doing what's required of him. Now stay where you are and wait for my arrival." Truman's end of the line clicks off and I'm left in the dark hospital room with nothing more than a frustrated fly for company.

"Tonight the stars seem overcome, I cannot see the light. Your face

4

no longer fills my eyes; I'm losing all my sight…" Scar's song sings eerily in the back of my skull, reminding me of past events. Deven is still alive. He's preparing an army to destroy the world. Once he finds out I've survived, all hell will break loose.

I've been exhumed to face death again.

I lie on the unmade cot and wrap my skeletal body with the scent of Kyle's warmth. It's the only comfort I feel in the damp chamber, surrounded by dark hallways and empty waiting rooms. The half-heart remaining in my chest thuds repetitively, and I find another tear sliding down my cheek. This time, I don't brush it away.

Part of me wishes I could slip back into my coma and dream of bright things again; Kyle, sunlight, health, the feeling of contentment. Instead I've been revived to stare into a world of darkness and destruction, a world I've begged to forget. *No Feeling. No Regret. Just Strength.* It's the slogan of a deceived world and heartless society. For without feeling and regret, there is no strength. There's nothing to overcome and fight for.

"Katrina, Ave, thousands of your people are dead," my fogged memory tells me. *"Everyone you love will suffer and be destroyed; Cathy, Callan, Sarah, Kyle, Matthew. They will burn and so will you."*

I sob and bury my face in a pillow drenched with Kyle's scent. My mind gives in to exhaustion and I slip away, this time to a place made of windless plains and dusty wastelands, where there is no thought or hope.

I've been lying in silence for a couple of hours when all of a sudden, the door to the room opens. In strides four figures covered from head-to-toe in plastic suits with breathing tubes looped around their heads and protective masks covering their faces, as if they're about to clean a toxic spill of some sort. They stare at me. They grab my arms and heave me off the cot.

I look at them in a state of disillusion, terrified. I open my mouth to scream but all that comes out is air. Confusion is more blinding than darkness.

"Blue-Jay?" A hand touches my shoulder but I flinch and yank away. All masked faces blur into a cloud of voices and quizzical gazes. "What's wrong with her?!"

"She's in shock. The trauma of all this is too much. She's horribly dehydrated and underweight. We need to get her to the aircraft and give her some decent medical care immediately," Truman's voice speaks. "237, you need to come with us. We're going to take you someplace safe. Cora?" He shakes me.

I don't respond. My vision flickers and the numbness returns. I forget how to walk. My legs quiver and give out beneath me. Someone catches my fragile body before I hit the ground and lifts me into their large, muscular arms. This man isn't wearing a suit like the others. He's different.

I'm carried through the dark corridor, down several flights of stairs, and out the swinging, glass doors. A burst of stark, autumn air slaps against my half-naked figure. I glance at the passing ground, gazing with a mixture of sadness and morbid fascination at the piles of feathered carcasses. How did the birds die and why?

"It's going to be okay, Blue-Jay. You're safe now. They told me you were being taken care of. I had no idea that this part of Sector 5 had been evacuated. I promise, you will never be alone again. I'll protect you. I will," my carrier tells me with a thick accent. "You're a living miracle."

My head rolls lazily. My eyes are transfixed on the aircraft parked in the street. It's huge with metal siding and rotating turbines, the same ship my father designed. Surrounded by abandoned vehicles blanketed with grime, the machine seems alien among the apocalyptic landscape.

"She must first be disinfected," Truman says as the entrance to the plane opens. "Radioactivity is still extremely high in these parts and though her body is immune to the effects, I don't want to risk further contamination."

I'm carried through the airship. The glow of florescent lighting flickers off my oily skin. Dry, re-circulated air blows in my face. Everything is white; crisp, clean and impersonal. I look around with unease and cling to the body of my escort. He cradles me and follows Truman down the narrow corridor. I'm small compared to his overly built structure. He towers six-inches above my head, masculine and strong. I know him somehow. His touch is familiar to me.

"Who…are…you?" The words roll off my tongue wearily, a faint tremor in the back of my mouth. "We know…each other?"

"Yes," he replies in a sad tone. "We've known each other since we were kids. Don't you remember me, Blue-Jay? I don't look *that* different."

"I cannot see you. My eyes aren't working right. I'm sorry."

"It's okay. You've been in a coma for a long time, but you'll heal. You always do."

I catch a glimpse of his eyes. They're ice-blue. "Tell me your name. I'll remember your name."

"Matthew." More sugary, familiar syllables.

I smile and allow tears to return to my blood-shot eyes. "How could I forget you, Matt?" I reach up and touch his face. It's covered in stubble and scabs. "You haven't shaved in a while, have you?"

He laughs. It's deep and loud like a clap of thunder. "No, but I'll shave for you." His voice is rich with Australian heritage, no longer the voice I remember. "I'd do anything for you, Cora, anything at all."

"Where's Kyle?"

He pauses. I feel his arms flinch beneath me. "We can talk about him later."

I'm taken to a medical clinic in the back of the plane; a small room with a bed, several IV pumps, and cabinets overflowing with antibiotics and gauze. A nurse wearing white scrubs is waiting for me when I arrive. She smiles a sympathetic smile and motions to the showers located in the clinic's bathroom.

"Can you bathe on your own?" she asks me. "If not, I can help you."

"I'll be fine." I look at the blurry faces around me; tired, anxious, and terrified. My courage is gone and the only thing I want is to be happy again, that smiling girl running through a field towards the boy she loves. Everything I once clung to has been erased with the wind.

"I'll set some clothes by the door." Matt touches my shoulder and this time, I don't pull away.

"Tell me one thing," I say. "How many have died?"

He stares at me, deciding whether or not to relay the truth. "Half of the United States population. Millions perished a year ago when Deven unleashed his nuclear missiles. Everyone else has either died from the Regiment's invasion, starvation, or radiation poisoning."

"I've been dead for a year?" I choke on my own words. Shock vibrates through my limbs. I've lost a year of time; missed a birthday, skipped Christmas. For months I've been out-cold, while the world went to hell. "Are they still alive; Cathy, Scar, Callan...?"

"Yes. They're fine. Cathy and Geode are in California, living with

7

Sarah's parents. Scar, Sarah, and Seth are with Kyle, leading our troops against the Titan. And Callan is still fighting alongside Deven. Don't worry, Blue-Jay. You haven't lost anyone else."

"Not yet." I shuffle slowly towards the showers.

"I'll bring you some food," he calls after me. "And a book or two."

I nod and slip into the bathroom, locking the door shut behind me. Shakily I remove the bandages covering my chest. The wound is still ugly and discolored. I cringe and force myself to look away from the plunging chasm.

"No Feeling. No Regret. Just Strength. This is nothing more than a battle wound, a meaningless scar to add to my collection," I mutter. But no matter how many times I say it, I know it isn't true. There is meaning to my imperfection.

I turn on the shower and glance at my face in the bathroom mirror. I hardly recognize my eighteen-year-old self. My face is pale and gaunt, and my body reeks of sweat. What happened to Cora Kingston? Was she lost playing Deven's game? Now all that's left is a bird-boned creature; frail, wounded, and scared.

Hesitantly, I slide beneath the flow of water. It pounds on my shoulders, soaking my hair and steaming off my flesh. I close my eyes and turn the heat on high. The steam thickens. Water drips into my wound. I disregard the pain and allow my anxieties to be washed away.

Shock. It's what Truman says I'm experiencing. But I don't feel any different. Actually, I don't feel anything at all. Not anymore. From the moment I woke up, everything has felt like a nightmare. None of this is my reality; not the airship, the desolate towns, war, the Titan. It's all some sick daydream my diseased mind has conjured. It's like living in Deven's game.

The floor beneath me shakes as the aircraft experiences turbulence. Bottles of shampoo rattle on their shelf, towels tumble from a set of cabinets, and the water in the toilet swishes back-and-forth. I grip the sides of the shower to steady myself.

"Don't give up. Keep fighting. You're braver than this," Kyle's memory whispers. *"Be strong and courageous. We will not be defeated."*

I lift my chin and allow the torrents of water to fall across my face, masking the effusive tears in my eyes. I clutch the incision between my breasts and sob. Without Kyle, I'm lost. He's the only one capable of piecing me back together.

"I can't do this anymore!" I scream.

The plane dips and throws me against the wall. I bash my head on a tiled corner and sink to the puddle-covered floor. I stare into space, confused and exhausted. My body aches from starvation. My skin stings beneath the boiling rain. *We will not be defeated.*

"Blue-Jay, are you okay in there?!" Matthew knocks on the bathroom door.

I don't answer.

"Cora?!" He jiggles the knob frantically. "Answer me!"

I breathe heavily. My eyelids begin to close. The end has come and this time, I can't save the world. I'm no longer 237. That number is only a mark on my skin. I can no longer claim to be Cora. She died months ago. What am I now as this half-hearted, bag of bones?

It'd be easier to lock away my feelings, to bury them in the back of my soul. It's who I was created to be, numb and emotionless. Love was never meant to be a part of my vocabulary. What used to be a twinge of friendly attachment has grown into an ecstasy of need.

"I'm coming, Cora! I'm coming." Matt slams his body against the panel. I hear the hinges groan under his weight. "Don't move!"

I sink lower until my head is resting on the shower's floor. With every expansion of my lungs, the stitches in my chest stretch. The hole opens and closes like a mouth full of black teeth, grinning at me with pink, healthy flesh. What little remains of my heart belongs to Kyle and I know that what beats in his chest belongs to me as well. We're each other's missing puzzle piece.

The bathroom door is ripped open. Matthew stands in the threshold and gazes at me with crippling panic. He snatches a towel off the floor, steps into the shower, and kneels beside me. He wraps the cloth around my naked figure, conserving my modesty to the best of his ability.

Singeing water beats mercilessly on his back as he lifts me from the floor and cradles me against his wet chest. I sob. My body is limp in his arms. I bury my face in the hot fabric of his shirt and allow him to comfort me.

"I know you're scared. You can be scared with me. I'm strong enough for the both of us," he whispers and combs his hands through my dripping hair. "Everything is going to be alright. You will heal. You will fight. And you will see a happy ending. I swear. We'll get through this."

I nuzzle my head beneath his chin but when I look up; his face isn't the one I'm longing to see. I want his piercing, blue eyes to be replaced with soft hazel. I want his short, brown hair to be replaced with blonde. He will never be Kyle.

"You're so beautiful."

His lustful remark catches me off guard, even if I am only partially conscious. I feel his hand on my leg. He grips my bare thigh, not sensually but protectively. I look at him. He looks at me. His hands move up my towel-covered waist, and rest on my neck. I stare at his mouth in panic as he leans towards me. I can't kiss him. Not again. I don't love him.

Matthew is inches from my lips when he suddenly stops and kisses my forehead. When he pulls away, he frowns at the shock on my face. "You didn't think I'd…take advantage of you, did you? I'm not like that. You know me, Blue-Jay. If I want to kiss you, I'll try to ask first."

Flustered and confused, I scoot away from him and struggle to climb from his lap. I take one step forward and slip. I fall backwards. Everything goes dark.

"She's a strong one, she is." The nurse's voice penetrates my sleep. "A bullet to the heart, starvation, dehydration, a concussion; she survived it all. I wish more people in our country were like her. So many have died already."

"So Cora *will* heal?"

"Of course. She's like you. Her cells will regenerate, her heart will strengthen, and her body will recover from malnourishment."

"Will she be the same?"

"No one's ever the *same*, Matthew. After everything this girl has experienced, it's a miracle she's still sane. No average human being could've survived after seeing what Cora has seen."

A needle pierces my wrist. Something pumps through my veins, reviving my aching limbs. I sigh in my slumber, content with the feeling of comfort. It's as if I can feel the torn tissues of my skin weld together and my blood rehydrated. Even my tongue grows damp again. I'm being fixed from the inside.

Once my eyes have refocused and my brain defogged, I awake from my forced rest.

I'm lying in the medical clinic's single bed; wearing cargo pants and a black, Prime Way t-shirt. My clean hair is braided and my wound has recently been bandaged. A single tube trails from my vein to a clear bag hanging from a rack above my head.

"What'd you give me?" I ask the nurse. She's standing by the door, reading an old *Entertainment Weekly* magazine. I doubt more issues are being printed now that the world has fallen into chaos.

"A drug Stonecipher Incorporated designed to work with your altered-genetics. It stimulates and hurries the healing process," she answers. "I've never seen it take effect so quickly before. When I redressed your wound, took out your stitches, the incision had already scarred-over. You almost look healthy again."

I twist onto my side and slowly rise to a sitting position.

"There's my Blue-Jay!" The twenty-year-old saunters into the clinic with a tray of food. He's changed into a set of armor; thick, metal plating that has been battered and stained with blood. "You look…normal."

"And how did I look before?"

"I'd rather not answer that." He blushes as he sets the tray in my lap. "I made your favorite; Mongolian Stir-Fry with extra bean sprouts, fruit cocktail with all the pear-slices removed, and the darkest chocolate I could find. I even fixed your coffee the way you like."

"You cook?"

"Since I was living alone in DC, I had to learn how to feed myself. Go ahead. Eat."

The moment I taste the food, I almost forgive Matthew for the incident in the shower. The stir-fry melts off my tongue, spicy and warm. My empty stomach devours everything that enters my mouth. I spoon the steaming noodles down my throat, searching the tray for more. I'm starving.

"Whoa, slow down!"

"I haven't eaten real food in a year," I tell him between bites.

"Sure, but I doubt you want any of it to make a reappearance. Just ease up a bit. You're not a pig."

I roll my eyes and slowly chew a mouthful of vegetables. "Better?"

"Yes. Better," he laughs.

I pause and rest my fork on the tray. "Are you ready to tell me now?"

"Tell you what?"

"What's happened? Where's Kyle? Does he even know I'm alive?"

"Lots of questions." Truman appears in the doorway. He's wearing his signature pinstripe suit and has his mousy-brown hair slicked back with gel. "Patience."

"I've been in a coma for a year!" I shout. "I need to know what's happened, what's changed, who's dead and who is still alive. Please. Tell me everything."

"The truth is ugly…"

"I'm strong. I can handle it. I always do."

"The world is not how it used to be," Truman answers grimly. He sits in an empty chair and motions to a map plastered above my bed.

I turn and gaze at the continent with baffled terror. The entire east coast has been painted black, blotted from existence; a severed limb. Webs of ink stretch across the country like an uncontrollable cancer, tangles of death in the midst of abundant life. Red spots are drawn over cities and towns. Blue lines cut the landmass into pieces, dividing the once prosperous nation into a puzzle of quelled vitality.

"It's gone?" I look at the two men, hating the answer in their eyes. "Everything?"

"All that remains is radioactive rubble. There were no survivors. One minute, people were driving home after a long day at work, and then, there were no homes to go to, no traffic to complain about. Nothing. Half of the United States just ceased to exist."

"I saw the missiles launched," Matthew admits. "The blast seemed to ignite the air on fire. I watched as cities were torn apart, people killed, civilization stifled. The Titan's Regiment colonized towns and slowly moved westward out of the Dead Zone and into what was left of America. After a few weeks, they invaded Chicago. Deven has turned the city into his private fortress. He built a concrete wall around the perimeter, either killed or enslaved what few occupants remained, and used the buildings to house his weapons and army. There was nothing Kyle could do to stop him. It was too late."

"We're attacked every day, either by the Regiment's nuclear-missiles, officially titled Erasers, toxic gas, or mutated animals. People are dying and the world is scared. If the Titan conquers us, there will be no hope for this earth. We are being killed by our own mistakes. I should've wiped out the Prime Way Program when I still had the chance."

"No, we're being killed because you allowed fear to corrupt your judgment!" Matt rebuffs. "This invasion is not taking place because people like me exist. It's happening because you imprisoned my kind. All it took was one misanthropic lunatic to offer them an escape. Your prejudice towards difference is what's causing us to crumble."

"We were meant to invade and conquer the world, to take over. Truman's right. We should've been massacred before any of this could happen," I mutter.

Truman shakes his head. "You are not to blame. You're the only thing separating us from extinction." He sighs and glances gloomily at the map. "Kyle said that your race would one day save humankind. He was right."

I stare at the floor and try to make sense of this new world. My errant heart aches with a pain I've never felt before, empty and desperate. Like my country, half of me has been destroyed. Deven caused this pain. He took what once was whole and created a dystopia.

"When Washington DC was vaporized, Marner accepted the role of president. He's turned Salt Lake City into the nation's Capital; now titled Dimidium, which means *half* in Latin. It's a strange place now. Legionaries and humans walk the streets side-by-side, living together, working together. A military base was built outside city limits to separate war-activity from the citizens' daily life," Matthew tells me.

"Is that where we're going?"

He nods. "You'll like it. Out of every place still standing, it's the most normal; movie theaters, restaurants, shops. There is a lot you need to see."

"Will Kyle be there?"

"No. He and his division have dropped off the grid. We haven't seen or heard from them in weeks," Truman says. "But don't worry. They were headed for Sector 9 which is notorious for bad connection. They'll contact us soon."

"And what about me? When will I join my troops?"

"We'll talk about that later. Right now, your focus needs to be on healing." Truman stands and flashes a sincere smile. "The world wouldn't be the same without its Blue-Jay." He turns and walks out the door, leaving me alone in the clinic with Matthew and the friendly-faced nurse.

"Feel like showing me around?" I rise from the mattress and remove the needle from my arm.

"We can do that later. You need to rest."

"I've been resting for months." I lace up my boots and move towards the exit. "Come on."

"Fine, but then you're coming back to this room and getting more medical care. I'm not losing you again." His demeanor suddenly changes from the highly ranked soldier he's become to the boy I remember training with all those years ago, when we were still children playing a game we thought was fun.

As we leave the clinic, I glance over my shoulder at the reconfigured map. Those zigzagging lines, ink blots, and red circles. They all seem like the unspoken skeleton, the corpse of what once thrived. I don't want to forget the past. History is the only thing separating the world from a relapse.

I follow Matthew down the narrow corridor, this time on my own two feet. The floor trembles. Lights flicker. He smiles at me with that electric grin that once made me want to erupt into flames and turn to liquid at the same time. But even *it* has lost its warmth.

"I'll show you the control center. It's my favorite room in the hovercraft, lots of machines and people." He turns down another hallway. "The world has finally embraced us and our technology."

"I would've rather been left invisible than be the cause of destruction," I say. "We aren't like them, Matt; no matter what they say. We're not…human anymore. Our blood is different. *We* are different. Just look at me! I've been shot, starved, poisoned; and I haven't died! Why is that? Why do I keep escaping death when so many people are dying around me?"

He doesn't answer and walks in silence until we reach the entrance to the control center. With a relieved look on his weary face, he opens the door. "Welcome to the new world, Blue-Jay."

The room is larger than I would have imagined, with high ceilings and windows overlooking a magenta sunset. Projected screens cover the walls, flickering with icons and symbols. Men and women are seated at metallic workspaces with their hands sweeping across the holographic images, typing codes and drawing lines with their adroit fingers.

I glance down at the ground, almost suffocating by my own

astonishment. The floor is glass. Clouds hang suspended beneath my feet, golden with the sun's final beams. Swirls of green landscape mix with the florescent hues of the sky. For the first time in months, the world looks beautiful. It's not dark and corrupted. It's perfect.

I sink to my knees, wanting desperately to feel alive again, to be with Kyle. My world is black. It's empty and dark. But with him, everything is a sunrise. We're stronger together.

"So hold me close, my dear so sweet. And keep me safe from fear. I need you now more than ever before…

"Danger seems so near."

CHAPTER 2

Divided. It's the first thing I notice about America's new Capital; not the snow-capped mountains on the horizon or the hum of car engines, but the concrete wall rising from the earth. It towers two-hundred-feet in the air, severing old shopping complexes and cutting through once busy intersections. Like a python, it traps what remains of Salt Lake City in its slithery embrace. Why was it built? To keep its inhabitants safe? Or to stifle the fear of the outside world, where everything is a matter of life or death?

"This wasn't what you were expecting, was it?" Matthew asks as we walk through the urban war-camp. Fire crackles in rusty trash cans. Soldiers, man and program, jog through the streets with glowing weapons strapped to their backs.

"I didn't think we'd be stationed in the suburbs, if that's what you mean?" I step over a broken mailbox and make my way across a weed-infested lawn. The cul-de-sac may be seaming with war-activity, but it feels empty and dark. I look at the houses around me, expecting to hear the laugher of children from the neighborhood playground or see the ghosts of Mr. and Mrs. Jones grilling burgers on their patio. But I don't. The grill is cold and the only things playing are the memories of a lost civilization. Everyone has been evacuated, embraced by the protective barriers of Dimidium. Now all that remains are the remnants of a once prosperous society.

"This place isn't *that* bad. We have running water, electricity, comfortable housing, plenty of food, and enough vacant territory to conduct military exercises. Marner has equipped us with everything we'll need to protect the country."

"Or what remains of it," I mumble as an airship flies overhead. The turbines shimmer with a blue hue as the machine disappears into the sea of clouds.

"Most soldiers look forward to coming back after an excursion. The world has changed, Blue-Jay. There are few places like this still on the map." He smiles and salutes a Legionary unloading provisions from an old postal van. "Dimidium keeps life as normal as possible. People have jobs, schools for their children, entertainment, and a stable government. It's a rarity nowadays."

"They won't be stable for long. Deven is invading. He's wiping us out."

"Not yet. Our job now is to contain chaos, to protect what few strongholds we still have. Kyle is driving the Regiment east, back into the Dead Zone. His troops are keeping us safe. Besides, more teenagers are volunteering to be programmed. The adult soldiers would too if their genetic-makeup were pliable. Our army is growing, Cora. We're becoming stronger. Soon, programs will become the majority. No more hiding...ever."

We're like weeds, overgrowing and suffocating the life out of humanity. Could something like us truly be the world's greatest salvation and downfall?

I remember spring in Maine and how all the dorms were infested with ladybugs, but not the red ones Katrina loved to paint. These were orange. They crawled arrantly through the vents and clung to our windowsill. They scattered the floor, adhered to the walls, and squeezed their round bodies into the light fixtures. I hated them and overtime, I saw fewer of the original insects. Then one spring, I didn't see any. The foreigner, the genetically-altered became the majority. All traces of the authentic race vanished. God created man with human strength and senses. I am what occurs when science oversteps its bounds.

"We'll stay within the Capital tonight." Matthew's voice pulls me from my reverie. "Truman will meet us at Counsel Hill, where Marner's office is located."

"We are going *into* the city?"

"Of course," he snickers. "It's not like we're freaks now. Look around. Do you see a division? Skin color, blood, genetics—none of it matters! We're working together to survive and conquer."

I glance at a crowd of soldiers warming their hands by a fire. They laugh amongst themselves; man to teenager, red to orange, authentic to foreigner. Matthew is right. The world has changed.

"Come on. You still have a lot to see."

I stroll down the monochrome avenue with Matthew by my side. He rambles on about the building of Dimidium, but I hardly pay any attention. Everything in sight is so similar to life at Prime Way. The human part of my brain hates it, but the other half bubbles over with excitement.

Recruits of all races and blood types salute me as I pass. Some smile. Others nod with approval. I stare at them in utter confusion, partially shocked by their recognition. Could the Blue-Jay still have merit in this age of time?

We leave the bustle of the neighborhood war-camp and move towards the main road. I watch the scenery change from apocalyptic suburbia to urban decay. Trees and overgrown flowerbeds are replaced with rubble and deserted roads. The moment our feet leave the perimeter of the subdivision, we are immediately submersed in eerie silence. Here there are no faces, no clamor of armor, nothing.

"A scout from the city is coming to pick us up," Matt tells me. He tucks his hands in his pockets and curiously observes me with his electric-eyes. "You're not still mad at me, are you?"

"No." I lift my face to the sky, watching the silvery clouds roll across the horizon. Shapes form. Lines zigzag across the blue etch-a-sketch. For the first time since my awakening, I breathe.

The rumble of an engine meets my ears. It's the only sound to be heard among the towers of mangled buildings and vacant streets. I squint my eyes against the glare of the sun, spotting a jeep in the distance. The driver is clad in the same uniform armor as my troops wear and is carrying an electric spear. The tip sparkles with energy the closer the vehicle approaches.

"Byron, what took you so long?!" Matthew yells as the Legionary pulls to a stop in front of us. "I was beginning to think that I'd have to *walk* to Dimidium's gates!"

"There was traffic," he answers sarcastically. When his dexterous eyes find mine, a star-crazed grin spreads across his suntanned face. "Hi...I'm Byron. You're Cora, right? I've seen pictures of you around town. They do not do you justice. You're *really* hot." His heart races. I can hear it pounding in his chest. "Legion has told me so much about you!"

"Are you seriously flirting with your commanding officer?" Matthew scoffs. "You'll address her as Brigadier General."

Byron's russet skin turns to ash. He fumbles for an apology. "I'm sorry...uh...Brigadier." Already sweat is beginning to glisten on his shaven head.

"It's fine. I definitely do not need another title to add to my list of names. Please, call me Cora or Blue-Jay or 237. I'm not above you."

His stress melts away and is replaced with a soft glow of admiration. He smiles. "Legion said I would like you."

"You know Kyle?" I lean forward to hear his response with hands shaking. "Where is he? When'd you last see him? Is he alright? Please. Tell me."

"He trained me before the attack. I was in his special division until I was hit with a chunk of exploded airship." Byron turns his head to show me the scar on the back of his skull. It's disfigured and fairly fresh. "I was sent here to recover while Legion traveled to Sector 9. Don't worry. He'll be back."

Matthew checks his watch and frowns. "We better get moving. Dimidium's gates will be closing soon and I don't want to be left out here after dark. A few of the Titan's Injections roam these parts."

I climb into the backseat of the jeep, still trembling at the mention of Kyle's name. He is alive. He is fighting. And he will come back to me. No matter what bad news I hear today, those few words have broken through my darkness.

"He loves you, doesn't he? And you love him?"

I glance up, catching Byron's gaze in the rearview mirror. I imagine Kyle's eyes staring back at me, those hazel pupils overflowing with life. I used to take them for granted, abused the privilege of looking at his face and hearing his voice. Now I understand what longing feels like. It's a rupturing chasm of anxiety; wanting to touch him, to laugh with him, to be the girl I was with him. Now he's gone and the world we once faced together has changed into a hellhole of radiation and death. But even now, when everything falls apart, I find myself admitting to the greatest weakness of all. "Yes. I do."

Matthew cringes and the handle bolted into the jeep's ceiling snaps in half. He holds the broken pieces in his hands with a mixture of embarrassment and guilt, as if he'd just crushed a baby bird. "Byron, I think you may want to have Management lease you another vehicle. This one is falling apart."

I stifle the laughter building in my throat and quickly hide my smile from view. It's easy to do. Joy seems rude among the morbid landscape, like giggling at a loved-one's funeral.

"I don't think my jeep is the problem," Byron says. He cranks the ignition and speeds away from the curb. I watch the subdivision fade into the distance, along with the playing memories and nostalgic ghosts. They are scars to the nation.

The tires of the Capital's vehicle bounce over potholes and debris, weaving through dead traffic and driving by stop-signs. I lean my head out the open window to feel the cold, Utah air on my cheeks. It numbs my face instantly.

"How far is the city from here?" I ask as we pass an old shopping-mall. It's deserted. The parking lot is empty and the motion-activated doors open and close aimlessly. All that once mattered to the world is lost; wealth, popularity, the next fashion trend. How shallow and superficial has humanity become? Instead of caring about each other, we chose to place our trust in fleeting and transient habits. Are Deven's psychotic philosophies all targeting the corruption of mankind? Did my father create us with the purpose to reprogram society, to form a terra nova?

"You'll be able to see the wall once we reach the interstate. Dimidium is only a few miles downtown," Matt tells me.

We pass vacant schools, churches, and office-complexes. Their once welcoming thresholds have turned truculent and menacing. A chill shoots down my spine when I notice a pair of yellow eyes gazing at me from the dark window of a nail salon. An Injection; the Titan's blood-thirsty scavengers, the beasts that terrorized me for months in Deven's game.

"I am dauntless. The girl with the braid is not afraid. Nothing shall put me down," I repeat in my head. *"Be the Victor, not the Victim."*

"Keep driving. They won't attack unless we seem vulnerable."

My heart races, pounding beneath its stitches like a marching-band. I close my eyes until we have driven out of the suburbs. *This is all a game. Deven wants me to lose.*

More desolate streets appear as we reach the interstate. The once busy intersection is as silent and barren as a depleted airstrip. Several abandoned cars are stacked in the median. Bags of decaying garbage are piled by the curb. Silence. Emptiness.

"Look ahead, Blue-Jay." Matthew points to the horizon. "See what you and Kyle have done."

Mountains loom in the distance like sharp teeth ready to devour all who dare to approach them. A godforsaken cityscape stretches before me, towers of brick and skeletons of metal. Then I see the wall. It rises from the earth, a fortress of rock and iron surrounding the main district of Salt Lake City. Peaks of skyscrapers peer hesitantly over the barrier's rim. Airships hover above the settlement, blazing with lights and technology. Dimidium.

I sit in silence and watch as the wall grows closer. We drive through the outer rim of the city, past a vacuous homeless-shelter and several exhausted businesses. Sound bellows from inside the fortress—car horns, laughter, and the hum of electricity. I've arrived at civilization.

"Welcome to the new world!" I remember Matthew's words. *"No more hiding."* It's like telling me not to breathe. I'm not myself anymore. I've lost too much, been shattered into a million pieces. But just because I'm broken, doesn't mean I'm unfixable. I only need to find the rope that holds me together.

"Everyone is very strict about security around here. They'll do an eye-scan and some other crazy stuff. Don't be scared. It's only protocol," Byron says. His wound gazes back at me like an eye on the back of his head.

"I'm not scared of anything."

Matthew smiles. His white teeth flash beneath his stubble-covered cheeks. I know what he wants to say, *"Oh there's the old, intrepid Cora."*

Bravery isn't for the fearless. It's for the daunted times of life when you have the choice to either conquer your insecurities or allow them to defeat you. I will not be defeated.

A gate to Dimidium appears at the end of the interstate, a rectangular opening in the concrete barrier. The words *'Nos superfuerant eam omnia'* are engraved above the threshold, along with a graffiti drawing of *the sword and the arrow*. *'We survived it all'*, in Latin.

Soldiers wearing white uniforms and Plexiglas helmets are stationed at the small outpost with guns ready. Others patrol the ridge of the wall, watching for the risk of a possible attack. They recognize the jeep and immediately ready themselves for the mandatory security procedure.

"This gate isn't as tough about newcomers," Matthew tells me as Byron pulls to a halt in front of the guards. "Just go with it."

"Numbers 1889 and 226, returning with 237. I'd hurry and let us in. The Blue-Jay has a meeting with President Marner she has to get to." Byron musters a pleading smile. "Come on, Davis and Carter. You know Matt and me. Open the door."

One of the Legionaries laughs. "You know the drill, man. Lift your sleeve."

Byron rolls his eyes and unclasps the armor covering his right bicep. They hold a scan to the numbers, tracing and deciphering the ID chip programmed into his skin. A green light flashes. He's been identified as a citizen of Dimidium. "Took you long enough."

The guards complete the same procedure with Matt before turning their attention to me.

"Arm please."

I roll up the sleeve of my shirt and allow him to press the scan to my tattoo. It flashes. The laser-beams comb across my skin, reading the black ink as if decoding my DNA. Once my identity has been confirmed, the soldier smiles and types something quickly on his keypad.

"Welcome to the Capital, General Kingston." He bashfully lifts a strange device to my face. "If you don't mind, I need an eye-print before entry. It'll help Management set all the locks to your living quarters and such. Another identification detail."

I nod and fit the machine to my eyes. I stare into what seems like nothingness. Then, there's light. It spreads through my pupils, engraving the print of my stare into its database.

"What if we could have chosen our fate? Would you be who you are today?" Kyle's voice rings through the soft tissues of my brain. *"Time to set selfishness aside. Forget about me for now. There is a difference*

between bravery and courage. Bravery is facing your fears. Courage is doing so with integrity. Have integrity, Cora, and never forget who you were born to be."

"I could never forget." I feel tears in my eyes and quickly pull away from the machine. The young Legionary looks at me curiously, baffled by my reaction.

"Let them in!" He motions to a pair of soldiers perched at the top of the wall. Slowly the gate doors open, allowing us passage into Dimidium. "Enjoy your stay, Cora."

The jeep's engine roars to life. Byron waves at the guards and drives us through the opening and into the city. I breathe heavily and cling to the hole in my chest. It aches. Why must I be fragile? In a world where teenagers run faster than animals and are stronger than machines, shouldn't my body be indestructible? It's a detail my father must have overlooked when brainstorming our design.

Matthew turns in his seat and smiles at me. "Cora, you're in Dimidium." His deep, Australian voice is overflowing with childish excitement, as if he's just revealed the puppy hidden in his parents' garage. "You're going to love it here!"

I focus my gaze on the floorboard, afraid to face my surroundings. If I look up, I'm consenting to reality. There will be no going back. My vision of the world will change. "Has Kyle seen this place?"

"Of course. He stayed here for two-months before traveling to Sector 9."

I sigh and slowly lift my face. When my eyes meet the metropolitan landscape, I gasp. Towers of glittering glass arise on either side of the road, skyscrapers of mirrors and structures shimmering with lights. Huge mega-screens are mounted on the sides of buildings, flickering with high-resolution images. A picture of Kyle and me flashes onto the electric billboard with the caption—Join the Movement. I almost giggle at the sight of us, both dressed in white with a soft smile on our lips. *The sword and the arrow.* Even more than the Blue-Jay, the simple icon has become a symbol of united hope.

People swarm the streets, stopping at crosswalks and breezing through alleyways. I notice a teacher waiting on the curb with her class of children. They all hold onto a yellow rope with smiles riddled across their innocent faces. Are they going on a field trip even in this dark time?

"How many people live here?" I gawk at the city, marveling at the height and splendor of the skyscrapers. Cars drive past us. Others seem to hover. Truman was right. Kyle and I updated the nation into a new age, where our technology is embraced, not persecuted. We were the missing link.

"Three-hundred-thousand," Matthew answers. "We receive more refugees every day."

I smile to myself and stare out at the population of humans and Legionaries. They mesh together like the weaves of a basket, or a braid; different but at the same time so alike.

"Look, it's the Blue-Jay!" The schoolchildren squeal with glee as we stop at a red-light across from them. They shout my name and salute me with small hands. Even the teacher beams with excitement. "Blue-Jay, will you sign my shirt?! Would you take a picture with us?! Blue-Jay?!"

I wave at the crowd. Other pedestrians pause and stare at me wide-eyed. They know who I am and yet they're not running away.

"I'll get us out of here. I doubt you want to sign autographs." The moment the light turns green, Byron presses the accelerator and the jeep lurches forward. "We're not far from Counsel Hill. If I had a hovercraft, I could get you there in minutes; but Management says I'm not *qualified* to own one."

I look at the airships drifting above the city. Pixel images flash across their glass floors, showing pictures of Kyle's army battling the Regiment. I notice a man standing by the road with a transparent keypad. It glows as he glides his fingers across the holographic surface, moving icons and typing words. "These are my father's inventions."

"Yes. We recovered some of his research after a raid on one of the Titan's outposts. Marner collaborated with Stonecipher Incorporated to produce what you see here. Practically everything has been revolutionized: transportation, security, agriculture. We're almost as advanced as the Titan. Soon, we may actually be able to put up a decent fight."

It's as if I've walked into another dimension, a world where the Blue-Jay thrives and *the sword and the arrow* are victorious. The wall is the illusion. Marner has created a haven from Deven's wrath, tricking its occupants to believe in safety. We are not safe.

The sky has turned a purple hue by the time we reach Counsel Hill.

It's the largest skyscraper of them all, built in the center of Dimidium. It climaxes into the twilight sky with lights ablaze. Windows shimmer with the colors of the horizon. The steel structure stands against the scenic canvas, more intimidating than the distant mountains. A tribute to progress.

Byron stops the jeep in front of the building. "It was nice meeting you, Cora." He grins back at me with a collage of sympathy and affinity. "If I see Legion before you do, I'll tell him about today."

"Take care of yourself, Byron."

"I'll try but you know how wars go. Each day could be your last."

"Then why do it?"

He shrugs. "You're someone worth fighting for."

His answer sends a piercing pain through my chest. It's what Kyle told me a year ago, when the world was still oblivious to our existence and Deven was nothing but a conniving science-experiment. Now people die for *the sword and the arrow*. They die pursuing hope, a glimmer of light on the distant horizon. They die for me; whether I am dead or alive. The guilt is unbearable.

"You can't save everyone, Cora." Again Kyle's voice penetrates my thoughts. *"It's a scar we'll have to bear until the end of time."*

"My body is made more of scars than flesh and blood."

Matthew climbs out of the jeep and walks towards the entrance of Counsel Hill. "Are you coming?"

I nod and follow him inside the building, crippled by the emptiness in my thoracic-cavity. Fear drips through my arteries and veins. They shall not defeat me. I must conquer the daunted.

The lobby of the tower is as extravagant as the exterior. Metallic light fixtures hang from the high ceilings. Expensive paintings adorn the stone-gray walls. Stiff, plastic furniture crowd the many waiting rooms and work spaces. I gaze around the room, astounded by the glamorous architecture. People stroll past me with scowls on their faces and ties wrapped painfully around their necks. Clicks of heels echo across the marble floor, mixed with the squeaks from mine and Matthew's boots.

"What is this place?" I spin in circles, feeling microscopic among the stern grandeur of the building. Legionaries ride up and down the escalators. Adults hurry across the lobby with beads of sweat on their brow. I even notice a couple sitting erotically on an overstuffed sofa, casting flirtatious looks and whispering things that cause them to giggle.

"This is America's control center. Everything is based in this building—our military, Truman's operations, Management, the City Council, Stonecipher Incorporated, Marner and his employees. It's all here. We're standing in our nation's remaining stronghold."

"You really believe in this place?"

"Don't you?"

"I don't know what I believe anymore." I sigh and watch the couple in the waiting room enviously. "Why are we here? What does Marner want with me?"

"There's only one way to find out." He points to the security checkpoint separating the lobby from the rest of the building. "Hold your head high. It makes you seem taller than everyone else."

"I'm not a kid anymore, Matt."

"No. I guess not. The young Cora was savage and fierce, with pouty brown eyes and crooked teeth. You're much stronger than the girl I used to know, and beautiful." He smiles. "What am I going to do without my Blue-Jay?"

"Find a new one."

My blunt response catches him off guard. He stares at me with a hurt expression on his handsome face. I almost feel guilty for smothering his complement, but I've reached my breaking point.

"That was cruel," Kyle's memory scolds. *"You mean a lot to him."*

I shake away the voice and move hastily towards security where two guards in white uniforms are waiting. Matthew follows. He allows one of the officers to scan his tattoo.

"Name please."

I stare into the masked faces of the soldiers, angry at Matthew and his love for the Capital. "Brigadier General Cora Kingston, number 237." Intensity shoots through my body, awakening the programming buried deep within me. Buzzing fills my ears. My senses enhance. A flood of unnatural serenity washes through my brain, cleansing my thoughts of control. I don't want to fight it. I'm stronger when I embrace my creation. It's less painful. No Feeling. No Regret.

"We have a meeting with President Marner," Matt tells the human. "Charles Truman is waiting for us on Level 10."

"You've been granted admittance, 226." The guard types something on his transparent keypad and inspects me with a scowl on his thin lips. "I'll need to complete a few identity tests to give you clearance, General."

"What are you going to do? Test my DNA, scan my scars, and check my eye-print again?"

"If it comes to that."

I open my mouth to rebuke the man, but Matthew plants his hand firmly on my shoulder.

"Stop. This isn't the place to pick a fight. We're their guests. Be respectful," he whispers in my ear. "Do what they say and everything will be fine."

I glare at him and roll up my sleeve. The soldier scans my numbers, identifies my eye-print, and keys dozens of codes into his holographic tablet. They're trying to decide the same thing I am. Is 237 a threat or an asset?

"I need you, Kyle! Where are you?!" I scream into the darkness of my mind. The pain in my chest is agonizing. I claw at the wound with my fingernails, secretly hoping to tear through the source of discomfort. It doesn't stop.

"Give me your hand." The guard grabs my arm roughly and jerks me towards him.

Instinctive, I cringe and throw my knee into his stomach. My body is seized with electricity as the programming takes effect. I lose all control. My fists slam against approaching officers, knocking them helplessly to the ground. Legionaries rush towards me with guns aimed, but I maneuver myself out of their grasp. My vision dilates and refocuses so that everything is magnified. I can see the pores on the Counsel Hill's secretary's chin and the spit glistening off the couple's lips. Heartbeats all around me. Heavy breathing. Screams.

Time seems to slow as I move. I run like lightning, leaping over shoulders and ducking beneath legs. For a brief second, I don't feel anything. I'm weightless, invincible, and painless. Nothing hurts. Even when the surrounding soldiers close in on me and begin firing bullets at my broken body, I stay clear of mind. It's an exhilarating feeling to know that even as battered as I am, I'm still powerful.

"Stop it, Cora! This isn't you!"

"I refuse to fight my design." I close my eyes and allow altered-

genetics to consume what little humanity remains in me. This is my identity.

As if unlocking a vault in the back of my brain, images and emotions I had forgotten rush through my clear head, drawing away the thrill of the programming.

I see myself driving Aunt Jen's old station-wagon, laughing and singing to a song on the radio. The windows have been rolled down, allowing the warm California breeze to turn my loose hair into a whirlwind of brown tangles. Kyle is sitting in the passenger seat, smiling and scrolling through the music on my iPod. His blonde hair is unruly and his eyes are hidden beneath a pair of my turquoise sunglasses. With a press of his finger, 'Surfing USA' by the Beach Boys blares through the speakers.

He snickers and sings at the top of his lungs. "If everybody had an ocean, across the U.S.A. Then everybody'd be surfin', like californ-I-A..."

"That was horrible!" I shout over the roar of music.

"Why don't you give it a try?"

The both of us laugh as I begin singing. Our voices carry across the highway and over the beaches of Santa Barbara. Glares are cast. Obscenities are yelled as we drive by. Kyle shouts and throws his head back with a crooked grin on his face. Summer has never felt so warm.

"I bet I could outrun this thing," he says and clings to my hand. His touch fills me with life and a sense of normality. It's addicting. "I'm serious."

"Yeah, right?!"

"We'll have to find out one day."

"Sure...one day." I look at him, having a sudden desire to lean over and kiss his smile. Our hair beats against our faces and the blaring music drowns the whistle of wind. But even among the perfect commotion, I hear his thoughts so clearly it's as if he's screaming them in my ears.

'I love you for who you are; the good and the bad. There is beauty in your imperfection.' His boyish smile and gentle eyes meet mine. Tall and built as he is, there's a kindness about him

that reveals his originality. 'You make me stronger.'
   "Sing to me again. I like your wailing."
   He smirks and begins singing the last few verses of the song.
"All over La Jolla, at Waiamea Bay. Everybody's gone surfin',
surfin' U.S.A..."

My reverie is ruined by the yank of arms around my waist. I scream, feeling my chest tear apart. Blood pours from my wound and immediately soaks my shirt. I'm shoved to the marble floor of Counsel Hill's lobby with the barrel of a glowing gun pressed to my back. I glance around the room with tears in my eyes, sad that the programming has lost its buzz.

Matt grabs my exhausted figure and pulls me from the ground. He shouts at the soldiers around us to back away and get a medic, but they stand steadfast with terrified expressions engraved on their faces. "She's unstable! Her body is still suffering from exhaustion and trauma! Please, help her!"

Medics rush to my side. They spray an adhesive to my wound, instantly welding the gaping hole together. An intense pain ripples through my torso.

"You heard the man! Back off and give the young lady some room!" Truman appears in the mob of artillery with an imperturbable look in his puffy eyes. "President Marner does not appreciate tardiness or disruptors of the peace."

"I'm sorry," I mutter sincerely. "It's my fault."

"Of course it's *your* fault! I didn't see anyone else terrorizing my employees." He shakes his head and clips a silver box to my belt. Without leaving time for questions, he inserts a needle into my wrist and attaches a tube from the box to my vein. "Take all the medication from this treatment. I do not want to risk another programming mishap because of your health and mental sanity. Now let's go. We can bleach out that blood-stain later."

The soldiers stare at us warily, some with their weapons still aimed. I don't blame them. It's my fault I'm weak of mind and body, unable to control my urge to conform. I just want to feel something that's worthy of being felt. Even if I have to fully relent to my genetics to experience the rush of lost memories, I will gladly do it. A kiss from Kyle or a hug from my dead parents is worth turning back into a monster.

"You're going to be okay, Blue-Jay." Matt wraps his sculpted arm around my shoulders and supports me as we follow Truman towards the escalator. "Allow your body to rest. You're safe here."

"What if I hurt someone?"

"You won't. Once you heal, everything will be back to normal." He's lying. Nothing will ever return to the way it used to be.

I'm in a daze as the two men lead me up several flights of stairs, down sumptuously furnished hallways, and through another lobby. Secretaries are seated at glass desks, typing feverishly on their futuristic laptops. Is that what this is, the future?

Truman stops and speaks briefly with a guard stationed in front of a large, oak door. He glances back at us and forces a smile. "President Marner is ready to see you now, Cora."

I unravel myself from Matthew's embrace and attempt to retain my composure. I re-braid my hair, button my jacket to conceal the blood-stain, and breathe until my brain is fully alert. I cannot appear weak. I am representing my race. "I'm ready. Let's do this."

Truman nods and opens the door.

A sudden gust of perdition explodes through my body as I walk into the president's office. I look down at my chest. "Keep yourself together," I tell my heart, begging the pain to stop.

"Good afternoon, General Kingston."

The voice punctures my confidence. I lift my head to face the man who wanted my people locked away, saw us as monsters; inhuman and without rights. I expect to feel hatred towards him, but I don't. This is my chance to win his respect. As much as I want to spit in his dark-skinned face, the thirst for acceptance drives away the urge for revenge.

Holographic screens hover above Marner's desk, flickering with faces and maps. The walls across from me are glass, overlooking Dimidium and the deserted landscape beyond. Airships float past the windows like silver clouds, shimmering in the sunset. I'd say that the office is breathtaking if it weren't for the man seated before me. His displeased grimace is hidden beneath his black goatee. His stormy eyes burrow into mine like a pair of freshly sharpened daggers.

I stand in the center of the room and force my fiery tongue into temperance. Angst bubbles in my stomach like acid, chewing and grinding at my patience. Our feelings are mutual.

"It's good to see you again, alive and well. Apparently you've regained your strength considering your little exhibition downstairs." His pretentious tone echoes through the room. He types something on his computer and the screens vanish, fading into oblivion. "My people had already begun mourning your death."

"Well, I'm glad I was able to spare them from more sadness." I hold my head high, trying to speak as Kyle would. He always knew how to talk to authority. Not me. I normally say things that end in disaster. "Congratulations with your presidency, Sir. I know you'll do your absolute best to protect this country."

"No insults? I was certain you'd be difficult with our...negotiations."

"Times have changed. If you're willing to see my race as equal and promise our freedom after the war, I'll cooperate."

"You're willing to agree to an armistice?" He leans back in his chair, searching my expressions for humor or dishonestly. "237, the little programmed smart-mouth who terrorized my last year as Director of the CIA, wants a truce? That's a little out of character, don't you think? But since I need your support, I'll accept your terms."

"Why am I here?" I ask with an austere voice. "I should be with my troops but instead, Truman and Matthew insisted that I come to this place. Why?"

"There are some things we need to discuss. My people look up to you. Your face has inspired hope for a brighter future. So no matter how reluctant I am to admit, we're equals now in power and rank."

His paradox makes me want to laugh, but I refrain.

"This city is all that remains of prosperous America. Of course it has been revised to the world's new standards, thanks to the work of your father. We have jobs, transportation, technology, electricity, and an abundant supply of food and water. Besides the nightly curfew and security procedures, we've been able to erase the effects of war from our citizens' lives." Marner plucks a peppermint from a bowl on his desk and pops it into his mouth. "Those surviving in Sectors beyond Dimidium are living through hell. Our armies do what they can to help but I'm afraid that things are past repair. Outbreaks of panic have swept across the country. People are either dying by the Titan's hand or their own. So if violence and starvation isn't enough to condemn this nation, the radiation in our atmosphere is. Half of our boundaries are unusable because of the

31

bombing's aftermath."

"What about Kyle? Have you been able to locate him?"

"Not yet. He was headed into Sector 9 which is a potential Dead Zone. The radiation levels are insanely high which means that the people still living there are dying from radiation poisoning and other unpleasant ailments. Dimidium's satellites and communication devices are useless in that district."

"Why would you have allowed him to go there?!" I ask. Even the medication being pumped through my veins does little to ease the discomfort in my chest.

"That's how you differ from him. Legion does what is right, even if it means risking his own life. The day he arrived at the Capital, he came to me while my troops were preparing for an attack on one of the Titan's outposts. He said, *'Our job now is to contain the virus and heal those infected, not risk more innocent lives. We give aid. We drive Deven's army into the Dead Zone. And once the country has reached some stability, we strike the Regiment'*. That's actually what he's doing now in Sector 9, giving aid to those suffering from radiation poisoning, starvation, and improper living conditions. He is a hero and a natural born leader. Everyone, including his troops, loves him." Marner leans back in his chair and gazes at me in silence. His dark physique is a silhouette against the colorful cityscape. "You, Cora, are unlike him in every way."

"Why do you want me here then?!" I blurt out. "If I am so inadequate, why bring me inside your city? You could have easily left me to die in that hospital. Why didn't you?"

He responds simply by saying, "I made a promise."

"So what now? When can I rejoin Kyle? I need to be useful."

"Oh you will be." The president presses a button on his desktop. The door to the office opens and Truman and Matthew stride in, both with timidity engraved on their faces, as if they know some dark secret that will trigger my enhanced fury.

"James Stonecipher has arrived, Mr. President. He's ready for his first session with 237."

"He what?!" I turn to Marner. All eloquence flees my mouth as my tongue catches fire. "What is Stonecipher doing here? Shouldn't he be in a bar somewhere or lurking in his desert fortress?"

"He lives in Dimidium now. Since his company is reviving our society, it only seems fair to permit his occupancy."

"You allowed that perverted pyromaniac into your city! What, do you want the world to…explode?! And what did Truman mean by *a session*? If that man is even allowed in the same room as me, I'll probably tear his head off!"

"Pipe down, 237. Though we may be equals, I have jurisdiction here. There are rules you must abide by, protocol you're required to follow." President Marner glances out the window at the sinking sun. His pupils ignite with the horizon's hue, giving his cold face an ethereal touch. He is an embodiment of this new world; numb, adaptable, fake, as deceiving as a newborn viper. All seems harmless until he sinks his fangs into your flesh.

"Damn all of you! I am not your Blue-Jay, General, or any other title you concoct to claim me! There is only one reason why I'm fighting and it's not for you or your precious city! I'm leaving this awful place the moment Kyle returns. I refuse to be your blue-feathered puppet!" I grit my teeth and clench my fists. Blood and energy stampedes through my body, heating my anger to a boil.

"Shouldn't we tell her now?" Matthew asks. He stands in the corner of the office like a guilty toddler, instead of the empowering tower of lean muscle I've always known him to be.

"Do you want her to erupt in flames?" Truman mutters.

"If you allow me near fire obsessive James, I just might." I turn and walk towards the exit. "I'll be…wherever I'm supposed to sleep. Wake me when Kyle's location is discovered."

"You won't be leaving the city, Cora." Marner's macabre voice stops me. "I made a promise to Kyle, the day he reenlisted as Legion, that I'd keep you under Dimidium's protection until you were fully healed. No grand escapes. No fighting. You're here to stay."

A stabbing pain of realization pierces through my chest. I can't leave? Kyle's request has trapped me under Truman's rule? Battling the discomfort of acceptance, I respond with the nectar-sweet denial I hope to be truth. "You're lying."

"Believe me. It'd be easier to allow you to leave as you please. I would much rather you fight outside my walls than to be a disturbance within."

"So you're going to lock me away until my heart heals?"

"Of course not," Truman cuts in. "Matthew and I will escort you wherever you desire to go within the city. Shopping, parties, theaters; you can do it all. Think of this as a vacation. As soon as you are functioning properly, you'll be allowed to join our troops."

It isn't a surprise that Kyle has done this to me, chain me to the confinements of the Capital for my own well-being. I should be furious but it's hard to hate someone who has become my core. I'd probably do the same to him.

"There is another option," Marner tells me. "Everyone has had to find their place in this new world. Some have chosen to work in production and agriculture and lead simple lives. Others who were once poverty-stricken are now some of the wealthiest members in our society. Life has changed. It's time for you to decide who you are. Are you the Blue-Jay, a figure of significant influence? 237, the scar of a program that no longer exists? Or are you nobody Cora Kingston? You see, this nation needs some hope. I can't give it to them but you can. So if you're determined to leave this place, I'll be happy to comply. I've already scheduled a tour across the country to cities still in my jurisdiction. You'll put on a smile, say a few motivational words, kiss a baby or two, and travel to the next town. I know it's not the blood-splattering action you're used to, but it is a form of fighting."

"What will I get in return?"

"For every speech you give and every session with Stonecipher you attend, I'll allow you one treatment of medication to hurry your healing process."

I stare at him, hating the smug smile on his dark-skinned face. He knows I won't refuse his offer. The incentive is far too precious to lose over pride. I can already feel the changes within my body from the first vial of serum. "Anything else?"

"Truman shall be your guardian. Stonecipher, your mentor. And Matthew will protect and guard you at all times. You must respect them and behave as a young lady if you are to receive treatment. Do we have an agreement?"

"This will be the last deal we ever make." I shake his hand, promising myself never again to trust the word of a politician. Equality? Honesty? His universe revolves around deception and deal making. "I'm not as weak as you think I am."

"Prove it."

It's a challenge I'm willing to take. If this new world associates strength with the Blue-Jay, it is what I'll become. I will adapt and evolve until I turn into an unstoppable powerhouse. I refuse to allow Marner the satisfaction of watching me crumble.

"James is waiting, Cora." Truman opens the office door as a sign for me to leave.

Without saying another word to the president, I turn and walk out of the room with Matthew following close behind me. He attempts to grab my hand as we make our way down the hallway, but I quickly return his gesture with a hateful glare. He's a traitor. His loyalties now lie with President Marner. Not me.

"Well I'm glad that's over!" Truman laughs as we step onto an escalator. His lips part into a relieved smile and the stress in his puffy eyes slowly disappears. "The next few months will be fun, all of us traveling together. We aren't bad company. Matt here can play a *mean* game of charades!"

"Sure, I'm as good as you are at flirting with women. How many more lies are we going to tell today?" Matthew snickers. "Remember that lady in Boston?! You tried to talk to her and…"

"Okay, okay that's enough! We don't want to alarm Cora on her first day here."

"I just agreed to be a bloody spokesperson," I scoff. "You're forcing me to endure training-sessions by a psychopath! And it's a matter of time before you coat me with makeup and dress me in frills! Yes, I'm a bit alarmed!"

Before they can respond, I step off the escalator and move across the lobby. People stare at me as I stride past them, some still holding weapons and others grabbing for their cameras. The way their jaws droop and eyes bulge would normally make me uncomfortable, but today is different. I don't feel self-conscious among their normality. Instead, their dumbstruck expressions fill me with confidence.

I pull off my leather jacket and drape it over one shoulder as I exit Counsel Hill. Night has fallen across the city. Lights flicker. Cars and flying machines dart through the streets, shining with trails of blue and white. People pass beneath the glimmering skyscrapers wearing colorful clothing and club-wear. Curfew is in a few hours and yet everything is so alive. It's captivating.

"Good evening, gorgeous. Need a ride?"

I cringe as a hovering limousine lowers in front of me. The back window rolls down to reveal a repulsive face; two inquisitive eyes hidden beneath a pair of sunglasses, thin lips, and a nose that has recently been perfected by plastic-surgery. The playboy billionaire smiles and slicks back his dark hair with a fire-printed handkerchief. His once clean-shaven face is now covered with neatly trimmed stubble. Seeing him sends a chill up my spine.

"You look a little lost, Cora Marie." Stonecipher's sunglasses perch at the end of his snout as he gazes down at me from his floating vehicle. "It's good to see you alive and well. I was worried after you and Kyle never returned to Tree Gap."

"What do you want, James?"

"Haven't you heard? I'm your new mentor! I shall turn you into a proper and eloquent young lady. God knows you need it," he chuckles.

"Why don't you shut the...!"

"Cora! Stonecipher!" Truman and Matthew emerge from the building. They join me on the curb and quickly greet the latest addition to our entourage.

"Climb in." James opens the door to the vehicle. "Pardon the wine bottles and piles of paper. I have a deadline to reach and have been working nonstop. Medicine, weapons, technology—everyone seems to want something from me."

I step inside the hovering car and sit as far away from Stonecipher as possible. The interior of the machine resembles the luxury of a limousine with leather chairs, a top-notch stereo-system, and an expensive alcohol collection. The glass floor is littered with bottles and garbage.

"Buckle up. My chauffer is an aggressive driver," James tells us with a heavy British accent as the hovercraft begins rising upward into the flow of air-traffic. Once above the skyline, the turbines rumble to life. With a press of the accelerator, the vehicle lurches forward.

"How does this thing work?" I stare at the city beneath us, entranced by the swirl of lights.

"It operates on magnetism. An entire iron grid has been installed beneath Dimidium to support this new form of transportation. All off-grid airships are much larger and run on nuclear-power." Stonecipher's eyes are fixed on me, as if I am more intriguing than the marvelous sight below. "All of these are Patrick Kingston's inventions. He was a genius man."

"So people tell me," I mumble and lean my head against the window.

Truman coughs as if to break the tension building in my chest. "Dinner is being served at seven o' clock in our complex's dining room. I think duck is on the menu. Does anyone *not* like duck?"

Disregarding his question, I ask one of my own. "When is our first session, Stonecipher? I want another dose of medication."

"We'll start at dinner. Come dressed to impress me. I want to see how pretty you can make yourself look on your own. Think of this as a beginner test."

"Shouldn't we be doing more important things?"

"Kyle handles the *important* things and we do what we can on the sidelines. Darling, sorry but you're benched at the moment. The only way you will get back in the game is by following your coach's training. And right now, I am your coach." He laughs at the grimace on my face. "You'll learn to love my eccentrics, Cora Marie. I can be quite a fun companion when the circumstances allow it."

The car dips and plunges into the Capital's suburbs. I grip my seat as the limo zigzags left and right, squeezing through alleyways and arching over stacks of piled rubble. Two minutes later, motion ceases. I feel the hovercraft sink to the ground and the doors click open.

"Welcome to your new home."

CHAPTER 3

My apartment is hardly anything to brag about. It's an old conference room with a toilet and sink screwed crudely into the crimson-painted wall. Thick, dusty carpet covers the floor. Old blueprints lie in a heap in the far corner. It feels like Dimidium, a city built over a city; a futuristic society constructed on the skeleton of old America. I hate it. Nothing should be recreated.

"I hope you like your room. I spent my first week here preparing it for when you'd wake up," Matthew told me as we climbed out of Stonecipher's limo. *"I guess I didn't want to believe that you were gone."*

I lock the door of the room with my eye-print and toss my jacket onto a plastic chair. Few pieces of furniture occupy the space— a bed covered in white sheets, two metal lockers, a desk, nightstand, several mismatched chairs, and an antique mirror. When the world ended, these office buildings were converted into public housing. They're drafty and smell horrible but are much safer than the homes beyond the wall.

A pile of canned fruit cocktail is stacked on the desk, as well as a vase filled with wilted lavender. Books and popular magazines form pillars on either side of the lockers. Matthew has outdone himself. He's even left a CD-player and a collection of dusty albums beside my bed.

I glance out the open window at the sparkling skyline, almost smiling at the billboard mounted on the adjoining building. It's Kyle and me, both gazing dreamily at each other like the couple in Counsel Hill. We look fearless and ridiculous in our white clothing and glossy skin. I want to hate the altered-image but I can't. It's too perfectly unrealistic to despise.

Consumed with aggravating exhaustion, I begin to pull off my clothes piece by piece. Dinner is in an hour and my appearance is far from *pretty*. I feel so out-of-place here, even though my race has been welcomed back into society. Maybe it's me? What if I don't belong anywhere? I know with Kyle, I never felt like a pathogen. He is the adhesive binding me to my originality.

I moan with frustration as I wiggle out of my green cargo-pants. They slide to my ankles and past my socks. I lift my stained tank-top over my head, pulling it past my face and braid. After ripping the IV from my wrist, I'm left in the center of the room wearing nothing but bloody gauze and striped panties.

"Forever and always," I whisper to myself before sentimentally unraveling my hair. It's longer than I remember. Instead of hanging several inches over my shoulders, it now drapes my chest. Time has passed. Things have changed. Nothing will ever be the same.

I walk towards the mirror, afraid to see the naked half of my body. I know what to expect—scars, bruises, and brandings. But what my eyes observe first about my figure aren't the markings littering my flesh or the hole between my breasts. I see my ribs and the muscles protruding from my skin. I see a gaunt frame and a sunken stomach. I see a reflection of someone I had hoped I would never become.

"So this is me?" I ask the mirror. My hands comb across my tattoo and the white lines streaking my torso like chalk tallies. I touch the rounded scar on my shoulder caused by a stray bullet, and gently inspect Deven's branding on my lower back. For fifteen-minutes I stand in front of the looking-glass, feeling and remembering each scar. Some have meaningless memories while others define my identity. They tell me who I am.

Gently I prod the scar-line caging my heart inside my sternum. The empty pain returns, that dull ache radiating from within my core. How can I spread hope when I myself have none?

Watching the clock on the wall tentatively, I go to the lockers. They have recently been stocked with a range of clothing and accessories. I'm glad. My shopping abilities are close to none.

I remove an amber dress from the rack. It's simple and feminine with a frilled neckline and pleated skirt. If I am to win Stonecipher's game and receive my medicine, I must play by his rules. I refuse to fail at something as ludicrous as a beauty contest.

The next half-hour I try hopelessly to better my appearance. I shower, shave my legs, attempt to curl my hair, and spend what little time left playing with the bottles and compacts of makeup. They are like beakers of genetic formulas and vials of serum. What does what? Where should I dab the purple powder and where do I smear the black stick? Most women know these things before they reach adulthood. Not me. I was transformed by a program. They killed the girl inside me.

Remembering a few tips Sarah had shared last summer, I dust my face with a sheer foundation and accent my eyes with mascara. It's the best I can do.

I slide on a pair of embellished flats and clasp a golden bracelet around my left wrist. As soon as I am satisfied with my work, I leave the apartment and travel downstairs to the reserved dining room.

"Were you all waiting on me?" I push through the doors and stride towards the long, mahogany table with newfound confidence. Matthew grins. His eyes twinkle like Christmas lights. For the first time today, I return his smile.

"You look lovely," Truman says and rises politely. He seems less stiff than usual. His suit has been replaced with slacks and a yellow button-up.

"Not bad for a fierce little savage," Stonecipher smirks. He sits at the head of the table, hunched over a bowl of chowder with a glass of vodka in one hand. "I can almost see a woman in you."

"So you approve?" I sit at the opposite end of the buffet. A plate of roasted duck has already been prepared for me.

"Maybe. You still have a lot to learn. Appearance is only a small part of what I will teach you. You must hold yourself like a leader, strong and empowering. Beauty is eye-candy. Words fuel revolutions." He laughs. "What'd you do to your hair?! You look like you just walked out of a London night-club. I am trying to build a responsible and mature image for the Blue-Jay, not a sexy clubber. So lay off the hairspray next time, darling."

"She looks fine, James." Matthew casts a sympathetic glance in my direction.

"I'm not here to make her *fine*! I'm here to make her marvelous! Does *that* look marvelous to you?!" He points in my direction and gulps another swig of alcohol. "Time for our first lesson."

A new tray of silverware is set before me; complete with an assortment of knives, spoons, and forks. They glimmer in all shapes and sizes. I've never seen so many utensils at one time.

"Etiquette is the key to success." Stonecipher lifts his cup of vodka and theatrically raises his pinky. "Though you probably think me a bit silly, manners are not reserved for the Queen of England. You must learn some if you are to progress with this tour. Believe me. A rugged, Plain Jane like you will hardly be accepted as a General, much less a political icon. You must be glamorous, eloquent, fit for the role of a princess. Nothing less than a Kate Middleton will do."

"Maybe we shouldn't have hired James…" I hear Matthew whisper to Truman. He's right. The wealthy pyromaniac will be dead by the end of the week if they continue to allow him to tutor me.

"Now let's take a look at the silverware, Cora Marie."

"What is this going to accomplish?" Truman asks skeptically. "She will be meeting with suffering Americans, not dining with your Queen. Why don't you focus on eye-contact or proper speech habits?"

"We do this *my* way or no way," Stonecipher blurts in a drunken voice. The right sleeve of his blazer is soaked with chowder, smearing white across the red tablecloth. "It's time to turn the beast into a beauty."

His remark sends me over the edge.

I grab a steak knife from the tray of utensils and throw it with abnormal strength. Ferocious. Rugged. Savage. Whatever people say, I know one thing for certain. I never miss my target.

A loud crack echoes through the dining room. Stonecipher's eyes are wide with shock as he glances at the knife pinning the collar of his jacket to the back of his chair, centimeters from the skin of his neck. He tries to pull away but is held in place by his fire-print ascot. Silence.

Matthew bows his head and presses his hand over his mouth to muffle his deep laughter. Truman sighs and nonchalantly adds another spoonful of sugar to his tea. James Stonecipher is frozen. He looks at the knife, then at me with his jaw drooping. Without warning, he begins laughing. His boisterous chuckles shake the table, vibrating across the roasted duck.

"That went perfectly," Truman mutters sarcastically over the roar of Matthew's and Stonecipher's laughing.

Angry and slightly embarrassed, I stand and drop my napkin onto the plush floor. I turn and walk out of the dining room with my ears buzzing. I'm sick of this place. Everyone I care about is away fighting my battles while I stay here, useless and weak.

I go to my apartment and quickly change into a pair of shorts, a sports bra, and tennis shoes. After braiding my hair, I ride the elevator down to the gym. It's empty. I guess in the middle of an apocalypse, fitness isn't people's number one priority.

Dust fogs the air as I open the glass doors to the patio. A crisp, autumn breeze blows through the room, washing away the musk of emptiness. Airships float above the housing-complex, shimmering like stars in the black sky. This city is a futuristic oasis in a desert of ruin, a flashing light on the desolate grid of earth's circuit-board.

Trying to forget my emotions, I pound my fists against a punching-bag. It's flimsy and built for human strength but I continue to hammer it with my achy limbs. I kick the sack against the wall and sling my elbow into its rubbery torso. It swings back and forth, provoking my programming.

Sweat drips from my skin. My lungs pant and my fragile heart races. I haven't been in a gym in over a year. I know that my body is weak. I know that the strain of exercise could hurt me more, but the rush of endorphins is intoxicating; to move, to breathe, to embrace a past identity. I release all control and allow 237 to make a reappearance. Adrenaline pulses through my veins, reviving me back to life.

"Quiet. They'll hear you," I whisper as I jump off Aunt Jen's porch. Sand meets my feet. The roar of tumbling surf echoes through the night.

"Don't worry. We've never been caught before." Kyle lifts his surfboard over one shoulder. The moon's rays flicker off his bare chest. "You ready?"

"When have I not been ready?" I laugh and sprint towards the beach. He follows with an incandescent smile on his face.

I stop to pull off my tank-top and shorts before dashing into the ocean. Waves slam against my waist, spraying my body with salt. I glance back at Kyle, lift my arms above my head, and dive into the chilled depths.

Water consumes me. It seeps into my pores, soaks my bathing suit, and creeps through the creases of my lips. I love it here; swimming beneath the stars, submerged in lively silence. The vulnerability isn't threatening. It's warm and surprisingly human.

"Are you sure you can keep up?" I emerge from the ocean with eyes stinging. Kyle paddles towards me on his surfboard. He slows to a stop and slips into the water, joining me among the rippling surf. I splash him. He grins and dunks me under. I feel his hand on my shoulder and for the first time all summer, I get an odd fluttering sensation in my stomach.

"I think you're part fish or something," he snickers.

"Like a mermaid?"

"More like a siren." He tries to swim away as I grab his head and shove him under the ocean's surface. His arms wrap around my waist and drag me below. We hover weightlessly beneath the waves, eye to eye. I touch his face with my wrinkled fingertips. Even in the middle of the sea, I feel his warmth.

Silver minnows dart past us, racing with the current like cars on a speedway. Kyle points upward and clutches my hand. We swim to the surface. I climb onto his board with my legs dangling in the water. He smiles and props his weight against my thighs.

"I'm glad we came here," he says. "I wish I could live in this moment forever."

"It doesn't have to end."

"Of course it does. Everything ends. I'm just glad to have now." He gazes up at me. His smile vanishes and is replaced with worry. "I don't want to lose you, Cora. You're all I have. You die. I die too."

"You'll never lose me. We're a team, remember?"

"Nothing is perfect in this world...except us."

I slam my hands against the punching-bag, groaning as the impact ripples through my body. Sweat glistens off my stomach. Bruises and blood cover my knuckles. The programming is losing its effect. I'm coming down from a high, returning to this hell.

One more kick sends the bag crashing against the wall. The chain breaks, causing the sack to fall limply to the floor. I clutch my chest, cringing at the pain pulsing through my core. I can't withstand this any longer; the sadness, anger, desperation.

"Why didn't you make me stronger, Dad?" I shuffle over to the strength-training equipment and lift a set of twenty-five-pound-weights from the rack. They're the lightest I've ever trained with.

"I thought I might find you in here," Matthew says from the doorway. He watches me with sympathetic eyes. "You're hurting yourself, Blue-Jay."

"Are you going to tell me to stop, to rest until my heart is healed?"

"Would you listen?" He snickers and leans against an old treadmill. "Cathy called me an hour ago. She wanted to know how you're doing. Apparently she and Geode went to the beach this morning. Sarah's parents drove them to Kyle's outpost in Los Angeles."

"I'm glad she's safe," I say and drop my weights. "Matthew, what happened the night of the attack? You, Geode, Scar, and Seth were all taken out of our cell. Where'd you go? How did everyone end up in the battle…except you? I remember hearing your voice before I passed out on the Titan's satellite. You were there."

He nods and rubs his neck nervously. "After we were escorted from the Titan's Hall, Scar and Geode knocked out two of the guards and Seth and I finished off the others. We were separated after that. I followed a pair of soldiers to the roof where I saw the hovercraft. It was blasting your screams and I was afraid that Deven was hurting you…so I boarded the ship."

"That's it?" I gaze at him skeptically.

"No, I slew a dragon on the way! Of course that's it. I'd do anything to keep you safe," he tells me surely with a touch of sadness trailing on his accent. "I wish you trusted me more. We were best-friends once. What changed?"

"We chose different sides. You decided to join Marner and defend his new America, not fight alongside me. A strong leader recognizes the strengths of others, but you don't see mine. When you look at me, you see that brave little girl facing Deven Lukes in the Arena. I'm not that person anymore. I only want the opportunity to sacrifice for the people I love. Why can't you see that?! This hole in my chest is nothing but a…glitch. It doesn't cripple me. It makes me stronger and gives me a purpose. I made the decision to save a life, better than killing without reason. Help me escape, Matthew! Get me out of this place! Let's find Kyle together!"

"Why, so you can hook up with him and disappear? I'm not an idiot! I know what will happen once this war ends. You'll marry Kyle, move away to some exotic location, have ten kids, and grow fat in your old age! He will stifle you, Cora. You'll become a silly housewife!" He laughs mockingly. "Oh, I forgot. You're terrified of intimacy! Have you ever even kissed him? Sorry, I guess I was worried for nothing!"

My face turns red. I grit my teeth in an attempt to muffle the curses building on my breath. When he moves towards me, I battle my fists to my side, resisting the urge to slap him across the cheek.

"We weren't designed to settle down. You know that. Our bodies aren't created for domestic life. We probably can't even produce children. If you don't believe me, look in the mirror. Besides a few extra scars, we haven't aged since Prime Way closed. What if we stay like this forever? Do you want your future kid, if you're able to have any, to see you like…this?"

"I can't change my genetics!" I shout.

"I'm not asking you to…"

"Then what are you asking?!"

"I want you to choose fruit cocktail over a braid," he whispers. His blue eyes burrow into mine, searching for the answer he'll never find. "Choose me."

"I'd rather you ask me to stop breathing."

I turn and dash onto the patio. Curfew has blown out Dimidium's lights, trapping the housing-complex in the shadows of the monochrome cityscape. I spot the window to my apartment high above, glowing yellow. My eyes narrow. My heart races with adrenaline. The challenge is too hard to resist.

Like a flustered bird trying to escape from a garage, I scramble up the side of the building. One jump launches me ten-feet in the air. A slight kick throws me from one wall to another. I race upward, fast and breathless. Matthew's voice echoes below but I ignore him. Why must everyone be one identity plastered over another, one secret buried beneath a treasure-trove of lies? You think you know them until something peels back their layers, revealing the ugly inside.

Speed ruptures through my body. Buzzing fills my ears. My senses enhance. I refuse to abnegate myself. This is the Blue-Jay. This is what I've become. I'm only weak when I pretend.

I fly through the night as if I were born with wings, twisting and spiraling towards the open window like a shadow among the darkness. My fingers claw at the creases in the bricks. My sneakers scrape against the side of the complex. My muscles ache. My chest throbs; but I climb story after story, listening to the sounds of the families living within the building. Children whimper in their sleep. Babies cry. Men and women worry silently. My problems are nothing compared to theirs.

Is what Matthew said true? Am I afraid of allowing Kyle into something more than my thoughts? For so long I wanted to believe that my life was better off fought alone, that I was too dangerous and unstable to protect anyone other than myself. I didn't want to love. It was easy to become numb to this world, to live as if I were dead. All it took was a taste of hope and a touch of humanity to bring me back to life. Kyle changed me. He made me real again. We both met with baggage but over time we were able to carry each other's burdens. I learned to open myself after being sealed tight for a decade. His unsure demeanor was replaced with confidence. Together, we healed.

I reach the windowsill and climb inside my apartment. Anger surges through my arteries like melted steel. Pain explodes beneath my sternum. I groan and shuffle across the room, grabbing a can of fruit cocktail off the desk. I pry it open and begin eating the fruit with my fingers. It tastes sweet and familiar like a lost memory gliding down my throat. But remembering Matthew's words, I quickly spit out the food and dump the remains in the trashcan.

"You will be forced to sacrifice everything," a voice whispers in the back of my head. *"Nothing will survive this war, not even you. Kyle will wither away to an empty corpse. Matthew will disappear. And earth will fade away until all that remains is a pile of depleted history. How can you even smile knowing your future is destined to end in tragedy?"*

"I smile because this is how I save the world," my heart responds. *"Hope is my bow. I refuse to be the arrow that's not aimed."*

A package has been left on my bed. Curious, I rip open the top and dump the contents onto my nightstand—a syringe and a slip of paper reading: *Accept this as a peace offering. Your mentor, James.* Desperate for another dose of medication, I push the needle into the vein of my left arm. The serum pumps into my body. I can feel it racing through my limbs towards the hole in my chest, healing the damage within. Every time I follow orders, I'll grow closer to freedom. I will be with Kyle again.

"Blue-Jay, are you in there?" Matthew knocks on the door. His voice sounds as if he's been crying. "Can we talk?"

"Go away!" I pull off my tennis shoes and throw them angrily against the wall.

"Please let me inside. You need to understand."

"Leave me alone, Matt!" I tear off my sweaty clothes and toss them in an empty hamper. "You've changed and I don't like the person you've become."

He stands in the hallway, speechless. His hand touches the door-knob and twists it to the right. A gust of stale air flows into my apartment, causing chill-bumps to wash over my naked figure. I hold my breath as the hinges creak and his shadow appears. A twinge of panic ruptures through my torso as the tips of his shoes cross over the threshold. He's entering my room.

As I reach for the empty syringe lying on my mattress, the door closes and Matthew's shadow vanishes. I heave a sigh of relief as I hear his footsteps down the corridor.

Shakily I open the set of lockers, finding something new among the piles of expensive clothing I had gone through before. Kyle's book-bag. Stonecipher must have had it sent from his home in Nevada.

I smile as I unzip the pack and begin sorting through the tangle of clothing and personal items— pictures, passports, a seashell still covered with sand. I unravel a gray t-shirt from the pile and slide it over my head. It hangs loosely at my thighs, oversized and consumed with the smell of sandalwood. I'm glad to have a piece of him. It helps remind me who I am.

After switching off the lights and placing a classical music album in the CD-player, I crawl into bed and bury my body beneath the piles of clean sheets. Sleep is a nightmare. I can't face it alone. So my eyes stay open, gazing at the billboard outside my window until dawn appears on the horizon.

I think of Sarah and Cathy, both living in a war they don't understand. I think of Kyle on the battlefront, leading our race against Deven and his army of Injections. I was created to fight with guns, not with words. My role now in this world is harder than I could've possibly imagined.

The next day comes faster than I would like. I dress to fit Stonecipher's prestigious standards before walking down the hall to Truman's suite. A guard scans my eye-print before allowing me inside.

"Good morning, Cora Marie." James rises from a floral-print sofa and straightens his golden tie. He musters a sober smirk and motions for me to take a seat in a velvet chair. "Have you eaten breakfast? I have everything from oatmeal to caviar."

"Some oatmeal would be great. Thank you," I say before sitting in the sunroom. Windows line the walls, all overlooking Dimidium's agricultural district. I watch workers move between rows of plants, hauling water and seed to different greenhouses. It seems out-of-place amidst the untouchable grandeur of the city.

"An improvement in your manners. I'm impressed." He hands me a bowl filled with steaming mush and watches me eat with skeptical fascination.

Truman looks up from his desk and smiles pleasantly in my direction. Matthew stands behind him like a guard-dog. His fastidious gaze is focused on the rug beneath his feet, remorseless and unforgiving. He was brutal and in return, I broke his heart.

"Let me introduce you to your new stylists, Sasha and Raena."

Two women emerge from an adjoining room with clothing draped over their arms and palettes of makeup in their hands. They both are incredibly tall with dark skin and frizzy black hair.

"Girls, show Cora Marie how she should look when speaking to the nation."

Before I can protest, the stylists attack me with their powders and creams. My face is painted with an array of colors. My hair is unraveled and properly curled. Even my nails are painted a dark shade of blue. In a matter of seconds, my entire image changes.

"What do you think, General Kingston?" Raena lifts a mirror to reveal my new reflection. It catches me by surprise. The face is not my own. It's been modified to look sweet and glamorous, a mask to cover my sunken features. My eyes seem bigger and more golden, like those of a young child. My skin is youthful and my lips are rosy. The image in the mirror radiates with gentleness and luring confidence. It's deceiving.

"Your appearance will make people *want* to pay attention to what you have to say. Look at yourself! You are beautiful. One word from you will entrance millions," Stonecipher exclaims enthusiastically. "From now on, Sasha and Raena will do your makeup daily. You will dress in the clothing I provide. And you shall wear your hair down, not in a braid. Do we have an understanding?"

I swallow the lump in my throat and nod.

"Good. Now to move on to more important things." He sets his glass of sparkling water on the coffee-table and eyes me skeptically. "Tomorrow you shall make an appearance on Dimidium's television-network…"

"You want me to talk on TV?!"

"Don't worry. I already have your speech prepared and programmed into the teleprompter. All you have to do is read what I've written."

"You'll do fine. Everyone will be so excited to see you that they won't care what you say," Truman tells me. "Remember who you are to them. Become their icon and they will embrace you."

"Exactly!" James paces around me critically. "Sit up straight. Uncross your legs. Put your hands in your lap. Yes, that's better. Hold your head high. You're not ashamed to be in my presence."

I roll my eyes as he continues to blurt out rules on etiquette and speech habits. I'm forced to endure hours of training—when to properly make eye-contact, how to eloquently deliver an address, what fabric and color goes with which season. It's exhausting.

"I have one more lesson prepared for today!"

"Thank God…," I mutter, causing Truman to snicker.

Stonecipher kneels by my chair and removes the shoes from my feet. "Don't you dare kick me." He takes a pair of diamond-studded pumps from Sasha and cautiously slides them over my soles. "You've walked in heels before, haven't you? I want to make sure you move gracefully. There's nothing uglier than a clumsy girl in stilettos."

I stand and stride across the room, not once tripping or wobbling. My balance has been enhanced. I can hop on a wire and not slip. "Am I graceful enough?"

"You move like a stampede of rhinos," he laughs. "Imagine you are floating, not stabbing the floor. Try again."

After several attempts, I manage to waltz across the apartment lightly. Stonecipher claps and musters a pleased smile. It's the first time he's ever looked at me with something besides lust.

"I think you're ready for your first outing. Well done, my dear." He pats me on the back and subtly slips another package of medication into my hand. "The Blue-Jay will be a success. This tour will motivate our world back into a civil society."

Truman nods. "She's ready."

CHAPTER 4

Powder clings to my skin. Hands combs across my face and arms, erasing everything the world may deem ugly. Hair-extensions are pasted to my scalp. Padded clothing is layered over my skeletal frame, camouflaging my sickly figure. Faux breasts are shoved into my bra. I hold my breath as a can of aerosol is emptied over my head, molding and hardening my new locks into a glossy curtain of chocolate curls. The lights of the vanity are blinding. The chaos unraveling in the studio reminds me of an army preparing for an attack. People rush past my dressing room, tapping their clocks in a final countdown. I know this shouldn't scare me. Cora Kingston, the Blue-Jay, is considered dauntless but here I am, trembling beneath layers of manufactured makeup.

"It's not too late to run away," my insecurities whisper. *"You can find Kyle on your own. What's holding you here—medicine, expectations, Matthew? Who elected you savior of the world? Your place is with your people. Run. Leave. Never look back."*

Fake nails are plastered over my own. Sasha sews foam-inserts into the shoulders of my blazer and on either side of my hips. She moans before zipping the back of my skirt. "You're so skinny! I will try to hide the fact that you're still recovering. It's difficult though. The world needs to see that their leader is healthy but…well, you're not."

"I'm sorry."

"It's alright. I like challenges." She raises the neckline of my blouse and drapes a string of metallic beads over my chest to distract from the lump of gauze beneath my clothing.

"Remember to make eye-contact with the audience. Sit up straight and be pleasant. A single smile will cause the nation to fall in love with you," Truman babbles. His calm demeanor is annoying. "Don't worry. We've practiced your cues and blocking a million times. You are ready for this, Cora."

"Once you heal, you can leave. You'll be with Kyle again," I tell myself as Raena glues voluminous eyelashes across my lids. *"Breathe. This will all be over soon."*

I try to think of him as the stylists alter my appearance—waxing my eyebrows and accessorizing my body. His face slowly emerges from the vague chasm of my mind. I see his boyish smile that could make even the hardest heart melt, those sparkling hazel eyes, and his thick, blonde hair. Memories sketch the details. I remember his molded, slightly oversized nose and the occasional pimple that sometimes appears on his forehead. His imperfections are what make him so perfect. They're what keep him human.

"We are finished. You look ravishing!"

I rise from the chair to face my newest reflection. What I see is shocking, alien, a limpid glimpse of illusory stamina. I appear to be normal and beautiful, which is something I've never been able to confess. My skin looks healthy and my body is no longer starving; a perfect hourglass figure. My hair is thick and sleek. When I smile, my face ignites with robust color. Though my wardrobe is surprisingly simple—a striped blazer, chiffon blouse, red stilettos, and a fitted, black skirt; I feel stunning. I feel magnificent. I feel like a girl.

I stare at myself in the mirror, inspecting different angles of my new image and modeling various stances. Like a vain peacock, I continue to admire my own vanity. Embarrassment sears across my flawless face when I notice Truman's inquisitive eyes watching me.

"You're not screaming," he observes. "Do you like what you see?"

"It will do," I answer in an indifferent tone. "This isn't what I was expecting. I thought Stonecipher would dress me in something flamboyant and ridiculous."

"A costume would only exploit you, Cora. By wearing normal clothing, you've transformed from a rugged war-hero into a confident celebrity. The nation needs to see that their leader is healthy and approachable, charismatic."

"Five-minutes!" someone shouts from the hallway, causing a surge of anxiety to flood my nerves. Five-minutes until the Blue-Jay is unveiled. Five-minutes until my choice is set. Once I walk onto that stage, there will be no running away to fight my battles. I'll be stuck living as a masked icon until Kyle returns and my heart heals.

Sasha and Raena, with flustered emotions, quickly powder my nose and weave a small braid in the curls of my hair. It's a silent salute, the only thing branding me as myself.

"Now remember…"

"Make eye-contact with the audience. Sit up straight and be pleasant. A single smile will cause the nation to fall in love with me," I blurt out.

"Fear regret more than failure, Cora. You are the wall separating this country from true desolation. We survive. We fight. We carry on in the midst of an apocalypse because of the hope *the sword and the arrow* emit. Rise to the occasion. Become hope for the world to see," Truman tells me. He looks at his wristwatch and motions to the open door. "It's time."

I nod and sneak a final glance at my reflection. "Here goes nothing," I say before walking into the bustling corridor. *No Feeling. No Regret. Just Strength.*

Immediately I am consumed with a crowd of people. They stick microphones to my blazer and hurry me towards the stage entrance. I can't breathe. I don't want to breathe. Maybe by accident I'll suffocate myself and fall back into a place of warmth and happiness, a place where Kyle is there to remind me who I am. Life is purgatory. Death is final. How do I live so deeply that my scars and fear only impact how radiant and passionate I thrive?

Every human desires a branding, something to claim them and give them a purpose and identity. Maybe that's all we ever wanted? Could a yearning for acceptance truly be the cause of this disaster? My father may have been my designer, but he didn't determine the corruption of my race. He built our potential but it was our own selfishness that gave us a destructive purpose. The Prime Way Program isn't the killer. We are. We've allowed the darkness within us to take control of our humanity and emotion. It has decided our fate.

My eyes dart from face to face, trying to find familiarity among the blur of bodies. I can't do this. I can't stand up and confront the dying nation I've partially destroyed. Visibility is against my nature.

"You'll do fine. Stay on your feet, keep your eyes open, and you will make it through this." Truman walks hastily by my side. "Show them how *real* you are. Prick your finger if you have to! Allow them to see that your people are as fragile as we are, as human as we are. That's all I ask."

"But we're not! I'm finally beginning to see that. For as long as I can remember, I believed I was no different from you and Stonecipher. I believed that my alterations were only mental, that the physical aspect of me was still the same. Now I realize that everything about me has changed."

The backstage door opens. I glance one last time at my entourage of stylists before slipping into the darkness of the studio. Once the exit is sealed, I turn to face the silver curtain separating me from the cameras. No turning back. No running. I'm trapped.

Cautiously I creep forward and peer through a crease in the fabric. The studio set is basic—several overstuffed chairs, a plush couch, and large screens playing feed from the battlefront. Lights comb across the stage. Crewmembers rush back-and-forth, adjusting cameras and testing the teleprompter. I see a famous talk-show-host preparing for the interview. She's thin and petite with short, blonde hair and a pleasant smile. Acid dampens my mouth. My nerves go haywire.

"I'm surprised you came." Matthew emerges from the shadows. He musters an awkward smile and looks at me guiltily. "I thought you'd run. After what was said the other night, I knew you wouldn't stick around because of me. I was a jerk and I'm sorry. I want us to be friends. Please. You're the only family I have, Blue-Jay. I couldn't live with myself knowing I lost you too."

"Running is for cowards," I respond.

I need desperately to trust him, to have a friend among the chaos of Dimidium. I want us to be like we used to be—a team, two kids trying to survive the horrors of the Prime Way Program together.

"I have something for you." Matthew digs in the pocket of his coat and pulls out a wad of silver chain. "Cathy sent this to me a few days ago and told me to give it to you when the time was right." He unravels the jewelry and carefully clasps it around my neck.

I smile as I rub the star pendant between my fingers. It's a tribute to Katrina and a silent salute from my cousin. I'll wear it like the braid in my hair, in honor of the people I love.

A light flashes backstage, warning me of my oncoming cue.

"Good luck, Cora. I'm proud of you." Matt crosses his arms over his chest in a salute. "Stand tall. There's no need to be nervous. Everyone is here because of you."

I embrace him. His touch calms my flaring nerves. I pull away and step towards the parting curtain. The cameras flash green. With a fake smile drawn on my lips, I walk onto the stage and into America's skeptical gaze.

> *Laughter is like a fresh breeze. It cleans through my body, making everything feel alive and good. I forget my fears, the heights I'm reaching, and the danger if I fall. Life suddenly becomes beautiful—the sunset beyond San Francisco Bay, the headlights shimmering like fireflies below, and the calluses on my palms from climbing.*
>
> *"Come on, Cora! This may be a once in a lifetime experience. We can't miss it!" Kyle grabs my hand and pulls me higher, both of us scaling the side of the Golden Gate Bridge with abnormal agility. "I'm not going to let you fall. You're safe with me."*
>
> *I smile and race past him, running across steel cables and leaping from beam to beam. He chases after me with stars in his eyes. Together we climb. Together we fly. Together we fall. Like morning and night, like sand and water, like the sword and the arrow—we fit together.*
>
> *"Hopefully no one will spot us up here. We'd have a lot of explaining to do." I reach the top of the arch, marveling at the vast landscape before me. "Can we glue our feet to the ground and stay forever? I don't want to leave."*
>
> *"I could endure forever with you." Kyle lifts himself onto the platform and grins at the awestruck expression on my face. He tiptoes towards the edge of the arch and peers down at the water below. "I bet I could make one epic cannonball from this height."*
>
> *"Don't you dare! I'd kill you if the jump didn't kill you first." He snickers and steps onto a thin cable suspended over the*

bay. It trembles beneath his weight. "Sometimes it takes risking everything to conquer the unconquerable. We remember those who overcame their fears. I want to be remembered."

"As an idiot who fell off a bridge?!"

"No, as an idiot who lived!" He spreads his arms wide and gazes up at the twilight sky.

"Please. Come back," I plead. "If you fall and die…"

"I won't. Nothing, not even death, could take me away from you. I promise." As he begins to move towards me, he slips.

My heart stops as I watch his body flail. A scream rumbles inside my chest but is trapped before leaving my mouth. I reach for his arm desperately. I'd rather fall to my death than be without him.

His hand grabs mine, yanking me to my knees and towards the edge of the platform. I close my eyes and wait for the rush of air, weightlessness, and then the sharp impact of rippling water. But it never comes. I'm left dangling from the side of the bridge with nothing at the end of my arms. Kyle has disappeared.

Panic consumes my thoughts as I stare into the dark abyss below, watching for a splash among the waves. No, he can't be gone. We were supposed to last forever.

"Please bring him back!" I yell a prayer in the back of my mind. "I'm in love with him! I shouldn't be ashamed but I am! Don't take him away. If you allow him to live through this, I promise to confess everything. He means the world to me."

As if on cue, I hear a muffled groan and see movement in the scaffolding below. Kyle's body scrambles from beneath the arch and reaches towards me. Anxious and relieved, I clutch his wrist and pull him up beside me. He collapses on the metal platform with his hand cupping the back of my neck. I land on top of him and stare at his pale face with tears in my eyes. Our lips are inches apart and even though I made a promise, I can't bring myself to kiss him.

He breathes heavily. His chest rises and falls. I want to slap him for making me confess something even I myself never wanted to admit. Is that what I've been feeling all along—that twinge of need and desire in the center of my chest, beating and longing

*for something I cannot have? Is that what love should feel like,
or is the word "love" really just to describe the race of emotions
a human experiences during a physical relationship? If that's
true, love doesn't describe how I feel about Kyle. He is a
promise, a connection fused deep within myself that I couldn't
undo even if I tried.*

*"Don't you ever do that to me again! I'd rather have you
than be forced to remember you."*

*He nods and brushes the hair from my face. "Let's go surfing
next time, okay?"*

"How about we stay home and watch a movie?"

He laughs. "I'll make the popcorn."

Spotlights blind me as I prance onto the stage. I smile and wave at the
hundreds of cameras crammed into the television studio. Their lenses
focus on me from different angles, capturing the celebrity essence of
Dimidium's Blue-Jay. My heels click obnoxiously on the wooden floor. I
grit my teeth, wishing that the flashback had lasted longer.

"It's such a pleasure to have you on the show today, Miss Kingston."
The talk-show-host rises from her chair and hugs me. I adjust the
hemline of my skirt and sit on the empty couch, sweating beneath my
padded layers of clothing.

These are the people who once cringed at the thought of my
existence. They created what I've become. One thought, a single
inclination that science could perfect humanity, fueled the Program.
Their discontentment gave birth to destruction.

Be hope for the world to see.

"Thank you. It's an honor to be here. Even in the middle of a disaster
like this, it's so wonderful to see civilization prosper," I read off the
teleprompter. I've been practicing all morning, trying not to say the *gasp*
and *laugh* cues. "Much has happened over the past year and I know
many of you have suffered. We're living in a dark time but my people
are doing what they can to contain the Regiment. We will fight this war
and we will win."

"It is such a comfort to know that the future of America rests in your
capable hands. Beautiful and a soldier—what is your secret?"

"Lots of coffee," I say with a smirk.

The talk-show-host places her hand supportively on my shoulder.

"All of us are honored to have you and Kyle as our leaders. Tell us, what inspired the Blue-Jay?"

"Growing up, I always had a problem with climbing trees. I'm surprised no one shot me down thinking I was a turkey-buzzard or something..."

Recorded laughter echoes through the studio. I know it's fake but I smile at the sound.

"Over the past year, the Blue-Jay has grown into something more than a nickname. It has become a pseudonym of hope in our state of despair. *The sword and the arrow.* Both are...bigger than life. They symbolize everything we stand for—courage, honor, hope, and acceptance. We are united and that is what makes us strong. I promise that as long as I live and breathe, I will fight for our freedom."

"And what about Legion? Has it been hard to be away from him?"

"Of course it's been hard," I read. "I haven't seen him in over a year. The last time we were together, I was dying. Before that, he was dying. Without him, I feel like half of a picture. We are nothing alike. But we are, somehow, a part of the same entity."

The woman shakes her head in awe. "What a brave young woman you are. After all you've been through, why do care about us? You could easily join the Titan and wipe out humankind."

I stare at the teleprompter, waiting for my dialogue to appear. It doesn't. The screen has turned black. I look at the talk-show-host. She leans forward to hear my response. This is all a setup. They've introduced me to the world only to ask this one question. I should have expected my exploitation to end in a game of truth or dare. Could I lie? Would anyone care as long as I say what they want to hear?

Silence falls across the room as I move to the front of the stage. I feel their propitious stares as I wrestle apart the neckline of my blouse, showcasing the scar that almost suffocated the life from my body. It sends a message stronger than words.

"Pain is unlike any emotion known to mankind. It demands to be felt. We can't escape its touch, no matter what we do or how we act. But sometimes our greatest pain becomes our greatest strength. It's a choice we all have to make. Do we allow hatred and angst to transform our hurt into suffering? Or do we turn our discomfort into a scar that will give hope to the hopeless?" I look down at my chest, trying to find the words to describe the agony my wound causes. "Unlike other afflictions, I'm proud of this pain. Every breath I take, it reminds me who is still alive because of a choice I made. That is why I'm here today. I fight for who I love…and he loves you."

"Liar," something whispers in the back of my mind. *"You don't want to feel this hurt any longer. I can take it all away. No more suffering, anger, love. You'll be painless. All you have to do is allow me to consume what remains of your human genes. Stop resisting. You're stronger when you don't pretend."*

Something moves in the back of the studio. For a brief moment, I feel a sharp sensation in my abdomen as the figure rises from his chair. Is it my imagination or could the shadow belong to the devil himself? No, Deven is too smart to risk coming here. He doesn't even know I'm alive.

Buzzing fills my ears. Anger stampedes through my veins as I gaze at the image. I'm not scared of him. He will burn to the ground, reduced to nothing more than insignificant ashes. Doom to the Titan.

I am asked a few more questions before the interview ends. When the cameras turn off, I heave a sigh of relief and stumble wearily backstage. I hardly have time to relax before Sasha and Raena force me to redress. As soon as my hair has been brushed and my makeup redone, Matthew and Truman escort me out of the building to a hovering limousine. Fans line the curb, screaming and clawing at my clothes as I pass by. Their hands touch my skin but I can't feel them. Their screams blare in my ears but all I hear is the steady rhythm of my own breathing.

"Hold onto me," Matt says as he guides us through the crowd. "It'll be over soon. Our train leaves within the hour."

I duck my head to avoid the flash of photography. Truman opens the door to the awaiting vehicle and I climb inside, quickly hiding my face from view. People tap the glass windows. They study me with paltry fascination instead of fear. I'm more than visible. I'm conspicuous, like a neon marquee in the middle of a dark desert.

"You were marvelous tonight," Truman says as he slides into the limo. He locks the car door as soon as Matthew is seated and grabs a can of soda from the stocked mini-fridge. "Your parents would be proud of you, your brother too.

"My family means nothing anymore," I whisper.

My dad only cared about perfecting society, designing what I'd become. I know my mom loved me but she's dead now. Callan is part of the enemy. My own brother betrayed me and now I'm back to where I started a year ago. Alone.

"I'll be your family, Cora. You don't have to be alone anymore. We can face the world together," I remember Kyle saying. He always wanted to rescue me from myself. Even in the darkest times of our lives, he was able to see the girl beneath my masks; and in all honestly, the only thing a girl wants is to love and to be loved. He gave me that.

The crowds outside the limousine go wild with excitement as Stonecipher emerges from the studio. He smiles and gives high-fives to some of his squealing fans, stopping occasionally to sign an autograph and have his picture taken.

James Stonecipher's wealth and occupation have bought him celebrity status.

"Goodnight, America!" he shouts. "Keep the beer cold! I'll be back in a few weeks!" When the valet opens the back door of the limousine, Stonecipher smirks and walks to the front of the vehicle. He crawls into the passenger seat and stands up, sticking the top of his torso out of the sunroof. "Party at my place next month! Who's coming?!"

Screams blast from the mass of people. Hands shoot into the air, waving frantically in response to the man's question. Stonecipher laughs and says goodbye to the citizens of Dimidium. Once the hovercraft begins to rise off the curb, he plops into his seat with a satisfied grin on his haughty face.

"Great show, Cora Marie! You did exactly what you were supposed to do." He reaches into his pocket and hands me a syringe. "I think you've earned this."

Anxious and relieved, I stab the needle into my left arm. The medicine pumps through my body, once again healing the chasm in my chest. It's addicting. The weariness in my limbs disappears, the fatigue fogging my brain melts away, and a sudden gust of health rushes through my lungs.

"Next time you speak, try to be sweeter. Your intense monologues were quite unsettling," Stonecipher tells me. "We should be at the train station in a few minutes. Tea anyone?"

Days, weeks—they all fade into a blur of rehearsed speeches and desolate cities. A month passes and I hardly notice. Each moment is spent traveling, speaking, and enduring the envious stares of suffering people. The world has become hell. Injections roam free, bombs spread disease, and with every hour, Deven conquers more of this country. I miss the brightness and ignorance of the past. I miss my dorm at Prime Way, Katrina and her paint-smeared clothes, Callan's suntan, laughing with Kyle. It's hard to laugh now. I wake up to a plush train-car while civilization rises to face starvation, radiation, and the fear of death. How will flowery words and a painted face fix what my race has destroyed?

I stare outside the window of Stonecipher's train as we pass smoking ruins and piles of decaying bodies. The Regiment has invaded two more Sectors, colonized towns, and bombed three of Kyle's military outposts. They've moved out of the Dead Zone and all I can do is hope, pray, and deliver speech after speech to receive medication. My heart is healing. I can feel it inside my chest—tissues welding together, cells regenerating. In a few weeks, I'll be free.

Legionaries are everywhere; rushing through train stations, guarding public housing, walking the streets with guns strapped to their backs. Some are younger than thirteen. They fight while I'm trapped inside a routine of fake smiles and halfhearted gestures. I look at each of them with a flutter of adrenaline, wanting desperately to see Kyle among their metal-clad masses. But I never do.

After an appearance in Santa Fe, I cried. Children were clawing at the stage. Blisters covered many of their faces, a side-effect of radiation poisoning. I couldn't handle it; the misery, the guilt of causing this. I hid myself and bawled until my eyes were red. Matthew found me. He said, "Don't numb your emotions, Cora. There is power in compassion." It hurts to feel. Sometimes I want to embrace the programming and allow the pain to wither away.

Truman and Stonecipher have especially grated on my nerves. Their critical remarks, insincere compliments, and heartless jokes make my blood boil. Truman is less repulsive to be around, unlike James who only laughs and mocks my performances. They don't understand. Even Matthew seems blind. He may have Legionary blood, but he's no longer the soldier I remember him to be. No matter how many nights we stay up talking, I will always feel a barrier between us. Like Dimidium's wall, he has blocked out the brutality of our reality and at the same time, he has blocked out me.

"You've done this twenty times, Blue-Jay. Why are you nervous?" Matthew asks as he clips a microphone to the collar of my lace-dress. "I can see it in your eyes. You don't like being here."

"Truman didn't tell me that we were coming to Dallas," I answer and glance warily around the deserted cafeteria. A tangle of Scrub High School banners are piled by the empty vending machines. Crumbled paper and empty food trays cover the dusty tables and floor. A year ago, this place was filled with teenagers who only cared about their social life and sports. Now the students who once roamed these halls are either dead, recruited into Kyle's army, or hiding away in their family's basement. They never knew what was coming. One moment they were watching their team's football game and the next, they were hiding with a radio, listening as the Titan blew half of the country off the map.

"Why should it matter? Dallas is just another city. People aren't dying from radiation here but they are suffering from a shortage of food. Dimidium is trying to send what they can to the local outposts but our supply is short." He smirks and pats the gun strapped to his hip. "Deven should know not to mess with Texas!"

I smile and nudge a forgotten textbook with the tip of my shoe. Math, my least favorite subject. "Kyle went to this school. His family doesn't live too far from here."

"Gosh, I totally forgot. I'm sorry."

I shrug. It helps to drive away the stab of agony in my chest. "I never really think of Kyle as having a life before me, but he did. This was his home, his past. I just feel like I'm standing in his graveyard of memories, if you know what I mean?"

Matt nods. A sudden wave of sentiment floods his face. He snickers. His blue eyes shine with remembrance. "Ian and I had some good times growing up. Our older brother, Cody, never wanted to do anything with us. Ian was always the one who took me to the beach, drove me home from school, and even taught me how to ride a bike. I think we even went camping once before my parents died."

"You've never talked about him."

"No, he's my graveyard. I buried my family's memories the moment I was recruited into the Prime Way Program. It was easier to forget them. He and Cody sent me to live with my grandparents as soon as they graduated from high school. I hated them after that." He tilts his head and gazes at me with a flash of amusement. "You've never talked about your family either. I guess we grew up with a mutual understanding. Neither of us asked questions."

"Maybe it would've been better if we had." I toy with the star-charm dangling from my neck and straighten the fitted skirt of my white dress.

Matthew glances at his wristwatch and motions to the door leading to Scrub High School's courtyard. "It's time. You know what to do."

"I've memorized Stonecipher's speech word for word," I say. "Be the Victor, not the Victim."

As I move towards the exit, I take one last look at the empty cafeteria. It's as if I can see Kyle among the ghosts of the past. He moves between the rows of tables with a tray full of junk food. His hoodie is old and his jeans are ripped. A skinny boy with shaggy, brown hair trails close behind him. They mumble insults at the jocks and laugh. Normal, real, misunderstood—he was human.

I touch the doorknob, feeling a warm sensation spread through my body. It immediately vanquishes all fear and doubt. Kyle is the provenience of my hope. Even if he is thousands of miles away, being a part of his memories suddenly brings light to my darkness. For the first time in weeks, I can smile with sincerity. I can speak freely for what I believe in.

"Forever and always," I whisper as I walk through the set of doors and into the courtyard. Legionaries and civilians are stationed along the sidewalk, protecting me from a distance. Some salute me as I pass. Others stare. Like the hundreds of other soldiers I've met, they're filthy, armed, and clothed in metal.

Cars have been stacked to form barricades around the school. Ash fogs the air. In the distance I can see the skyline of crumbled buildings, like jagged teeth on the smoky horizon. Grass grows from beneath debris. It's the greenest I've ever seen, a riposte to the chaos and horror of war.

I follow the path to a makeshift stage constructed in the parking lot. Already a crowd has gathered. They are much thinner than the citizens of Dimidium and look as if they haven't bathed in months. How will I appear to them—rich, spoiled, a monster living off their suffering?

"Cora, come here for a moment!" Truman calls from behind the crudely built platform. "There are some people I want you to meet."

A group of newly programmed Legionaries are waiting for me when I join Truman's side. They haven't fully adhered to their genetic-alterations. Some are still extremely weak. Their eyes scan me skeptically as I greet each of them in the way Stonecipher had instructed.

"These are some of Dallas' home-troops. They've been recruited and programmed to protect their city," Truman tells me. "Ron Thatcher, number 3001, is head of their division." He motions to the largest of the bunch, a tall boy with black hair and beady eyes. I notice an old football jersey beneath the plates of his armor.

"You went to school with Kyle, didn't you? He talked about you once or twice."

Ron looks at me with a blank expression and nods. "We were in home-room together. He came to a few of my parties."

"Oh, you're the guy who beat him up. I remember now. You threw him into your swimming-pool. It must be humbling to fight for a man you used to publically humiliate." His shock makes me smile. "Now if you'd all excuse me, I have a prior engagement."

Truman shakes his head in awe as I turn and step bravely onto the stage. Silence breezes through the schoolyard as I find my stance behind an old teacher's podium. This has become routine.

"Good afternoon, ladies and gentlemen. It is an honor to be here today," I begin. The words flow off my tongue as fluid as my mother's lullaby. Every gesture, every smile, every articulated syllable—all part of my performance. It means nothing anymore.

The gaunt people stare up at me with squinted eyes and unenthusiastic smiles. Their lack of excitement makes me uncomfortable. I blurt jokes, shout motivational quotes, and yet they remain silent and dead-faced. Why isn't this working? It's always worked before.

"I know things seem bleak but we must rally together!" I yell. "We cannot be defeated!"

My voice fades away as a crisp autumn wind blows from the east, stirring the dust and leaves into a cloud of ashy rubble. It floats across the parking lot, caressing the hoods of parked cars and dancing off the pavement. No one seems to notice the swirling debris, or realize its significance; except me. Something as timeless as a gust of wind, as memorable as the tattered American flag rippling over the school, as persistent as the foliage springing up from the cracks in the asphalt—can live forever.

"When darkness thrives, a hero must arise. We are the change that will shape the world. Without us, everything will die. There is meaning to our imperfections, our quirks, our glitches. We have purpose, Cora. Nothing can take that away for us," Kyle's voice echoes in the back of my head.

I gaze at the audience of Texans, noticing a familiar face among the crowd. He's watching me with curious eyes, a play of a smile on his thin lips. I've seen him before; from a photograph, memory, a brief encounter. He is Kyle's friend—Michael Stevens.

I forget the remainder of my speech as Mikey moves towards the stage. He is tall and gangly. His dark hair has been cut short and his once pale skin is now a medium tan. Questions swarm my mind. Has Kyle been here since the attack? Could his best-friend know his whereabouts?

"The Titan will fall and we will claim our nation once again. Thank you," I say quickly before unclasping my microphone and climbing off the platform. A knot forms in my stomach as I push through the mass of people. Mikey is the only connection to Kyle I've encountered over the past month. To even talk with him will give me peace.

"Blue-Jay!" a small voice squeals giddily.

I flinch as a little girl races out of the sea of bodies and entwines herself around my legs. Two oversized hazel eyes stare up at me, both hidden beneath a curtain of matted hair. She giggles and tugs at the hem of my dress.

"Lucy, come back!" Mikey rushes from the crowd and scoops the child off her feet. She screams angrily as he tosses her over his bony shoulder. "I'm sorry. She's a wild thing." He looks at me and musters a shy smile. "You're Cora."

I nod, watching the little girl squirm. She moans and kicks repetitively. "May I hold her?"

"Uh…sure." Mikey pries Kyle's sister off his body and sets her gently in my arms. Immediately she adheres to my torso, burying her head in the crease of my neck. "Her name is Lucy."

I laugh as the child runs her tiny hands through my hair. She toys with my necklace and fingers the lace around my shoulders. I've always been awkward around children; but when I hold Lucy in my arms, an unknown emotion bursts inside my chest. She shares Kyle's blood. That makes her special, familiar, and in a way, mine.

"Blue-Jay!" she squeals again.

"Yes, Lu. I'm the Blue-Jay," I say.

"Kyle?! Where's Kyle?"

"I don't know." I look at Mikey. He's observing me with glazed eyes. "Have you seen him? I've been traveling for a month and haven't heard a thing."

"Not recently. He's supposed to meet me at an outpost in Sector 7 next week. I've been recruited as his division's Director of Communications." He snickers. "Kyle has always been horrible at keeping in touch. Maybe I can help change that."

"Whenever you see him, please send word to me. I need to know he's alive."

"Of course." Mikey motions to the group of home-troops gathered behind the stage. "I'd be like Ron if my body would adapt to programming. I've already gone through the procedure twice and not once have I experienced any changes. The doctors have given up on me. I guess I'm stuck fiddling with computers." He snickers with a twinge of bitterness. "You're lucky to be able to fight. I'd much rather die with a gun in my hands than watch helplessly as the world goes to hell."

"Mikey, my mom wants us to come home! Julia's back from the outpost with our weekly rations." A boy jogs from across the parking lot. He's tall for his age with ice-blue eyes, shaggy dark hair, and Kyle's soft features. A shotgun is slung over his shoulder. "Who are you talking to...?" He stops and stares at me in shock. The blood drains from his face. "What is *she* doing here?"

"Benji, this is Cora."

"Yeah, I know. Her face is plastered on every corner from here to Fort Worth," he scoffs.

"What's up with you, man? I know we're living in an apocalypse but you can at least have some manners. Your mom would have a cow if I told her that you've been sassing a commanding officer."

"She is my brother's mutant girlfriend! Kyle left us for *her*!"

"Grow up or go home!" Mikey shouts. "Kyle didn't leave us for nobody, Benji. Now stop whining and either be polite or scram!"

"This is her fault." The boy glares at me before walking away. He grabs his gun and moves quickly towards the school, not once looking in my direction.

"I'm so sorry. I didn't know…" I set Lucy on the ground. She gropes my legs and clings to my hand. Unlike Benji, her eyes light up when she sees me, as if I'm a part of her family.

"Don't worry about it. That kid has been a mess since the war started. We've all been living together, you know, for safety reasons. I've tried to be a big brother to him but I'll never take Kyle's place," Mikey tells me. "Are you doing anything tonight?"

"I leave for Memphis at eight o' clock."

"Great. Why don't you come and have dinner with us?"

"Are you sure that's a good idea?"

"Positive. Kyle would want you to meet his family. Besides, I think General Kingston should see how people like us are living. We eat at six. You know where the Chase's house is located. See you later." He lifts Lucy onto his hip and turns to leave. "Oh and if it means anything, I'm glad Kyle found you. You changed his life, Cora, for the good. I'm still a little jealous that my best-friend has a hot girlfriend and superpowers but…I'd rather him have those things than me."

"You're a good guy, Mikey."

He shrugs. "Now remember, dinner is at six o' clock."

"I won't forget."

CHAPTER 5

Suburbia. Rows of houses, tangles of streets—a monotonous plain of shingled roofs and once manicured lawns. I've never understood the mindset behind the *American Dream*. How are cloned buildings, a cookie-cutter lifestyle; desirable? A sense of acceptance, belonging? How could I understand something so foreign? I've never truly belonged anywhere.

"Why are you doing this? They don't want to know you," a voice inside me whispers as I climb out of Stonecipher's limo. *"You are not their type of human, Cora. They will hate you and what you did to their son. You're the reason he never came home."*

I grab a bag of rations from the backseat and nervously toy with the star dangling from my neck. The neighborhood is silent, masked by evening shadows. It makes me uncomfortable.

"Are you sure you don't want me to come inside, Blue-Jay?" Matthew asks. He hands me my cardigan and glances at Kyle's house warily. "I don't like the look of that place."

"I owe a debt, Matt."

"No you don't." He steps out of the vehicle and faces me. His eyes gaze into mine with a mixture of desperation and sympathy. "You didn't take Kyle away from them. He chose to become one of us. You didn't cause this war. Deven did. You don't owe them anything!"

"Then I owe it to myself," I say and force a smile. "Aren't you tired of guilt? Wouldn't you do anything to feel peace again, to be able to breathe without suffocating? Experiencing Kyle's past might unlock the handcuffs binding me, help me to see things clearly again. I need this."

"Emotions don't handcuff us, Cora. It's something much bigger than that. I know. After I was recruited into the Prime Way Program, everything changed. There was a part of me that wanted to relinquish all control, allow the programming to dictate my every move and feeling. I tried for years to fight it, to feel a sense of freedom. But it never came. Those thoughts implanted in my brain ate away at my self-conscious until I wanted nothing more than to follow orders. Our alterations are our handcuffs. We will never overcome them."

"I refuse to believe that."

He shrugs. "Believe what you want. I know what changed me. If I hadn't had you to support me through training, I would have killed myself. You gave me the motivation to keep fighting. You became my will to live."

"I'm glad I was able to help someone," I smirk. "Now don't worry about me. I can take care of myself. Cora Kingston is dauntless, remember? No Feeling. No Regret. Just Strength."

"You're not as strong as you used to be…" He slides into the limo and quickly salutes me. "I'll pick you up at seven-thirty."

As soon as the car has disappeared into the sea of nostalgia, I sigh and begin my trek to the front of Kyle's house. It looks deserted from the road, a crumbling structure covered in peeling, white paint. Wooden slats have been nailed crudely over the windows. Weeds consume the yard and flowerbeds. Rusty rubble clutters the driveway. It must have been beautiful in its prime. Now all that remains is a dilapidated skeleton, a fortress for the surviving family within.

I stop midstride and pull a stolen syringe out of the bag of food. I've been waiting all day to indulge in its sweet rush of health and serenity. The emptiness in my chest is too painful to bear any longer. Matthew's right. I have lost the strength that once branded me as myself. The old Cora was fearless and intimidating. Now I'm weak, fragile, a woman consumed with feelings. I've become the most agonizing thing of all—a girl.

I slide the needle into my arm and hastily pump the medication into my body. As I hurry to discard the syringe, I catch sight of a face staring at me from the cracks in a boarded window—Benji. His ice-blue eyes watch me angrily as I approach the door to his home, almost daring me to enter.

A knot forms in my stomach as I step onto the front porch. My nerves erupt in a frenzy of anxiety. Without hesitation, I knock on the battered door. The creak of footsteps and the jiggling of locks meet my ears. I hold my breath as the entrance is unsealed and two bodies appear.

"Hurray! Blue-Jay is here!" Lucy darts out of the house and hugs my waist. She wraps her small fingers around my wrist and pulls me towards the threshold. "Come. I want you to play with my dolls."

"After dinner, Lu." Mikey looks at me and grins. His awkward demeanor melts away, leaving a handsome persona to his slender frame. "I knew you'd come."

"I was hungry."

He laughs and steps out of the doorway. "Come on in. Everyone's waiting to meet you."

Lucy drags me inside. I hold my breath as my feet meet the plush floor of the living-room. The carpet is stained and reeks of mildew, but there's something sentimental to its imperfection. An old couch is shoved in the far corner of the room, next to a powerless TV set. Crates of rations, a cot, and several stacks of firewood lay next to the ashen fireplace. This was once a home.

As I stand unsurely in the center of the space, a middle-age woman saunters out of the kitchen and inspects me with critical, green pupils. She's tall, lean, and dressed in worn clothing. Her frizzy, brown hair is tied back with a piece of red ribbon.

"Cora, this is Kyle's mom, Alice Chase."

I muster a smile. "Thank you for inviting me to dinner, Mrs. Chase. It's a pleasure."

"I didn't invite you. Michael did. You should thank him." Her voice is cold and hateful. It stabs at me like a dagger.

"Mr. Daniel, come meet Cora!" Mikey calls to a man watching from the top of the staircase. He resembles Kyle the most with graying blonde hair and soft features. When he sees me, his eyes widen with curiosity, not hate.

"You're a long way from home, aren't you?" A girl in her early twenties emerges from a backroom and collapses on the sofa. She's very pretty—tall, lean figure with curly golden hair and pale eyes. "Did

Dimidium get too crowded for you, Blue-Jay? Got tired of all that food and safety, huh?"

"Goodness, Julia. Mind your manners," Daniel says as he descends the flight of stairs. He walks towards me and shakes my hand politely. "It's nice to meet you, Cora. I am very glad you could join us for supper. We are more than happy to share what the Lord has blessed us with."

"Speak for yourself," Julia mutters.

"If you aren't willing to sacrifice some of your food, I don't mind giving her my rations for the night. It'd be an honor to serve a soldier." A slender lady wearing an oversized sweater moves out the shadows. She looks at me with a pleasant glow in her tired eyes.

"This is my mom," Mikey tells me as he embraces the pallid woman. She rests her head against his chest and smiles. Her aesthetic expressions cause my nerves to subside. The Stevens Family has a natural peace about them that makes the hatred in the room disappear.

"Dinner will be ready in a few minutes," Alice says as she heads into the kitchen.

"May I help? I brought some bread and fresh vegetables to contribute." I give Julia the bag of produce, ignoring her scowl and prejudice.

"No. You stay here. This is something I can do without help from…your kind." Alice rolls her eyes before leaving the living-room. Her last remark feels like a slap to the face. My kind? Does she still see us, even her son, as being monsters?

"We haven't had bread in months!" Julia exclaims as she searches through the sack of food. "And where'd you find vegetables?! The crops around here were ruined by radiation months ago."

"James Stonecipher, my mentor, has his train stocked with fresh supplies weekly."

"Wow. I doubt our meager rations will measure up to your expensive taste," Julia scoffs and rises from the couch. "My brother sure knows how to pick 'em."

I bite my tongue, trying to contain the surge of anger pulsing through my body. Tears dwindle beneath my eyelids. Pain pricks my confidence. They have no idea what I've been through.

"Try to understand. They're still mad at Kyle for never coming home," Mikey whispers. "One minute he's a runaway and the next, he's pronounced dead. Then out of the blue, he's a superhuman hero ready to protect the earth from a misanthropic villain. You being here, reminds them of what happened to their son."

"Then why did you invite me to come?"

"They needed to meet you, Cora. Trust me."

I look at the stained floor and notice a ladybug crawling at the base of a cluttered coffee-table. It's orange. The foreigner, the genetically-altered has become the majority. It's how they see Kyle and me. We are the mutated original, the weed suffocating their race. I know they hate what we've become. I see it in their eyes, that prejudice that once forced me into exile. We will never belong among them.

Benji and Lucy sit by the fireplace with an old board-game. I watch the two children with fascination. It's almost as if I can see Kyle playing with them, moving his game piece with a playful grin on his face. I hear him laugh and imagine his memory cradling Lucy in his arms and pulling Benji into a headlock. They miss their older brother and I stole him away from them.

Dinner is served a few minutes later. I sit in Kyle's empty chair and wait patiently as bowls of rice and beans are passed around the table. Everyone is silent. The quake of distant explosions causes the chandelier above my head to swing back-and-forth. I listen to the blast of falling bombs with a knot in my stomach, remembering the attack on Deven's camp—the deafening screams, the smell of burning flesh, explosions that could blow your body into a million pieces. People are dying tonight.

"This must not be what you're used to eating." Alice spoons a pile of canned chicken onto her plate and stares at me coolly.

"Actually I'm given the same rations as you are, with the exception of the vegetables and bread Stonecipher gives me. Everyone is low on supplies, even Dimidium. The only thing that gives them an advantage is their ability to grow their own food."

"Any news from that great Capital of ours?" Daniel asks sarcastically.

"Not that I'm aware of." I eat a forkful of rice. It's bland and tasteless.

"Do you have any family, Cora?"

"No. They're all dead," I answer hastily. "My parents were murdered when I was a kid and my brother was abducted by the Titan a year ago."

"I'm sorry. My eldest son, Harry, and his wife went missing when the war started. They were living in Oklahoma City at the time. I haven't heard from them since," Daniel tells me sadly. He's lost two children to the effects of the Prime Way Program. No wonder he despises my kind. "But I guess everyone has lost someone either to sickness, radiation, poisonous gas, or the Titan's raids. An outpost was built not too far from here so when the bombs get bad, we go there for shelter. We've been lucky to survive this long, unlike some of our friends who died during the first attack. It's been hard. We rarely leave our home unless we are going into town to gather our weekly supplies, which doesn't provide us with news from outside our sector. Have you seen battle?"

"No. I've been relieved of my duties for the time being. Instead I have been traveling the country, speaking to survivors."

"We need help, not words. Your people don't seem to be winning this war!" Julia shouts. "Seriously, where's Kyle when we need him? He's supposed to be some sort of hero now. Why isn't he fighting? Where is he?!"

"I don't know. I haven't seen him in over a year," I say. "But you should be proud of him. He's risking his own life to save the country."

"He should be here with his family," Alice mutters.

I want to yell at all of them, tell them how Kyle has sacrificed his own life on their account. He ran away from home because of them. How can they blame his disappearance on me? They pushed him away.

"Did it hurt, you know, becoming…what you are?" Benji asks.

I shake my head and take another bite of rice. "I don't remember exactly what it felt like. It happened really quick, like an electrical shock. I remember the preparations for the procedure and the aftermath, lots of needles and bright lights. That's all."

"How long have you been like this?"

"Since I was eight-years-old. Prime Way liked to recruit children at the beginning. It was easier to brainwash them, I guess." I force an irritated smile and drink from a plastic cup. Their questions are beginning to annoy me. I'm not here to be interrogated.

"So…" Julia sets down her fork and looks at me with a prejudice gleam in her eyes. "How long have you and my brother been together?"

"Almost two years."

"Have you slept with him?" Her question startles me.

I choke on a piece of chicken and gulp the remainder of my water.

"Excuse me?!"

"Julia!" Alice yells and looks at her daughter with shock. "How dare you…!"

"Come on! All of you were thinking it! What do you think Kyle's been doing with this girl for the past year, holding hands?! My little brother found himself a…"

"Julia, you better shut your mouth this instance! I can easily lock you outside," Daniel snaps.

I clench my teeth together, trying to retain my composure before unsealing my lips. Anger ruptures through the chasm in my chest. I hold my breath to keep my programming from being unleashed. Now is not the time to lose control.

"To answer your question, no. My relationship with Kyle is different from what *you're* used to," I manage to say. "We don't need to sleep together to love one another. Can you say that?"

Her face turns red. She puckers her lips and stares at her plate aghast. I shouldn't give her another reason to hate me. I want the Chase Family's acceptance because deep within, a piece of me hopes to be a part of their family someday.

"Why were you taking drugs?" Benji inspects me with cold eyes. "I saw you do it before you came inside. You stuck a needle into your arm."

Everyone at the table stops and looks at me with gaping mouths. I can almost see their thoughts above their heads, like critical teleprompters. *'Of course delinquent Kyle would end up with her. How could we have expected any better?'*

I can't handle their skepticism any longer.

My fingers reach to the top of my silk blouse and begin undoing the buttons one-by-one. The fabric pulls away from my chest, revealing the scar between my breasts. Silence fills the room as their curious eyes gaze at my wound. Alice blocks Benji's view with her hand, but it's too late. They have all seen enough of the mark to know my pain.

"None of you know what I've been through so don't judge me. I'm only here to do what Kyle would want."

Lucy hops out of her chair and taps my shoulder impatiently. "Can we play dolls now, Blue-Jay?"

I nod and lay my napkin on the table. "Of course." I glance at the faces around me and gracefully rise to my feet. "Thank you for dinner."

Without asking permission to leave, I follow Lucy into the living-room and sit with her on the floor.

The child pulls a basket of Barbie-dolls from beneath the couch. She cradles one wearing a pink sundress and brushes its long, brown hair. I rummage through the collection and remove a doll with blonde hair and a missing arm. The moment I touch its plastic body, Lucy squeals and knocks the toy from my hand.

"What's the matter?" I try to retrieve the figurine but she pushes it out of reach.

"That one's dead! Titan killed her!"

I look at the little girl, noticing fear within her large, hazel eyes. "It's alright, Lu. You don't have to be scared. You're safe." I lift her into my lap and hold her tiny figure in my arms. She clings to my finger. Her touch sends a stampede of unknown emotions through my arteries. Maybe there's more to life than fighting. Could I ever experience joy to the fullest, like waking up to a family or coming home after a long day to receive a sloppy, wet kiss from someone who loves me? A year ago, the thought would seem revolting. Not anymore. I've found the person I could endure forever with. He turns something as uncertain as our future, into a beautiful dream. No more nightmares. When darkness thrives, love brings hope of a brighter tomorrow.

"Can you stay with us?" Lucy asks as she toys with the curls in my hair. "I like you, Birdy."

The revised nickname makes me smile. "No. I must leave, but we'll see each other again. I promise. Next time I come, your brother will be with me."

She crosses her arms over her chest in a salute. I laugh and playfully toss her onto the ripped sofa. She giggles. The sound brings warmth to the dreary house.

"Cora." Mikey emerges from the kitchen. He watches Lucy and me with an amused grin on his boyish face. When I meet his gaze, he motions to the staircase. "Do you want to see it, you know, Kyle's bedroom? Not to be weird or anything. I just thought that since you haven't seen him in a while…"

"It's not weird." I climb to a standing position and adjust the hem of my skirt. "Show me."

He heaves a sigh of relief and awkwardly moves towards the flight of stairs. I follow him. As we reach the second floor, he glances at me and tilts his head to one side. "May I ask you a question?" When I nod, he continues. "What's it like?"

"To be in Dallas?"

"No, to be a Legionary?"

I shrug. "It's suffocating. When you're not battling your programming, you're constantly worrying whether or not you'll be hunted down and killed or if you will be the one hunting and killing. But it has its perks too. I can run faster than any known animal. I can jump high and balance on wires. I can see and hear things miles away, notice changes in my surroundings that you probably wouldn't. I can speak and understand every language known to mankind, am knowledgeable on every aspect of war and strategy. The list continues."

"That's amazing! It sounds like something Kyle and I dreamed about when we were kids. Both of us were geeks, if you didn't already know. He built a tree-house in my backyard to hold our Vulcan meetings. Sometimes he'd even wear a red, superhero cape."

I smile, imagining my overly built Kyle running across the yard with a red sheet tied around his neck. "Maybe you'll be like us someday."

He shrugs. "I hope so. Normality is overrated."

We walk down the dimly lit corridor, past closed doors and baskets of useless items. Everything is so real, so domestic. The abandoned socks, piles of unwashed clothes, a stray teddy-bear in the threshold of Lucy's bedroom—it causes the threat of war to vanish. This is a home. It's a place where people belong. Seeing something as insignificant as a bobby-pin on the floor makes me miss my own family. But they will never come back.

Mikey opens the door to Kyle's and Benji's bedroom and flips the light switch. A florescent bulb illuminates the cluttered space. "His side of the room is exactly as it was when he left. No one has touched a thing."

The moment I step inside, I smell Kyle. It's a strange thing to describe, that sudden familiar whiff of sandalwood fogging the dusty air. I scan the space, wanting to remember every detail—the old action-figures posed on the windowsill, the pair of muddy sneakers at the foot of his bed, even the stack of textbooks on his nightstand. This is the bedroom of a normal, teenage boy.

I finger a *Harley Davidson* keychain resting on his desk and notice a cowboy-hat nailed above the closet door. My ears begin to buzz. I almost curse as a rush of adrenaline shoots through my body. Why can't I be allowed a few moments of peace? In an hour, I'd welcome the programming but not now, not when I finally have a connection to Kyle.

Suddenly, Kyle's bedroom fades away. My programming unlocks another precious memory. I forget reality as I'm sucked into its accepting embrace. Once I realize that the past is a place to be visited, not relived; it will have no power over me.

> *Sand between my toes—the pinnacle of solace, the felicity of life, a paean to the vague joy I once felt long ago. It's an exhilarating feeling to walk onto the beach in the fading light of a sanguine sunset, to hear the eurhythmic roar of tumbling surf. I belong here. Not among the waves or California nightlife, but among my family and a world that accepts me.*
>
> *"Hurry, Cora! We're starving over here!" Callan shouts from the picnic-table.*
>
> *Tiki torches are staked in the sand, casting fiery light across the shoreline. Aunt Jen stands by the smoking grill, laughing at something Sarah had said. Cathy tosses a Frisbee and Barbie chases after it with tail wagging. Kyle looks at me and waves. His skin is as tan as leather, making his teeth glow like newly birthed stars.*
>
> *I walk from the side of Aunt Jen's bungalow with a plate of steamed oysters in my hands. A breeze sweeps across the Pacific, ruffling my hair and tossing the skirt of my dress in a frenzy of white linen. I smile and hike towards the awaiting crowd. They procure Cora from 237, from the layers of washed emotions and painful scars. With them, I know who I want to be.*
>
> *"Would you pour me some of that lemonade, Callan?" Aunt Jen sits at the table and begins smearing mayonnaise on her burger. She looks pretty tonight, healthy and alive. I've braided her long silver hair and tied the ends with blue ribbon.*
>
> *My brother pours a glass of drink for our aunt and grabs greedily at the platter of seafood. "Yum, oysters! You outdid yourself, Sis." He cracks open a shell and slurps the contents dramatically.*

"Don't eat too much, Cal. Remember what happened last time?" I slide into the space beside Kyle and spoon a pile of potatoes onto my plate. He touches my hand and entwines my fingers with his. I clench my lips together to hide a smile, but his laughter sets it free.

"I'm staying with Sarah if he gets sick again," Cathy says before biting into a cob of corn.

"We may all be staying with Sarah if he gets sick!" Aunt Jen giggles. She glances at me and nudges my foot from beneath the table. "You and Kyle are planning to stay with me forever, right? I don't know what I'd do without you two."

"We won't be leaving," I answer and turn to Kyle for confirmation.

He nods. His altruistic eyes burrow into mine. "You're stuck with us."

Callan tickles Sarah's neck with the tail of a half-eaten shrimp. She scoffs and shoves him playfully. Laughter takes the place of words as we eat beneath the sunset. Aunt Jen tells stories. Sarah shares riddles. Kyle and Cathy snicker and flick crumbs at pesky gulls. It's all so perfect.

"Kyle, you're from Texas. Don't you know any line dances? Better yet, can you square dance? I can totally imagine you wearing red boots and a cowboy-hat," Callan jokes. "Come on. You must know one or two. Show us!"

"I'm horrible. My best-friend took me to a hoedown when I was twelve. That's all. Not all Texans live on cattle ranches and line dance to Home-on-the-Range after dinner."

"Fine. We won't play Home-on-the-Range." Sarah digs through her tote and pulls out an iPod and a set of small speakers. "Lucky for you, I'm a huge country-music fan."

Kyle rises and reaches for Aunt Jen's hand. "May I have this dance?"

She chuckles and climbs from her seat. As music begins to play, Kyle twirls my aunt and promenades her across the shore. We laugh as they kick their feet and swing their arms back-and-forth.

Callan and Sarah join the dance. They lock arms and spin in

*a circle. The sun highlights their silhouettes as they prance
along the beach, past blazing torches and away from the picnic.
Barbie nips at their heels, barking and chasing after them. It's
amusing but at the same time, beautiful. This is my family. These
are the people I love. I'd die for them a million times over.*

*"Dance with me, Cora!" Cathy grabs my hand and drags me
away from the table. She giggles as we mesh with Aunt Jen and
Kyle. We weave between each other, laughing and clicking our
heels. Kyle wraps his arms around my waist and twirls me. We
spin, facing each other with smiles on our faces.*

*I feel his pace slow to a stop. Even with beats blaring, he
sways me back-and-forth with the rhythm of the waves. I place
my hands timidly on his neck, daring him to kiss me. It's a wrong
desire to have. I shouldn't want to kiss him. What I am feeling is
a lie.*

"Did you mean what you said about us staying here?"

*"I want to. This place is perfect for us. It's easy to forget
Prime Way when we're surfing and having picnics but our pasts
won't go away. We still have to face them. I just worry that one
day someone will come looking for us and we won't be ready.
They could hurt your family."*

*"We can't run forever. As long as we're careful and stay
under federal radar, I think we can hide here. I've been training
how to blend in most of my life. We'll be okay."*

*"Sometimes I forget who I'm talking to," he smirks and pulls
me a few inches closer. "This is the first time I've ever seen you
in a dress. You look...pretty."*

*I touch his broad shoulders, giving him one last chance to
kiss me. This could ruin everything. The friendship I've
treasured over the past year could suddenly become something
more, something that could threaten the emotional wall I've built
around myself.*

*"Aren't you going to dance with me, Kyle?" Cathy pleads.
She beams with a childish smile as she kicks sand at our legs.*

*"Fine. I'll dance with you, Squirt!" Kyle scoops her up and
tosses her over his shoulder. She squeals as he races towards the
rolling surf. Together they crash into the waves, colliding with*

the wall of tumultuous foam and salt. Laughter. It's the most hopeful sound I've encountered over my sixteen-years of existence. Compared to the sunset, the sparkling ocean, the summer breeze caressing my skin—it outshines them all.

Cathy splashes Kyle in the face and glides smoothly with the surging current. He grins and hugs her small figure. She giggles as he dunks her underwater. They've adopted each other, as brother and sister. I've never known acceptance like this, where someone could love a complete stranger.

"Cora, help me!" my cousin exclaims as she climbs up Kyle's back and wraps her bony arms around his head. Her auburn hair sticks to her face like seaweed.

"I'm coming!" I wade knee-deep in the ocean. Waves beat against my legs, soaking the hem of my sundress. "You two are..."

Before I can finish my sentence, Kyle tackles me. He jumps out of the waves, knocking me into the surf. I smile as my mouth is filled with salt water. Together we climb. Together we fly. Together we fall. Like morning and night, like sand and water, like the sword and the arrow—we fit together.

"You're going to pay for that!" I shout kiddingly as my head emerges from the Pacific. I cling to the wet fabric of his shirt and with Cathy's help, manage to shove him back into the watery depths.

We are a family.

The flashback subsides, leaving an empty pain in my chest. I cringe and squeeze my eyes together. If only the programming could last longer, instead of forcing me to return to my desolate reality? The world shouldn't feel this dark. It should be bright and good like summertime, like days I spent lying in the sun with Kyle by my side. But maybe my world has always been this dark. The only difference is that now, I can't run from it.

"Cora?" Mikey touches my shoulder. "You've been silent for the past ten-minutes. Are you alright? What happened?"

I lift my head, seeing that I'm still standing in the center of the room. "I'm fine. It was nothing."

He stares at me dumbfounded. His eyes search mine for the truth.

"It's almost seven-thirty. Your people will be coming for you."

I nod and nervously toy with Katrina's charm. "Will you send word to me once you know Kyle's location? I need to find him. Please, it's important."

"Of course. His division uses radio frequencies to communicate. Do you have a military issued transmitter? Messages can only be sent and retrieved by using the device. It's a new product from Stonecipher Incorporated."

"Truman keeps all weapons and technology locked away. I'm not even allowed to hold a dinner-knife. They treat me like a toddler on house arrest."

Mikey snickers. "That's okay. I have one you can borrow." He opens the closet and digs through a pile of duffel bags. "I hid all of my tech-stuff in here. Benji protects it for me." He removes a rectangular device from the clutter, along with an earpiece. "This transmitter has its own frequency. Once I know Kyle's location, I'll call you. To contact me, all you have to do is dial: MS1. It works like a telephone."

"Thanks. I'll keep it on me at all times," I say as I tuck the items in my pockets.

"Be careful out there. The east is a dangerous place. You haven't seen war until you pass into the Kill Zone. I'm pretty sure that's where you're headed."

"Don't worry about me. I've survived this long. I won't die until the Titan is dead."

"I believe it," he smirks. "I'm glad Kyle chose you. You're different from the rest of your kind. I don't know but there's something about you that makes me want to save the world." He blushes and awkwardly fiddles with a button on his shirt. "You may not realize it but…you inspire bravery. You give people a reason to fight. Remember that when you're facing your enemies. We rise against hell because of what you and Kyle stand for."

"I hope you still think that after the war is over," I say. A car horn blares from the road outside. Matthew has arrived. "It's time for me to go."

After saying a brief goodbye to Mikey and the Chase Family, I leave the house and walk down the sidewalk to Stonecipher's awaiting limousine. I climb inside and heave a sigh of relief. The emptiness in my chest brings tears to my eyes but I quickly brush them away. My programming is bursting at the seams, begging me to run away and fight. It hurts.

"Were they nice to you?" Matthew asks. He watches me from the opposite side of the vehicle.

"Yes. They treated me as if I were already part of the family."

"That's great." His lips form a straight line. I doubt he'll ever forgive me for breaking his heart. Part of me is angry because of it. I may not love him the way he wants, but I still care. He's like a brother to me. We've been friends since the beginning of Prime Way. I can't lose him, but I also can't lose Kyle.

"Are Truman and Stonecipher waiting on the train?"

He nods. "They were video-chatting President Marner when I left. Apparently Deven attacked one of our outposts in Sector 4 last night. Everyone living there is dead."

It feels like a punch to the stomach. More people have died. Soon the entire nation will succumb to the Titan's power. Everything will end.

Matthew scoots towards me and conjures a genuine smile. "I didn't mean what I said about you not being as strong as you use to be. I've been saying a lot of dumb things lately." His accent is heavy.

"You're right. Believe me. I wish I could return to the girl I once was. You'd like her a lot more."

"I like you now, Blue-Jay! You haven't changed completely. Part of you is still the girl who fought Deven in the Arena, the girl who jumped from trees. Don't lose that identity! You're strongest when you embrace your creation." Sincerity flows from his words, causing the pain in my chest to strengthen.

"Why can't you love him instead?" my programming whispers. *"Kyle doesn't understand how you're wired. Matthew does. With him, you'll never feel pain or sadness. You will be strong. It's what you want. Embrace it, Cora! You're only weak when you pretend."*

"No," I say aloud. It silences the voice in my head. I can't allow 237 to take control of me just yet. I'm going to escape soon. Marner will not be my handcuffs. I'll run away, find Kyle, and fight until the war is won. Now that I have a contact, it will only be a matter of time.

The dark city of Dallas passes outside. I lean back in my chair and watch as the bombed neighborhoods are replaced with crumbling skyscrapers and rubble-filled alleyways. Streetlamps rise powerless on either side of the road, like metal trees without their leaves. I'm glad to be leaving this place. It'll be easier to breathe in a location meaningless to me.

A few minutes later, we arrive at the station. Stonecipher insisted that we travel by train for safety reasons. I've liked being able to sleep in the same bed every night.

Matthew and I step out of the vehicle and enter the building. Old newspapers clutter the floor. Dust hangs in the air. It's a dreary atmosphere on the verge of being terrifying. I'm so used to deserted places that this almost feels like home.

We walk through the main terminal to where our train is waiting. It's a stunning piece of machinery, long and silver like a mechanical bullet. Matt and I both seem to relax as we board the locomotive. Desolation is suddenly replaced with familiarity.

"Good. You two are back on time," Truman says from a booth nestled beneath a large computer screen playing a broadcast from Counsel Hill. A half-eaten plate of pork rests in front of him, beside a glass of brandy. I lied to Alice Chase. The food I'm given is better than what Dimidium indulges, compliments of James Stonecipher. "Has the chauffer driven the limousine into the cargo-hold yet?"

"He's doing that now," Matthew answers as he grabs a soda from a bucket of ice. "Do you want anything, Blue-Jay?"

"Coffee." I collapse at a vacant table, exhausted. Matthew hands me a cup filled to the brim with black liquid. The smell sends a wave of peace through my aching body, reminding me of normal mornings in California when I'd wake up to find a pot brewing on the stove.

"Why all the sad faces?" James enters from a set of sliding doors and casts me a quizzical look. "What's wrong, Cora Marie? Did dinner end in failure? You better not cry and ruin your makeup. Sasha and Raena aren't here to fix it." He snickers and motions to the high-tech screen. "Haven't we already seen this broadcast, Truman? I'll make a call to Marner in the morning and see if he can give us something better to watch. Any requests?" When none of us respond, he adjusts his orange tie and grabs a cinnamon-roll from the buffet. "Everyone's mute...wonderful."

I lean my head against the window as the train's engine rumbles to life. Silently it rolls down the tracks, away from Dallas and into the night. I clutch my wound, hoping to squeeze the pain from my heart. I'm tired of traveling, enduring speech after speech, town after town. When we stop for a restock, I will sneak away. It won't be hard. I'll run until I find decent housing. Then I'll call Mikey, wait for a destination, and find Kyle. I'd rather be on my own with a gun in my hands than treated like a spoiled prisoner. I must fight or I'll die.

"How was dinner this evening, Cora? Did you find what you were looking for?" Truman asks.

"No. I didn't. Now if you don't mind, I think I'll go to bed." I rise and walk towards the door leading to the sleep-car. Slumber is nonexistent. I haven't slept since I woke up in that empty hospital. I'm too scared of what I might see if I close my eyes.

Passing my bedroom, I move from car-to-car to the back of the train. I've spent every night here, watching the moving landscape with minor fascination. The space is built like a sunroom with glass walls and overstuffed chairs. I normally keep the lights switched off and sit by the windows, thinking and begging my programming to allow me another vivid memory. They never come.

I sink to my knees at the base of the wall. The floor barely trembles, as if the train isn't moving at all; one-hundred-and-eighty-miles-per-hour and I hardly feel a thing. It makes me wonder if my father really was a monster. He designed so many things for destruction and yet created inventions that can be used to better the world. How can someone cause the end and yet pave the way for a future?

"Tonight the stars seem overcome. I cannot see the light. Your face no longer fills my eyes. I'm losing all my sight," I sing quietly. "You say it will end one day come near. You say we'll both be fine. But all seems lost and evil here. They're drawing between us a line…"

The doors behind me open. I grow silent and wait for my visitor to speak. No one's ever come to look for me here. Matthew must have followed me. He's been shadowing me for a month.

"Enjoying the view?" I ask without looking over my shoulder.

"Not especially." It's Stonecipher's voice that replies. I cringe as he approaches my side. Why couldn't it have been Matthew? I'm not in the mood to listen to James' narcissistic rants.

He sits on the floor and offers me a bottle of whiskey. "You look like you might need a drink?"

"It doesn't affect me. You know that."

"Sure, but the idea of drinking will make you feel better." He offers the alcohol once more and I take it willingly. "You're welcome."

I lift the vile to my lips and gulp the poison within. It burns my throat like acid, trailing into my stomach with a drowsy effect. The aftertaste sends a shiver up my spine. I cough and hastily return the bottle to Stonecipher. He laughs and takes a swig of the drink. I know I should hate him, but tonight, I'm too exhausted to care. For a few moments, the tension between is expunged.

"You seem like you're ready to beat someone up."

"A little," I say. The taste of whiskey still lurks in the back of my mouth, hot and heavy like a pile of embers. "It's that instinct engraved in my brain. I think my dad gave me an overdose."

"Your father never wanted this for you, Cora Marie. Please understand that." When Stonecipher looks at me again, all traces of sarcasm and shallow humor have vanished. His words are filled with compassion. "Tell me something. Why does Deven Lukes hate you?"

"Because he thinks I'm his competition," I answer. "He was recruited from an orphanage in New York City a few months after me. We were the top in our classes, always trying to beat the other at something. Though he was a jerk and a total bully, he wasn't psychotic, more like a weird kid with a fetish for torturing lizards and playing in ant-piles. Teachers loved him because he was fearless and horrifying. We hated each other for years until ninth-grade, when he suddenly showed an interest in me. I was a mess at the time and wanted to be liked by someone so…we dated. It wasn't a real relationship. I followed him around and he pretended like he cared. The whole time he knew about the chip in my back and was waiting for the right time to remove it. The opportunity never came so he dumped me, challenged me to a match in the Arena, and when I won, he decided that we were mortal enemies. That's his story. He must be the winner of every game to be happy. And to him, winning this war and killing me will be the final victory. It's how his insanity functions."

"Sounds like a stupid motive, if you ask me." James snickers. He gazes out the window at the passing tracks. "There's a lot you don't know about me, Cora Marie. I wasn't always this crazy."

"Did you have a fetish for torturing lizards and playing in ant-piles too?"

"No, I spent more of my time trying to impress a girl." He pulls a chain from beneath the collar of his shirt with an expensive diamond ring dangling from the end. "After your parents died, I met a beautiful woman at a banquet in Atlanta. She was attending with her father, who was a well-known scientist, and I'd like to say that it was love at first sight. The only problem was that I was thirty-one-years-old at the time and she was seventeen. We fell in love and entered a courtship. She was planning to graduate from high school before we were married." He laughs. "You know, most people thought she was after my money. I didn't care. I wanted to spend forever with her. She made every day worth living. Honestly, you're like her in many ways—headstrong and determined."

"What happened?"

"We were never married," he answers with tears in his eyes. "The day of the ceremony, I got up and drove myself to the church. I had the ring in my pocket and walked down the aisle with a smile on my face, ready to see my bride. But she never arrived. I waited for hours at the altar even after the preacher left, but my flame never made an appearance." He pauses and gulps another swig of alcohol before resuming his story. "They found her car at the bottom of a lake, empty except for a veil and the remains of a wedding-cake. Apparently she and her father had been driving to the church and ran off a bridge. A few days later, I buried two empty caskets."

"No one ever found them?"

He shakes his head. "I spent thousands of dollars trying to recover her body. I had search teams scanning the lake for weeks. They were never discovered which made me think that somehow she was still alive. So I invested in agencies across the globe, trying to track a girl that may have no longer existed. Again, my searches failed. She was pronounced dead, making me a forever bachelor and an almost widower. That is my story, Cora Marie. It's how my insanity functions."

We sit in silence. I take another swig of whiskey, allowing the burning sensation to dull the ache in my chest. Whether it's programming or lost love, we both have pain we'd rather not share with the world. They are our scars.

"I have something for you." Stonecipher reaches into his blazer and removes a silver bracelet. It's plain and elegant with *the sword and the arrow* embossed in the metal. A year ago I would have gagged at the thought of wearing jewelry and makeup. Now I'm forced to wear them daily.

"It's not what you think," he smirks and presses the icon welded onto the bracelet. Immediately a green light flashes upward, forming a holographic screen in midair. Pixels flicker as they piece together an image. I watch in awe as Kyle's and my face appear suspended above the piece of jewelry. It's the photograph Katrina took after he was programmed.

James touches the symbol again and the image changes to one of my brother, then to a picture of Cathy and me lying on the beach. He continues to scroll through a database of photos, each flashing with its own color and memories.

"This is a prototype. I had it made just for you," he says as he clasps the jewelry around my wrist. "You and Kyle left a lot of photos at my house when you were abducted by the CIA. I want you to be able to carry them around with you at all times, to remember what the world looked like before the war. This bracelet is waterproof, bulletproof, and practically indestructible. Think of it as a peace offering. So can we be friends now?"

"Yes, we're friends." I smile at my mentor. Tomorrow I'll probably regret the decision to end conflict with Stonecipher, but right now, I'm glad to have someone else on my side. He's earned more of my respect. "May I have another sip?"

"Be my guest." He passes the bottle, watching me swallow another painful mouthful of alcohol. "Whiskey is definitely not your drink."

I laugh and rest my back against the base of a plush chair. Outside the moon has reached its prime, casting silver light across the empty landscape. We pass farms, cities, miles of woods and smoking rubble. For hours I watch the train-tracks melt into the gloomy distance. James stays with me, enjoying the quiet more than conversation. In a way, I appreciate his presence.

"Do you see that?" I lean forward, gazing in horror as a plume of fire appears on the horizon. It lifts silently into the sky, rupturing into a cloud of ashes and brimstone. The train shakes. I cover my head as a crystal chandelier drops from the ceiling and shatters on the floor. Deven is making another attack.

"You have got to be bloody joking!" Stonecipher leaps from the ground and yanks a fire-alarm attached to the wall. Sirens blare. Lights flash. He opens the door to the adjoining car. "Hurry! We don't have much time!"

I follow him through the train, stumbling with every explosion. Buzzing fills my ears. My muscles tense. A calm alertness washes through my blood, waking me from fear. The Titan has unleashed his Erasers. If we don't get off the tracks, we are all going to die.

"What's happening?" Matthew steps into the hallway from his bedroom, half-dressed. He shoves a pair of shoes onto his feet and buttons his pants.

"That Lukes kid is going to ruin my train!" Stonecipher shouts hysterically. He pulls out his phone and immediately taps into the locomotive's control panel. "We'll stop in Little Rock. It's only a few miles from here. Hopefully we can make it that far without being blown to bits."

"The Titan is bombing further up the tracks!" Truman appears from the dining car with a glowing gun strapped to his shoulder. "If that's not bad enough, his Regiment is gassing the countryside." He hands us each a re-breather and gives weapons to the two men.

"Don't I at least get a knife or something?!" I ask as a discharge sends the four of us crashing against the walls of the corridor. "I've been trained for situations like this. Let me fight!"

"Not today," Truman answers. "Matthew, don't let her out of your sight."

The train grinds on the tracks, accelerating to a dangerous speed. I'm thrown to the floor with every explosion. Gunfire can be heard from outside. Blasts of energy ricochet off the train's metal siding, causing the lights above me to flicker intensely.

"We're not going to make it!" Matt yells as a bomb tears the caboose to pieces. He grabs my arm protectively and pulls me to his side. "Maybe if we disconnect the cargo and sleep-cars, the engine will be able to go faster!"

"We need those cars! How are we going to survive without food, transportation, or clean linens?! I'm not amputating my train!" Stonecipher protests angrily.

"Either we find a way to escape the Kill Zone, or we die. It's your choice?"

Stonecipher sighs and glances at the holographic screen of his phone. "Fine, but we better get moving. I'll start surgery in exactly thirty-seconds."

Truman nods and leads the way into the dining car. The moment the doors are sealed, Stonecipher keys something into his device. I watch as half of the locomotive is disconnected. It falls into the distance, taking away our exquisite rations, modern supplies, and my cursed makeup.

I lean against a table, bracing myself as the train picks up speed. James immediately stumbles towards the bar and begins stuffing an old grocery bag with bottles of liquor and packs of nuts and crackers. Truman sits at a booth and toys with his transmitter. Mine is still hidden in my pocket.

I breathe jagged breaths. With every shutter of a distant explosion, a wave of terror ripples through my body. It's painful. I shouldn't be scared, not now. War is what I was created for. My programming should drive these emotions away. Why isn't it working? Have I changed so much that even my genetics have lost their potency? Even when I was being tortured in Deven's game, I felt evidence of my alterations—a calm mind, intensified movements, that obnoxious buzzing in my ears. Now in the midst of a petty bombing, I'm as shaken as a puppy surrounded by fireworks.

Matthew watches me from the steaming buffet. There's something deep within his eyes that gleams with understanding. He knows what's happening to me. I can almost hear his voice in my head saying, *"You know how to fix this, Blue-Jay. Why are you suffering when you know there's an escape?"*

Having an escape can sometimes be harder than being trapped. Knowing I can run makes the battle harder to fight. Like all humans, I want to live. The ambition to survive is stifling the importance of compassion, of sacrifice. I'm not like Kyle. He's selfless, a leader, and contains a moral sense of duty I've never known. My goal is to live until my nineteenth birthday, save as many people as I can, and somehow keep surviving until I've reached an old age; if that's even possible now that the War of the Titan has begun.

I move towards a window and gaze out at a valley of burning rubble and mass destruction. The train is speeding down the tracks at two-hundred-miles-per-hour and yet I can still see the blur of smoke and the flicker of flames consuming the countryside. Legionaries race across the battlefield with weapons strapped to their bloody armor. I can hear their yells and screams for help as bombs continue to hammer the landscape. They fight. They die. And there's nothing I can do to save them.

"Cora, get away from there!" Matt shouts as a surge of energy blasts against the side of the severed locomotive. He flies across the car like a shadow or a gust of wind, catching me as the impact knocks me backwards. His touch sends a flash of mixed emotions through my body—hate, annoyance, humiliation, and them a rupture of passion in the depths of my heart. It makes me furious.

"I'm fine!" I shove him away and hastily climb to my feet. "I can take care of myself! Just because I'm dressed in frilly clothes and have gauze taped to my chest, doesn't mean I'm weak! I am still capable of fighting!"

"Here she goes again," Stonecipher mutters as he guzzles a bottle of beer. "We'll be arriving in Little Rock any minute. Grab what you want. We may not be coming back."

I glance at Matt angrily as the brakes to the train begin to pulse, slowing our speed. He follows Marner's commands. He's allowed to carry a gun. He knows his identity, something I am struggling to discover. Maybe that's what I envy most about him. Matthew Marx has embraced his genetics and therefore, has succumbed to painless emotions and manufactured strength.

Truman rises and motions for all of us to follow him to the sealed exit. Outside, the landscape gains definition. I see the outlines of deserted vehicles, grotesque piles of decapitated bodies, and the charred remains of exploded homes. Debris clutters the streets. Smoke and poisonous gas fog the air.

"We'll be using our re-breathers from this moment on." Truman fits the device over his mouth and nose, and adjusts the elastic strap around his head. We all do the same. "Things are going to get rough once we enter the station. If the Titan is making an attack, civilians will be panicking. We must stay together. Matthew, protect Cora. Her well-being is number-one priority."

The door clicks open. A gust of toxic, acidic air slams against my face. It's the same poison Deven unleashed on me and my troops while we were suffering in the jungle outside his camp. Many of my people died from the effects of the chemically-altered toxins.

"The past is vast and absolute. It has no power over me," I tell myself as I remember the months I spent wasting away in an overgrown building, dying of starvation and infection. I've never known physical pain as agonizing as what Deven caused. He killed me and yet I'm still breathing.

"Stay close," Matthew orders as the platform outside the train appears. People flood the terminal in chaos. They stare at Stonecipher's locomotive, hopeful for reinforcements that haven't come. Soldiers rush amongst them with re-breathers adhered to their faces. War has conjured a fear that sends darkness rippling across the earth. I can feel it, as suffocating as the poison in the air. If bombs and guns aren't the death of us, our own fear will be.

Another explosion sends a shower of plaster across the frantic mob. They must've been taking refuge here when the attack began. Sleeping bags and survival equipment are stacked in the corners of the station, all left behind by civilians trying to escape imminent death.

I step off the train, staring aghast at the masses of terrified human beings. Children squeal as their parents drag them through the sea of bodies. The elderly are crushed beneath stampedes of panicked feet. I sense everything—blood splattering the concrete floor, the whimpering of a young girl hiding beneath a trash bin, eyes wide with horror. *There is power in compassion.*

"Cora, come back!" Truman shouts as I wander away from the terminal in a daze. I'm immediately caught in the current of the crowd, being pulled towards the exit of the building; shocked and confused. Claustrophobia sets in. My ears buzz as my programming takes effect.

A division of Legionaries appear a few yards ahead of me. I doubt I know any of them. My original race was destroyed the night of the first attack. These recruits probably never saw Prime Way. They just have a vague, vestigial knowledge of a program ended long ago.

As I'm swept along with the chaotic riptide, I hear a voice that sends a wave of desperation through my veins. Familiar, sugary syllables caressing my sensitive ears like a warm embrace. I dig my heels against the cement, forcing myself into a still position. I listen. Again I hear his deep voice, a twinge of a Texan accent trailing on his commands. Kyle. He's here.

I peer over heads, anxious to catch a glimpse of him. I jump and shove my body through the masses, following the sound of his voice. He's so close. After months of searching and suffering, I've realized one thing. Love never dies.

"Kyle…" The word rolls off my tongue as his face appears in the mob. I forget to breathe, forget to move, forget the panic and destruction surrounding us. All I see is him—those tired hazel eyes that once sparkled like stars, unruly blonde hair, stubble-covered cheeks, and an overly built body covered with battered armor. It's him. He's alive!

Tears flood my eyes as I stare at him. Even among the deafening noise, I'm able to hear his heartbeat. It sounds like mine, broken yet strong like a steel drum. My vision enhances so I can see the sweat on his brow, the pores around his nose, and the cuts on the side of his neck. His breathing is shallow, struggling because of the toxins in the air. He's not wearing a re-breather.

I rip off my mask and scream his name. I wave my arms and shout as loud as my vocal cords will allow. He glances in my direction but doesn't see me and continues to yell commands at his division of recruits. A stab of pain pierces through my chest as I try to climb over a wall of horrified civilians. I'm so close. I can't lose him again.

"Don't leave me!" I scream as he moves towards the exit of the station. "Kyle, stop!"

He pauses and scans the crowd, listening intently to the wail of sirens and mixed voices. "Did you hear that?" he asks one of his soldiers. "I could've sworn I heard….forget it. It's just my mind playing tricks on me." Before I can reach him, he turns and leaves the building, disappearing into the night.

I stumble against the side of the corridor with tears streaming my face. I clutch my heart, sobbing as my last piece of humanity is ripped from reach. No one notices as I sink to the floor. I'm just a girl, weak and feeble and unable to fight for the people I love. The Blue-Jay, 237, General Kingston—they are all names of a restricted identity. I'll do whatever it takes to get to Kyle.

CHAPTER 6

Fire swallows the city, consuming everything in a cloud of orange heat. Ash rains from the charred sky. Screams seize the night as missiles drop like arrows into the earth, blowing away life as easily as the petals of a dandelion. I'm dragged through it all with tears streaking my face. I feel as if someone has dropped a fifty-pound-weight down my throat, crushing my sternum and rupturing the arteries in my chest. Emptiness replaces my fear with an overwhelming darkness. Kyle's gone.

"We must go back!" I shout as Matthew leads me away from the train station. "Kyle is here!"

"We'll find him again! Kyle can take care of himself. He's survived this long without our help. A few more days won't be the death of him," Truman yells in response as we run down a road littered with empty vehicles. "Keep moving! The Regiment is invading! If we don't reach Legion's outpost within the hour, we are all going to die!"

Matt grabs my shoulder and faces me with concerned eyes. "Do you want me to carry you?" It's almost an insult, another jab aimed to criticize my choice to withstand my programming.

"No, I'm sure I can keep up!" I glare at him as a blast of energy explodes the car to my right. The detonation throws us all to the pavement, with an impact that knocks the breath from my lungs. Shards of broken glass slice my skin. My ears are deafened by the power of the explosion. Blood gushes from my nose as I roll onto my side to see the damage caused. My body is still intact.

Stonecipher curses from among the ashen rubble as the ground begins to quake. His words are muffled as he rises to his feet. I recognize four words. "The Titan is coming."

"Get up!" Truman adjusts the power of his rifle and aims at the approaching shadows. Already I see movement within the crumbled skyscrapers of Little Rock. Like ants, Deven's army marches out of the ruins with black metal covering their heads and bodies. I stare at the virus of demons. This must be what hell looks like—dark, painful, fire lapping at my heels, soldiers loyal to the devil himself. Is my brother among them?

Before I can force my legs into motion, Matthew scoops me into his arms and sprints towards a cluster of office-buildings. I want to scream at him to release me but my tongue refuses to move. I'm paralyzed. Have I endured so much physical trauma that my body has decided to quit functioning?

Matt zigzags between cars, leaps over smoking craters, and ducks beneath pieces of crashed airships. I grip his neck and peer over his shoulder, watching Truman's and Stonecipher's silhouettes until they fade into the distance. A year ago, I wouldn't have cared about their well-being. Now, they seem to be the only piece of family I have left. My parents are dead. Callan has betrayed me. Kyle is gone. And the world I once envied has been revealed to be a gruesome and vulnerable place. War strips away our masks. It either tears us apart or brings us together.

A hovercraft soars overhead. Its propellers are blazing with blue lights as it disappears into the sea of skeletal structures. The Titan has arrived. Even with several miles separating us, I feel his presence like a knife to the stomach. Why has he come, to kill Kyle's Division? Or is this the usual invasion procedure? Wherever Deven walks, death follows.

"We're not leaving them, are we?!" I ask as 226 stops between two of the office-complexes. He sets me on my feet and reaches for his gun.

"They'll catch up with us. Don't worry. My orders were to keep you safe." He notices my wheezing and hastily gives me his mouthpiece. "What happened to your re-breather?"

"I lost it at the train station." I suck a few mouthfuls of fresh air before returning the device. "Deven unleashed his poisonous fog on me and my soldiers when we escaped his camp. After weeks of daily gassing, I think my lungs developed immunity to the toxins."

"You've never talked about what happened during those months. What did he do to you?"

"Things you wouldn't believe." I clean the soot from my face and wipe the blood from my nostrils. My ears are still deaf. "What I experienced…" Before I can finish, he lunges at me and cups his hand over my mouth. I gaze at him wide-eyed as he shoves me against the wall of one of the buildings.

"Quiet. An airship just landed in the parking lot," he mutters. "They brought those dog-creatures with them. Do you want to see?"

I nod and pry his fist from my lips. Together we slide down the alleyway, past crates and stacks of garbage, to the corner. My heart pauses as I glance around the edge of the structure, only to race to an unhealthy speed. There stands the man who set fire to my world, destroyed my life, and killed everything I've ever cared for. *Doom to the Titan.*

Deven saunters from the hovercraft. He's dressed in black armor with a gladiator helmet on his head. This is his game, his arena; a lucid moment in his madness. He must conquer the world to satisfy his wounded ego.

A faction of soldiers pace around the futuristic plane, followed by Injections on metal leashes. They snarl and snap their blood-stained teeth, anxious for a bite of human flesh. Their thick coats are matted with filth and their eyes glow like embers in the dim light. They were bred for horror, for death. No feeling. No regret. Just unmovable instinct.

"Another successful invasion. Once we occupy every Sector, there will be no stopping us. The nation will be ours. Goodbye America," Deven snickers. There's a newfound confidence about him that I've never seen before, menacing and malicious. His demeanor sends chills down my spine. One word from him and the entire country will be erased from existence. No longer is he a bully fighting for my place as top in our division. He has become as dangerous as a nuclear-bomb.

"Shoot him," I whisper to Matthew. "Kill him while you have the chance."

"Now is not the time. If I start shooting, so will his army. Two people against a thousand armed Legionaries are not beatable odds. We have to wait."

Deven stops and looks in our direction. I feel his pupils scan the side of the office-building. He senses my presence like a wolf searching for his prey. For several minutes he stands in silence with his eyes transfixed on our hiding place.

"Come and find me," I say in my head. *"I'll break your neck with my bare hands."*

"I'll video-chat with Squad 19 as soon as Little Rock's perimeters are secured." The Titan turns and moves towards the airship. "Grab what you can! We're leaving! Contact Cain in Sector 2 and tell him to meet me in Chicago."

Moments later, the hovercraft lifts off the ground and vanishes into the canopy of black clouds swirling above the inner city. My chance to kill Deven has once again slipped out of reach. As long as he breathes, death will continue to rage.

"So what now?" I sigh and lean against Matthew, exhausted. We are both covered in sweat, blood, and ashen debris. My curled hair is tangled and singed and my luxurious clothes reek of smoke.

"We need to find Truman and Stonecipher and get out of here while we still have a chance." He pulls a radioactive knife from his belt and attaches it to the side of my pants. "You have impeccable aim, Blue-Jay. If something happens, I trust you'll know how to defend yourself with something as small as this. Just don't do anything stupid, okay? And…break off your heels. You can't run in shoes like those."

"This is what happens when you allow James Stonecipher to give me a makeover," I scoff as I tear the heels off my shoes. "Do you have a hair-tie?"

He casts me a sarcastic look and motions to his short hair. "Sure, I have a bunch of them in my purse. Let me get one for you…"

"Don't be a jerk." I roll my eyes and quickly braid my hair, securing the charred ends with a bobby-pin. "How long do you think we have until the roads leading out of the city are blocked off?"

"It doesn't matter. Our destination is only a few miles away."

There's a sonic detonation in the streets beyond the office-complex. I step towards the opening of the alley, gasping at the scene before me. The skyline of skyscrapers that once shimmered like diamonds on the horizon is now burning with flames, crumbling to piles of useless rubble. Pillars of smoke reach like fingers into the night, tendrils of dust turning the poisonous air into a charcoal fog. Even with my ears ringing, I hear the wail of dying people.

"We must do something! He's killing everyone!" I shout as another missile bombs the downtown district. The explosion sends a pulse of energy in all directions, flattening the burning buildings to piles of steel and concrete. The ground trembles. Flames extinguish. And the screams die until the world is blanketed with silence. It's over. The Titan has won.

"They're coming after us!" Truman and Stonecipher appear at the edge of the adjoining road. They wave at me and point to a hovercraft trailing behind them. The machine is shooting balls of blue energy, blasting the surrounding pavement into clumps of rock. "Run!"

"Not yet," I whisper as I rip Matthew's gun off his shoulder. He yells at me as I sprint from the safety of the alleyway and into the complex's parking lot. I aim the weapon and fire electric charges at my father's invention. They bounce off the silver plating like rubber balls. Nothing will be able to destroy the plane. It was made to be indestructible.

"A distraction. It's the only way to keep Truman and Stonecipher alive," I think. *"For Kyle."*

I remove the knife from my hip. It flickers with radioactivity. I scan the landscape, strategizing my next move within a matter of seconds. This is what Matthew meant when he said, "Don't do anything stupid." I must be bad at following orders.

The airship soars towards me like a charging bull, beaming with insidious nuclear power. Its turbines spin rapidly, becoming a blur of florescent blades. I drop Matt's rifle and race towards the machine at top speed—eyes narrowed, fists clenched. My ears buzz. My senses enhance. And with a single surge of consuming strength, my programming takes effect.

Fierce. Fearless. Intimidating. Altered-genetics rush through my veins, adhering to my nerves and human membranes like dye. I lose control as instinct manifests itself. One jump sends me flying onto the hood of a charred truck. My body leaps into the air, spiraling towards the approaching hovercraft with abnormal speed.

Images flash through my clear mind, polluting the programming's intense focus. Pain pierces my brain. I clutch my head in midair and slam against the hood of Deven's machine.

Warmth. It covers my body in radiance. Sunlight. Bright ethereal rays, burst from the cloudless sky and wraps the world in clear, halcyon splendor. I smile as I climb from the surf, wading through the waves with familiar strides. Sand sticks to my feet like glue, hot with the tropic's summer glare. I grab a towel off the shore and wrap it around my body. I've never been to this place before and yet, my scarred heart tells me differently. Is this a past memory or a glimpse into my future, a dream I've yet to have?

I glance down at my hands. The tips of my fingers are wrinkled from swimming, but there's something different about my palms that causes me to stare with a mixture of curiosity and terror. I'm wearing a wedding ring—a silver band sparkling with diamonds. What is this place?

A flock of seagulls glides past me and disappears into the lush jungle canopy beyond the beach. Cliffs can be seen further along the shore. Waves slam against their rocky bases, spraying foam in all directions. An ecstasy of emotions ruptures in the depths of my chest. This must be a dream. I could've never been to a place as perfect as this.

In a confused daze, I wander towards a white building set away from the ocean. It's a house— big and beautiful with a wrap-around porch, large windows overlooking the Atlantic, and a hammock swinging lazily in the breeze. Could this be my home?

"There you are, Cora! Your husband's looking for you." Cathy appears at the entrance of the house. She's aged several years. Her scrawny figure is now tall and lean, and her auburn hair hangs long down her back. The tattoo on her right bicep is beginning to fade. "I'm glad you're home."

Metal slaps the breath from my lungs as I slide down the front of the aircraft. I stab my knife into the glass windshield, smiling as cracks vein across the dashboard. Pain continues to pulse through my head, scattered with images of unknown places. I grip the blade, allowing my programming to swallow all aspect of my humanity. Once this battle is over, I'll fight it back into the chasms of my consciousness.

"It can't be…" The pilots gaze at me with shock through the hoods of their black helmets. They thought I was dead. Sadly for them, the Titan told them wrong.

I kick off my shoes and climb up the front of the plane. A buzz of energy darts through my limbs, intensifying my motions. It washes away all emotion, giving me the edge I've been longing for. Easy. Consuming.

The airship dips to the left, knocking me across the slick surface. I cling to the rim of a glowing turbine. Heat explodes from the gun-system, blasting the ground beneath me to dust. I look towards the office-complex, seeing Truman and Stonecipher as they vanish into the alley. They are safe.

"Time for you to die," I mumble as I pull myself onto the side of the hovercraft. Wind beats against my back, threatening to throw me into oblivion. My knife is only a few feet out of reach. If I can somehow retrieve it, I'll be able to crash the airship.

With one leap of faith, my genetics propel me towards the cracked window of the machine. I reach towards the hilt of the blade as I fly weightlessly in midair. My body is in slow motion as I yank the knife free from the windshield. The glass shatters instantly, slicing my skin and stabbing the injected soldiers within the plane. Three seconds is all I have left before I plummet to the pavement below.

I take a deep breath as I begin to fall, and stab the weapon into the dashboard of my father's invention. Sparks emit from the holographic screens and technological devices. The glowing turbines grow dim, deadening the flying vehicle. I push myself away from the chunk of metal as it lands like a meteor in the parking lot, catching fire in a crater of cement and smashed cars. I'm left falling through the sky with limbs flailing. The impact of my landing will kill me. I'm too high to survive this free fall.

"Cora!" Matt races beneath me with his arms outstretched. He stares up at me in panic as I fall towards him. *"I will not let you die,"* his fear seems to say.

I squeeze my eyes shut and wait for the pain of impact. I expect to feel sadness or fear or terror, but I feel nothing as I fall through the air. I'm numb. Not even the thought of losing Kyle or the end of the world brings regret to my heart.

Matthew catches me. My figure slams against his chest like a tumbling boulder. I knock him to the ground, both of us landing on the ashen pavement with pain rippling through our bodies. My stomach is in knots. Glass protrudes from my bleeding skin. I moan and glance at his dirt-smeared face. He breathes heavily and gently touches my neck. We are still alive, and so are Truman and Stonecipher.

The door to the airship slides open manually. Four soldiers scramble out of the wreckage, some with blood oozing from their armor. They spot us and aim their guns, firing balls of blue energy in our direction.

"Run!" Matt shouts. He leaps to his feet as the enemy charges towards us, and pulls me up beside him. We both sprint in a mad dash for the alleyway, weaving between chunks of rubble to avoid being blown to pieces. "Faster!"

"Don't tell me what to do!" I rebuff as I snatch the gun I had dropped earlier off the ground. I pull the trigger. Nothing happens. I curse and toss the piece of metal aside. "We're not going to make it!" I scream as I glance behind us at our pursuers. My programming flickers through my blood-stream, enhancing everything to its max. I run as fast as my legs will carry me with my eyes focused on the entrance to the alley. I begin counting down the seconds until safety. *"5...4...3...2..."*

Matt and I race into the narrow enclosure. Stonecipher has stacked a pile of crates by the opening and is dousing them with the alcohol he brought from his train. An entire bottle of vodka is emptied over an old trashcan. Truman yells at us to keep moving but I stop to watch James.

"What on earth are you doing?!"

"Buying us some time." He pulls a lighter from his pocket and ignites the pile of tender. Flames spread across the tower, forming a flaming barricade against our attackers. "Move it, girl! They won't stay confused for long!"

The four of us leave the alleyway and travel down another tangle of streets, ducking into abandoned shops to keep out of sight. We find an old parking garage still stocked with vehicles. Matthew hotwires two parked motorcycles. Seeing the bikes remind me of Kyle, but again I feel nothing—that stark emptiness in my chest that once drove me to madness. Now it feels powerful and exhilarating, like a dose of Stonecipher's healing-serum.

"Quiet. They've followed us," I say. Footsteps can be heard at the entrance of the garage, mixed with the whisper of voices and the clang of armor. "Get down."

We hide ourselves beneath a navy convertible, watching as the soldiers appear. They pause and scan the space. Their masked heads are menacing—blank and faceless. I feel a surge of adrenaline pulse through my body, thirsting to kill. My ears buzz. My programming flairs. It wants to be released. I can't control it any longer. The rush is too intoxicating to withstand.

"We can sneak around them. No one has to die," Truman writes on a slip of paper. He gazes at me pleadingly, almost as if he knows the thoughts swarming my brain.

I look at him as my hands begin to shake. It's too late. My genetics have taken effect. There's nothing anyone can do to stop what is about to happen. "I'm sorry," I mutter in response as my body rolls from beneath the car and sprints towards the squad of injected teenagers.

Like a bird, I spring off the ground and wrap my legs around the first soldier's neck. I do a backbend, throwing his body over my head and onto the cement. With a twist of my ankles, I snap his spine in half. This is my identity. This is who I was created to be—dauntless, invincible, and victorious. Killing is a minor detail. One moment I'm a pretty teenage girl wearing cashmere and the next, I'm fighting like a savage. They may try to change my appearance but they will never change my blood.

The next two deaths come quicker than the first. I kick and twist, snapping spines and crushing necks. This time, I don't lose a tear. Regret and remorse are the last emotions to cross my mind. These people killed millions. They deserve to die.

I pull a knife from the belt of a dead soldier and thrust it into the stomach of my final victim. She crumbles to the earth, limp and bleeding. Her helmet rolls off, revealing her face. She's not much older than me—brunette and pretty with an upturned nose and thin lips. Darkness floods my confidence. A feeling of utter anguish stabs the boundaries my programming has formed. I killed her.

I stumble away from the bodies, confused and desperate. What have I done? How could I have allowed this to happen? Kyle would've been able to control his alterations. Why can't I? Why is painlessness such a temptation?

Truman and Stonecipher crawl from beneath the convertible. They stare at me with gaping mouths, shocked by the brutality of my actions. Fear has replaced respect. They will never look at me the same way. Even Matthew gazes at me with disapproval, as if becoming the girl he loves has turned me into a monster unfit for attention.

"We need to leave. More will be coming." I avoid eye-contact as I straddle one of the motorcycles. Matthew climbs in front of me and cranks the ignition. Moments later, the four of us are speeding away from Little Rock and into the deserted suburbs.

Embrace it. Withstand it. Two choices that will either save me or be the death of me. It's like deciding whether to choose Matthew or Kyle, emptiness or pain, strength or love. Now is the time to make a decision. Do I choose to become my father's creation and live with an emotionless heart, or do I choose to fight for my humanity?

There was a time I believed that my scars would disappear, vanish as if nothing had ever happened. But life doesn't work like that. What happens to you, changes you. There's no going back. It may sound simple, but it isn't. I've spent years trying to erase the choices I made— the lying, killing, and wanting to become something I'm not. It's an occupational hazard that anyone who has spent their entire life learning how to hate, eventually becomes bad at learning to love.

I want more than anything to be happy again, like the days I spent with Kyle in California. Happiness seems like the most natural thing in the world when I'm with him, but the strangest and most impossible thing when I'm not. Now I feel like I'm trying to breathe in a place with no oxygen. I gasp, but the air is empty and deceiving. After a few minutes, I will suffocate.

The light of dawn appears on the horizon as Matthew drives through a vacated neighborhood. Construction equipment is piled by the curb beside half-built homes and overgrown lawns. I cling to the fabric of his shirt as he slows to a stop in the middle of the road. Truman and Stonecipher park beside us. They've yet to say a word to me, as if I'm a criminal on my way to prison. We are fighting a war, and I will do whatever it takes to keep the people I care about safe. Kyle is courageous. I am only brave.

"The entrance to the outpost is around here somewhere…" Truman climbs off his bike and wanders towards the structure of an unfinished house. We follow him hesitantly, weaving between wooden posts and a rusting bulldozer.

"Thank you for saving my life," Stonecipher whispers as we walk through the skeletal building. The final rays of moonlight fall across his filth-smeared face, revealing a sincerity I've never seen before. "No one has ever risked themselves for me like that, Cora Marie. What you did was courageous beyond all measures. So whatever people may say in the future, you will always be my hero."

"I killed six people tonight, James."

"How can we expect to win this war if we aren't willing to exterminate our enemies? You did what you had to do to save us. That, in my opinion, is worthy of honor not persecution. I believe in *the sword and the arrow*. I believe in hope. You are hope." He salutes me. "Be the Victor. Not the Victim."

I muster a smile. His forgiveness eases some of the pain in my chest.

"I found it!" Matt shouts from the backyard. We go to where he is standing; beside a lopsided, portable bathroom. The blue building is covered with ash and looks as if it hasn't been used in a decade.

"You've got to be kidding?!" I gawk as Truman opens the plastic door. "Ian Marx created this, didn't he? There was one exactly like it outside his house in Florida."

"Yes. We used his designs when building different escape-routes out of the outposts. This is just a backdoor. It's the most accessible," James says as he moves into the box and fits himself through the toilet. "Very creative idea, if I do say so myself." His head disappears into the small hole.

"I'll see you both at the bottom. Cora, I have a feeling you're going to be surprised by what you see." Truman goes inside next. He climbs down the opening, leaving Matthew and me alone.

I lean against a wooden beam and breathe a sigh of relief. The sun shimmers on the horizon. It breaks through the darkness, reviving the world to life. "Do you hate me now?"

Matt shakes his head. "No, I don't hate you; even though you did lose both of my weapons." He wraps his arm around my shoulders. "In the future, can you try to follow orders, Blue-Jay?"

"I doubt it. I'm not very good at following orders."

We sit for a few minutes in silence, watching the sunrise with meager fascination. Even when the earth is swarmed with chaos, the sun will continue to rise and fall. Infinity is forever. Forever is always. And always is a promise engraved in the core of my existence.

As soon as I have retained my composure, Matthew and I climb down the tunnel and into Kyle's military outpost. Florescent bulbs line the interior of the tube. The hatch above us is sealed shut the moment our feet touch the concrete floor below. I glance around at the many awaiting faces, almost dumbstruck by the hopeful awe in their eyes.

Arms cross. Hands pat my back. Legionaries surround me, all young and radiating with support. "Welcome to outpost-gold, Blue-Jay." They smile and beam with excitement. We've never met and yet when they look at me, it's as if I've been a part of their family for a lifetime.

"Come. There's a lot you need to see." Matt grabs my hand and leads me away from the crowd of soldiers. They watch us move down the hallway, still glowing with the addictive humility and leadership Kyle emits. Prime Way trained me to fight with hate. Kyle trained these teenagers how to fight with purpose. He gave them intention.

The narrow corridor opens like a cathedral, widening into a room the size of a football stadium. Balconies are stacked along the plated walls, revealing levels of control centers and living space. The ceiling forms a pixel dome, playing a broadcast from Dimidium. Hundreds of humans and Legionaries walk among the various rooms. Some carry baskets of rations and medical supplies while others have holographic tablets and transmitters. It holds a kind of beauty I've never seen before.

I walk among the masses of people in line to receive their breakfast, still marveling at the technology surrounding me. Re-circulated air blows against my face as I stare up at the ceiling. Voices echo through the underground courtyard, forming a lively song. It takes away the darkness of the world above. People are surviving because of what Kyle's army is doing. I want to be a part of them.

"It's pretty amazing, isn't it?" Matthew asks. He stands beside me, scanning the elaborate architecture with equal intrigue. "President Marner had dozens of outposts like this built when the war began. Each is made to accommodate a thousand refugees and is equipped with a medical clinic, soup kitchen, and a full work-out facility with a swimming pool."

A group of children rush past me. They are clean and dressed in pastel-colored clothing, bright and fresh like a sunrise on the Pacific. Like Dimidium, there is a fine line dividing life in the outpost from the horrors of war beyond its rock confines.

I watch a pregnant woman saunter from the mob of survivors with a plate of food resting on her swollen belly. She moves towards me wearily and smiles. Her face is kind and framed with strands of frizzy, black hair.

"Thank you for fighting for my babies' futures," she tells me. "I'm having twins. My husband and I have decided to name them Kyle and Cora, after the heroes that made their birth possible. Without you, Blue-Jay, we wouldn't be alive right now." She salutes me and wanders to a table set away from the chaos. Her words form a knot in my stomach. These people see me as being their leader, a hero. I've done nothing to earn their respect.

"Cora!" Sarah appears in the crowd. She waves and runs towards me. Her blonde hair is tied back in a ponytail and her once sick body is now strong and healthy. She's dressed in gray armor and has a gun strapped to her side. So much has changed, I hardly recognize her. She has become a part of my race.

Seth follows behind her. His mousy-brown hair hangs long over his forehead and his face is clean shaven. He smiles. His soft eyes glow with youth. He and Sarah both have *the sword and the arrow* tattooed on their left wrist in blue ink.

"I've missed you both so much!" I embrace them, trying not to squeal with excitement. It's been a long time since I've seen a familiar face. I had almost forgotten what they looked like.

"You're alive," Sarah whimpers. "Everyone told me you were going to die. I didn't want to believe them." Tears form in her eyes as she hugs me a second time. "How are you?! Kyle has been worried sick. He's going to be ecstatic when he finds out you're alive!"

"I saw him briefly at the train station but he didn't notice me. Where is he now?"

"We're to meet him in Sector 7 in a few days," Seth tells me. "Our division was separated when the invasion on Little Rock began. The outpost outside of Minneapolis is our rendezvous point."

"I'm just happy you're still breathing!" Sarah laughs. "You are a walking miracle, Cora."

"It's time for us to go," Matt says and touches my shoulder. "Truman wants us to meet him in the medical clinic. You desperately need some antibiotics."

"I'll be in the hospital ward, if you want to stop by!" Sarah shouts.

The next hour passes in a blur of dimly lit corridors, sterile rooms, and needles dripping with chemically-altered healing. I'm decontaminated, coated with various creams, and pumped with serums of every kind. A nurse slices off my charred clothing, revealing the scar between my breasts. From the outside, it appears healed; but I can still feel the emptiness within. She sprays me with a clear liquid. It sinks into my skin, healing my cuts until they are nothing but thin, white lines. The singed ends of my hair are snipped away before being braided. None of it arouses me from my shock-induced daze. I stare at the white walls, unable to feel anything. My programming has faded and yet I remain numb. I know what I must do, but my body is paralyzed in place— motionless.

I change into a pair of nude-colored heels and a fitted, silver dress before joining Truman in the waiting room. He is sitting in an overstuffed chair while reading the first chapter of *'The War of the Worlds'* by H. G. Wells. When I cough, he looks up and musters a fake smile.

"Did you want to speak with me?" I ask.

"Yes. We have a few things we need to discuss." He points to the sofa across from him. "Please, take a seat. This won't last long."

I sit and stare at him impatiently. "I'm sorry for what happened in the parking garage…"

"That's not why I wanted to speak with you," he tells me. "I've decided to cancel the remainder of the tour. It's become clear to me that you are not emotionally stable enough to endure several more weeks of traveling. You never did have time to fully recover after being wounded. You need to rest. So instead of going to Memphis as planned, we will be traveling to New York City. My penthouse survived the initial attack. You will be safe there while you finish healing."

"You're going to lock me up?! I've done everything you've asked! Why are you doing this?!" I yell. Anger explodes through my body. He cannot treat me like a prisoner. I'll run away.

"You haven't slept in weeks, haven't eaten. Matthew and I have noticed. There's something that's happening to you, Cora. You're not acting sane."

"You think I'm crazy?!"

"No, but I think you're on the verge of doing something stupid. How can you expect to lead an army when you're battling against yourself? I advise that you dig deep and settle some problems within your own mind." He stands and motions to the two guards in white uniforms stationed at the door. "These nice gentlemen will escort you wherever you want to go. Think of them as handcuffs." Before I can argue with him any further, he vanishes down the winding corridor.

I scream obscenities at Truman and bury my face in the palms of my hands. *"Be brave. You are brave,"* I tell myself. *"The time has come to choose your fate. Embrace or withstand? No more games. No more walking the tightrope between two identities. The time has come."*

I rise, brush the wrinkles from my clothing, and face the guards with a scowl on my face. "I'd like to go to the hospital ward, if you don't mind."

They nod and lead me from the room.

The building stretches, for what seems like miles, in all directions; forming many levels of terrain. I stride down Plexiglas hallways, across rock arches, and beneath natural waterfalls. One moment I'm walking on metal and the next, I'm stepping on dirt. Some sections of the outpost are composed of caves with ceilings dripping with stalactites, while others look like the interior of Marner's hovercraft. The architecture is truly genius.

"That's the hospital ward." One of the guards points to an opening in the side of a stone wall. The door is marked with a red X. "We'll be waiting here."

I go inside the chamber. The room is half the size of the outpost's atrium. Beds clutter the space, all occupied with the sick and wounded. Legionaries rush from patient-to-patient, bandaging cuts and administering medication. Sarah is among them. She smiles and motions for me to approach her.

"Great. I'm glad you're here. I could use your help with cleaning this burn." She hands me a pile of gauze and a pack of ice. "You took medical classes at Prime Way, didn't you?"

"Yeah...I was top in my class," I say as she uncovers her patient's wound. The girl's stomach has been scalded by one of the Titan's Erasers. When Sarah touches her blackened skin, she screams and looks at me with tears in her eyes. "You're going to be alright," I tell her. "Be brave. It'll be over soon."

"It hurts," she sobs as her burn is coated with a hybrid-aloe mixture. She writhes and tries desperately to push Sarah's hands away. "Make it stop!"

"Hold her down, Cora. I can't stitch up the gash if she keeps moving."

I kneel beside the bed and grab the young girl's hand. "What's your name?"

"Hannah," she mumbles between gasps for air.

"Listen to me, Hannah. You have to be strong. I know it hurts. Look," I pull down the neckline of my dress so she can see my scar. "It'll hurt like hell for the next few minutes. But if you can push through the pain, Sarah will fix you and all this will stop! Can you be brave?!"

She nods. "I can be brave like you."

Sarah looks at me and smiles. "Hold on, little one. Count to forty and this will all be over." She goes to work the moment Hannah starts counting—sewing the gash, pumping her with antibiotics, and wrapping her wound with gauze. "I'm going to give you a tranquilizer to help you sleep. When you wake up, you'll feel as if none of this ever happened."

The girl turns to me as Sarah sticks a needle into the vein of her arm. "Thanks, Blue-Jay." Her eyes close. She slumps against her pillow in a peaceful, painless sleep.

I stare at her, feeling a twinge of envy and despair bubble inside my chest. These people need a hero; even if that hero is a confused, teenage girl with a major identity crisis. It doesn't matter to them who I was or the problems I have. If I choose to stand for light instead of darkness, for hope instead of fear, for love instead of hate—they will follow me to the ends of the earth. All along I've been focusing on my inadequacies instead of embracing my strengths. There is meaning to my imperfection. There is beauty in my flaws. There is strength in compassion. Bravery may be self-serving, but it has the power to rally millions of people to face their foes.

"You've changed," Sarah says as she places a pack of ice on an elderly woman's forehead. "I spent months with you in California but I never really knew you, Cora. The person Kyle talks about isn't the girl who claimed to be my best-friend's sister." She passes me a bottle of pain relievers. "I'm not mad, I just…wish I had gotten to know the *Joan of Arc* figure everyone adores."

"You do know her. I haven't changed much." I place a few pills in the hand of a girl sprawled on a cot with a bandage taped to her arm. "Have you heard any word from Callan?"

"Not since the night of the attack. The Titan must have him on lockdown. I expected that he'd at least send a goodbye note or something. Don't quote me on this but…I think I may be in love with him." She glances in my direction and forces a smile. "This war has wreaked havoc on relationships. Take you and Kyle for example. You're supposed to be a team and yet you haven't seen each other in over a year. What are you going to do when you're finally reunited?"

"Thank God for bringing the two of us together," I answer. "How was he the last time you saw him?"

"Tired. He doesn't sleep, just patrols the camp like a pacing guard dog. His rations disappear but no one ever sees him eat or drink. I worry about him. He's a strong leader but gives away too much of himself to survive. When I join the rest of my division, I'll talk to him about taking a few days off. Maybe once I tell him you're alive, he'll come visit you on leave." She fills a patient's canteen with fresh water and adds an extra blanket to the cradle of a newborn babe. "Kyle saved my life, you know? He programmed me when my organs began to fail. It's a blessing but at the same time, a curse. Becoming a Legionary has given me health and enhanced abilities but…I've seen things, horrible things that I will never forget."

The ground quakes. Dust falls from the ceiling as bombs pound the earth above. Sarah shouts orders at some of the younger Legionaries and rushes around the room, doing her best to calm the wounded. I try to make myself useful by rocking the cradles of crying infants and comforting the elderly, but I still feel useless. All I need is a single command to set me free.

"What can I do to help?!" I ask as another explosion shakes the foundation of the outpost. "Give me a command, Sarah! This is what I was trained to do."

"I can handle things here! Go get some rest. I'm sure you need it." She rummages through an old filing-cabinet and tosses me a box of syringes. "Get well soon, Cora." The container in my hands passes along an unspoken command. She wants me to run away, to join Kyle, to fight alongside the people I love. *Be the Victor. Not the Victim.*

After saluting Sarah, I turn and walk into the corridor where my guards are waiting. They look at me suspiciously before leading me to my bedroom. I follow with a smile on my face. It won't be long until I break free from Truman and Marner. They can't control me any longer. I am the Blue-Jay. I am dauntless. Nothing can put me down.

My apartment reminds me of a hotel room—clean, tidy, and impersonal. The walls are solid rock, crudely hidden beneath cheap paintings and light fixtures. The queen-size bed is covered with a thin, purple quilt. And the wardrobe has recently been supplied with a few changes of clothes.

I kick off my shoes and pace around the room. Outside the window of my door, I see the backs of my guard. Their presence makes me uncomfortable. I could easily render them unconscious and hide their bodies in the bathtub. It's what Truman's expecting me to do, another reason for him to lock me away in his godforsaken penthouse. He wants me to fail his tests.

"What's wrong with you?" I ask myself as another shock of pain pierces through my brain. "Why is this happening?" My programming dwindles on the verge of appearing, but I quickly stifle the urge.

I go to the closet and find a bathing suit among the items, remembering what Matthew had said about the outpost having a swimming pool. The thought of my body soaring smoothly through the water sends a ripple of energy through my exhausted frame. Sleep is the last thing I want to do at a moment like this. I haven't gone swimming in over a year.

The red, one-piece bathing suit is a size too small and squeezes my torso like a corset. It's the best I can find so I quickly re-braid my hair, snatch a towel from the bathroom, and join my guards in the hallway.

Weightless. Tranquil. Silent. I hold my breath as I sink beneath the surface of the pool, submersed in warmth. The lights flicker across my skin as I glide through the water. My body twists and turns, swimming slow laps. I close my eyes and allow the chlorine to consume my emotions. I don't want to think. It's easier to focus on the movement of my arms and the repetitive kick of my legs.

"This isn't over," a voice in my head whispers. *"You can't escape."*

I blow mist from my nostrils and propel myself across the pool. My feet pound the water. My arms lift and fall like the turbines of Deven's airship, drawing me away from my confusion and into the only comfort I've ever known—the racing of my heart and the rush of fatigue exploding through my blood. I was made to be physical, to sweat, and to find relief in pain. But the pain I feel now is anything but comforting. It's hollow and empty, seaming with the darkness I've hidden beneath my layers of masks and scars. Unlike most battles, I can't run away.

Another stab of discomfort pulses through my brain. I cringe and scream as a flash of light fills my pupils. No one can hear me. I will drown beneath my waves of confliction.

> *I'm standing in the middle of a battlefield, red with blood and smoking with ashes. Blasts of gore splatter my armor. Screams of dying soldiers pelt me with fear. I spin, scanning the chaos with teary eyes. Arrows fly from my hands like bullets, killing to protect. The remnants of Dallas lay behind me. All that remains of the city are charred buildings and radioactive rubble. Everything is gone.*

> *"Cora, tell your division to retreat to the ruins!" Kyle shouts at me from a barricade of demolished vehicles. His face is smeared with sweat and grime, battered and worn from days of war. He lifts his sword and yells something that sounds like a battle cry.*

> *"I'm not leaving you!" I scream as a bomb blasts an old military tank to my right, emitting a discharge that knocks me from my feet.*

> *"If we don't move now, we are all going to die!" Callan yells. My brother heaves me to my feet and drags me away from the confines of the barricade.*

> *"Better to die with the people I love than survive alone."*

My lungs burn. I cough for air as my face emerges from the tepid water. My body trembles. My head aches. What's happening to me? The memories playing through my mind are not my own. Am I hallucinating? Is this what happens when a person reaches their breaking point?

I float on my back and stare at the tiled ceiling, waiting for the discomfort to subside. It doesn't. Instead, another surge of torment scrapes across the soft tissues of my brain. There's no way to mask my pain. I scream and with a final breath of oxygen, drop beneath the illuminated surface.

Movement ripples through my body. I gasp and clutch my swollen stomach with a combination of fear and amazement. Life is growing inside of me. I'm defying my destructive purpose. Instead of killing, I'm creating.

"She moved!" I exclaim, laughing at my own joy. "I felt her kick!" I look down at my expanding torso, noticing a diamond ring on my finger. The gems are the size of my fingernails.

Hands reach around my waist. They comb over my belly, feeling for signs of activity. I hear laughter, a deep explosion of contentment echoing from behind; and though I try to find familiarity within the sound, my mind has built a wall between all recognition.

"What should we name her?" my husband asks.

I try to face him but my neck is stiff, almost as if my mind has refused to give away his identity. "Kate," I answer. "I think we should name her Kate, after Katrina."

"Sounds perfect."

Again my daughter kicks. Her small heartbeat pounds in my ears. Wife and mother—two words I never wanted to exist in my collection of titles. But now, I've embraced them. This is my baby. I loved her before I even knew she would exist.

I claw desperately for the side of the pool and heave myself onto the concrete ledge. Water drips from my hair and slides down my flesh. I pant and rub my eyes, trying to wipe away the horrific images. Nothing my own mind has conjured has ever felt as vivid as this. Am I experiencing a glitch like Kyle? I don't understand. Why is my programming allowing these glimpses to be released?

"You're becoming very predictable, Blue-Jay." Matthew saunters into the room with a towel draped over his bare shoulders. "What are you doing here?"

"Things always seem better when I'm wet," I say and toy with the star-charm dangling from my neck. I slip into the pool and watch as he climbs stealthily into the water. He barely makes a splash or ripple as he disappears beneath the surface. Kyle would have done a cannonball, not moved with such rehearsed and fluid motions. It's proof of Matthew's genetics, his origin. Like me, he was the first of the Legionary race. We are wired differently from the others, been indoctrinated for too long of a time. Our own minds have been invaded, consumed, programmed. *Once it's entrenched in the system, there's no tearing it out.* Matthew and I are all that's left of the Originals. We are the last of our kind.

"You've already talked with Truman, haven't you?" He floats beside me with a guilty look in his ice-blue irises. His Australian accent flickers, changing from the voice of my best-friend to the brother of Ian Marx. "I'm sorry…"

"Let's not talk about it now, okay?" I paddle around him, allowing the warmth of the water to caress my healing skin. "For the next few minutes, can we just be friends and not worry about the war?"

"If that's what you want," he smirks and dunks beneath me, skimming the shadow-strewn floor like a bareback flounder. I dive after him. The both of us swim side-by-side, spiraling in the light like two fish in an aquarium. Chlorine burns my eyes as I stroke past him. He smiles and races me to the furthest corner of the pool.

A shock of torture slashes through my body once again, attacking my brain with the pain of a thousand needles. I writhe and build a mental barrier between my thoughts and the rage of my altered-genetics. It tugs at my nerves and stabs at my muscles, trying desperately to gain control. It can't have me. No one can.

"Stop! Go away!" I scream into the depths of my mind. *"I choose to embrace my humanity, not whatever is lurking inside my memories! I choose to love."*

Matt grabs my hand and pulls me to the surface of the pool. His arm brushes against my leg as I emerge from the water. His touch sends a race of inhuman emotions through my chest. I look at him, still seeing that ten-year-old boy I befriended as a child. What I am feeling isn't real. It can't be real.

My programming is unleashed in a final surge of adrenaline. I can't control my body. It lunges forward and wraps itself around Matthew's neck. He stares at me with surprise as I thrust my mouth against his, kissing him with more passion than I've ever felt before. I scream at myself to stop but I've lost control. My lips move unwillingly, forcefully. What have I done? What am I doing?

I feel Matt's arms around my waist, locking me in a protective embrace. He presses my back against the concrete wall and kisses me with equal effort, as if he's been waiting for this moment for a decade. His hands cup my face and comb through my wet hair. His heartbeat pounds against my scarred chest, as wrong as a skeleton-key in a car's ignition. My heart is saved for its other half, the only thing capable of stealing away my emptiness and making me whole.

"Embrace it, Cora. This is how it should be," my programming whispers. *"Matthew understands you. He's wired the same way. With him, you'll never feel pain or heartbreak. You'll be free. No more feeling. No more regret. One choice will end your suffering forever. Choose to embrace."*

"I can't allow you to suck away everything worth living for. Love is worth the pain," I answer as my lips continue to kiss unwillingly. *"I choose humanity instead of power, emptiness instead of strength. I choose Kyle."*

As if slicing the chains binding me, the effects of my alterations suddenly fade. I regain control of my body and open my eyes to see the illuminated water of the pool and a blurred, cross-eyed view of Matthew's face. He holds me tight, kissing my mouth as if the key to immortality lies between my teeth.

"Stop!" I rip myself away and stare at him, confused by his smile. His sultry breath blows across my face as I plant my hands firmly on his shoulders.

"There she is," he mutters and kisses me once more. "I knew you were still in there, Blue-Jay. Kyle hasn't completely changed you."

"Let go of me!" I shout as he nuzzles his face in the crease of my neck. I lift my knee into his stomach and kick him away from the side of the pool. "That kiss was an accident! Don't start thinking for one minute that I actually love you!"

"Deep down, you know you have feelings for me. I felt it! You couldn't have kissed me like that without it being intentional. Admit it. You love me. Why do you keep lying to yourself?!" When I reach towards the ladder, he grabs my waist. "Tell me the truth…"

"I've already told you. It was an accident, nothing more. Kissing you is like kissing my brother. That's all. I love Kyle and I always will. So stop touching me and pretending that there's even the slightest chance that we could be together, because there's not!"

His joy melts into an angry scowl. He nods and lifts himself onto the concrete ledge. "Fine, but I doubt you've ever kissed Kyle the way you just kissed me." He snatches his towel from the ground and leaves the gym, slamming the door shut behind him.

I curse and crawl out of the pool with my blood boiling. Guilt weighs on my shoulders, mixed with anger and a strong sense of rebellion. Matthew may be right about me never kissing Kyle with as much passion as my programming forced, but not for long. I will prove him wrong.

Later that afternoon, Stonecipher's train is recovered and hidden a few miles down the tracks. I say goodbye to Sarah and Seth, inhale a final breath of freedom, and endure an awkward trek to the locomotive. Truman babbles about his penthouse's accommodations, James fiddles with a lighter, and Matthew maintains an angry silence. I'm glad to be forgotten for a few moments. My head aches. Pain consumes my heart. If I were able, I'd run away and never look back.

Wind cradles my body in a freefall. Pavement flies towards me, dusty and covered with rusting cars and pieces of crumbled rubble. The ruins of a city rise in all directions, like jagged teeth ready to chew me to bits. I'm tumbling through the air. My legs push against the cracked glass of skyscrapers, propelling me across the avenue like a swooping bird. I grab hold of an electrical wire and swing in a low arch towards the frozen traffic. I'm wearing gloves. A bow and a sheath of handmade arrows are strapped to my back. This should scare me—the fluttering of my stomach, the strain of muscles, and the fear of falling to my death. But I'm not scared. I'm not scared of anything.

The images feel like shocks of electricity. They flash through my mind and then disappear as if they never occurred. What am I turning into? Why is this happening?

Coffee swirls in my mug, black and bitter. I glance out the train's window at the passing landscape. New York is a day's ride away. By tomorrow morning, I'll be in an elaborate prison built thirty-stories off the ground, in a city that has long since been blown to ashes.

I tap the icon engraved on my bracelet. Images form in midair, showing pictures of Kyle and the people I've left behind. I try to touch their faces but my hand passes through the screen. They are a memory, a piece of me that has been locked out of reach. I will find them and one day, things will be different. Like my flashbacks, life will be warm and beautiful again.

"What's wrong?" James asks as he sits across from me. He sips from his cup of tea and watches my expressions curiously. "You seem upset, and not just at Matt and Truman."

"May I ask you something?"

"Ask away." He pours a pack of sugar into his drink and waits patiently for me to respond.

"What if I told you I was experiencing…glitches, you know, like Kyle?"

"What sort of glitches are we talking about?"

I lean forward. My voice is barely above a whisper. "I've been seeing things, none of which have ever happened. There's a horrible pain in my head and then it's like I'm looking into the future. What could cause this? You knew my dad and how his programming worked. Please, I need answers. I feel like I'm losing my mind."

He chews on the side of his cheek, deep in thought. "The Prime Way Program altered you in two ways. It mutated your genetics so you'd be able to run at impossible speeds, have enhanced senses, and so on. Your brain had to be programmed, not only to implant instinct and strategic knowledge, but to level your mental capacity to match with your body's abilities. Side-effects happen when your level of programming falls less than that of which your body requires. Glitches, on the other hand, occur when your level of programming reaches full brain capacity."

"Is it dangerous?"

"I don't believe so," he answers. "Your father created the injecting and programming process, not to breed super-soldiers, but to create a perfect and superior human-race. That was its original purpose. What you are experiencing now is a bonus ability, a gift. Don't tell anyone. Keep what you are seeing a secret. You may be able to use it to your advantage one day."

"So I'm not turning into a freak or anything?"

"Not at all," he laughs. "Wait a few days for the boost of programming to adhere. After that, you shouldn't have any problems."

CHAPTER 7

Music blasts through the penthouse, unlocking a new level of intensity within me. I grab a steak knife from the sink and plunge it into the kitchen table. I crouch low on the floor with sweat glistening off my bare stomach and begin sawing off a leg of the furniture. Sawdust clogs my vision. My fingers bleed as I rip the pillar of wood away from the expensive countertop. I breathe heavily as I slice the plank into an inch-thick piece of bendable plywood. It feels lightweight in my callused hands as I crawl from beneath the lopsided table and perch my half-naked body on a silk-covered lounge chair. Swiftly, I carve away the sides of the stick, narrowing the limb and widening the handle. Like a madwoman, I slice nicks on both necks and lay my project on the magazine-strewn coffee-table.

I sprint across the living-room and rip the gray curtains away from the wall-length window. They fall to the carpeted floor, waiting for my knife to shred them to pieces. I do so, tearing the fabric into long slivers. I weave the cotton strands into a single cord and hastily fasten it to either end of my whittled form.

I gather the remaining splintered wood from the ground and carry it into the kitchen. Steam curls from the pot warming on Truman's stove. Metal boils inside the basin, bubbling and splattering the tiled backboard with silver dots. I scoop the silverware from the drawers and carefully lower each object into the molten mixture. They vanish one-by-one, liquefying into a deadly drink.

Pouring some of the solution onto the marble countertop, I quickly use a pizza-cutter to slice the silver into sharp triangles. I brush the shards into the water-filled sink, cringing as a cloud of steam blows across my face. It dampens my hair and underwear, smearing my makeup into a gruesome ring of black around my bloodshot eyes.

I wipe the perspiration from my face and walk towards the bedroom. I snatch a pillow off the waterbed. With a single movement, I stab the cushion and retrieve a handful of goose feathers. Their ethereal fibers wisp gently across my skin, deceptive of their new purpose.

A different song blares from the penthouse's speakers. It's livelier than the first, causing a newfound sense of anger and envy to flow through my healing chest. I curse and work faster—attaching silver tips to the slivers of wood, weaving feathers to the fletching of the arrows, testing the power of my bow by shooting at a picture of Truman fastened over the fireplace. It works perfectly every time, each dart piercing his skull with precision.

I sew a pillowcase into a makeshift quiver before hiding my handmade bow and arrows in the hall closet, along with a backpack full of provisions and survival equipment. I'm escaping tomorrow. I have a weapon, a transmitter, and a destination. All I have to do is find a way out of my cell. As soon as I'm free, I'll travel to Sector 7 and find Kyle. I refuse to be a prisoner any longer. I've served my time, done my duty. There's nothing holding me here.

"It won't be long now, Kyle. We'll be together again," I whisper to myself with tears in my eyes. Loneliness is more crippling than emptiness. I've been here alone for more than a week. Occasionally Matthew will bring me a bag of groceries or a new book to read, but he doesn't say a word. He leaves the rations, relocks the elevator, and disappears. Stonecipher and Truman returned to Dimidium once they encaged me. They'll video-chat me sometimes. Besides the news they release, I remain clueless as the Titan continues to invade my country. I hate seclusion. I blast music to drown the fearful silence. My thoughts are my only companions and they scare me more than a thousand of Deven's soldiers. I am my own worst enemy.

Wearily I saunter through the vacant apartment; beneath the rooftop swimming pool, which has turned a murky green hue, and across the plush living-room. Sumptuous velvet couches clutter the space, along with a flat-screen television and a metallic lamp. Books are stacked on the floor. Empty movie cases and wads of garbage form piles at the base of a million-dollar sculpture. I've done everything to wipe Truman's prestige from the interior of the building, but it's impossible. All the mess in the world couldn't stifle the rich atmosphere of New York's remaining penthouse.

I lean against the wall of glass overlooking the desecrated city and toy with the charm dangling from my neck. My body is constantly pumped with Stonecipher's healing serum and yet fatigue continues to fog my brain. Though I haven't had another programming mishap, I can still feel that twinge of temptation in the back of my head, longing to be released. What have I done to deserve this? Why must the world be so cruel? I'm suffering, constantly battling every burden dumped on my shoulders. Normality is dead. Prime Way is nonexistent. Numbers, names, titles— they consume my emotions in a frenzy of tears and pain, a stigma disgracing my identity. This game has lost its thrill. It's no longer an exercise meant to challenge my strengths, or a battle of the mind. This is a war and I'm being sucked into the destructive embrace of my own inadequacies. It'd be easier to release my humanity but I choose to stand firm.

Morning breaks on the horizon, a splash of color to the charred ruins of New York City. The crumbled, indelible structures form black silhouettes against the blood-red canvas. The world seems dead. Not a single person has been seen in the debris littered streets below. I'm like a flower growing inside a fire-pit, a beating heart amidst ghosts.

I've stared at this scene for days, watching old Broadway posters drift through the frozen traffic and cockroaches scurrying out of gutters. Wind whistles through the skeletal cityscape like a wail of imminent death, warning me of my approaching fate. I imagine what New York must have looked like before the bombing, alive and bustling with activity. Kyle stood here a year ago. He saw the life before the death. How could we have been so foolish to have become comfortable in our ignorance? One small mistake transformed our identity. It woke us up, after destroying our home.

The plasma-screen television beeps and flashes with light, warning me of an oncoming video-call. I trip over a fur-covered sofa and snatch my robe from beneath a pile of sawdust. I cover my bare figure before racing around the apartment in a desperate attempt to hide the evidence of my project from view. I toss everything suspicious into the trashcan and replace the missing table leg with a stack of novels. As soon as the penthouse looks somewhat tidy, I fetch a box of stir-fry from the fully stocked fridge and take a seat beneath the murky swimming pool.

Truman's face appears on the screen. He gazes down from the television with a nuance in his obdurate eyes, as if seeing me has brightened his morning. It's a surprise, especially when he smiles and salutes me. What have I done? Who's died?

"Good. You're awake. I was afraid you'd still be in bed." He shuffles through a stack of papers on his pixel desk, glancing at me nonchalantly.

"I never went to sleep," I rebuff and stuff my mouth with a forkful of noodles. "What do you and Stonecipher want now? I thought by locking me in this plush cage, we wouldn't have to speak to each other."

"I doubt you'll ever get rid of me, Cora Kingston. We belong to the same world now." He watches me with a pleasant smirk on his lips, as if he knows something that will bring light to my darkness. "I have a surprise I think may cheer you up."

"Are you going to release me?"

"Better," he answers. "Kyle is coming to see you."

I choke on a piece of carrot and stare at him wide-eyed. My tongue remains motionless as I fumble for words.

"He called Marner a few hours ago from a hotspot in Sector 7. Apparently Sarah and Seth arrived at their rendezvous point and shared the news of your survival. He's on a train as we speak."

I bury my face in my hands, trying to hide my joyful tears. Kyle is coming for me? We're going to be together again after a year of being apart? *The sword and the arrow* united? The weight on my shoulders is lifted. I don't have to keep fighting this war alone. Kyle is coming and together, we can face the world. "What time will he arrive?"

"Roughly seven o' clock," Truman tells me. "That's all I have to say. I'm sure you have plenty to do so I'll go ahead and log-off. Just keep in mind all he's been through over the past year. Kyle may not be the same person you remember." He smiles as the screen fades to black.

I collapse against the back of the sofa, breathing a sigh of relief. Tonight, I won't be alone. Tonight, everything will be better. Tonight, I'll be with my family.

"Only a few more hours." I tug at the end of my braid, suddenly feeling a wave of panic wash through my twisted stomach. The penthouse is a mess. Kyle shouldn't have to see this. I want him to arrive at a clean home; to a girl he's proud to love.

I leap off the couch and immediately go to work—cleaning, tidying, and reorganizing every closet and drawer in the apartment. I wash the dishes piled in the sink and scrub the floors. I mend the shredded curtains, patch the goose feather pillow, change the sheets on the bed, and spend hours washing the fish tank above the bathtub. I finish around two o' clock. The penthouse looks perfect.

There's a rock of anxiousness within my chest, grinding at my emotions. Unlike everything I've felt over the past few months, it's not painful. Instead it's hot with feelings and bursting with excitement. I am so terribly human.

The next three hours are spent on my appearance, a montage of expensive clothing and red lipstick. I shower, curl and straighten my hair a dozen times, paint my nails, and try in a failed attempt to do my makeup. What has happened to me? A year ago, I wouldn't have cared if I met Kyle wearing muddy boots and a sweat-soaked shirt. Now I'm acting like a love-struck, teenage girl.

I change my clothes four times, rummage through racks of dresses and boxes overflowing with shoes. I finally decide on a navy, A-line skirt and a chiffon blouse. After sliding on a pair of red heels, I glance at my reflection in the bedroom vanity. The person staring back at me is the identity I once longed to obtain—young, normal, with large, brown eyes that sparkle with innocence and a smile that radiates with the bliss of youth. It's everything I'm not, a mask to hide the imperfection within. Why is an appearance so deceiving? Behind every beautiful person, there are a multitude of scars.

My hands find their way to the hole between my breasts, a chasm plunging through my core. All the makeup in the world couldn't hide the ugliness of the mark. But how could I hate the scar that saved my world, saved the only thing worth living for? I am one piece of the puzzle. My other half will tonight make me whole.

I go to the kitchen and search through an old cookbook, finding a recipe for chicken casserole. It's the one thing I know I can make without failure. I follow the instructions and as soon as the dish has been placed in the oven, I furnish the lopsided kitchen table with the two remaining sets of silverware, a liter of soda, and a pair of candles. It's already six o' clock. In an hour, Kyle will be home.

The clock ticks. Each second melts away with overwhelming anxiousness. I remove the casserole from the oven, arrange the food in a somewhat tasteful display, and sit on the couch to wait. I weave a small braid in my hair and stare at the steaming dish, listening for the buzz of a moving elevator. Seven o' clock comes and goes without a visit from Kyle. I tell myself not to worry, that his train may be late arriving; but fear still looms in the back of my mind like a virus. He can't leave me to fight this hell alone. I'm not strong enough. My need for him may be my greatest weakness.

Sarah's question flashes through my brain, causing a stab of nervousness to rupture through my torso. My fluttering butterflies morph into a stampede of wild stallions, trampling my excitement into a whirlwind of anxiety. *"What are you going to do when you and Kyle are finally reunited?"*

I haven't thought about it until now. Kyle has felt so distant, like a nostalgic memory I've been chasing. Not anymore. We are going to be together again after months of searching. *"I will always find a way back to you, Cora."* It's what he told me before our lives fell into chaos. He is coming back, but once we're face to face, what will we say? How will we act? So much has changed since the night in the thicket, since we were last Kyle and Cora—my feelings, our identities, the world. When he walks into the penthouse, will I embrace him? Will I kiss him? Will we stand frozen and gaze at each other without words to share? All I want is to be close to him, a part of him. I want our cells to braid together like living thread. I want our ribcages to break open and our hearts to merge as one entity. In a world where darkness thrives and heroes die, all I want is him.

Hours melt away in lonely silence. The casserole ceases steaming. The ice encasing the bottle of soda melts. I pace the living-room, glancing at the sealed elevator with an unfixable pain in my chest. Why isn't Kyle here? Where is he?

Classical music explodes from the penthouse's speakers, drowning the emptiness of the building with a lively string quartet. I blow out the candles burning in the center of the kitchen table and practice shooting arrows at the portrait of Truman. Eleven o' clock passes, adding another load of worry to my shoulders. I sit on every piece of furniture, flip through half-a-dozen magazines, and count the bird carcasses floating in the rooftop pool. New York City is consumed with darkness, as lifeless as a pile of ashes. This apartment is the only place still fueled with electricity. Everything else is dead.

I collapse against the wall-length window, sliding to the floor with my knees to my chin. My stomach growls as I stare at the sliver of moon hovering above the crumbled cityscape, clocking the east coast at midnight. My excitement shatters into a million desperate pieces. Kyle should be here by now! Like everyone else, has he decided that I'm worthless and unfixable, unwanted? This war has stolen everything from me.

Claire de Lune by Claude Debussy echoes through the apartment, causing memories to play through my mind. Words, faces, emotion—they send a mixture of warmth and anguish through my bones. I can't handle the pain any longer.

"Stop it!" I scream as I throw a bookend at the stereo system. The device falls to the floor and shatters into a pile of useless rubble. Once again silence swallows the room like a virus, consuming my life until I know I am on the verge of suffocating. I must escape this place before I fall into insanity. My thoughts are more dangerous than anything Deven may attempt.

Memories dwindle at the edge of reminiscence. Unlike previous flashbacks, these are ones I've never forgotten. They are engraved in the tissues of my brain like tattoos, claiming and welding me to my past. I've tried for years to carve the images from my self-consciousness, but they are embedded in my programming, in my identity. They define everything I am.

"Experiment 237 is ready for operation." A faceless nurse leans over me, shadowing my eyes from the blinding lights. She stabs needles into my bare skin and pumps me with various serums and chemicals. The pain sends a blast of terror through my bones. I squirm and scream, only to be shocked by a low voltage of electricity. I've been tied to the table like a specimen for dissection. My childish body is no longer my own. It's been sterilized, branded, and turned into a science experiment. I chose

to be recruited. I chose to be rescued from my foster home and transformed into a superhuman creation. Why, to have revenge on the people who killed my parents? To be wanted by someone again?

"She's so young," the nurse whispers to Doctor Winslow. "Do you think an eight-year-old will be able to handle the programming?"

"She has undergone many tests to ensure her ability to adhere to the alterations. There shouldn't be any problems." The doctor fastens wires to my head and covers my mouth with a breathing-mask. He gazes at me blankly, scanning my naked figure with a crazed gleam in his eyes. "Begin the procedure."

I panic at the sound of his command, watching in horror as the nurse keys a code into the lab's computer system. Yellow liquid flows through the tubes attached to my body and enters my bloodstream. At first, I don't feel a thing. Then a searing pain flashes through my veins. I writhe in agony as my genetic-structure is altered. The chemicals seep into my cells, causing every muscle in my body to tense and harden. A burning sensation blasts through my nerves. My heart races and my vision blurs. I scream and beat my heels against the slick surface of the table. The pain is unbearable. I am going to die.

"She shouldn't be feeling any of this!" Winslow shouts and begins ripping the IVs from my flesh. "We need to put her under. Raise the level of programming ten-volts and lower serum dosage! Her DNA is mutating too quickly."

My body begins to shake. I clench my teeth and moan as a shock of energy pulses through my brain. Like a surprise punch to the face, the programming renders me unconscious. I fall limply against the examination table, unaware of my painful transformation. My mind becomes a database. Amidst the comfort of forced sleep, I become a Legionary.

"I claim myself," I mutter and glance out the window at the vacated streets. "They can't have me. No one can."

At one o' clock, the gears in the elevator begin to turn, humming with electricity within the shaft. I climb from the floor and stare at the sealed exit with my hands trembling. I forget to breathe. A surge of happiness washes away my despair. He's found me.

The machinery ceases and the doors open, sliding apart to reveal the face that has haunted my memory for months. I gaze at him—his battered and overly built body, his unruly blonde hair, the exhaustion that has stolen his youth and aged his persona. He looks at me with water in his bloodshot eyes. His exhaustion is replaced with relief, a kind of love I've never felt before. His chapped lips part in an altruistic smile as he steps out of the elevator and into the corridor. I don't know what to do. My feet are cemented to the floor. My tongue is heavy with words I've been waiting to say. Before me stands my family, my home, the only person worthy of forever. Could this be a dream, another gust of programming? Or is Kyle really here to rescue me from myself?

"Hi," he whispers with tears streaming his cheeks. He drops his duffel bag and moves towards me. With every step, my burdens fall to the ground and my handcuffs disappear. I race forward, wrapping myself in his familiar embrace. He cradles me against his armored chest, protecting me from the brutality of the world. No more fear. No more suffering. I am safe.

"You're alive. I knew you wouldn't give up on me." He holds my head in his hands, smiling at the braid in my hair. His touch releases tears of my own. I sob and bury my face in the crease of his neck.

"I've missed you so much," I whisper and cling to his waist. Allow me to be pressed against him for all eternity. I'd be content to spend the rest of my life in the comfort of his embrace. "Never leave me again. I can't do this alone. I need you, Kyle."

Then without guilt, pity, or fear, I kiss him. And he kisses me back. I laugh, feeling a rush of childish glee stir within my chest. It blows away my darkness and floods my emotions with light, with a glimpse of my old self. For the first time in ages, I become the girl scaling the Golden Gate Bridge, the girl singing to songs on the radio. I become Cora.

"Sarah and Seth told me everything," he says as he wraps his arm around my shoulders. "They told me about your revival and rescue, the tour to bombed cities. I even watched a rerun of your interview in Dimidium on my train ride here. James definitely put you in the spotlight." Kyle snickers.

"Thanks to you, I've had to deal with his sarcasm and stupid fire-jokes for the past month-and-a-half!" I nudge him playfully and kiss his cheek. "Don't worry. I understand why you put me under Truman's guardianship. I'd probably do the same to you. Just remember, you don't always have to protect me. We can fight this war together. We're a team. You're the sword, I'm the arrow."

"I can't live without you, Cora. If you had died…" He stops himself and musters a weary smile. His face seems different. He looks older, worn, saddened by the horrors of war. His hazel eyes have lost their sparkle and his once incandescent smile no longer glows. His humanity has been chiseled away.

"What's happened over the past year? Have you received any word from my brother? How are our soldiers? Where is the Regiment located? I want to know."

"Can we talk about all that in the morning? I haven't slept or eaten in over forty-eight hours."

"Of course. Go sit on the couch. I'll fix you a plate of food."

"Thanks." He kisses me before shuffling into the living-room. He tosses his luggage beneath the coffee-table and collapses on the silken sofa. His armored body looks alien compared to the prestigious splendor of the penthouse. "You look very pretty tonight."

Blood rushes to my cheeks as I spoon a pile of casserole onto a ceramic plate. I cast him a blushing smile before placing the dish in the microwave. This still feels like a dream—his presence around me, the familiar words exchanged. It's as if nothing has changed. Deep down, we are still Kyle and Cora, constant and untouchable. Forever and always.

"Things haven't been the same without you. Truman and Stonecipher have treated me like a puppet. Marner is the devil and Matthew is…well, Matt. They believe I'm mentally unstable and need rest. Do they seriously think that locking me in a godforsaken penthouse will help me recover?!" I say as I fill a cup with tepid soda. "Look at me. Do I look sick and unstable to you?" I glance over my shoulder at the couch. Kyle is lying on his side, fast asleep. I stare at his battered figure, cringing as the emptiness in my sternum returns. He is dead to the world, trapped in the halcyon of slumber. It's selfish of me to want to wake him. If I could, I'd crawl into his chest and become one with his flesh, enveloped by the warmth of his normality and the beating of his scarred heart.

I kneel beside him and brush the hair from his forehead. My fingers glide over his sunken cheeks, tracing the many cuts and bruises. He is the definition of courage. Everything about him is sacrifice. He'd give his own life to save a complete stranger. That may be what I love most about him. Even in the middle of an apocalypse, he has chosen integrity over power.

I pull the boots from his blistered feet and unclasp the armor covering his arms. His skin is pale and splattered with dry blood, and his biceps are smeared with the aged ashes of bombed cities. When I remove the plating encasing his torso, I cough from the stench that emits from his body. He hasn't showered in weeks. Gore and sweat ooze from his pores, forming an odor that brings a grimace to my face. It creates an image of war I've yet to experience. Kyle truly has gone through hell.

Gently I unfasten the sword from his hip and cut the stained shirt from his chest. He's lost an unhealthy amount of weight. His ribcage protrudes from his muscular frame. With every breath, his abs stretch beneath his epidermis, showcasing every tendon and vein. It scares me.

When he stirs in his sleep, I catch sight of a marking on his wrist. Like Sarah, Seth, and Scar, he has *the sword and the arrow* tattooed on his left forearm in blue ink.

My hands press against the scar on his chest, sliding curiously to the leather chain tied around his neck. A wooden charm dangles from the strands of rabbit skin, engraved with the icon that has transformed the world. I made it as a gift for his seventeenth birthday. After all this time, he's still wearing it as a tribute. I've never been forgotten.

"Goodnight, Kyle." I tuck a cashmere blanket around his weak figure and sit on the edge of the sofa. I yank off my red heels before lying down beside him. Like a child, I find my place against the form of his body. For the first time since my revival, I can finally sleep. Dreams don't scare me as long as Kyle is around to take them away.

Immediately I tumble into a still and peaceful slumber. Kyle's hand remains entwined with mine throughout the night. His touch wards fear from my mind, protecting me from the terror of my own thoughts. Morning arrives, bright and clear on the horizon of ruin. I am still curled on the couch when I hear the sizzle of bacon and the faint melody of *'Surfing USA'*.

My eyelids flutter open, scanning the illuminated living-room with curious fascination. Kyle stands in the kitchen. He's showered and changed into a white t-shirt and a pair of jeans. I watch as he scrambles eggs and pours a mug of freshly brewed coffee, singing while working diligently over the stove. If we managed to survive this war, would we have a home like this? Would I awake every morning to the sound of his voice? *There's nothing perfect in this world...except us.*

"You're up early," I say before rising drowsily to my feet. Blinding sunlight glistens off the furniture. I squint and stumble towards Kyle, tripping over my discarded shoes. "Did you sleep okay?"

"I don't sleep much nowadays." He glances at me and smiles. "I was starving so I thought I'd make us some breakfast. Are you hungry?"

I nod and prop myself against a barstool. He passes me a plate of food. I eat slowly. His fork shovels the rations into his mouth, cleaning the dish in a matter of seconds. I stare at him wide-eyed as he devours another helping of breakfast.

"When was the last time you ate a meal?" I ask as he gulps a liter of water. "Sarah told me that you haven't been eating, that your rations disappear but no one ever sees you consume them."

"I haven't eaten in over a month," he tells me. "It didn't seem right. People were starving all around me, children younger than Lucy. I couldn't fill my stomach when theirs was in the process of eating itself, so I gave my food to them. I'm fine. A little hunger never killed anyone."

I swallow the lump in my throat, suddenly feeling very self-conscious in his presence. He's been slowly starving to death while I've lived in luxury. What am I compared to him?

"You have no idea how much I've missed you." He grabs my hand, enclosing my fist in the warmth of his palm. It sends prickles of electricity across my skin. "They told me you wouldn't survive. I didn't believe them. I couldn't. I love you, Cora. You mean everything to me. I want you to know that."

"I love you too," I say without hesitation. All I want to do is kiss him over and over again, somehow finding a way to weld my shattered heart to his. Can love last even after the sun fades to black and the earth crumbles to dust? Can infinity be forever and always?

He leans against the marble counter and drinks from his mug of coffee. Color is beginning to return to his sunken cheeks. His sad eyes regain the sparkle I remember. "To be honest, I haven't been the same since the night of the attack. I've seen things that...forbid me to sleep. I've killed people, so many I've lost count. Deven has destroyed everything…except you. He can't have you. I won't let him." Kyle sighs and stretches his arms behind his head. "Everything is so dark."

"I still believe in light," I whisper and comb my fingers through his wet hair. A smile spreads across his face, stirring life within me. I've missed everything about him. "We don't get to choose what is real. We can only choose what we do about it. As long as there is breath in my lungs, I will fight for us."

"Don't let anyone tell you that you're weak, Cora. There has never been a stronger girl to walk the earth." He leans forward until we are inches apart. "You're someone worth fighting for."

"Promise you'll stay with me. I don't want to be any further away from you than this."

"If I could, I'd sew us together so we'd never have to be apart. But if that were the case, I'm pretty sure we'd have trouble finding clothes to wear." He motions to the collar of my blouse. "May I see it?" His cheeks grow crimson with embarrassment as I unbutton the fabric over my chest.

"It looks like yours, doesn't it?" I say as his eyes inspect the scar. His fingers hover above the disfigured skin, tracing the outline of the mark in midair. "Go ahead. Touch it. I won't bite."

"Doesn't it hurt?"

"Sometimes, but not now." I press his hand against my wound, allowing him to feel the repetitive pulse of my heart. When he glances up, I set my palm on the crease of his chest. Two puzzle pieces, inches from being joined together. His is mine and mine is his.

I climb onto the marble counter and face him at eye level. *"Kiss me. Please kiss me,"* I find myself silently pleading. *"You don't have to ask permission anymore. I love you and that'll never change. Kiss me the way my programming kissed Matthew. Let me prove to myself that I can be…"*

My thoughts are interrupted by the warm sensation of his mouth easing against mine. His lips linger, almost as if waiting to receive a sign of approval before continuing. I wrap my arms around his neck and return the kiss. We remain silent and steadfast in the kitchen, innocently exchanging affections. After a few minutes, he pulls away with a smile on his face.

"Do you want to get out of here?" he asks. "We're in the middle of

New York City without anyone to tell us what to do and where to go. Let's forget the world and…just be us."

"Are you going to guard me to make sure I don't escape?"

"Like always, if you run, I'll chase after you. I'm not losing you again, Cora. Where you go, I will go also." He kisses me and motions to my wrinkled clothes. "I drove my motorcycle from the train station. It's parked downstairs, so you may want to change. Don't get me wrong. You look gorgeous in that outfit but I think you might be more comfortable riding around NYC in pants."

"What, you wouldn't like to see me straddling a motorcycle in this skirt?" I laugh at his blushing expression and saunter towards the bedroom. After changing into jeans and a faded *Rolling Stones* t-shirt, I follow Kyle into the elevator. He types a code into the system, beginning our descent.

The lights flicker as we move downward. His hand slips into mine and for the first time in weeks, I don't have a desire to escape this place. If I ran away, I'd only run back to him. His presence gives meaning to my pain, light to my dark world. Is inner darkness truly an absence of light, or is it caused by allowing fear and hatred to consume human emotions? Maybe love isn't weakness. Maybe it is the strength that powers life. Beyond the blackness within all of our hearts, there is a seed of hope, of good, a desire to love and to be loved. That desire has kept me from falling into insanity.

Ash fogs the vacated lobby. Furniture and piles of debris scatter the once polished floor. I step out of the elevator and accidentally crush a dusty coffee-cup. Kyle grabs an old newspaper from a stack of abandoned luggage. Luxurious splendor has been replaced with gloomy nostalgia.

"The Giants won fifty to twenty-four at their last game," he tells me before tossing the stained newspaper aside. "It's sad to think that there may never be another football game."

"As long as man exists, there will be football."

We walk through the lobby, past an empty reception desk and out the sliding doors. Morning has forced a moist chill over the ruins of the city. Sun glistens off the metallic structures. Silence drags an eerie atmosphere into the graveyard of civilization. I look up at the towers of shattered glass, suddenly feeling a slap of realization. For months I've stared at this scene—the car-strewn roads, deserted skyscrapers, the occasional gleam of an Injection's yellow eyes in the darkness of the alleyways. It's always been out of reach. Not anymore. Radioactivity has driven the humans out of the Dead Zone and yet, I've been forced to remain.

Kyle moves towards a motorcycle propped against a rusting bike rack. He climbs onto the vehicle and cranks the ignition. The hum of the engine seems to be the city's remaining heartbeat, the last spark of life among the desolate rubble.

"Are you coming?" he asks and pats the seat behind him. I straddle the bike and wrap my arms around his waist, noticing the sword strapped to his side. He's grown up. The Prime Way Program made a man out of a boy, but this war forced that man to become a leader.

"Hold on tight." He presses the gas and the bike lurches forward, speeding away from the sidewalk at high speeds. I cling to the fabric of his shirt and rest my head against the arch of his spine. Wind beats against me. I laugh as we zigzag through frozen traffic, weaving between cars and racing down empty avenues. There is normality amidst destruction.

Sandalwood wafts from his clothes, familiar and comforting. The aroma is a memory. It holds everything I've ever treasured. I'm close to him, so close I can feel the warmth of his body. He feels different from how I remember. His muscles are larger and his skin is cluttered with new scars. Even inwardly, I notice a twinge of change to his usually optimistic persona. There is a wall barricading his emotions. He is growing numb after experiencing so much death. I can't lose him.

New York City flies by in a blur of ash and dust. Old hotdog stands and tourist booths line the curb. Kyle stops long enough for me to grab an Empire State Building snow-globe before continuing our tour of the downtown district.

The day passes in a montage of laughter and apocalyptic scenery. We climb the Statue of Liberty, walk through deserted Times Square, shop at places on Fifth Avenue that neither of us could ever afford, visit several museums, and cruise through China Town. Around three o' clock, we pull over at an abandoned deli to scavenge for food. The only edible things we find are a few bags of chips, several bottles of soda, and canned pickles. We sit on the sidewalk beneath a faded canopy to eat.

"Today has been great," Kyle says and casts me a genuine smile. "Even though this city looks like hell, I've had fun exploring it with you. Maybe it wouldn't be bad living here. The radioactivity would drive away predators and obnoxious neighbors. We could survive on our own, scavenging for food and living in Truman's penthouse. Everything we need has been left for us."

"You'd do that, leave your army and come live here with me?"

"Not until the war is over. I can daydream all I want but truth is…I have a nation depending on me. I have people I have to protect." He sighs and opens his bottle of cola. "I'm selfish when it comes to you, Cora. All I want is to stand beside you forever. But there comes a time when our happiness must be sacrificed for the well-being of others. Bravery is self-serving. Courage is sacrifice. I believe in the impossible odds, the chance that integrity will stifle darkness and restore the broken. I don't know exactly what I'm supposed to do. I only know what I can do."

I stare at him, feeling a slight twinge of jealousy within my chest. I'm not the only one he's fighting for. He sees me as a distraction from his duties, the girl of his past and future. No wonder he feels distant. He's blocking me out to keep his emotions intact.

"Mikey told me that you had dinner with my family. What'd you think of them? They weren't mean to you, were they? My parents can be…"

"They were very hospitable," I assure him. "Lucy is the sweetest girl I've ever met. Mikey and his mom treated me as if I were already part of the family. Julia and Benji seemed to hate me and so did your parents, but they'll warm up once I prove to them that I'm not a monster."

"You don't have to prove anything, Cora." Kyle rises to his feet. "We have a few hours of daylight left. Feel like a drive through Central Park?"

Trees form canopies of tangled branches among the urban debris. Ponds scatter the park, all shimmering with the sun's golden rays. Roads arch over stone bridges and loop around a massive green space. Art sculptures pose gracefully among overgrown flowerbeds. Time stands still.

Kyle parks the motorcycle next to a waterless fountain. He lifts me off his bike, tossing my body effortlessly over his shoulder. I scream and beat my fists against his back, giggling as he spins. Happiness replaces all fear. Together we climb. Together we fly. Together we fall. Like morning and night, like sand and water, like *the sword and the arrow—* we fit together.

"Put me down!" I laugh and wrap my legs around his waist. "Have you gone crazy?"

"I'm just glad to be with you again." He lowers me to my feet and plants his hands firmly on my shoulders. His eyes burrow into mine, suddenly replacing my glee with serious attention. "Listen. In case something happens to me, there are five things you need to know. Number one, meeting you was the best thing that ever happened to me. You gave me a purpose and a reason to live. Everything I am today is because of you. Number two, if I had to choose between you and saving the world, I wouldn't be able to give you up. Not to save a billion lives. Three, know that whatever happens, I will always find you again. Four, I love everything about you. Five, would you…"

"What's going on? This isn't goodbye. We're alive and together. What else should matter?" I kiss his cheek and run my fingertips through his windswept hair. "Let's enjoy the rest of the day and not worry about the end of the world, okay? What do you want to do?" I motion to a gigantic boulder protruding from the earth a quarter-of-a-mile away. "How about a race, you versus your motorcycle? Loser has to jump into the penthouse's rooftop pool."

"You want to drive my bike?"

"Sure. Why not?" I place my hands on the vehicle's handlebars and crank the engine. "Let's see if you're as fast as human transportation."

He snickers and crouches down in a runner position. "Ready when you are, darling."

"I'm always ready." I clutch the gas and thrust the motorcycle into motion. The wheels spin. A puff of carbon emits from the exhaust pipe. I lean forward and watch the speedometer rise. Wind slams against my face. The landscape morphs into a swirl of colors.

Kyle races after me. He leaps over park benches and shoves his body through a barren hedge. His legs blur into a shadow of moving limbs. Fast is hardly the right word to describe his speed. He moves like a phantom or a wild animal, swift and silent and pursuing his prey.

The bike rattles as it reaches its max, groaning beneath layers of metal plating. Kyle sprints past me. He throws himself over a ravine in a mad dash for the boulder. As much as I'd like to let him win, the competitive side of me refuses to relent.

Brakes squeal, slowing the motorcycle to a stop. I slide off the vehicle and bolt after him. Sweat glistens off my skin. My heart races and my lungs swell with air. I jump from the ground and into the treetops. Like a bird, I soar from branch to branch, climbing higher in the spindly canopy.

"Cheater!" he shouts as I do a backbend in midair and land lightly at the base of the boulder.

"How am I cheating? There weren't any rules!" I smile and dash up the rocky slope. Kyle grabs my ankle and crawls over me, reaching the top of the massive boulder with a smug grin on his face.

"You cheated!" I scoff and kiddingly punch him in the stomach.

He wraps his arms around my waist and sinks to the solid ground, holding me against him. I nuzzle my head beneath his chin and stare at the impeccable view surrounding us. Even the crumbled skyline of New York City seems to hold a morbid beauty. Ash and dust may have stolen civilization, but nature continues to fight back, surviving the scars of man.

The silence of the park is deafening. I imagine children laughing and tossing Frisbees in the green space, dogs barking, joggers prancing down the narrow paths. They're dead, vaporized, blown from existence. Being here is like standing in a graveyard. Millions of people are gone and yet I remain, alive to face their killer. Even with Kyle behind me, I can't feel at peace. We're at war and I will fight until the Titan is dead or until my heart stops beating. It's my purpose. There is no way to escape fate.

Storm clouds are brewing on the horizon. A damp, acidic breeze wisps across my skin. I compress myself against Kyle's chest, attempting to drown my doubts in the safety of his touch. Matthew's wrong. I could be intimate with Kyle if I wanted to, and maybe I have in some ways. I've shared everything with him. He knows more about me than anyone in existence. Emotional intimacy is harder for me to give. I was designed to be physical, not pour out my heart like a sappy girl. Even so, a part of me wants to prove Matt wrong, justify the kiss at outpost-gold.

"I'm sorry for leaving you at the hospital, Cora. At the time it seemed like the right thing to do. People were dying and I knew that if I didn't do something, mankind would be exterminated. I couldn't be selfish. After sitting by your side for over a month, I forced myself to give up. But please know that leaving you was the hardest thing I've ever had to do." He strokes my braid and musters a sad smile. "We held a memorial service at Prime Way for Katrina, Ave, and the other Legionaries who died in battle. You were one of them. Everyone stood on the beach and placed candles in the water. While bombs exploded in the distance, we were silent. You should've seen it, eight-hundred flames floating among the waves. It was…beautiful."

"Did you send away my candle?"

"No, I kept it in my pocket. I never even ignited the wick. You weren't dead to me yet." He leans back on the rock floor and stares up at the overcast sky. "We've been through so much. I hope people remember us fifty-years from now. I hope the world remembers Prime Way, this war, and most of all, I hope they remember how differences can redefine history. Our pasts haven't hindered us. They've made us stronger. To conquer, one must have something to overcome. We've overcome the Prime Way Program, Marner's persecution, death, and even ourselves. We are the victors even if we die tomorrow."

"I don't feel very victorious right now, Kyle. Look around us! Everything is gone! We may survive but that doesn't make us alive. I want to be happy again, not spend the rest of my life worrying about safety and starvation and the next attack. Nothing will ever be the same."

"Why should it be? We've broken barriers. We've transitioned the world into a new age, a place where our kind can live in unison and humanity has the ability to thrive! Once this war is over, we'll have the foundation to build a home better than what the past could offer. We will find peace in our darkness. In the face of death, we will discover life." He sighs and gazes at the storming horizon. "I've seen what Prime Way has caused, the repercussions of one man's actions. But I've come to realize one thing. Your father isn't to blame for all this. You've seen Dimidium. That's what he was trying to create all along, not this bloody apocalypse we're facing. He created our potential but we determine our purpose. Glitches, side effects—they're not caused by problems with our level of mutation. They reflect what lies within our hearts. Evil festers. Love thrives. Strength is only derived from our intentions."

"What's happened to you?" I look at him with awe, dumbstruck by the empowerment flowing from his tongue. "You've grown wise in your old age."

He laughs and rolls onto his side. I lie beside him with my eyes transfixed on his gleaming smile. He whispers a joke and all I want to do is glue my body to his and stay with him forever. Seriousness melts away, sending a prickling sensation through my limbs, as if they've been asleep for all this time.

"My faction of troops cannot wait to meet you," he tells me. "When I left camp, they were all asking me when you were coming to visit. You'll like them. They all work as a team and protect each other, like we do. Sarah has taken the role of lead medic in our division. Seth is head of security. Mikey is our new director of communications. Deirdre is combat strategist. And Byron, once he recovers from his head injury, will be in charge of technological advancements. We've been traveling the country for months, trying to force the Regiment back into the Dead Zone."

"Has it worked?"

"Not as well as I hoped. It's as if the Titan knows our every move. His army usually foils our attacks before they can be made. I'm starting to think I have a spy among my soldiers. How else would Deven know our plans?" He shakes his head and scowls. "There's no way we can win this war if information continues to be leaked. We will all be annihilated."

"So what's next? Once you leave, where will you go?"

"I'll return to my division and together, we will rescue your brother. He's not who you think he is, Cora. A few days ago, he contacted me. He wants to be with Sarah and help us defeat the Titan."

"Why?! He betrayed us! What makes you think that he won't do it again?"

"Something he said," Kyle answers. "I don't know why but...I trust him. We all make mistakes. Either we choose to move on or we become so consumed with our own inadequacies, we murder our tomorrow. I forgive him. I want to bring him home. That's my plan."

"Why won't you let me escape? Why are you keeping me here? We can fight this war together! *The sword and the arrow*, forever and always."

"You don't understand. You haven't seen what I have. Once you do, there will be no going back. Deven will come after you. He won't stop until you are dead. In his eyes, our entire species must be eradicated. I can't let him hurt you. You're my reason to fight, the only thing in the world strong enough to motivate me to face this hell! If I lose you, I'll die." He places my hand over the tattoo on his forearm and looks at me with tears in his eyes. "There's no life beyond a world without you, just purgatory."

"Then let's run away! You don't have to keep doing this. Our race can leave the country and form a colony on some deserted island. None of us have to die or fight. All you have to do is stay. Stay with me, Kyle. Don't leave."

"There's something you need to see." He rises to a sitting position and pulls off his shirt. The sight of his bare chest sends blood rushing to my face. "If my efforts are in vain, why do I have these?" He turns to show me the fresh scars slashed across his back, thin white lines forming a drape of pain over his spine. "I was captured a few weeks ago by a squad of enemy troops. They took me to a Regiment outpost outside of Minneapolis, tied me to a post in the center of the camp, and one-by-one, they whipped me. Cain gave the first thirty-five lashes and then the Elite had their way with my body. Before the other soldiers even began, I had been beaten two-hundred-twenty-two times. I don't even remember the last hour of the whipping. After the five-hundredth slash, I passed out. When I came to, I was lying in a ditch fifty-miles outside city limits; bleeding, dehydrated, and half-naked. A note had been stapled to my chest with the words: *The cross brings crucifixion*, written in red ink. Deven made me an example. Instead of a public execution that would bring even more chaos within his militia, he humiliated his opponent. He knows the influence we have over the nation. We have become a beacon of hope, a symbol of victory. The world rallies behind us. All it takes is a spark of uprising for the Titan's power to diminish. I am not ashamed of what I believe and I will fight for what is right until the day I die. I believe in the impossible odds." He cups my face in his hands and searches my eyes for a sign of understanding. "We can't give up. We must keep fighting."

I look at him with a mixture of anger and resentment. He's locked me away from a war he's determined to win, endured torture without once allowing me to share the burden, and has refused the love I've fought desperately to obtain. For a year he's wanted me. But when I finally want him, his attention is elsewhere. The pain is more intense than emptiness, broken as if someone has shattered my heart with a hammer. *"Please want me. Please remind me who I am. Please let me fight for you."*

"When are you leaving?" I croak. His presence suddenly feels agonizing. It knocks the breath from my lungs. *I need him now more than ever before. Danger seems so near.*

"Tomorrow morning," he tells me guiltily before sliding on his t-shirt.

I nod and toy restlessly with the star-charm dangling from my neck. My chest aches with desperation. A knot forms in my stomach, so intense it makes me nauseous. Maybe if I give Kyle a reason to stay, he will. Maybe if I reveal my love to him, he won't leave me alone.

"We should go. It looks like a storm is coming." He climbs to his feet and motions to the black clouds forming above the remnants of the Empire State Building. A flash of lightning veins across the sky, followed by an earsplitting clap of thunder. He grabs my hand and the both of us jump off the boulder. We walk to where his motorcycle is parked.

Central Park is soon replaced with empty skyscrapers and deserted roads. Lightning strikes. Thunder rumbles. An eerie light filters through the city, dead and cold. Rain begins to fall, soaking us instantly. I clutch Kyle's waist as we speed through Manhattan. I must give him a reason to stay. I can't lose him to the tragedy of our lives. When darkness thrives, love brings hope of a brighter tomorrow.

Kyle curses when the engine sputters. The motorcycle slows, coming to a stop in the middle of the street. Rain pounds onto our shoulders. A fog of ash and dust lifts from the pavement.

He inspects the gauges and releases an irritated sigh. "We're out of gas. Looks like we'll have to walk the rest of the way home." He helps me off the vehicle and begins walking in the direction of Truman's penthouse.

"You're going to leave your bike?"

"I'll come back for it in the morning. There must be a spare can of fuel around here somewhere." He looks at me and offers his arm. I grab his hand and follow him through the ghostly ruins. Water streams our skin. Lights flash in the sky, illuminating the city in electrical flashes. We move in silence, both breathing heavily amongst the ashen smog. I lean my head against his shoulder, disguising my tears with the fall of rain. Maybe if I fake a smile, he'll love me enough to stay.

"We must attract bad luck," I shout as a bolt of lightning sparks off a building to our left. "…and possibly electricity!"

He laughs. It's not as genuine as I remember. The old Kyle radiated with sincere joy. When he laughed, he made me feel like the funniest person in the world. Not anymore. He's lost his sparkle, his human edge. His soul is sad and dying, suffocated by the trials of this new age. Maybe he needs me now more than I need him. Maybe it's my turn to bring him back to life.

I jump onto his back, wrapping my arms around his neck and my legs around his torso. "I'm tired. Kyle, would you carry me?" I kiss his wet cheek and cling to his muscular body like a hundred-thirty-pound backpack. *"Give him a reason to stay."* It's my new mission.

"I'll carry you through any storm." He glances back at me with a mischievous grin on his lips. "You might want to hold on. I've had a few power kicks since we were last together." His heart races. His limbs shutter as his programming takes effect. With a single motion, he shoots forward, sprinting at speeds I never thought were possible. I grip his shoulders to keep myself from falling.

He leaps off the pavement and pushes himself against the side of a skyscraper. Weightlessly he propels us backwards, zigzagging from structure-to-structure with agility I've never known a Legionary to possess. We soar above the deserted streets like a pair of gulls, rising higher into the sea of steel skeletons. I watch aerial New York pass below, and smile at the fluttering sensation in my abdomen.

Torrents of rain swirl around us in slow motion. Gravity becomes nonexistent. Kyle flips in midair and slams against the window of an office-complex. An adrenaline crazed shout explodes from his lungs as he drops into a freefall. I scream and dig my fingernails into the skin of his biceps, panicking as the earth approaches. He's going to kill us.

In a matter of seconds, his hands unravel me from his spine. My legs flail as I plummet towards the car-strewn street. Moments before impact, Kyle pulls me against him. I forget to breathe as his feet meet the road. He lands like a meteor, cracking the cement as if it's nothing more than a thin layer of ice. I'm left hovering feet above imminent death with his arms clutching my waist.

"You've been holding back," I gasp and stare up at his sweat-soaked face.

"I didn't want to freak you out. My glitches have enhanced everything." He breathes heavily. A sparkle flashes through his pupils, igniting his smile with the optimism I fell in love with.

"Gosh, you're hot." Blood rushes to my face. I want to shoot myself for saying such a thing aloud. I climb to my feet and stumble towards Truman's apartment building. Kyle follows me through the dusty lobby with a blushing smile on his lips. He keys another code into the elevator and we begin our ascent to the penthouse level.

CHAPTER 8

Minutes feel like hours. Silence blares in my ears, provoking new emotions. Kyle leans against the wall and stares at the sealed doors. He glances at me awkwardly before stashing his hands in the pockets of his jeans. I bite my tongue, trying to bury my embarrassment beneath the weight of my thoughts. Why do I feel this way? Shouldn't I be able to admit my attraction to him without being overcome with guilt? My programming doesn't control me any longer. I claim myself.

"Prove Matthew wrong. Give Kyle a reason to stay," my self-conscious whispers. It permits the feelings bubbling inside my chest. *"You're alone with him. This is what you want. He's leaving tomorrow. Now may be your last chance to prove that you are the only one worth fighting for."*

I will not lose him again.

As if discovering a newfound wave of confidence, I shove Kyle into the corner of the elevator and fit my mouth to his. He looks at me with shock before returning the kiss. Our lips move together, fusing as if they'd never divide. His hands comb across my back, stirring my excitement to a boil. I stick to his body like a tattoo, meshing our hearts to form one entity. Regret is the last thing on my mind.

He holds my face and kisses me over-and-over, until our lips are raw. His warmth sends prickles of electricity through my veins. I want to freeze this moment and live forever in the simplicity of his touch. Why should we worry about tomorrow? Why should the next few hours be consumed with Deven's darkness? All that matters is the pulse of our hearts and the huff of our breathing. Together, we can forget the world.

When the doors slide open, Kyle lifts me off my feet and steps into the corridor. He pushes me against the wall of the hallway with enhanced speed, accidentally shattering an intricate vase. I laugh and kiss him again. Truman is going to be furious.

My fingers glide through his wet hair. My emotions race to a new level. I tug at his wet shirt and pull the sopping piece of fabric over his head. His bare chest presses against me. The heat sends a thrill of adrenaline through my body. It drives away the chill of the rain and the gloom looming in the back of my mind. 1026 completes 237. The sword unites the arrow. Kyle is a part of my identity. To lose him would defy everything I am.

"You were wrong about me, Matt. I'll prove it," I think to myself before lifting the back of my t-shirt. Kyle grabs my hands and pulls them away from the hem of my clothing. I kiss him harder and shake my wrists free of his grasp. Again I attempt to remove my top, but he plants his palms firmly on my waist to keep me from undressing.

Determination mixes with hormones. Anger rages, causing my desire to heighten. I force him into the living-room and onto the sofa. My lips dwindle on his cleanly shaven chin as I pry his fingers away from my hips. *"Don't you want this too, Kyle? You say you love me. Prove it!"*

As if answering my silent question, he rolls from underneath my body and walks hastily to the wall-length window. The muscles in his bare back are tense as he stares out at the storming city. He remains wordless. Every second of silence grinds my shattered heart to dust. Why doesn't he want me?

"I can't." His eyes remain transfixed on the clouded cityscape. "You don't realize how hard it is for me to be around you without wanting to," he pauses. "But I love you enough to say no."

"We could die at any moment! All it takes is another bullet or explosion to end our lives. Why wait for a future we may never have?"

"Because I want to believe we'll have a future, Cora! I'm not ready to admit defeat. This is one thing Deven can't steal from us." He shakes his head and collapses in the chair across from me. "I'm not ready to grow up completely. Can't we just…enjoy being together? We used to have so much fun before all this mess started. Is it alright if we continue to have fun, starting tonight? I'll make dinner and we can listen to music or watch a movie. What do you think?"

"Are we still allowed to kiss?"

"Of course. You're my girlfriend, not my best-friend's dog," he snickers. "So can we call a truce?" When I nod, he grins and kisses me a final time before walking to the kitchen.

My lips are glued into a permanent smile for the remainder of the evening. Kyle and I make charred hamburgers, laughing as we accidentally drip ketchup onto our new change of clothes. We blast rock music while shooting spit-balls at the portrait of Truman and waltz to an old Frank Sinatra ballad. As soon as we've listened to every vintage album in the penthouse, we sit on the living-room floor with several blankets and a tub of peanut butter to play a quick game of Truth or Dare. After he braids my hair and I reveal secrets he never knew, we watch the sappiest movie in Truman's collection. Kyle falls asleep halfway through the film and I get bored so I start counting the dead birds in the rooftop pool. Maybe he's decided to stay. Maybe he'll want to have days like this forever.

Midnight rolls around. We both shuffle drowsily to the dark bedroom and collapse onto the water-filled mattress. I crawl beneath the silk comforter and into his arms, praying that tomorrow night I'll fall asleep with him beside me. He sighs and slips his hand into mine. We lay side-by-side with the light from the window illuminating our silhouettes, silent except for the breath trailing from our nostrils. He can't leave me here alone. We need each other; to sleep, to breathe, to live.

I touch the numbers tattooed on his right bicep and slowly drag my hand to the scar on his chest. He kisses my forehead and stares up at the ceiling. The moon's silver beams outline the profile of his face, faultless and stalwart. He is my family and I love him now more than ever before. It doesn't matter what happens to us. I know who I am because of him. I know who to fight for.

"Are you scared, Cora?" he asks. I know it's a test. He's trying to determine whether or not I've broken free from my programming.

Dauntlessness has always been my mask, armor to hide myself from the brutality and pain of the world. I've been told from the beginning that fear is weakness. If felt, it could get me killed. But I've come to realize that fear isn't what destroys us. It's the actions that derive from fear that determine our fate. Maybe admitting our insecurities is the first step to reviving humanity, healing what has been lost.

"Yes," I whisper. "I've been terrified for months. Nothing has felt familiar or safe. It's like I've been walking through a battlefield with bombs exploding all around me. I never know which step will blow me to pieces." I feel his nose sliding along my jaw and his lips press against my ear. I don't want him to stop so I keep talking. "I'm afraid to sleep because of the nightmares I know will play through my head. I'm afraid of facing Deven because of the memories I know he will force me to remember. I'm afraid of my past and future, afraid of what my father has created. I'm afraid that my brother will always hate me. I'm afraid of what I am, what the world wants me to be. I'm afraid of my programming. I'm afraid to be alone. I'm afraid of…losing you."

"You'll never lose me. I promise." He brushes the hair from my face and gazes at me with a gentle gleam in his eyes. "We're going to be alright. Remember, we still need to have our first date."

"What do you call this?"

"The pre-date initiation," he snickers. "After this war ends, I'll take you to dinner and a movie. I might even buy you flowers."

"Oh you Texans, always wanting to stick to tradition. I'm happy titling this as our first real date. Both of us are healthy and not slowly dying. It's perfect."

"You're perfect."

"Are we going to be *that* couple, you know, the boy and girl who everyone thinks are annoying because they constantly have sappy conversations?"

"That's the best thing about it! There's no everyone. They're all dead!"

"Great. That makes me feel better," I scoff and rest my head on his shoulder. He laughs and cradles me against his chest. I smile. It's the realist thing my body can convey.

"Would you think I'm weak if I told you that I'm scared too?"

"No. I'd think you were the strongest man alive."

He smirks and glances out the bedroom window at the crumbled city. A shimmer of light appears on the horizon, then vanishes in a cloud of fire and smoke. The explosion sends a chill down his spine. "I can't save everyone. That has been the hardest thing for me to overcome. I'm looked at as a hero and yet in battle, soldiers and civilians die. I fight because it's what is right…but inside, I'm a mess. I want to protect everyone, keep the world safe. It's my fatal flaw. I can't let people die."

"That's not a bad thing."

"It is when you're surrounded by death every second of every day," he tells me. "I wish I were like you and Matt and had the ability to forget my feelings; but I'm not wired like that. I feel everything in excess, ten-times a normal human would experience an emotion. Pain cripples. Compassion suffocates. Love becomes so delirious, it works like a drug. I shouldn't even be here now. Truman warned me not to come. He knows how hard it'll be for me to leave."

"Then stay or take me with you. We're stronger together." I lean over his body and salute him. He strokes the weave in my hair. It's everything we are.

"I've missed you." He lifts his head and kisses me. His lips linger, gliding over mine with equal passion. Unlike with Matthew, kissing Kyle feels right. There's no regret. All I feel is a fluttering sensation in my stomach and warmth in my chest. This is a memory I'll treasure, the moment I decided I wanted Kyle to be my forever.

"You can sleep, Cora. I won't let dreams hurt you."

I kiss him a final time before finding my place against the form of his figure. He wraps his arm around my waist and tucks the silk comforter over my shoulders. I close my eyes. The fear of darkness is replaced with the thud of Kyle's heart and the rise-and-fall of his breathing. Together, without words or touch, our hearts become whole. We fit together.

"I hear our worlds will come to an end. I hear our deaths are so. They think we are a threat to them. Is this a game, I don't know…" The song plays through my mind as I tumble into a still and peaceful slumber. I've given Kyle a reason to stay. If he truly loves me, he won't leave me here alone.

Dawn ignites the bedroom with golden hues, penetrating my sleep with overwhelming light. I stir beneath the piles of sheets. My arms stretch across the mattress in search of Kyle's warmth, but the other side of the bed is cold. I sit up and glance around the space, noticing a pile of his clothes on the carpeted floor. I hear the gurgle of brewing coffee and smell the sweet aroma of fresh pancakes. He hasn't left! He's decided to stay. For the first time in ages, someone has chosen me.

I smile and roll onto my back. Laughter wells inside my chest, an uncontainable joy that explodes within me like a nuclear bomb. I clutch the silk comforter over my mouth to stifle my girlish giggle. All I want to do is jump and squeal and run through the penthouse like a child on Christmas morning. I want to embrace Kyle and kiss him as if I'm trying to demonstrate mouth-to-mouth resuscitation. I don't care about Deven, this war, or the death looming outside my door. Nothing matters anymore! Kyle is here. Together we will fight. Together we will survive. And together, we will endure forever.

As calmly as my excitement will allow, I slide off the bed and rush happily into the living-room. It's empty. I walk into the kitchen. A mug of coffee has been left on the counter beside a plate full of steaming pancakes. A note is lying beside the food with the words: *forgive me,* scribbled neatly in Kyle's handwriting. I can't breathe. I can't move. My legs are frozen in place, cemented to the floor with the pain of realization. There are an infinite number of words to describe heartbreak. Mine can be expressed with three syllables—agony.

Feral emotions pierce through my abdomen, crucifying all traces of happiness from my body. I lean over the trashcan and cough up the contents of my stomach. Despondent darkness suffocates the twinge of life still pulsing within my heart. I stumble against the stovetop, knocking Truman's coffeemaker to the tiled floor. It shatters and splatters black liquid across the kitchen. I weep and clutch the hole in my sternum. Kyle's gone? He didn't choose me?

Anger trembles through my limbs. Tears burst from my eyes, streaming my face like hot waterfalls. I scream and wipe the dishware off the counter. Silence drives me to madness. Loneliness becomes a bullet to my chest, a torturous and meaningless scar. I'm a caged bird, fed lies and deceptively fondled. Kyle left and locked me in this cell. Instead of the team that once inspired hope, we've become victims of the Titan's wrath, victims of our own choices. He's no longer fighting for me. He wants to save the world and all I want is to survive this hell. I'm tired of playing these games, suffering human emotions to feel a glimpse of blissful acceptance, and scraping away my own identity to satisfy the cravings of others. Forget feeling! Shun regret! Embrace strength!

I moan and kick over the kitchen table, hearing another crash. My snow-globe is lying in a pile of shards beneath the flipped furniture. I kneel beside the souvenir and scoop the broken pieces into my hands. The miniature Empire State Building no longer holds a perfect memory. It's as dead as this city.

My legs crumble. I collapse on the floor and cry, surrounded by crushed ceramic and hot coffee. I can't be with the man I love. My life is nothing but sadness and tragedy. It'd be easier to die and slip into a state of delirium, a place where pain no longer exists.

"Embrace your design," my programming whispers. A rush of manufactured adrenaline races through my arteries, dulling my discomfort. *"One choice will end your suffering forever. Give in. Erase your emotions. Become who you were created to be, strong and fearless. You were destined to be the prime of mankind. Why should you allow love to destroy your potential? Relent. Kill Deven. Transform into the soldier you've always wanted to be."*

"All this hurt will disappear?" I mutter between sobs. "I'll be strong again?"

"You'll be the best of your kind, an original Legionary. It's what you want. You'll be wiped clean of this pain. All that will remain is an unquenchable fire, fueled by instinct and anger. No feeling. No regret. Just strength. The Prime Way Program created the best of you, Cora. 237 is more powerful than any other name."

I pull my knees to my chin and stare up at the swimming pool. A Blue-Jay is floating among the murky water, its blue feathers forming a rippling cloak around its decaying body. It's what I will become if I continue to pursue human strength. Forget emotion. Allow myself to be washed clean. It's what I want. No more pain. I choose to embrace.

As if unlocking a vault within my genetics, a searing pain pierces through my entrails. I arch my back and writhe on the floor with my nails clawing at the carpet. My mind resets, erasing emotions and reloading my programming. I scream as an electric shock vibrates through my head, stabbing my brain with agonizing ferocity. My muscles twist and squirm under my skin like infuriated serpents. Shocks of energy flash through my veins, catching my blood on fire. Light darts beneath my flesh, consuming all human genes and reconfiguring my design.

I gasp as another dose of adrenaline pumps through my body, awakening my senses. Intensity adheres to every thought and movement. Power replaces weakness. Like a corpse rising from the dead, I drag myself off the floor and crawl up the side of a chair. Sweat drips from my pores. My lungs pant.

I soar off the ground and onto Truman's bookshelf, crouching among the piles of novels with primitive characteristics. My reflection stares back at me from a shattered mirror. I flinch at the sight of my face. It's changed. All innocence and youth have fled my features, leaving a fierce and powerful persona. For the first time in months, I look like myself.

Buzzing fills my ears as I do a back-tuck off the shelving. I smile and jump ten-feet in the air, latching myself to the ceiling fan. I hang upside down and unravel my braided hair, allowing the brown locks to hang loose. I think of Kyle to test my new self for heartbreak. I feel nothing, empty of every painful and blissful emotion. Altered-genetics no longer causes strife within my body. It coexists, allowing me the control and instinct I need to survive an apocalypse. The Prime Way Program fabricated my race to withstand a disaster. Kyle's Legionaries are a new breed. They are weaker than the programs my father created. Matthew and I are the last of our kind. We are Originals.

"No more glitches," I smirk and flip off the ceiling. I land on the coffee-table with my eyes narrowed and my fists clenched. Physical discomfort has disappeared. Determination floods my thoughts. It's time to escape. I will find Kyle's Division, save my traitor brother, and face the Titan. I'll kill him slowly, slicing off limb for limb until he apologizes for destroying my life. Deven will die.

I turn up the radio and sprint into the bedroom. With abnormal strength, I rip off my clothing and change into a pair of jeans, combat boots, a black sports bra, jacket, and leather gloves. I toss the remaining clothes into the bathtub and soak them in hairspray. With the flick of a lighter, I set fire to the heap of silk and cashmere.

After grabbing a blanket, a bar of soap, two rolls of toilet-paper, and Stonecipher's memory bracelet; I lock the door to the bedroom and grab my equipped backpack from the closet. I sling my bow and quiver of arrows over my shoulder and move hastily into the kitchen. Like a thief, I scavenge through the cupboards, grabbing steak knives and packs of matches. As soon as I've gathered everything useful from the apartment, I turn the oven on high and allow gas to leak into the radioactive air.

"Truman is not going to like this," I snicker and punch a hole in the wall. I yank an electrical-cord from behind the sheetrock, forming a bundle of wires around my arm. I snatch a bookend off the cluttered floor and move towards the wall-length window. With a toss of my arm, I throw the statuette against the glass surface, shattering the barrier instantly. The only thing that separates me from freedom is an eight-hundred-foot drop.

After tying an end of the electrical-cord to a support beam, I step onto the penthouse's ledge. My hands dig the lighter from my pocket and hold it in front of my face. Fire flickers at the tip of the device, hot against my fingers. I smile and toss the flame into the apartment, stepping off the ledge the moment I hear the roar of combustion.

Heat explodes above me, emitting a discharge that blows me further away from the building. I twist onto my back and gaze up at the cloud of fire and ash. Wind cradles my body in a freefall. Pavement flies towards me, dusty and covered with rusting cars and pieces of crumbled rubble. The ruins of New York City rise in all directions, like jagged teeth ready to chew me to bits. I'm tumbling through the air. My legs push against the cracked glass of skyscrapers, propelling me across the avenue like a swooping bird. I grab hold of the electrical wire and swing in a low arch towards frozen traffic. This should scare me—the fluttering of my stomach, the strain of muscles, and the fear of falling to my death. But I'm not scared. I'm not scared of anything.

My gloved hands slide down the cord. My vision enhances, revealing every detail in my surroundings. I'm still hanging seven-hundred-feet above ground, certainly not a safe drop for any normal human. Lucky for me, I'm no longer normal.

I dangle at the end of the wire and swoop towards a neighboring hotel. The moment my feet touch the structure's metal siding, I release my grip of the cord. I crouch against the building and propel myself backwards, flipping in a diagonal to the other side of the alley. I leap off balconies and glide down windows. My body moves with perfected agility, every motion flawlessly executed. I jump and twist, approaching the pavement with controlled speed.

With a final kickback, I land on top of an abandoned Mercedes, denting the hood and crushing the windshield. Sweat soaks my clothing. My scars glisten in the morning sun. I've escaped. Deven has no idea who he's dealing with. I have become the name given to me. I've become the Blue-Jay.

I step off the car and move swiftly through the sea of vehicles. A red, Ferrari convertible is parked along the curb with its keys still in the ignition. The temptation is too hard to resist. I toss my backpack and weapon into the passenger seat before sliding behind the steering wheel.

My fingers dial MS1 into Mikey's transmitter and press the device to my ear. There's a buzz of static before a voice responds to my call.

"Good morning, Cora. Did you finally escape? I was starting to get worried," Mikey answers.

"Yeah, I'm outside the charred remains of Truman's penthouse as we speak. I need a location. Are you someplace secure where we won't be overheard?"

"My job is to keep our communications network secure! No one will hear a word we say." He pauses. "You sound different. Is everything alright?"

"I'm fine. Now if you please, I really need to start moving before someone sees the smoke from the explosion I caused. Don't ask questions. Everything's okay."

"We'll be camped at an abandoned marina a few miles outside Chicago, preparing for a raid on the Titan's city. I'll send you the exact location within the hour."

"You're going to rescue my brother?"

"That's the plan. Be here in forty-eight-hours if you want to participate. Now to discuss the fun stuff..." He chews on something crunchy and slurps carbonated liquid. "What are you driving?"

"A red convertible."

"That's going to get you killed. Once you exit the Dead Zone, ditch the car and find something more ATV. You'll need to stay off roads as much as possible, even travel on foot if necessary. The Regiment has satellites monitoring all major highways, interstates, and so on. How much artillery are you equipped with?"

"A bow, a dozen arrows, and five steak knives."

"You are really going to die," he laughs. "The world is an extremely dangerous place for a lone traveler, especially one of your ranking. Deven has sensors which can detect every mutated species in a hundred-mile radius. Every genetic-code filed in Prime Way's database has been loaded into his system. He'll know your whereabouts the moment you step onto his grid. All of hell will be chasing you. In other words, find a decent gun! That should be your number-one priority. Nuclear-powered and radioactive weapons are the only things strong enough to put a dent in the Titan's forces.

"Do not drink water from any reservoir, creek, or lake. Deven has pumped all water sources with toxic chemicals. Consume only packaged food and bottled water. Also, never be outside after the sun sets! Find a house with a basement, board up the windows, go downstairs into a windowless room, and stack furniture against the door. Do not start a fire. Honestly, don't even breathe. Injections are most lethal after nightfall. If Deven programs your coordinates into their brains, they won't stop until you've been shredded into a pile of flesh. Remember, everything can kill you! Don't trust anyone. Even civilians have become dangerous. If they think you're carrying something valuable or useful, they will attack and rob you. So travel light."

"Anything else I should know?"

"That's about it. Everyone's going to be so excited to see you, especially Kyle."

"You cannot tell Kyle I'm coming! I want...to surprise him. Promise me."

"Sure. I promise. It'll be our secret. Now you should probably go."

"I'll see you in forty-eight hours. Goodbye, Mikey."

"Arrive alive." His end of the line clicks off and I'm left sitting in the driver's seat, alone with a world of danger lying before me. No feeling. No regret. Just strength.

I crank the ignition and slam my foot on the gas pedal. Tires squeal as the Ferrari swerves from the curb and shoots away from the downtown district of Manhattan. Wind beats against my face, tossing my loose hair in a frenzy of brown waves. I adjust my sunglasses and turn on the iPod still attached to the vehicle's dashboard. An old rock song, a relic from the past, blasts from the speakers and echoes through the maze of empty streets. I smile, watching New York City slowly fade into the distance. It won't be long now. I'll have my revenge and this war will end. Doom to the Titan.

CHAPTER 9

Breathless. Suffocating. Water seaming with inhuman life. Cold tendrils embrace my body in a cage of frigid currents, pulling my limbs in unnamed directions. My lips are sealed together, separating my empty lungs from the airless abyss. My eyelids blink away the frost forming on my pupils, only to bring clarity to shapeless surroundings. I float through the darkness like a pale-faced ghost. Not even death could stop me now; not winter's bone or the threat of drowning. I am immune to it all.

I release a stream of bubbles from my nostrils. They drift like silver jellyfish towards the surface of Lake Michigan, giving direction to my sea of confusion. My emotions and thoughts are clean, blank, a white slate cluttered with only determination and instinct. I can't doubt my motives. I can't experience fear or hate or love. It's better this way. Without feelings, I'm safe. My body has become a weapon that no man or beast is able to tame, not even myself.

I paddle upward. My head emerges from the water and into the darkness of night, gasping for air. My breath is white in the frigid breeze. I steady my heartbeat and stare at the skyscrapers looming ahead. Chicago, once a thriving city shimmering on the shore of America's Great Lakes, has become the Titan's stronghold. Beauty has been replaced with evil, with a sense of dread and inferiority.

A wall rises from the downtown district. It towers above the rubble-filled streets and empty structures, separating the dying world from Deven's dictatorship. Lights flash from watchtowers built at strategic points throughout the city. Armed soldiers stand erect at their posts, their faces masked by shaded helmets. Silence screams in my ears. Though my heart has grown numb to emotions, I still feel a twinge of despair when I imagine the Chicago Massacre—clouds of smoke, children screaming, people dying by Deven's hand. He will die for his crimes. And once my arrow pierces his blackened heart, humanity will restore. The world has become his playing field. We are but pieces in his game.

The past forty-eight-hours have been hell. Once I left New York, earth became a place festering with lonely demons and the remains of mankind's mistakes. I drove one-hundred-eighty-miles before ditching the Ferrari at a roadblock. I traveled on foot until I crossed the black line dividing the Dead Zone from surviving civilization. For the remainder of the day I walked cross-country; avoiding towns, roads, and anything that might get me killed. Not once did I spot a living soul. Loneliness became habit. I stole a motorcycle from a Pennsylvanian dealership and pillaged empty houses for packaged food and bottled water. I spent the first night comfortably hiding in the cellar of an abandoned farmhouse. It wasn't until I crossed into Ohio that my presence was noticed.

A squad of Centurions found me and chased me across the state. I killed five of them and stole a nuclear-powered gun, three radioactive knives, and a pack of supplies. The Regiment kept me running for two-hundred-miles and when night fell, Injections began tracking my genetically-altered scent. I locked myself inside a suburban home located in the outskirts of Defiance, boarded up the windows, and hid in the basement with my gun ready. One of the beasts tore through the bolted door and destroyed the main floor, but I remained untouched. When morning dawned on the horizon, I left my stronghold. Light revealed the darkness within the home. Freshly killed bodies littered the kitchen floor—a man, woman, two teenage boys, and a little girl the same age as Cathy. They'd been murdered hours before I arrived.

My DNA was acting as a beacon. I figured that the only way to blot myself from the Regiment's grid would be to mask my encoded genetic-structure, or at least confuse the Titan's locating system. I gathered some of the family's blood and smeared it over my skin, gagging as the foreign cells mixed with my own. After I finished covering my flesh, I left the house and drove off road until I reached Whiting, Indiana. Most of the town's citizens were still locked inside their homes when I entered city-limits. I left my motorcycle in a parking lot and walked to a vacant wharf. Mikey told me to stay off road, so that's exactly what I did. I jumped off the pier and swam eighteen-miles across Lake Michigan to Chicago. I fooled technology. I beat Deven at his own game. My programming has become my greatest weapon.

I slip beneath the waves as an airship flies overhead. It sinks into the City with its turbines glowing red. Flecks of snow fall across the water's surface. A spotlight combs across the waves, searching for intruders, searching for me.

"What is your purpose, 237?" Crammer's didactic voice echoes through my head. I remember his game, those relentless drills used to engrain authority into my thick skull. I remember feeling a rush of panic at the question. If I answered wrong, I'd be punished.

"I shall destroy the Titan, even if I'm killed in the process. I will die a hero."

"You will never be a hero. It is not in your nature."

"I may be your soldier and creation but you do not determine my purpose! You do not choose my fate! Prime Way is over! Cora Kingston and 237 are dead! I now can choose who I am, who I will become. For once, I want to feel like I've done something good! You may have stolen my childhood and humanity, but you cannot have my heart...or my future. My programming doesn't define my identity. It's my weapon. With it, I shall bring your army to its knees."

"What do you think will happen once this war is over? Civilization will never accept your kind. There is only room for one intelligent race on this planet. You will either save humanity and be exterminated, or you'll massacre the inferior and take your rightful place on earth. You're from a different age in time; a superior being, an alien among men. A decision will have to be made. Do you save our original species, or do you continue the invasion?"

"Bravery is self-serving. Courage is sacrifice. If being courageous means sacrificing my own life to save billions, I will gladly do so. It's my purpose."

I paddle to the lake's surface and swim towards shore. My body slices through the waves without making a sound, strong and rehearsed. The weight of my backpack drags me beneath the waves. I struggle to keep my head above water as I near the concrete barrier separating the tumult of the ocean from the desolation of Deven's city.

My wet hands grip the bulwark, scraping away a fistful of algae. I moan and lift myself out of the water, collapsing onto the sidewalk with limbs trembling. A mixture of grass and dirt fills my mouth as I press my face against the earth. Heat rushes through my veins, warming me out of death's reach. I cough and climb wearily to a standing position. My boots are soggy and my clothing clings to my skin like bandages. I wring-out my hair and unfasten the glowing gun strapped to my hip. One flip of a switch arms me with enough nuclear-power to blast an army of men to dust.

I stare into the maze of vacant streets, locked in impenetrable shadows by towers of charred rubble. The Titan's City rises in the distance like a viper ready to strike its prey. Spotlights comb the ruins of Chicago, searching for human genes—for surviving life. I watch armed recruits march along the barricades. Their black armor transforms them from teenagers to demons waiting to kill me. Deven has destroyed the good in mankind, created monsters out of children. They all must die. The effects of the Prime Way Program will end and my sanity will be restored. No Feeling. No Regret. Just Strength.

Manufactured strength adheres to my fatigued muscles. Instinct clears fear from my mind, leaving only numb emotions and a thirst for revenge. I rush into urban darkness—ducking in and out of corridors, sliding beneath blockades of debris, climbing through skeletal remains of skyscrapers, all to avoid the illuminated eyes of the City.

I grab Mikey's transmitter from my backpack as I crawl beneath a rusting stack of vehicles. His location blinks red on the screen, only three miles from my current position. It won't be long until I'm reunited with my soldiers.

Grime plasters my flesh as I sprint past the Cloud Gate Sculpture. Instead of a colorful cityscape, the mirrors reflect only gray hues and crumbled structures. I gaze at the stainless form, wondering how many people had done the same. It's as if the deserted park suddenly becomes claustrophobically crowded with nostalgic ghosts. Imagined sunlight floods the park. Shriveled plants revive. I stand amidst the bustle of the past, watching someone else's memories rush through the courtyard. I see a group of students following their teacher, all talking or texting on their cell phones. A businessman passes through me. His tie is fastened tight around his neck, as if he'd been secretly trying to strangle himself. I spot a mother and her daughter sitting on a park bench, both feeding bread to a flock pigeons. They're dead now. The virus that began at Prime Way has spread across the country. Their ghosts will always haunt this place.

Voices echo from a nearby avenue, followed by terrified screams. I aim my gun in the direction of the sound and hastily hide my body in the shadows of an alley. Pain stabs through my chest as I inch towards the commotion.

"Stand against the wall!" someone shouts. I hear the sobbing of children and the frantic pleas of men. Women weep. Babies scream. What's happening?

Cautiously I tiptoe forward and peer around the corner of an apartment building. The road is empty except for a squad of Centurions and a few human survivors. Black figures cover the side of a shopping complex, permanent shadows engraved in the stucco. I stare at the scene, noticing the pile of ashes at the base of the outlines.

The prisoners are forced against the stained building. Soldiers divide the crowd like a pile of clothes, sorting the eligible recruits from the useless. Once the teenage survivors have been loaded into a cargo truck, the Titan's troops aim their weapons at the remaining captives. Prayers are whispered. Tears are shed. And one by one, the masses are blasted with balls of energy. Their bodies vaporize instantly. I stare in horror as innocent people are murdered before my eyes. Ash fogs the air. Agonizing wails fill the night. Even my programming isn't able to numb the despair in my heart.

"Move out!" an Elite officer shouts.

I squeeze my eyes shut and wait for silence. My wrist bumps against a windowpane, accidentally triggering Stonecipher's memory bracelet. A holographic image of Kyle forms in midair. His kind eyes burrow into mine, comforting my sorrow with his signature assurance. Do I still love him? No, I can't love anymore. I've sold my humanity.

A vicious growl rumbles from inside the apartment building. Two glowing amber eyes appear in the darkness, following by the gleam of barred teeth. My scent has been revealed. An Injection has found me at last.

I reach for my bow as the beast sneers. Its thick coat smells of rotting flesh and its paws are coated with dry blood. I step away from the creature and pull a homemade arrow from over my shoulder. These animals killed hundreds of my people, tortured me for months in Deven's game. They can't have me. No one can.

"Breathe. Just breathe," I tell myself as the Injection sits back in a lunge. "One shot. Aim between the eyes." I pull the arrow to my cheek and aim for the beast's soft spot. It snarls and pounces, clawing at my neck with its yellow talons. I release my grip. The arrow embeds itself between the creature's eye sockets, killing it instantly.

A cloud of toxic gas drifts through the streets. I cough and shield my nose and mouth with a black glove. I have come to a giant maze filled with fatal attractions. I'm a piece on a chessboard, the rat in a mousetrap. It's as if I'm reliving the horrors of Deven's game.

I scramble away from the carcass and sprint in the direction of Kyle's camp.

"You're fading, Cora. Don't give up!" Katrina's voice penetrates my clean thoughts. It startles me. I trip on a pile of discarded furniture, falling clumsily to the pavement. *"Remember what you promised? You said you'd keep fighting—for humanity, for Kyle, for me. Don't sell yourself! If you continue to drown your emotions in programming, you'll lose them forever."*

> *Images fill my mind, playing through my brain like an old film-reel. I see golden fields and a newly planted orchard. I watch people, young and old, push wheelbarrows and dig holes in the charred soil. Kyle is among them. He tills the dirt of a garden and helps Cathy cover sprouting seeds with damp earth. Mud smears his smiling face. Sweat glistens on his brow. He glances up and waves at me, calling my name with a sense of joy I've never felt before. Is this the future or a perfect dream my weary mind has concocted?*

"You want this, Cora. I know you do. You're still in love with Kyle. Don't let him go."

I push the voice from my head and climb achingly to my feet. The images cease. I brush the filth from my clothes and continue on my trek through the dilapidated ruins.

Kyle and his division have set up camp in a deserted marina, built beneath two parking garages, directly across the Chicago River. An old restaurant separates the ancient structure, complete with shattered windows, faded umbrellas, and molded food. The bow of a sunken ferry peers eerily over the river's surface. Corpses drift with the current, all bloated and unrecognizable. It's a place blotted from Deven's radar. In a few hours, my brother will be rescued and the Regiment will fall to its knees. This war will be over. I'll be free at last.

Dust fogs the air. Decaying food blankets the restaurant's lavish tables. This place was once considered an elite dining experience with expensive dishware and sparkling chandeliers. Wealthy men and women came to enjoy the waterfront view and a glass of their favorite merlot. I imagine their chatter, the clang of pots in the now mildew infested kitchen. Not anymore. All luxury has been drained from the business. The only thing that remains is a morbid, apocalyptic atmosphere cluttered with debris and the voices of genetically-altered teenagers.

I crawl beneath a table to observe the soldiers without alerting them of my presence. They hover above a fire blazing in an old caldron, laughing and discussing strategy. I spot Sarah sitting on top of a dessert cart and Seth whittling a piece of wood. Byron and Deirdre stand next to Scar, conversing with several new recruits. Kyle appears in the crowd with Mikey following close behind him. I catch my breath. I have finally achieved my goal. I've found my people, my friends, Kyle. Why am I not happy? For months I've waited for this moment. Shouldn't I feel some sort of joy, peace, a sense of belonging?

"You're emotions have been lost, remember? You'll never feel happiness again."

Kyle drops his weapons onto a stained table and collapses next to the fire. He toys with the wooden charm dangling from his neck and watches his recruits with a sad gleam in his eyes. His armor is more battered than I remember.

"Does Callan know we're coming?" Sarah asks. Her blonde hair hangs loosely around her pretty face, giving her an angelic persona. She fiddles restlessly with a radioactive pocketknife.

"Yes. I contacted him a few hours ago. He'll be waiting for us when we make our attack tomorrow," Kyle answers. He surveys an array of maps on a holographic tablet. "Get some sleep, everyone. We need to be fully alert when we face the Titan."

"Yeah, so we can pulverize that freak!" Byron shouts with an amused grin on his face. "Dibs on his airship! I'm flying to Australia to catch some gnarly waves after all this is over. Who's coming with me? Legion and Sarah, I know you two can surf…"

"If you get the airship, I want the state of Georgia. Humans can't live in it anymore." Seth snickers and gulps water from his canteen. "Perk of being a Legionary."

Everyone laughs. Scar strums a few chords on her guitar and Deirdre scoops a spoonful of stew onto a ceramic plate. I watch them, marveling at the smiles on their faces. How are they happy?

"What do you want, Deirdre?" Sarah asks.

"To be with my brother. President Marner said he'd release him from prison once this war is over. I just…want to be a family again."

"That's what I want too," Kyle says. "I want to be with my family." He leans against a rotting chair and continues to finger his necklace.

"So how was your visit with Cora?" Scarlet asks. "Is she alright? When is she joining us?"

"She's healthy and ready to fight," Kyle answers guiltily. "It was good…to be with her again. Hopefully we'll see her soon."

"Was she mad when you left?"

Kyle hesitates and tosses another piece of wood into the fire. "I don't think…"

"He wouldn't know," I say and rise to my feet. Everyone stops and stares at me wide-eyed, as if I'm a ghost or wandering spirit. "Your grand leader slept with me and then left before morning, all because it was the easiest thing to do. He was too cowardly to tell me goodbye." I drop my backpack and pile of weapons and saunter towards them. "He wrote a note and left me in bed…"

"Cora," Kyle looks at me in shock. The blood drains from his face. "What are you doing here?"

"Thought I'd pay the Titan a little visit." I stab my knife into one of the tables and gaze at him angrily. "What, surprised to see me? You didn't think I'd be able to escape, did you? Your weak little girlfriend was too human and fragile to combat a feat like this. Well, sorry to disappoint! I may have experienced a few glitches myself. You're not the only one capable of scaling the side of a skyscraper."

"First of all, we didn't *sleep* together! That term can be skewed quite dramatically. And believe me. I never intended to hurt you! I left because

I knew that if I waited any longer, I wouldn't be able to leave! Sure, it was the easier thing to do. But what'd you expect, Cora?! I couldn't stay with you forever. You knew that. And I've never thought of you as being weak! I promise. Honestly, I thought you were the strongest person on earth to fight this war in a way unknown to you. I admire your tenacity!"

"You left!"

"Only to keep you safe!"

"I never wanted to be safe! I wanted to be with you. That's all I ever wanted!"

Silence falls over the room. Everyone watches us with intrigue, waiting for the conversation to continue. I don't care if they hear. They need to know that their leader isn't perfect.

"How'd you find us?"

"Not all your soldiers are against my escape." I pull the transmitter from my pocket and toss it to Mikey. "Thanks for your help."

Kyle glances at his best-friend in shock and then looks at me with a mixture of anger and desperation. "Well, you're here now. Are you hungry? We have some stew left over from dinner. Sarah, would you plate some for her." He turns and motions to Mikey. "We need to talk."

I watch them disappear into the condemned kitchen before joining my friends by the fire. They immediately embrace me, bursting with questions and chatter.

"Welcome back, Blue-Jay!" Scar throws her arms around me. She smiles and brushes the soot from her armor. Her frizzy auburn hair is filthy and matted, and her gray eyes are bloodshot. She looks older than I remember, a woman in her early thirties rather than the twenty-seven-year-old who fought alongside me in Deven's game. Her touch is human and yet radiates with strength and domination. "I've missed you! How are things in the living world?"

"Pretty dead," I answer as Sarah hands me a bowl of soup. Seth and Deirdre pat me on the back. Byron gives me a bottle of water. The scar on the back of his head is barely visible beneath his thick, bleached hair.

"Have you met our newest recruits, Cora?" Scar motions to the crowd of onlookers. "That's Austin, Courtney, Naomi, and Dean." The soldiers salute nervously, all staring at me as if I'm a celebrity.

I greet them with routine ease before sitting on the mildewed carpet. "Where are the twins, you know, the ones with the green hair?"

"They transferred to the Los Angeles outpost to guard Cathy," Seth tells me. "Geode is planning to join us once we return to Dimidium." He grabs an old napkin and begins polishing his rifle. "This war is getting rougher by the day. I'm sure you've seen your share of death over the past eight-months."

"She was dead, remember?" Byron snickers. "You look pretty good for a corpse, Blue-Jay."

"Don't flirt with Legion's girl. He'll throw you to the Injections," Seth laughs.

"Nah, Legion wouldn't hurt me. We're pals."

"You are such an idiot, Seaweed!" Deirdre scoffs.

I eat in silence, listening to their banter absentmindedly. Kyle's and Mikey's voices drift from the kitchen. My enhanced hearing catches a few words from their whispered conversation—*Why'd you help her escape, I thought you'd be happy, Not your place.*

As always, I feel nothing.

"Your scar has healed nicely," Sarah says and sits next to me. "I'm glad you found us. Don't listen to what Kyle says. He missed you. I know he did. Deep down, he's happy you're here. Love has a funny way of showing itself."

"What makes you think we still love each other? We're fighting for two completely different things. He doesn't care for…"

"Don't say it, Cora." She sighs and shakes her head. "I thought the same thing when Callan joined Deven. The betrayal hurt. I wanted to believe that he loved me, that he did what he did because he wanted us to have a future together…"

"He did, Sarah. He loves you. Joining the Regiment was his way of securing your safety throughout the war. Deven promised him that you'd be together."

"I thought so." She smiles. "Kyle loves you too. He says your name before every battle. I don't know if that's romantic but…he is fighting for you. I've never met a more sentimental person. He's an amazing leader. We'd all give our lives for him."

"Why?"

"Each of us has our own reason. Scar and Seth follow him because of what he stands for. Byron is here because he believes Legion will destroy the Titan and restore the world. Deidre has seen Kyle's strength and chivalry in battle. And the other recruits follow him because of his honesty." She pauses for a moment to watch Byron toss a knife at an apple perched on Seth's head. "My reason is different from theirs. I'm not fighting alongside Kyle because he saved my life or because he's rescuing Callan. I honestly didn't know if I wanted to be in his division until I joined an excursion to the Dead Zone. We were passing through a town on the boarder of Sector 2. The Titan had attacked hours before we arrived, killing practically everyone. Blood trickled through the gutters. Smoke was so thick, it covered the sun. I've never been in such heavy darkness.

"I remember the silence as we moved through a burning neighborhood. Bodies scattered the pavement. Soldiers were vomiting from the foul stench. I didn't know how to react. Kyle told us not to be sad, but to be angry so that we'd never want this to happen again. As we were about to leave city limits, he spotted a group of children hiding in a dumpster. One of them was crying hysterically. He knelt beside her and told her everything was going to be okay. She replied by saying, *"it's so dark"*. That's when he pulled a glow stick from his pack, activated the device, and gave it to the child. He said, *"I still believe in light"*. Those few words proved to me that he was worth dying for. I knew there wasn't another person on earth worthy of defeating the Titan. Kyle stands for light. He is light."

I nod and glance towards the kitchen, noticing a twinge of jealousy within my chest. The world believes more in Legion than in me. How can I blame them? I fell in love with Kyle because of his good heart. Why shouldn't they? His kindness and compassion will be the death of him, while I'm left alive to endure my selfishness and anger. Is it better to suffer from love or hate?

"You don't deserve him. Treasure his love or you'll lose him forever." Katrina's words haunt my mind. She was right then and she's right now.

"Careful! You almost sliced my head off." Seth ducks as Byron tosses another knife at the moldy fruit perched on his head. "Save it for those awful Centurions!"

"Come on, you big chicken! If I decapitate you, I promise to give you my week's worth of rations. Do we have a deal?"

"That doesn't make any sense!" Seth flies onto a table and throws the apple at Byron. It slams against his chest like a meteor, knocking him to the floor. The occupants of the restaurant erupt with laughter. Their happiness remains a mystery to me.

Scarlet strums the strings of her guitar to hush the crowd of teenagers. She looks at me and smiles. We spent a lot of time together in Deven's game and yet, I know very little about her. There always seemed to be an unspoken rule between us, a wall of safety to keep our pasts a secret.

I listen to her play, each chord like candy to my ears. She sings softly. The lyrics add another dose of sadness to our morbid surroundings. When she reaches the chorus, I almost forget to breathe. The verse forces me to recall a conversation from weeks prior.

"Fire's hands have burned away, leaving me love-lost forever..."

I stare at her, trying to sort the questions swarming my mind. *"No. It couldn't be Scar,"* I think to myself. My eyes scan her armored figure in hopes of finding an answer to my hypothesis. *"She's the right age. The story would make sense."*

As if confirming my theory, I notice an object tucked beneath the collar of her breastplate—a chain. When she moves, I see a silver wedding-band dangling from the strand. It's all I can do to keep my mouth sealed. Headstrong, determined, daughter of a scientist—the pieces of the puzzle fit together. Scarlet Archer is the flame, Stonecipher's flame.

Kyle walks out of the kitchen. He looks at me and motions to a set of stairs leading to the marina below. "Cora, can we talk...in private?"

I nod and climb slowly to my feet.

"Don't be deceived by him again. He'll break your heart," my programming whispers as Kyle leads me to the lower level of the restaurant. *"You don't love him anymore. Admit it. Scream it. Believe it. Embrace the painlessness and thrive in the safety of comfort."*

"You're lying to yourself, Cora!" another voice shouts. *"Kyle holds your identity, your sanity. Without him, you'll lose everything! Remember why he left you in New York. He wants to keep you safe, keep the nation safe. You love him more than life itself. Remember..."*

It's so loud inside my head. Conflict rages beneath my skull, tearing apart the truth I once clung to. I try to lock away my indecision in the depths of my mind, burrowing my doubt in the soft tissues of my brain. Still they puncture my confidence. It doesn't matter how high I hold my head or how tight I purse my lips, I remain weak and vulnerable. Even my altered-genetics aren't able to tame my inner battlefield.

I follow Kyle through the dark marina, past empty boat slots and murky pools of water. He glances back at me occasionally but remains silent. It's as if I'm a delinquent schoolgirl being led to the principal's office for punishment.

He steps onto the deck of a rickety houseboat and forcefully helps me board. His hands guide me into the dimly lit cabin. Obscenities dwindle at the tip of my tongue but are quickly stifled by the sight of the living quarters. Oil lamps and stacks of maps scatter the ancient appliances. Holographic tablets project images onto the mildew-splattered walls. Glowing weapons are piled at the base of a rotting cot, along with bloodstained equipment and an old radio. Kyle's been sleeping here.

"Nice place," I say sarcastically as a roach scurries across the linoleum floor. "Was Truman's penthouse too luxurious for your liking?"

He rolls his eyes and unfastens the armor from his chest. "Be mad at me. Curse me. Slap me. Spit in my face. I don't care as long as you're safe! Look at me, Cora. How much more do I have to give to prove that I love you?! I've sacrificed everything for us! So please, save me the heartache of losing you again and get the hell away from here. What are you trying to prove, that you still have the ability to kill?! Violence only brings more pain."

"This is my brother you're trying to save! I have the right to be here."

"Revenge is all you care about—revenge on me for loving you too much, revenge on Deven for destroying our world, revenge on yourself. Don't you see it? You're so consumed with hatred for the past that you've driven yourself to madness. Congratulations! You've become exactly what Prime Way trained you to be. You've become Deven."

I slap him across the cheek, angry at the truth in his words. He stumbles backwards with a hurt expression in his soft eyes, and knocks a pile of dishware off the kitchen counter. Guilt emits a painful discharge. It ruptures within me, cracking the programming's boundary around my heart.

"Kyle...I didn't mean to....I'm sorry," I stutter and reach towards him. He grabs my shoulders and gazes into my eyes with desperation. His touch is forgiveness. It washes the intensity from my body and replaces my anger with peace. For a brief moment, I forget my reason for coming to the Titan's City. All I want to do is wrap myself in Kyle's arms. But that desire is quickly extinguished.

"What's happened to you, Cora?" His hands cup my face. His fingers comb sadly through my loose hair, pausing when they find the small braid woven among my tangles. He looks at me intently, fitting the puzzle pieces together. "Say you didn't..." His affirmation turns to shock. "You promised you wouldn't!"

"Don't you dare judge me. I had my reasons."

"Because I left to fight for the millions of people still alive?!" he scoffs. "This is your revenge? You decided to shut me out, embrace your programming and....forget. That's weak!"

"Call me whatever you like! This is who I am now! You can't lock me up. You can't toy with my emotions. I've finally become strong enough to defeat Deven!"

"But in the process, you've become just like him. I don't even know who you are anymore. The Cora I once knew would never sacrifice her humanity for power. I love the girl with the braid, the girl who gave me something to fight for. You're not her."

Fury trembles through my body, heating my emotions to a boil. Buzzing fills my ears. I want to scream and curse at him. I want to put him in a headlock and shake the words from his mouth. I'm not good enough. Maybe that's what hurts the most, knowing that my own desperation and hatred transformed me into something incapable of loving; and in the process, made me incapable of being loved. So instead of indulging in honesty and admitting to my flaws, I fight back with my only remaining weapon.

"Matthew likes who I've become! He wants me to be strong and fearless, not weak and fragile. He *loves* me for who I am, who I've always been! We're wired the same way!" I grit my teeth and step so close to Kyle, I feel his breath on my face. "Matt even kissed me! Did you know that? We made-out in the pool at outpost-gold. He thought I was good enough. So say what you want. Tell me I'm inadequate! Tell me our time spent together was a mistake! Tell me how you wish we'd never met!"

He stares at me. Tears glisten in the corners of his eyes. I expect him to shout and rush angrily out of the houseboat, forever giving up on us. But he remains steadfast, watching and inspecting me with unconditional emotions. Then when the silence is too deafening, he leans forward until his lips hover inches above my left ear. "How could I ever call you a mistake, Cora?"

There isn't an amount of programming strong enough to numb the sudden joy within my heart. It explodes like a bomb inside my chest, pulverizing the hardened walls around my feelings. Humanity seeps into my bloodstream, reviving a little of what was lost. I catch a glimpse of life, of hope, of future. My dark world shatters for a few precious seconds and is replaced with warm light.

"Please come back," he whispers. Timidly his mouth eases against mine, as if the solution to reversing my alterations lies in the genetic-makeup of his saliva. I don't fight it. With every kiss, a memory plays through my mind. For so long I've been embracing and resisting, relenting and fighting; all the time trying to form a tower of invincibility around my scars. But maybe strength was designed to be shared. Maybe the cure to my weakness is finding someone to fight this battle alongside me.

"He's changing you, 237! Don't be deceived. He makes you weak!"

Holographic lights blink restlessly on the nautical themed walls, trapping the room in an eerie, futuristic atmosphere. Kyle's slick armor rubs against my flesh. The salt of his sweat meets my tongue. His hands rest against the bare skin of my ribcage, sending a fluttering sensation through my stomach. I want his touch to release another rush of adrenaline, but my programming has sealed away all remaining emotions. It's my punishment for ever believing I could live without him.

"Good evening, America."

The voice startles us. We spin around, only to face the flickering screen of a 1978 television set. Static clears. A face emerges from the technological darkness—cruel eyes, a malicious smile, and the distinct features of Satan himself. How is the TV being used as a transmitter? The houseboat doesn't have electricity.

Deven chuckles. His metal armor encages his overly built body in a suit of invincible power. "It's been eighteen-months since the initial invasion took place. I've been lenient, allowed your little rebellion to exist. But now you've become a thorn in my side. I see you, all of you, all the time. I track your every move," he laughs. "You underestimated

166

me! I am god on earth! And in exactly twelve-hours, I will prove my power to the ultimate extreme. So get a good night's sleep! It'll be your last."

As soon as the screen fades to black, Kyle grabs a bookend and crushes the television, shattering the device into a thousand pieces. He looks at me wide-eyed. A cold-sweat breaks across his forehead.

"Suit up. We're invading the City tonight," he tells me and quickly grabs his sword from the floor. "I don't know what Deven's planning but we need to stop it."

"We? You want me to come?"

"It's your brother we're trying to save. Besides, would you listen if I said no?" He smiles and tosses me a set of armor. "Promise you won't do anything stupid. I can't afford to lose you again, Cora. You die. I die too."

"I promise," I say as I strap on the gray plates. "Send some of your troops to gather a body or two from the ruins. We need the human blood if we're to make it into the Titan's City without being noticed. Unless we mask our DNA, our genetics will get us killed."

"There aren't any bodies to gather. Deven had all corpses incinerated a few weeks ago, except for the ones floating in the river; and those are bloodless. Mikey concocted a shielding device to block us from the Titan's radar, but it is only able to hide us for an hour max. Scar might be willing to donate some blood. We can dilute what she gives and distribute it among the division."

"That'll work." I nod and activate my armor. Mechanically the suit consumes my body, molding itself to fit my form. It buzzes with electricity. The lightweight metal intensifies my every move. I finally feel whole, healthy and confident. Deven will die today. "Let's do this together. We're a team. You're the sword and I'm the arrow."

He salutes me. "Forever and always."

CHAPTER 10

Memories trickle through my thoughts. They ignite my senses, flaming beneath my skull with overwhelming clarity. Then all at once I'm submerged, as if I've jumped off a cliff into the tumultuous waves of the past. I see and hear things, some I never experienced in this lifetime. Dialogue twists from rehearsed to new conversation. Scenery morphs into unknown places. Details remain confused and unanswered. But I'm at peace.

"Cora," the voice belongs to my daddy. It rumbles through the confines of my brain. I see his silhouette amidst the mirage of my thoughts. He moves forward until the film of light sheds from his face. "You've been a busy girl these past few years."

"No thanks to you. Look around. You caused this war. Why? Why'd you want to create people like…me?! What was our original purpose; to one day destroy the earth? I don't understand. If you knew this would happen, why'd you do it?"

"God knew Adam and Eve would sin, but did that stop him from creating this beautiful planet? Did that stop him from creating man? He gave us a choice to choose our own purpose, whether for good or evil. I didn't know the future. Part of me hoped that mankind would be able to responsibly handle my research, use it to bring the world into a new technological age. I wanted to help make this planet a better place for you and your brother! I never intended for you both to get hurt. You were

meant to be safe, live a happy and normal life."

"That dream ended when you and mom died! All chances of us ever being happy, ended!"

"Don't underestimate yourself, Cora. You can overcome this. I know you can. It's your choice, your purpose, your fate. Choose good over evil! Choose happiness instead of strength. Light, no matter how small, breaks through darkness." He looks at me with a hint of a smile on his lips. "I love you, my child. Someday I hope you'll be able to forgive me."

"Answer my last question," I request as he turns to leave. "Did you know I'd end up this way?"

"I wasn't certain. My colleagues noticed your exemplary qualities and asked if we could use you as the initial candidate for programming. Of course that was out-of-the-question, but they persisted. Your mother begged me to send you to California to live with my sister for a few months. I was selfish and wanted you and Callan to stay with me in Miami. Weeks later, Mom and I were erased from the picture. I guess I knew deep down that...they'd take you anyways. To have Patrick Kingston's daughter in their Program would fulfill every vendetta," he answers. "I'm sorry for the mess I've made. All I ever wanted was to be a good father, not ruin your life."

The loose ends of my existence slowly fit together. My obsession with throwing blame, clears. It isn't my fault I'm here, not my father's research, bad luck, or a splurge of irony. The villains who deceived me and stole my future are dead. It's over. How could a lifetime of hatred end in a matter of seconds?

I look up at the conjured image of my father and silently say goodbye. He's gone, a finished chapter. Closure will separate us forever. So as I build enough strength to force away the memories, I say the three words it's taken twelve-years to mutter. "I forgive you, Daddy."

Eyes snap open. The landscape of my thoughts fade, only to be replaced with the darkness of dystopian Chicago. I'm crouched beneath the canopy of a dilapidated coffee-shop, both of my legs blanketed with fresh soot. Fog has settled over the ominous city. Every rustle of wind causes a chill to wash through my spine. Fear radiates from the towers of rubble. So many have died here. It's difficult to stay focused when everywhere I look I see the ashen shadows of the Titan's victims. My thirst for justice has never been so strong.

"Our perimeter has been secured," Kyle whispers as he emerges from the scorched building. His metallic helmet hides most of his face from view, except for those gentle eyes which remain visible beneath his visor. "Mikey's hacked into the Titan's satellites and security monitors. We're invisible for the time being." He kneels beside me and stares into the desolate avenue. "Have you coated yourself with Scar's blood? Byron and Sarah just used the last of what was donated."

"I'm covered," I say and string an electric arrow across my bow. I scan the wall of an office-complex, searching for signs of approaching Injections. They're close. I can smell them. "Has everyone gathered for infiltration?"

"Yes. They're waiting inside." He glances at me briefly and encloses my fist in his own. "Once you step foot on Deven's battlefield, he won't let you leave. Are you sure you're ready for that?"

"I've never been more ready," I answer with my jaw tight. This is the moment I've been anticipating for months. "Divide the division into two squads, one with the objective to shut down the Titan's current operation and the other to assist us in rescuing my brother. Both teams need to be equipped with artillery, transmitters, survival tools, any possible technology, and a complete escape route and rendezvous point. If one squad doesn't make it out alive, the other should have transportation or at least a planned path of travel. Mikey should set up a control center in this building to keep us informed of possible changes and events within the city so we won't be caught off guard. Scar and one of the newer recruits can stay and protect him."

"Seth, Deirdre, and three other Legionaries have already volunteered to target the Titan's mystery threat. They'll be invading the Regiment Labs built on the eastern boarder of the city. Sarah and Byron will join us. We will head towards the Sears Tower, which has been converted into Deven's headquarters and capital. The W Chicago City Center, which is only two-hundred-fifty-meters from the Titan's Capital Tower, has been redesigned as a recovery center for newly injected soldiers. It's where Callan is being kept."

"Once both objectives have been reached, where will we regroup?"

"210 South Canal Street, Union Station. We'll follow the railroad tracks out of the city. Leaving will be much easier than getting inside," he tells me. "Marner briefed me a few days ago on the Regiment's development. They have over thirty-thousand troops, twenty-thousand human slaves laboring in the city's factories, and a few hundred scientists administering injections and working to produce new weaponry. The ability to stay undetected is our only advantage. We go in, get your brother, and leave. No assassination attempts. Nothing to draw attention to our presence. Understand? We're outnumbered and outgunned. Until we can rally enough Legionaries together to form an army, we won't be confronting the Titan. Do we have an agreement?" Kyle stares at me intently, waiting for a sincere promise to roll off my tongue. He knows how badly I want to murder Deven. The desire pulses through my blood, a purposeful vendetta that must be achieved. "Patience. This war isn't over yet. He will be punished, just not today. We must do what it takes to protect our people."

"Don't worry. I won't compromise this mission." I pull a pair of digital binoculars from my belt and quickly scan the landscape for predators. "Follow orders, complete the assignment, and get out alive. But next time, Deven will die."

"You're not the only one who wants him dead, Cora. After everything I've seen, all I want to do is tear Deven to pieces. My mind rehearses his death every time I see a corpse or a puddle of blood. But I know that if I dwell on that darkness, it'll consume me. I was programmed to focus my energy on revenge. Every day I must fight that urge. It's the only way I can keep my priorities in check. I fight to save and protect the people I love, not kill the one man responsible for their pain. You must find it in yourself to do the same."

I watch a wad of stained newspaper blow across the pavement. It's more proof that our world has ended. Prime Way is over. The numbers tattooed on my arm are meaningless. Civilization is crumbling because of Deven's afflictions. I refuse to forget. He will die, and I will be the one to kill him.

Kyle pulls the binoculars from my eyes and forces me to look at his masked face. "All night I've been trying to concoct some profound final statement. But when I open my mouth, everything collapses. So I'll stick with honesty and hope to avoid an ellipse…"

I raise his helmet and quickly kiss his mouth, stifling his farewell before it can be muttered. I don't want another goodbye. We've been separated enough. It's easier to live in denial where we believe nothing is strong enough to tear us apart.

"Let's go save the world," I whisper.

Kyle helps me to my feet and together we enter the charred coffee-shop. Our blood smeared soldiers are standing among the blackened furniture, all dressed in Stonecipher's lightweight armor with weapons slung over their shoulders. Seth and Deirdre polish their helmets. Scarlet is seated in the back of the room with a pad of gauze taped to her vein, helping Byron piece together a broken rifle. Sarah and Mikey form digital maps on their holographic tablets. The others organize ammunition and medicine. The twelve of us will infiltrate Deven's impenetrable city.

"It's time." Kyle's deep, Texan voice shatters the unearthly silence. Every eye in the room focuses on him. The young Legionaries cling to his every word with admiration spilling from their pupils. "I don't know what more to say. We all know what we have to do, what lies before us. I'm proud to call each of you my friend. We've defied every odd, done whatever it has taken to protect the survival of liberty. So let's show the Titan what we're made of! Let's teach him not to mess with the US!"

"Sounds good with me." The wall to my right flickers with pixel tiles, revealing a camouflaged figure among the charred wallpaper. His suit is the same as mine, gray except for a strip of painted flames on his breastplate. He steps forward clumsily and attempts to manually open the visor of his helmet. A touchpad appears on his wrist. He presses one of the glowing icons and immediately the armor slides away from face, revealing his neatly trimmed goatee and mischievous smile. "It's nice to see you all again. You wouldn't believe the traffic I flew through to get here. Everyone all of a sudden owns an airship. Geez, you'd think roads didn't even exist anymore!"

"What in the world are you doing here, James?! You're going to get us all killed!"

"Dimidium was boring me. Besides, I thought you might need my help. I brought some extra supplies, technology, medicine—the usual." He sits down and props his feet on a lopsided table. "Do you like my suit? It's custom made…"

"How'd you find us?" Kyle cuts in. "Our location is classified information. Only Marner and Truman have clearance to our travel plan."

"There are other ways to find a division of genetically-altered teenagers," he remarks. "I could've tracked your DNA codes, used your issued Stonecipher weaponry as homing-beacons, or been following you this entire time. But I settled for a simpler method. I found you using the locating chip within Cora Marie's bracelet. Very handy indeed."

"You did what?!" I exclaim. "This entire time you've been tracking me?! That's low, even for you. I thought we were friends or...something."

"Don't get your knickers in a wad, darling. I only had the chip inserted in case I needed to save your skin. Think about it. I didn't interfere with your grand escape."

"But you followed me here!"

"Out of the kindness of my heart," he says in a sarcastic, British tone. "Please. I want to help. It's not like I flew all the way here, dodging missiles and battling those ferocious Injections, just to say hello. Even though in all seriousness, those beasts are quite terrifying. They're like wolverines on steroids."

"How long have you been here?"

"In this building, only a few minutes. In Chicago, several hours. The Titan's radar is no match for my airship's cloaking device. He has no idea we're here." James smirks and tosses Kyle a pack of rations. "Take a load off, Legion. Have a drink! Eat a sandwich!"

"We're in a hurry. Deven is planning another attack." Kyle removes his helmet and passes the food to Deirdre. "I won't refuse your help. We could use someone knowledgeable on technology and warfare. You can stay here and assist Mikey Stevens with communications."

"That suits my expertise. I'm happy to help blow a whopping hole in the Titan's invasion." He looks at me and musters a guilty smile. "Believe me, Cora Marie. The bracelet was a gift. There were no strings attached. I truly wanted to make amends. Tracking you was never my intention. I just wanted to keep you safe. I've seen too many of my friends killed over the years."

"Some never died, James." I lean forward and lower my voice to a whisper. "You didn't tell me her name was Scarlet. That's why you called her your flame, isn't it? She was your fire."

"How do you know that?"

"She's sitting in this room."

His eyes widen with shock and excitement as he scans the coffee-shop, pausing when he sees the trembling figure of his deceased fiancé. She gazes at him with a mixture of panic and tearful excitement. Silence overtakes the room. They remain frozen, trapping us all in an air of awkwardness. Kyle is the first to break the ice. He clasps his hands together and begins briefing the recruits on their mission. I try to listen but my attention is focused on James and Scar. Shouldn't they be embracing, crying and saying how much they missed one other? I thought love was like a disease. Once you caught it, there's no way of escaping its hold. But maybe Legionaries are the only ones susceptible to the forever sickness. We fall in love once. It's the way our brains are wired. And as much as I hate it, I wouldn't want it any other way.

"How exactly are we getting inside?" Byron asks. "It's not like we just walk through a door."

"Maybe we can," I find myself saying. "Mikey, are there any service entrances into the city?"

"Yes, but they can only be accessed from the other side of the wall. Someone would have to enter the city and manually open the door. And for them to do that without being killed, they'd have to be invisible to all sensors and cameras," he answers, suddenly realizing my plan. A smile of approval crosses his face. "That might work."

"What might work?" Kyle looks at me fearfully. *"Please don't do anything reckless. I can't lose you again,"* his voice repeats in my head.

I avoid his gaze and turn my attention to Stonecipher, who is still suffering from a state of shock. "James, would you mind lending me your suit?"

He nods and begins removing the plates of metal.

"Tell me what's going on!" Kyle shouts out of frustration. His mood shifts from charismatic to panic stricken. "Why do you want his suit?"

"It's our way inside," I tell him. "Someone needs to manually open the service entrance from within the city to allow everyone else access. With the armor, I'll be invisible. I can walk through the main gate without being noticed. It's a foolproof plan."

"Then let me do it."

"Kyle, you're twice James' size! It'd be like a grown man trying to squeeze into a pair of toddler pajamas. I can do this. Let me. For a year you've been risking your life to save this country. It's my turn."

"She will be invisible to all sensors, heat monitors, and cameras. No one will notice her presence," Mikey adds in my defense. "What better way for the Blue-Jay to reenter the Titan's playing field? He killed her once. Why shouldn't he have to battle her ghost?"

I smile and fasten the pixilated armor over my figure. It adheres to my form, as lightweight and responsive as a layer of flesh. I fit the helmet over my head, flinching as a computer screen appears within the visor. My sight enhances to compete with the armor's built-in scope. I've never been in a suit as high-tech as this. All at once I feel invincible, as if James' confidence has been programmed into the plates of radioactive steel.

"Once you're inside the city, follow State Street north three-blocks and turn right onto Madison Street. You'll find a service entrance where the wall intersects Michigan Avenue," Mikey instructs. "It should only take you fifteen-minutes to get there."

Before I can switch-on the armor's camouflage, Kyle grabs my wrist. He looks at me with a gleam of uncertainty in his hazel eyes. "Promise you'll be careful."

"Of course," I say without doubt. "Make sure you're there when I open the door. And please bring my bow." I press a button on my wrist's touchpad and immediately the pixels in James' armor begin to flicker, swirling with color until they match the scenery of the coffee-shop. When I look down at my body, all I see is the charred floor and a moldy napkin. I'm invisible.

Kyle stares through me. His worry brings a smile to my face. I move forward and wrap my arms around his neck, hugging him a final time. My touch catches him off guard. He glances down and embraces my invisible figure. As soon as his grip lessens, I slide away from his body and rush out of the building. I've finally been accepted onto the battlefield. And this time, I know how to fight.

Buzzing fills my ears. Sweat builds beneath the layers of indestructible armor. My lungs pant as I sprint through the maze of empty structures, leaping from rooftops and ducking beneath fallen debris. Computer generated icons flash through the interior of James' helmet, showing digital maps and diagrams of Old Chicago. I breathe. I run. Each step draws me closer to Deven's City. I can already see the wall, a rise of metal and concrete suffocating the horizon with darkness. My mind is clear of fear. For the first time in my entire life, all of my identities coexist as one, powerful entity. Nothing can stop me now. My programming has transformed my thirst for revenge into the ability to avenge.

I lift my hand in front of my face, but I see nothing. *"Come on, Dad. Don't let me down now,"* I think as the entrance to the City appears in the distance. Vehicles form a line from the wall's gate, all waiting to pass through security. I stare at the headlights and the rows of injected soldiers. There are so many of them. They swarm the fortress like ants, pacing inside watchtowers and spilling over onto the battlements. Kyle's right. We are outnumbered and outgunned.

Up close, the Titan's wall isn't so intimidating. The foundation is crudely built and the plaster is cracked. Graffiti clutters the gate's threshold. I even notice *the sword and arrow* spray painted among the hodgepodge of designs. *We are hope for the world to see.*

Cautiously I tread forward, weaving between cargo trucks filled with new recruits and sliding past an eighteen-wheeler stocked with fresh produce. I pass a Centurion directing traffic. He looks in my direction but doesn't see me. This plan may work after all.

Spotlights comb across the outskirts of Chicago. Glowing airships lift out of the city and disappear into the night sky. I watch a group of guards sort through the new shipment of teenagers, dividing the strong from the weak. It's as if Deven has restructured society to match that of Prime Way, a dictated civilization built on deception and the power of strength.

I join the lineup of armored soldiers and try my hardest not to bump against one of them. Together we move through the gate, past sensors, leashed Injections, and dozens of armed Elite. No one notices my presence. I remain a ghost as I walk into enemy territory. The thought of fooling Deven's technology brings a smile to my face. I won his game by using his own tactics against him. I cheated.

Cain, the man who killed my aunt and best-friend, appears in the mob of guards. His huge body is dressed in a white tuxedo, the uniform of the Titan's Elders, and a pair of expensive shoes. His face is as ugly as I remember—piggish nose, bald head, and a gruesome smile that looks as if it had been cut with a jagged knife. It's a struggle to contain my programming with him so near. All I want to do is tear out his heart, make him feel the pain he caused me.

Capital Tower rises ahead. It's the tallest structure in Deven's city, a black skyscraper lifting higher and higher until it disappears into the fog. I can barely see the lights at the top, two blinking prongs spearing the night sky. I once saw a picture of the building when I was schooling at Prime Way. My class was studying major cities across the United States, memorizing maps and strategically analyzing each location. At the time I wondered why we were learning such things. Now I understand that it was for moments like this. We were being prepared for war.

I move swiftly through the crowded streets, under train-rails and across bridges. People rush past me. I glance at their faces—new recruits, injected soldiers in slick armor, a group of exhausted adult laborers, and an Elite driving a motorcycle. No one sees me as I shuffle through the masses. Numbers, brandings, despondent oppression—they fill the debris-strewn roads. I try to harden myself to the darkness. I try to block out the screams of children, keep myself from noticing the ashen shadows splattered across the side of an apartment building, shield my face from the hanging noose constructed between two converted factories. I weave between streetlamps and beneath a mega-screen depicting Deven's face with the slogan, *Fight and Prosper* stamped on his chest. His taunting voice echoes through my head.

"You know you can't beat me, Sweetheart. I've already won," I hear him say. *"I branded you. I destroyed you. I own you. You're mine to control. This is no longer a petty child's game. The stakes are greater and this time, we're going all in."*

I jog up State Street. The buildings here have been remodeled as training centers for the Titan's army. I look through a window to watch a new shipment of recruits train. The interior of the gym is similar to the Ground Sector at Prime Way—rooms filled with punching bags and weight equipment, a padded ring for fighting exhibitions. It unearths memories of my past. I see myself fighting and feel the strain of muscles as I imagine blocking a blow to the face. I've changed since then. The world has changed.

An airship flies overhead, sending a gust of wind through the urban war-camp. Turbines blaze. I squint and duck into the shadows. Even my armor's camouflage can't hide me from the Regiment's searchlights. The pixels reveal themselves under heavy light. I check the watch within James' helmet. I've been within the city for thirteen-minutes. Kyle and his division could already be waiting at the door.

I break into a sprint as a train squeals down the rails to my left. A mob of Centurions are waiting by the tracks, laughing and prodding a woman in her early twenties. She's dressed in monochrome colors with a parcel of rations tucked beneath her arm. I watch them pull her hair with hatred boiling inside my chest. They've become like Deven. They prey on the weak. My own race has become my enemy.

"Leave her alone!" I shout angrily. They pause and glance around with bewilderment. Their confusion sends a rush of adrenaline through my body. *"Keep walking,"* I tell myself. *"Don't stop."*

As Mikey instructed, I turn right onto Madison Street and move towards the sequestering wall. It's not too late. I could still go after Deven. Kyle would be safe outside city limits and I'd have invisibility as an advantage. This war would end by a simple act of selfishness. *Bravery is self-serving. Courage is sacrifice.* Am I brave or am I courageous?

I heave a sigh and rush down an alley towards the designated service entrance. I break the lock and open the door. Kyle's face appears first. He slides through the narrow entryway with Byron following close behind him.

"Cora, where are you?" he asks and looks around desperately. His division forms a crowd behind him, each soldier fully equipped for battle.

"Sorry. I forgot to turn off the camouflage," I say. The moment I reveal myself, he relaxes and passes me my handmade bow and quiver of electric arrows. His smile is calming.

"Divide into squads. Team leaders, you know your mission. Once your objective has been achieved, regroup at Union Station. You'll know what to do from there. From this moment on, we are all under a silence band."

Before I realize what's happening, half of the recruits gather their artillery and rush silently into the streets of Old Chicago. I watch until they disappear into the fog. Their target is more crucial than mine. If they fail their mission, more people will die.

Kyle motions to Sarah and Byron and the four of us begin our trek to the heart of Deven's City.

It's strange to think that eighteen-months have passed since the war began. Technology has transformed the planet. Things that never seemed possible are. I look at Kyle now and am dumbstruck by what I see. He's become a man—tall and robust with defined muscles and handsome, stalwart features. Every time he glances at me, I feel like melting. It's as if I finally see him, the real him. I see the blonde scruff on his cheeks and hear the authority in his Texan voice. It takes my breath away.

"Do me a favor and become invisible," Kyle whispers. "I need you to be safe."

"Only if you're invisible too. We can share James' armor."

He laughs and removes his helmet. "Wouldn't that be a sight—two half-bodied soldiers wandering the city at night! We'd sure scare the *mess* out of some kids."

I smile and toss James' helmet behind a dumpster. I'd rather confront my enemies face-to-face. "This is the first time we've ever entered a fight together," I point out. "I like it."

"What happened to the silence band?" Byron interrupts. He lifts his visor and musters an amused grin. "I thought we were supposed to be *sneaking* through the Titan's hive, not patronizing it."

"Are you in command of this operation, 1889?" Kyle snaps with a hint of jest. "I didn't think so."

Sarah snickers. She clutches her gun and walks swiftly by my side. I know she is anxious to rescue Callan. It shows on her face, in her movements. "How far are we from our target?"

"A few blocks," I answer. "We'll need to find cover once we round this corner. The city's main terminal is just beyond the next building. Trains, civilians, soldiers—we'll be sitting ducks."

Kyle agrees and leads us into the shadows cast by a renovated housing-complex. Palpability is our only disadvantage. All traces of our mutated DNA have been concealed. Mikey's blocked our body heat from the Titan's sensors, and monitors security cameras to keep our presence here unnoticed. If we can reach Callan's cell without being seen, we might actually make it out of this city unscathed.

"How do we become invisible without camouflaged suits?" I ask myself, remembering the night of Deven's first attack. The answer suddenly becomes clear. *"We must become one of them."*

I stop beneath a clothing line to pry the armor from my body. I shed James' suit the way a snake would shed its skin, wriggling and tugging until the metal infused jumper slides over my ankles. Everyone stares at me with bewilderment as I brush the wrinkles from my ripped jeans and adjust the neckline of my sports bra. As if to pass along an unspoken message, I braid my hair.

"What are you doing, Cora? Now's not the best time to change your outfit!" Kyle speaks sharply. His expression hardens until all trances of youth vanish. He switches from caring boyfriend to stern, commanding officer. I've never seen this side of his personality. "Put those clothes back on."

"She knows what she's doing." Sarah moves towards me with a gleam of understanding in her pretty eyes, and begins undressing. Byron follows her example.

I remove some of the laundry from the clothing line and divide it among my squad. After sliding on a gray t-shirt, a pair of leather boots, and a baseball hat, I confront Kyle's confusion. "You said it yourself. We are vastly outnumbered and outgunned. If we want to reach our destination without getting shot in the back, we need to blend in, stay off-grid, and become flies on the wall. Technology is Deven's expertise. The only way to avoid contact with him is by using some outdated tactics. Let's make our own camouflage." I toss him a heather V-neck and a stained stocking cap. "It's worked before."

He nods and tosses his gun and sword to Byron. I watch as he unfastens the armor from his body, each layer shedding with rehearsed ease. The muscles in his arms tense as he pulls the suit from his pants, revealing definition I never noticed before. It's difficult not to stare at his bare chest, especially when I notice the words freshly inked on the right side of his ribcage. Before I have a chance to read the fine print, he meets my gaze and quickly hides the design from view. His response baffles me, causing my curiosity to heighten. What does the paragraph say? When did he have time to get a new tattoo? He already has two markings, Deven's emblem branded on his spine, and dozens of scars. There must be something urgent and significant about this new inking. Why else would he receive another tattoo before entering a warzone?

"Let's head to the train-tracks. I have a plan," Kyle instructs as he pulls the stocking-cap over his forehead. "If we get split up, do not try to complete this mission alone. The world doesn't need idiotic heroes. Go to Union Station and wait for the others to regroup. Understood?"

The moment we comply, a spiteful laughter echoes through the tenebrous city. Our eyes lift to the holographic screen mounted between two buildings. A breath catches inside my throat. Anger rumbles through my core, as strong and hot as a shot of whiskey. Deven appears above the maze of streets, a grotesque smile drawn across his thin lips. My desire for bloodshed reaches new extremes.

"Countdown has begun," the Titan states in a monotone voice. His head has been shaved clean and the tattooed flames that were once confined to the skin of his forearm have spread up his shoulder and across his chest. Every painful lash, hurtful remark, and devastating memory—they all resurface to drown my hope with darkness. A mere bully has morphed into the devil himself.

"Be prepared. In seven-hours, our invasion will be complete. America will come to a staggering end and our reign of supremacy will begin. We'll replace humanity with our race and once the planet succumbs to our power, we will rule the world." His declaration sends a shiver down my spine. "Tomorrow afternoon, governors will be chosen from my Elite to rule the nation's districts. Remaining children will be programmed, tagged, and shuttled to outposts across the country. Adults wanting Regimental Citizenship must enlist as caretakers, ambassadors, or laborers before the exodus…"

This is no longer a petty child's game. The stakes are greater and this time, we're going all in." Our choices tonight will either save the world or destroy everything we've striven to protect. The urgency on Kyle's face confirms my doubts. We are humanity's only remaining hope. Without us, Deven wins his final game. *"You know you can't beat me. I've already won."*

When the announcement ends, Kyle conceals his weapons inside a pillowcase and looks at us with rugged strength. "It isn't over. We still have a fighting chance," he says. "The other squad is targeting whatever is posing as a threat. We must trust that they'll complete their mission. Until then, our objective is still to rescue Callan Kingston."

"Then can we blow the Titan's fat head off?" Byron aims his glowing rifle at the empty billboard and clicks the power from dormant to active. The gun hums with energy. His eyes narrow, transforming his persona from jesting to recalcitrant. "I got something to fight for. Let's do this. Whatever it takes…"

"Whatever it takes," Sarah agrees. She crosses her arms over her chest. "Doom to the Titan."

I smile and salute my friends. "Be the victor, not the victim."

"No Feeling. No Regret. Just Strength," Kyle adds. "Now who's ready to get run over by a train?"

Crowds move steadily through the terminal. Trains come and go, carrying passengers across the bustling city. I am among them—a shadowed face, one of thousands, invisible. With my head down and my bow carefully hidden inside a rotting backpack, I move through the masses. Guards look in my direction but they don't recognize me as their enemy. To them I'm just another recruit or young laborer, someone they'd whip in training or starve in the slums. Soldiers pass by without a second look. They must be anticipating the end of the world. I notice the excitement on their young faces as they prepare to depart. Where are they headed; to celebrate with their friends at a local bar, night training, or their cushy apartments nestled in the outskirts of Old Chicago? They are the Elite, the only people Deven favors. That one aspect of their identity causes hatred to bubble inside my chest.

Kyle and Byron walk ahead, occasionally peering over their shoulders at Sarah and me. Together we make our way towards the rails. Airships soar overhead, illuminating the sky with blue and white hues. Frost forms patches on the damp cement. I breathe heavily as the four of us step off the departure platform and onto the tracks. Five-minutes until the next train.

"Are you sure this is a good idea?" I ask quietly as we move away from the terminal.

"No," Kyle smirks. "But it's the least dangerous plan I could come up with."

"Next to skydiving without parachutes and roping ourselves to the back of an Injection, right?"

"There's that cute sense of humor," he jokes. His expression softens. It calms my fears.

"So we just lie down on the tracks?" Byron clenches his teeth and stares at the rails fearfully. "Remember when I said, *whatever it takes*….well, that didn't include suicide!"

"Do as I told you and everything will be fine. It looks scarier than it is. Just hold on tight." Kyle lies on the tracks and musters a smile. "Tilt your head to the side so your face won't get shaved off."

Sarah and Byron lay between the rails, both trembling. I know I shouldn't be scared. I've done this sort of thing hundreds of times. It's what Legionaries do for fun. We risk our lives to feel a rush of adrenaline. Except now, having fun might get me killed.

I nestle myself between the tracks, breathing deeply to keep my heart rate at bay. The chill of metal meets my spine. Wooden slats press uncomfortably against my back. I toy with the star-charm dangling from my neck to keep my mind distracted from possible death. Wallowing in the dirt isn't how I'd want to spend the last four minutes of my life.

"We are invincible," I tell myself. It's a lie meant to replace my doubt with confidence. Though as much as I think it, my twinge of vulnerability continues to grow into a cancer of fear. *"Cowardice is not in my vocabulary. The Program made me strong. This world made me brave. Sacrifice made me courageous. I am the Blue-Jay, and nothing can shut me down."* This is my creed, my identity—my purpose.

I stare between my feet at the top of Kyle's head. He looks back and reaches out his hand. I grasp it, squeezing his callused knuckles until they turn white. The warmth of his skin eases the chill from my back. A single touch drives away all uncertainty. He runs his index finger across my palm as if to pass along a needed message. *Dead or alive, we are victorious.*

Lights appear further down the tracks, as blinding as the sun. They race towards us. I forget to breathe as the tracks vibrate, shaking my body as if I'm being tossed into a blender. I clench my teeth and tilt my head to one side. *"Hold on tight. Keep chest pressed to the bottom of the train. Don't die."* Fear wrenches within my stomach. A scream catches inside my throat. I gaze up at the starry sky and try to lose my anxiety among the streaks of constellations. *"Breathe. Just Breathe."*

"Grab on and don't let go until I tell you!" Kyle shouts as the train's grate nears his ankles. He doesn't make a sound as the locomotive swallows him whole, sucking his body beneath the rumbling cars. Horns blare. A spotlight combs across my figure. I groan from the painful vibrations.

Then, it's my turn.

I flatten myself against the tracks, avoiding the grate as it slices the air above my face. Wind whips the baseball cap from my head, grinding the hat beneath hundreds of screeching wheels. The sound brings tears of horror to my eyes. I've been shot, sliced, tortured, and yet the thought of being crushed to death suffocates me. The same way Kyle has aviophobia, I'm claustrophobic.

Before I have a chance to second guess myself, I lift my hands and grab hold of an axle. Immediately I'm yanked into motion. My body is dragged across the rails, the skin peeling from my spine. Blood soaks the back of my t-shirt. I scream and pull myself off the ground and against the oil smeared train-car. Pain pulses through my nervous system, but discomfort is unimportant. All that matters is escaping this situation alive.

My feet press against the sides of the locomotive to keep from slipping. I glance down at the tracks, a blur of brown and gray flying past at fatal speeds. Wind continues to beat against my wounded back. Chains rattle. As time passes, my muscles strain. I won't be able to hold on forever. Soon my arms and legs will grow weary. I will fall and I will die.

"Cora, are you okay?!" Kyle yells above the noise. He climbs from axle-to-axle until our bodies are inches apart. His cheek and forehead are bleeding. "Why are you bloody?!"

"I scraped my back! Don't worry. I'm fine!" I shout in response, my voice shaky. He tilts his head and looks at me skeptically. I can't let him worry. "What about you? Are you…alright?"

"We're all great, you know, just hanging out. Thanks for asking!" Byron calls from further down the tracks. "Legion, how much longer do we have to ride this thing?!"

"A few minutes! I've already checked our location on my transmitter. Once the train slows, we let go. I'll say when," he answers.

My fingers have turned an unnatural shade of purple. My muscles ache with fatigue. I breathe heavily and tighten my grip. I can't fall. I won't fall. *"Cowardice is not in my vocabulary. The Program made me strong. This world made me brave. Sacrifice made me courageous. I am the Blue-Jay, and nothing can shut me down."* I repeat it over and over until my fear disappears and the pain in my joints lessens.

Brakes squeal. I lurch forward as the locomotive reduces speed, and grab at a rusting chain to steady myself. Kyle glances back and nods. It's time.

"Release!" The command unravels my hands from the steel rod. I grit my teeth and drop off the car, falling against the tracks with a loud *crack*. Agonizing pain sears through my ribcage, forcing a moan from my mouth. I lay unmoved as the train passes overhead, disappearing down the rails and into the dismal city. Am I still in one piece? I feel as if I've shattered every bone in my body. Blood soaks my clothing. Bruises cover my flesh. I bite my lip and roll timidly onto my side, only to see the glossy walls of Capital Tower rising a block away.

Pressure spreads through my lower abdomen. It surprises me but at the same time brings an irritated grimace to my face. Of course this would happen now. As I'm approaching my target, humanity strikes back. When was the last time I used a bathroom, twelve-hours ago? I didn't notice the urge until now. Why must my body function as a teenager's should? It's another glitch in my design.

Sarah climbs slowly to a standing position. She brushes the dirt from her jeans and walks towards me. "Looks like we're all alive," she croaks before helping me stand. "Cora, your back is a mess! I have some first-aid in my bag. Wait a moment…"

"Whew, that was awful!" Byron stumbles in our direction. He unrolls the sleeves of his sweater and spits a wad of bile from his mouth. Except for the cut on his wrist, he is uninjured. "I'd rather be caught in a riptide than do *that* again. Gosh, I think I swallowed a rock!"

"Among other things," Sarah mumbles as she retrieves a bottle of medication from her backpack. She lifts the back of my shirt and sprays the liquid over my cuts. An excruciating sting occurs as my flesh pieces itself together, healing and regenerating until the wounds are nothing but fresh scars. "That looks better. Come over here, Byron. I'll fix that cut of yours." Her matted blonde hair forms a halo of gold around her face, giving her an angelic persona.

Kyle saunters to my side with oil and blood smearing his cheeks. He pulls the stocking-cap from his head and sits on the gravel. I lean against a lopsided electrical pole and gasp for oxygen. My body aches. Every breath sends a ripple of pain through my abdomen. If we were alone, I'd curl up in his lap and sleep until the pain subsided. *Nothing is perfect in this world…except us.*

"Our destination is only a few blocks from here. We'll have your brother within the hour." He glances up, noticing my frown. "What's wrong?"

I kneel beside him and lower my voice to a whisper. "I need to…use a restroom."

"Now?"

I nod, blushing with embarrassment. My face is hot. Humiliation nauseates my stomach.

"Come on. I'm not letting you wander the city alone." He laughs and rises to his feet. "Sarah and Byron, you both stay here and contact Mikey. He will relay details concerning entry into the W Chicago City Center. Cora and I will be back in a few minutes."

"Wow, Legion and Blue-Jay are sneaking off! The army's going to love hearing about this." Byron puckers his lips. His thick eyebrows crease together to form a single arch. "Try not to make-out for too long. You sure would hate for the Titan to find you…"

"I have to pee, you idiot!" I shout crisply, irritated by the pain in my abdomen. Sometimes I forget I have an explosive side, the part of me that throws knives at people's heads and slaps them across the face. I'm not especially kind or gentle or feminine, but I am headstrong and if I love something, I will give my life to protect it. That is probably the only personality trait Kyle and I share.

Byron's cheeks are red with mortification. Sarah clasps a hand over her mouth to muffle a giggle. I grab Kyle's wrist and lead him away from the tracks and into the tangle of crowded streets. We wander the block of offices, ducking into vacant businesses in search of a toilet. The air reeks of awkwardness, as if my need to *go* has unearthed a hidden truth, forced me to admit to my weakness. After walking the city for a few minutes, we find an abandoned subway terminal with a dilapidated bathroom. The stalls are covered with graffiti and the air smells of sewage and mildew. Still it's better than using a trashcan.

Kyle follows me inside the women's restroom and stands by the sink with a gun clutched protectively to his chest. He stares at the muddy floor as I rush into one of the dimly lit stalls. My cheeks flush as I lock the door and unclasp my belt. Embarrassment can hardly describe the humiliation I feel.

My jeans slide to the floor. I bite my lip as I relieve myself, clenching my teeth until a spring of blood trails onto my tongue. It tastes metallic and forces a grimace onto my face. If I could, I'd crawl inside my backpack and disappear. Pride is such a painful flaw.

I bury my burning face in my hands, listening as Kyle turns the sink faucet on and off. What does he think about me now? Is he secretly laughing, or is he as embarrassed as I am?

"Thanks for coming with me," I mumble to break the awkward tension. "I'm sorry."

"Cora, you are human. It's no big deal. You've seen me vomit, bleed, and crap myself," he answers. "The only thing you haven't seen is me naked…"

"And that isn't by choice." A new dose of humiliation floods my body with heat. Obscenities whisper from my mouth. I feel like hurling. Are my armpits sweating? That's gross! Why did I say such a thing? What's wrong with me? I should just cut out my tongue. That'd solve so many problems.

"What does your tattoo say?" It's the first question I can think of, something to draw his attention away from my seductive remark. "You didn't have it when you came to New York."

"No, I got it on the train-ride here. It's…a reminder of who I am. I thought that if I inked my identity on my body, I wouldn't forget." His voice is on the verge of laughter. "I'll let you read it after our mission is complete."

I stand and refasten my belt, steadying my breathing before exiting the stall. Kyle looks up and smiles, those gentle eyes burrowing into mine with sudden intensity. I shudder. He makes me feel vulnerable and weak in the knees. At first the feeling was delirious, as painless as morphine. Now it aches like the bruises on my spine.

"We don't have much time. The others are waiting for us," I say without meeting his gaze. "Humanity is on the brink of extinction. If Deven's threat is carried out, we will all die. He can't be allowed to win; not now, not ever. I won't let him."

Kyle places his hands on my shoulders. One palm envelops my acromion, his fingers stretching across my shoulder-blade. I've never noticed their size before, or how small I am compared to his muscular frame. He's over six-feet-tall and I'm only five-feet-six-inches. In my mind, our sizes have always been equal. That's far from the truth. A single squeeze from Kyle could shatter every bone in my body. The thought makes me furious but at the same time, fills me with curious, unshakable desire.

"Once your brother has been rescued and our troops have fled the city, I'm going after Deven. I couldn't tell you before because the others would hear," he discloses. "I want you to come with me."

"What happened to *not doing anything reckless*? I didn't think you wanted me to fight."

"I guess I'm bad at following my own orders." He tilts forward until our foreheads are pressed together. "You are not made of glass, Cora. This is your fight as much as mine. Besides, we're a team. We're stronger together." His next few words release as a whisper. "I never want to be apart from you again. A year was enough."

Timidly I place my hands on his hips, cringing as heat rushes to my blushing cheeks. He strokes my hair and laces my fingers with his. What if this is the last time we're ever together? What if we die tonight? If I only have a few hours left of life, I want to spend them with Kyle. *"Write your name on me. Claim me. It's the only branding I want to have."*

He wraps his arms around my waist and kisses me lightly. A thrill of emotions rises within my heart as I feel his lips ease against my neck, and the pressure of his fingertips against my cracked ribcage. I smile and glide my hands over his back, touching every indented scar and bulging muscle. There is no fear. There is no regret. With him, I'm safe.

A rush of adrenaline surges through my veins. It enhances my senses and intensifies my movements. I shove Kyle against the stained wall and fit my mouth to his. This time, he doesn't react with hesitance or shock. Instead he grabs my body and turns, pressing *me* to the wall. The impact surprises me. His weight pushes against my chest, sandwiching my figure between his torso and the cinderblock barrier. I can hardly breathe. My lungs ache. Maybe his strength *will* shatter my bones. I respond by kissing him harder.

The florescent lights flicker as Kyle lifts me off the ground. I entwine my legs around his abdomen and run my fingers through his short hair. He sets me on the bathroom counter. We kiss for what seems like forever; because as far as we both know, forever could be stolen from us at any moment.

CHAPTER 11

Wind slaps against my face as I peer over the skyscraper's ledge. Three-hundred-feet beneath me, South Wells Street and West Adams Street intersect; a collision of weary crowds and hovering vehicles. What once was the Sears Tower rises a few blocks away—ebony boxes stacked high into the sky, illuminated by holographic screens. The city is chaotic and ablaze with lights. Above the bustle, Chicago seems the same as it did before the invasion. It's all a lie. The opulence of Deven's center city is meant to deceive, to draw attention away from the enslaved laborers and the nationwide apocalypse occurring beyond the wall. Sensuous, grandiose, indulgent—they've replaced hope with fraudulence.

The roof of the W Chicago City Center hovers a hundred-meters away. It is our destination.

"We will have ten-minutes to get into the hotel, find Callan, and escape. Mikey will knock out all monitors and cameras on this side of the city. We'll be in the dark long enough to complete our mission without being noticed," Sarah relays. She crouches on the roof's ledge with abnormal agility. "Our only problem is getting inside. Legion, I suppose you have a plan since you led us up here."

"What, are you going to make us jump?" Byron smirks sarcastically. His smile fades when he notices the seriousness in Kyle's eyes. "You *really* want us to die tonight, don't you?"

"Security is thick on the first few levels. The roof entrance will provide us with easy access into the building. Besides, Callan's cell is room 2101 on the twenty-first floor. It makes sense to start at the top." Kyle glances at me for approval. His eyes glisten with a smile, reminding me of our kiss. Heat sears across my face. I still feel the print of his hands on my waist and the thrill of his lips against mine. I've kissed him many times before and never felt this warm, as if I could leap out of my skin with excitement. What made this time different? Why was a kiss inside a filthy bathroom so...right?

"There are very few things I'm afraid of, heights being one of them." Byron's face is white and his pupils dilated. His hands tremble as his programming takes effect. Confliction radiates from his expressions. I know the feeling—two identities and genetic-codes warring beneath his skull; fearlessness and humanity, bravery and courage. "I can't jump!"

"You've been trained for this. We all have," Sarah adds anxiously. "If we don't go now, our timeframe for infiltration will end. The mission will be compromised! We can't afford to lose this opportunity. Callan's life is at risk!"

"No. It's too far. I won't make it!"

"Fear is a human sickness. The only cure is facing it head on," I say. "I'll be the guinea pig and jump first. If I die, you know not to follow." My eyes narrow. A huff of breath trails from my nostrils as I back against the far corner of the platform. I lunge into a runner's stance and stare ahead at the distant roofline. Seven strides, a single jump, two-hundred-feet of air—it's time for the Blue-Jay to take flight.

Before anyone has a chance to stop me, I sprint forward.

The abyss of weightless danger swallows me whole. My stomach wrenches the moment my feet leave the ledge. I forget to breathe. My arms flail as I soar over South Wells Street. The rush is familiar, like the smell of Kyle's clothes or the taste of coffee. It surges through my veins. Same as every original Legionary, I am an adrenaline junkie.

My destination approaches. I feel myself begin to fall, descending rapidly towards the hotel. I prepare myself for the pain of impact and stretch out my legs to meet the gravel covered roof. The moment my feet touch ground, I relax my muscles and tumble forward in a roll. Rock pierces my flesh. Discomfort washes through my body. The pain is minor and expected. As I rise to a sitting position, I grab an arrow from over my shoulder and string it across my bow, aiming at whatever might be waiting for me on the rooftop.

I am alone.

Sarah lands in a wad beside me. She moans and brushes the pebbles from her skin. Byron follows after her, crumbling in a heap of strained muscles and bent limbs. He clutches his knee and curses under his breath. Before either of them rises from the ground, Kyle alights. He hardly stumbles and walks swiftly towards me. His perfected movements are envied. I've been training for nine-years and have never gained such agility.

"We are ready for infiltration," Kyle whispers into his headset. Immediately the lights of the hotel falter, dimming until the surrounding blocks are trapped in blackness. Byron tosses us each a flashlight. "Enter single file. Once we're inside, our silence is mandatory until we locate our target. Remember, we only have ten-minutes before power is reestablished. Countdown starts now."

The entrance is unsealed with ease. Kyle leads us into the unlit corridor and down a flight of stairs. Voices echo from distant hallways, soldiers rushing from their rooms in a sudden panic. I'm glad to hear them, to hear something rather than the beating of my heart and the repetitive huff of my breathing. Silence is uncanny. Darkness causes even the most logical thing to morph into a chilling nightmare. My worst fears are found in the dark.

Sarah switches on her flashlight. A soft, white glow illuminates the carpeted floor. To anyone passing by, we appear to be a group of irritated recruits, half-asleep and searching for a fuse box. Invisibility should fill me with confidence. But all I feel is unease, as if this is another trap in Deven's game. I refuse to be caught off guard again.

Footsteps pound in all directions. Flashlights flicker. The four of us move steadily through hallways and down another staircase to the twenty-first floor. Even though the pretentious building has been converted into soldier housing, most of the original extravagance has been kept intact. Rich beauty has lost its value in this new world.

Kyle motions to a metal door on my left, room 2101. It looks foreign compared to the luxury of the hotel's corridor. The entranceway has been locked using a high-tech security system. Yellow caution tape streaks the steel panel. We've arrived at my backstabbing brother's cell.

Byron rushes forward and attaches a decoder to the door's keypad.

Numbers and letters slide across the screen as the encoded lock is deciphered. Minutes later, the device flashes green and the door clicks open. Kyle glances at me with a smile on his face. *"We did it."*

I stare into the dark bedroom, unable to move. Callan betrayed me, chose to save his own skin rather than save the world. How do I forgive someone who left me to rot in a cell? He's the only family I have left and yet in some small way, I wish he had died too. It's easier to handle loneliness than a brother who sided with my enemy. Nothing, not an apology or weepy remorse, could ever wipe away the hurt he caused. So no matter what is said, I've lost him.

Sarah shines her flashlight into the apartment, scanning the room until the white beams fall across Callan's face. He shields his eyes and rises from a plush chair, fully clothed in armor with a pack strapped to his back. Sarah squeals and drops the light. She rushes into the darkness and throws her arms around my brother's neck. I hear sobbing and mumbled words. He has always loved her more, chose her safety over mine.

Kyle activates several glowsticks and a lantern before entering the suite. I lace my fingers with his to drive away the pain and insecurity looming in my thoughts. He touches the back of my neck as if saying, *"Everything is going to be okay."* And I believe him.

The door is closed once all four of us are inside the apartment. Byron sits on the king size bed. Kyle places the lantern on a nightstand and speaks briefly to Mikey on his transmitter. Sarah clings to Callan's arm, smiling with tears streaming her cheeks. My brother looks at me, speechless. I gaze at him in silence. A year has transformed his appearance. His dark hair, which was once short and spiked, is now long and drapes his forehead. His cheeks are covered with untrimmed stubble, his russet body tall and built. Scars clutter his skin. Dozens of names have been tattooed on his wrist; everyone he's lost from the effects of The Prime Way Program. My name is among them.

"Cora," he gasps. The blood drains from his face. His almond eyes are wide with shock, his hands trembling. "You're alive!"

"No. I'm a ghost," I snap coolly. The chilled sarcasm in my voice sends a wave of panic through his pupils. I can't help it. His selfishness almost killed Kyle and me.

"Deven told me you were dead. Thank God, he was wrong!" Callan embraces me. I flinch at his touch, fighting the urge to pull away. He squeezes my shoulders so tight, tears of pain fog my vision. "I'm so sorry, Sis. It's my fault you were hurt. I thought…choosing the Titan was my only choice. He told me Sarah was going to die if I didn't join him, that everyone was going to die. He promised to protect all of you. It was stupid of me to believe him."

"What happened to you, Callan?" Sarah asks. "Why were you locked up?"

"Share stories later. We need to leave. Time is running out," Kyle adds. "The others will be waiting for us at Union Station."

"We can't leave now!" my brother says. "The Titan is preparing to exterminate all of you, genocide humankind. Everyone is going to die! That's why he locked me up. I discovered what the Regiment was creating in their labs and tried to contact President Marner."

"Exterminate?! How?" Byron hops off the mattress frantically. "I've almost died *way* too many times tonight. No misanthropic psycho and his army of delusional teenagers are going to kill me!"

"It's already happening," Callan explains. "Unlike my father's mutating serum, the programming process tapped into your cerebral cortex. Strategic knowledge, reasoning, and emotion control were engraved in your Frontal Lobe and Limbic System. The Parietal and Occipital Lobes were programmed with fighting instinct, enhanced senses and movements. Your Temporal Lobe was the only part of your brain untouched. All this said, each of your brains emit a signal imprinted from the genetic-alterations. If tapped into, the hacker has complete control of your body's nervous system. He could wipe out your race with a single click. All he'd have to do is turn off the Medulla segment of your Brain Stem. Until now, the technology to combat this feat has never been in existence…"

"Deven's going to shut us down," I mutter. Pain stabs through my abdomen. I feel sick. He has control over me again. "He'll either kill or brainwash us."

"What about everyone else? How are they going to die?" Kyle croaks. I've never seen him so pale. "Aren't the Titan's soldiers susceptible to this…control?"

"No. Our brains haven't been rewired like yours. We were mutated, not programmed. As for everyone else, the Regiment will unleash a multitude of nuclear-missiles to erase the remainder of the United States.

First one is targeted at Dimidium. After the country has been cleaned, more Erasers will be launched. They will tear apart other nations and continents. In six months, earth will be conquered."

Byron stumbles across the room to a trashcan and vomits. The sound of his heaving sends a shiver down my spine. I cringe and lean against the wall, breathing deeply until my nausea subsides. There is no denying it. We are all going to die today.

"This doesn't change anything. Our mission still continues as planned. The others may have found the control panel and are shutting down operations as we speak. We can't lose hope," Kyle says to shatter the morbid silence. "Why should we give up? We've made it this far, spent a year battling the Titan's horrors without fatality. He may have stolen our homes, our friends, family, and futures. But here we are, stronger than anything he's ever created. We've never been defeated. Even if we die today, we are victorious. So let's fight until our hearts stop beating. Let's show the Titan what we're made of."

Sarah presses her tearstained face against Callan's chest. He embraces her, tenderly stroking her blonde hair. "I'm going to keep you safe," I hear him whisper. It's another lie. He can't keep any of us safe. Our lives are ticking away. One click is all it takes.

"Let's go," my voice commands in a strong tone. "I know everyone is scared. I am too. But what Kyle said is right. The other squad is counting on us. We must fulfill our mission." I cross my arms over my chest. "I believe in the impossible odds."

Kyle musters a smile and walks toward the door. I follow him. The five of us leave the apartment and retrace our steps to the roof.

The thought of death no longer fazes me. I expect to feel a sense of dread, anxiety, even sorrow. I feel everything but. Is it because deep down I've already made peace with the person I love, said goodbye? I may be open to dying, but never goodbye.

Does Deven really have my brain on a control panel? Now I'll never know if my thoughts and movements are truly my own. Maybe that's what scares me most. Death is simple and final. Mind control erases all self-purpose and determination, morphing my body into a thoughtless weapon. Deven could make me do *anything*. I'll no longer be his enemy. I will be his pet.

A gust of frigid air blows across my face as I step onto the roof. Night is breaking. Streaks of pink sunrise paint the distant horizon. I try to shrug off the fear weighing on my shoulders, and move hastily towards the ledge. Our time is running low. Once the lights come on, all hell will break loose.

"In case we die today, there's something I need to ask you." Kyle places his hand on the small of my back and leans close to my ear. His voice softens as it breezes through his teeth. "Would you...?"

A loud explosion interrupts his question. We turn, stumbling as a cloud of fire rises from the outer city. Energy surges towards us. The earth shakes, knocking all five of us to the gravel covered floor. Flames tear through buildings. Smoke fills the air. Screams replace the bustle below. I cover my face as fiery ash rains from the sky.

"The others," Sarah mumbles as another eruption blows apart a street of skyscrapers. "They exploded the labs...and everything else in that district. What if they didn't escape in time? They could be dead or dying!"

"We can't leave them!" Byron shouts and gazes at Kyle and me with a sudden look of horror.

"As far as we all know, they may have just saved the world and are waiting for us at our rendezvous point. Assumptions cannot be made," Kyle states sternly. "Do not mourn or worry unnecessarily. We are following protocol. Until we receive confirmation of their deaths, they *are* alive."

"We can't lose any more time!" Callan shouts as the hotel's power flickers to life. The screens projected on the side of Capital Tower buzz with static. A siren blasts somewhere among the maze of streets. "We're back online! If we don't keep moving, every soldier with two legs will be tracking us!"

"What's the quickest way out of here?!" I yell over the roar of chaos.

My brother smirks and fastens a black helmet over his head. "Follow me." He grabs Sarah and with a single jump, flings himself over the roof's ledge. I watch his body fall and disappear into the flow of hovering traffic.

"Is this a joke?!" Byron glances at the three-hundred-foot drop, heaving a mouthful of bile. Sweat drips from his temples. His skin has turned a sickly green hue. "How do I jump without...dying?!"

"Aim to land on an aircraft or vehicle. The moment your feet reach impact zone, relax all muscles in your legs so they won't snap in half. You learned all this in basic training." Kyle leads 1889 to the roof's edge. "All you have to do is jump. Let your programming do the rest." When Byron refuses to move, Kyle grabs him by the collar and shoves him into the chasm. He wails as his body is sucked towards the swirling pavement below.

"That was mean," I scold as Byron lands heavily on top of a cargo truck. "I'm supposed to be the *mean* one, not you. Pushing people off the roof is my thing."

Kyle laughs. "I may be a little meaner than you remember. Effectiveness comes before courtesy." He scoops me off the ground and into his arms. Hesitantly he steps onto the ledge, peering into the abyss of flickering lights and flaming debris. "I don't ask permission anymore. I just *do*."

"That can be a good thing…in some situations. But you know I can jump by myself. Daredevil stunts are an expertise of mine. I've been doing this sort of thing for a decade."

"I really don't care, Cora." His brow furrows. A smile plays across his lips. "Effectiveness, not courtesy." Before I can chastise, he falls forward. Together we tumble off the ledge.

The world slows. Wind, chaos, the churning of my stomach—they become unnoticeable. I am weightless again. My eyes dart from building to building. My arms cling to Kyle's broad shoulders. Windows fly past as we fall story-after-story. The road beneath, though raging with crowds and transportation, seems safe. Gravity pulls us down. I gasp as oxygen is ripped from my lungs.

"I trust you, Kyle. I will always trust you," I say silently. He grips my back as we approach traffic. Eyes lift. Car horns blast. I squeeze my eyes shut, awaiting the pain of impact. *"Together we climb. Together we fly. Together we fall. Like morning and night, like sand and water, like the sword and the arrow—we fit together."*

Kyle lands on the hood of a hovercraft. Glass shatters. Metal dents. He groans and sinks to his knees, with me adhered to his torso. I crawl from his grasp and rise to my feet. The vehicle has yet to stop moving. We're heading down South Canal Street. In a few meters, we'll arrive at our destination.

"Are you alright?" I ask as another explosion erupts in the distance.

Flames and smoke fill the dawning horizon. Morning is scabrous. "I
don't see the others. They must have already reached Union Station. Can
you stand?"

"Yeah, I'm fine." He climbs to an upright position and rubs his blood
splattered thighs. "My legs are a little sore, that's all." He unsheathes his
sword as voices shout in our direction. Lights race past us. Balls of
energy blast the air above our heads. We've been spotted.

I pull an arrow from over my shoulder and across my bow, fastening
a rope from my pack to one end. I aim for a Centurion leaning out of his
apartment window. "Hold onto me!" I shout as the hovercraft shoots
through an intersection. With a single release, my arrow pierces the
soldier's chest. He slumps against a metal rail, dead.

Kyle places a hand on the rope and the other on my waist. When I
nod, we both leap off the vehicle. There is a brief moment of falling
before the rope catches our weight. We swing across the avenue and onto
the bustling sidewalk. People pause and stare at us as we bolt through the
masses—two bloodstained teenagers who look as if they just crawled out
of the slums.

Union Station appears ahead, a gigantic building with a multitude of
columns and windows. Banners, bearing the Titan's insignia, hang from
the many ridges. Recruits and Regimental Citizens crowd the curb. Kyle
and I walk among them. As we climb the steps to the main entrance, we
spot Callan and the rest of our division hiding in the shadows. We join
them in silence.

"Are the others here?" I ask. They shake their heads in response. It
sends a rush of dread through my thoughts. "We can't afford to wait any
longer. We must leave."

"They're our friends," Sarah pleads. She turns to Kyle with tears in
her eyes. "We can't leave them here to die. They need us!"

"I trust Seth and Deidre. If they're still alive, they will find a way out
of the city. We can't risk compromising our mission. The explosions
may have killed our friends, but it also may have saved humankind. They
knew what had to be done. Bravery is self-serving. Courage is sacrifice.
If they sacrificed their lives to ensure we'd have another chance to defeat
the Titan, they demonstrated true heroism and courage. We shall
remember them with honor." Kyle motions for us to follow him. "It's
time for us to go."

"What if the control panel and bombs weren't destroyed? What if the Titan still shuts us down?" Byron adds. "We could be on our way to Dimidium and just...die!"

"It's a risk we have to take," I answer. Genetic signals, programming, brain hackers—it's surreal.

The five of us emerge from the shadows and enter the building. It's emptier than I am expecting. Few people fill the high-ceilinged lobby; a group of soldiers sitting on a bench and an Elder reading a faded newspaper. A knot of unease forms in my stomach. This doesn't feel right. Where is everyone?

Kyle notices the oddity as well. His lips purse together and his eyes narrow. The abnormal quiet sends a shiver down our spines. He gazes at me and mouths five words. *"Get everyone out of here."* Before I can follow the order, mechanical buzzing echoes through the lobby. I cringe with realization. We've walked into a trap.

The station's walls shimmer. Pixel camouflage disintegrates, revealing the hundreds of armed soldiers surrounding us. Energy hums as weapons prepare to fire. How did they know we were here? Who told them our plans? I glance at my brother for answers, but he looks as dumbstruck as I am. Kyle was right. There is a spy in our midst.

Guns aim. Energy hisses with potency. I forget to breathe as I scan the mass of faceless soldiers. This time, there is no escaping death. I won't wake up to find myself lying in a hospital bed. I am going to die. We are all going to die. It'll be quick and mostly painless. Fatality will hit and when I open my eyes again, I'll be in a better place with Kyle, Callan, Byron, and Sarah beside me. I will see my parents, Aunt Jen, Ian Marx, and my friends from Prime Way. We will be together forever and always.

"Doom to the Titan!" Byron yells and crosses his arms over his chest. Sarah and Callan do the same. *The Program made us strong. This world made us brave. Sacrifice made us courageous.*

All five of us lock hands and stare at the enemy with unwavering determination. Kyle's fingers slide between mine. I look at him and he looks at me, both of us silently saying goodbye.

Part 2—Kyle Chase

CHAPTER 12

There is an electric blast in the upper balcony. Blue fire emits from the station's walls, creating a discharge that throws my body backwards. I am weightless. I am dying. I am deaf. Embers curtain my clothes, gore splatters my face, and heat singes the hair from my head. For a moment I am soaring across the ashen lobby and the next, I am lying in a heap by the main terminal. Flaming carcasses scatter the stone floor. The heavy odor of charred flesh fills the air. Pain sears through my limbs as I scan the room for survivors. There isn't a soul standing.

"Cora!" I yell desperately, unable to see her body in the sea of decapitation. "Is anyone out there?! Byron, Sarah, Callan?!" I drag myself to a standing position and stumble across the lobby. My ears bleed. Smoke fills my lungs. Questions swarm my mind but their relevance and importance diminish the moment I see movement in Union Station's threshold. I grip my sword, ready to slay whatever may attack us next. No more of my soldiers will die tonight. I must keep them safe.

"Kyle!" Cora's arms envelop my waist. I feel her head against my shoulder. "We're alive, all of us. What happened? Where did the explosion…"

"I don't know," I mumble in response. My eyes are still focused on the empty doorway. Someone is here. I feel their presence, hear their breathing. Is it the spy who secreted information to our enemy, the traitor? Has Deven sent another invisible squadron to ensure our deaths? It doesn't matter who has tracked us here. They will die and we will escape alive.

"We better get moving. An airship is waiting for us in the ruins," Stonecipher's voice echoes from the shadows. His armored body appears, flickering with camouflage. "Don't look at me like that! Did you honestly think I wouldn't bring a backup suit?" The slats covering his face part, revealing his amused smirk. He steps over a pile of burnt armor and motions to the terminal's entrance. "Let's go."

"What are you doing here, James? Your orders were to stay at the command post!" I shout, still delirious from the explosion's impact. My head aches and my stomach wrenches. The discomfort is tenable, but I don't know how much longer I'll be able to contain consciousness.

"The other squad went offline," he answers grimly. "They're dead. I saw the first explosion and thought you might be in trouble. It's a good thing I followed my hunch. If I hadn't come when I did, you'd all be ash-shadows on the pavement."

"You caused the discharge?"

He grins and tosses me a cylinder cartridge—a nuclear-powered grenade. "I may have left one of these little surprises in the Titan's armory. It's set to detonate in five-minutes."

"They're dead?" Byron looks at me in a panic. His hands clutch his bloody shoulder where a fragment of shattered metal is embedded. "Seth, Deirdre…they're all gone?"

I nod, gritting my teeth as realization stabs through my chest. "Move out!" The command is emotionless, exigent, two words to erase the culpable pain in my abdomen. It's my fault more people are dead. My instructions murdered them. They followed me, only to die trying to save our world. The darkness is suffocating. Guilt presses on my shoulders. If this continues, I'll be crushed.

James hands me a glowing rifle. I take the weapon and move swiftly towards the terminal. Our window of escape is closing. If we don't exit the city within the next few minutes, fatality is certain.

The six of us sprint through the terminal, down dark corridors, and onto the vacated tracks. Acid and smoke clouds the air, burning my throat and liquefying my lungs. I can't see. My vision is fogged, but I continue to run. I can't give up. I won't give up. I believe in the impossible odds.

Another explosion shakes through the city. Buildings crumble. A plume of heat lifts into the pink horizon, spreading smoke across the morning sky. The Titan's armory has been annihilated.

I rush down the stretch of rails, heading towards the wall surrounding Old Chicago. The others follow. Callan grips my arm when I falter, steadying me with a twinge of zealous concern. He's not the traitor. He made a mistake and my clemency has turned a possible enemy back into a friend.

"Kyle, you're bleeding!" Cora squeezes my hand and frantically inspects the tear in my lower abdomen. Her voice fades into a muffled hum. I feel my legs weaken and slowly lower my body to the rusty tracks. Sarah unzips her pack and searches for medical supplies, James cuts the shirt from my chest, and Cora leans over me with desperation spewing from her tearful eyes. Her mouth moves but I cannot hear a sound. Shock, guilt, and injury drain the strength from my body. I shout at myself to keep moving, but my limbs are unresponsive. After a year of sleepless nights and slow starvation, my genetically-altered body has finally quit.

Byron and Callan heave me off the tracks. Sarah doctors my wound. James lifts a bottle of liquor to my mouth, and Cora stays glued to my side, mouthing things I can no longer hear. My head rolls forward limply. I'm fading fast. Legion, the world's victor, is no longer of use. Whether we survive this or not is all dependent on what remains of my division.

"We're going to be alright," Cora's expression seems to say. She gazes at me surely before aiming her bow at our approaching escape. I watch her walk, almost smiling at the human strength flowing from her movements. There she is, the girl with the braid. I've missed her.

The last thing I remember is being dragged through an opening in the concrete wall. After that, I blackout.

> *"He's a perfect specimen," Winslow gasps and shakes his head in awe. "What they said about him is true. His genetic-makeup is the most pliable we've ever encounter, besides 237's. Send word to Director Ramsey. He will want to observe this boy's programming."*
>
> *Whispers echo from the balcony above. What's happening? Has something gone wrong? Will they send me home? I can't go home, not now. I need to stay here with Cora. I must stay.*

"It'll take a few days for your genetic-alterations to fully adhere. Expect dramatic growth in everything; pain, muscles spasms, out-of-control hormones, headaches, and even thoughts of suicide. It is all normal. Your body is adapting to the level of programming, which in your case, will be higher than most. Fight through it. I'll prescribe some mitigates to ease the discomfort."

I squirm when he presses a syringe to the back of my neck. The needle pierces my flesh—an intense sting followed by a dull ache—and pumps yellow liquid into my bloodstream. These are my final moments of humanity.

"Your number will be 1026," Winslow tells me as he cleans my right bicep with an antiseptic wipe. "It defines you." He removes a tattoo gun from a tray of equipment and draws the pointed tip across my skin. For several long minutes, I endure the throbbing pain.

"Is this the boy Vince was telling me about?" Director Ramsey enters the laboratory. He reminds me of an icicle—frigid in demeanor, tall and slender with black hair, elongated features, and blue eyes so piercing, they could freeze me with one glance. His persona radiates with superiority. "Has everything we perceived about him...been accurate?"

"Yes. He is what we were hoping for."

The incumbent director inspects my naked body like a piece of raw meat, poking and prodding my limbs. His thin lips form a straight line. "Raise his dosage to the max and set intensity at level ten. Once he fully recovers, I want his progress monitored. We need to know how the programming affects his mentality. I expect a detailed analysis on my desk every week."

Winslow tapes electrodes to my forehead and temples, and secures a tangle of wires to my chest. "You won't feel a thing. The program has been modified so that the patient blacks out once the procedure begins. We had too many recruits die from pain during initial testing, or come out with unpleasant side effects. I've already injected your body with a brain stimulus. It'll keep your body actively responding to the alterations without requiring your consciousness."

Fear roars through my surety. Sweat soaks the Velcro over my mouth. I cringe and watch Winslow move towards the computer monitors. In a matter of seconds, everything I've ever held as truth will be recreated. I will no longer be Kyle Chase, normal and destined for destruction. Life will be new.

Director Ramsey stares at me as the machines around us buzz with energy. This is what I want. This is who I am. I'm a Legionary. No Feeling. No Regret. Just Strength.

Winslow flips a switch. Electricity sears through my head. I arch my back and writhe, passing out seconds later. Darkness cradles my brain in a plain of numbness and thoughtless dreams.

I awake.

I'm sprawled on a small, uncomfortable cot. The concrete walls surrounding me are bare. They make the dorm seem bland and impersonal, like a prison cell. Light streams through a narrow window. Another dusty cot is across from mine, but it's empty and stripped of bedding.

Tepid saliva fills my mouth. My eyelids are heavy. I twist onto my side and moan as a pounding sensation contracts beneath my skull. The programming's aftermath is definitely worse than the procedure itself. Every movement sends tears stampeding to my dry ducts. Even breathing is nauseating. I want to hurl the moment I rise to a sitting position. When will I know if I have changed? Nothing comes to mind, not a foreign word or a diagram of some sort.

I glance down at my body. I've yet to transform into the avatar displayed in Winslow's lab. My muscle mass is still the same. My strength is average. The only change is my wardrobe. I've been dressed in the Program's uniform. The sight of the t-shirt and combat boots sends a smile rippling across my face. It's official. I am finally a part of a system that wants me.

The numbers tattooed on my right bicep are intimidating. They claim me, marking me as a Legionary forever. Ink has never seemed so powerful. My parents would have a conniption if they knew I've gotten a tattoo, which may be a reason I like it so much.

My backpack, which is mostly empty, has been left by the

door. Security only allowed me to keep my cell phone case and a photo of my family. I place the few clothes I've been given inside a metal locker and tape the picture above my bed. It's the one thing that personalizes my apartment.

"Are you alive in there?" Someone knocks on my door. I hear their heavy breathing. Could my ears do that before?

"You can come..." Before the phrase is fully muttered, my door opens and a Legionary strides inside. He is short and stocky with a distinct, square jaw. His fingers clutch a clipboard.

"I'm Jonah Powers, number 983. Some retard pulled a prank and signed me up as 'Legionary tour guide'. So you get the amazing privilege of following me around all day and learning the basics of Prime Way survival. What's your name?"

"1026."

"Real name?" he smirks. "Only trainers and teachers call us by our numbers. They want to 'erase all past self and reprogram us with selfless discipline'. It's a bunch of bologna, if you ask me. I may be a freakish soldier but I sure don't have to sound like one."

"Kyle Chase. That's my name," I stutter. His bluntness catches me off guard. Are all people here so straightforward? I noticed Cora has the same tendency. She says exactly what is on her mind, whether it's good or bad. I like that. It's refreshing.

"Where are you from?"

"Dallas, Texas."

"Kyle the cowboy. Fits nicely," Jonah snickers. "So what possessed you to enlist in the Program? You don't look like a foster kid or rehab addict. Those are usually the losers they go for."

"Family problems."

"That's always a whammy. I've only been here for a month, still in the first level of training. I was recruited from an orphanage in New York, but believe me, I am no Annie. My story is the same as a lot of kids here. We're all just a big bunch of unwanted misfits." He laughs. "If I rank high enough in my training, I hope to progress and become a Strategy Major. Do you know what you want to major in?"

"I don't know what…"

"Oh right, you don't know how this system works. Sorry. I'll explain." He takes a deep breath and reads off his clipboard. *"Your training process is divided into three levels—Basic, Intermediate, and Experienced. It is designed to unlock all aspects of your programming. The first level focuses on an overview of all majors. You take courses in Survival 101, Combat, Strategy, Fear Tactics, Communications, and Medicine. At the end of the semester, you have a final in each class. Your overall grade determines your rank. There are twenty people in a division. Only the top ten are given active-status, which means that they are eligible for high action majors such as Combat and Fear Tactics, and later ranked as Elite soldiers. Those who were in the bottom ten are only allowed to pursue dormant careers like Communications and Medicine.*

"Intermediate training focuses on your designated major. In my opinion, it's the easiest level. All you do is learn an overview of your major and settle into the change of lifestyle. After finishing the course, you pass into Experienced which is all centered on perfection. It usually takes two or three years to complete. The entire training procedure lasts four years."

"What happens after that?"

"You graduate out of the system. It's the highest rank a Legionary can achieve." Jonah motions to the open door. *"We better get moving. If I don't complete the tour before dinner, Yuzek will make me run extra laps at tomorrow's training. And I hate running."*

"I heard Legionaries can reach speeds of seventy-miles-per-hour."

"So? I still don't like doing it."

I follow him out of my dormitory and into the bustling streets. Legionaries crowd the sidewalks. ATV vehicles weave through the scattered crowd. We walk past supply stores and armories, through a patch of woods and into the camp's training district.

"Welcome to the Prime Way Program. We pride ourselves on discipline, strength, and lots of blah, blah, blah…" Jonah flips through pages of typed information. *"During your rigorous*

training process, you will attend the Academy every day from seven o' clock to four. Afterwards you will join your division for physical training in the Ground Sector." He motions to a school-like building and a concrete tower. "During your initiation today, you will be evaluated and placed in a current division. Hopefully you'll be put in mine. It needs some decent recruits and not the idiots they paired me with."

I laugh.

"Our curfew is eleven o' clock every night, unless we have a camp-wide activity or otherwise stated by Director Ramsey. We must be in our dorms with the lights off, not in the girls' dormitories. My roommate was locked in confinement for a week because he threw a party in his girlfriend's apartment. Also, make sure you have your numbers scanned every time you enter and exit a facility or participate in simulated missions. It's another bogus attempt for the Faculty to keep tabs on us but...better to follow orders than face punishment." His smile refreshes as he tucks the clipboard beneath his left arm. "Now for some information that will actually be of use. See that building over there?" He points to a structure that has been converted from an old dormitory into the camp-store. "If you climb through the back window, you'll find a hangout we call the Computer Bar. A few years ago, a Legionary-legend named Christopher started the place undercover. It serves smoothies and has old laptops, which do not have internet access, and a pool table. Director Ramsey has allowed it to stay in operations as long as we behave ourselves. You should check it out sometime. Practically everyone goes there before dinner."

"Where is the cafeteria?"

"It's in the center of camp, next to the Administration Building. We are served four meals a day. Eat every bit. Our bodies burn so many calories it's hard not to lose weight. Drink lots of water, take your vitamins, and load up on the protein. The first week of training is the hardest since your body is still coping with the programming's alterations. If you don't properly nourish yourself, you'll pass out during training and find yourself in the infirmary; which is located beside the shooting

range." He hands me a pile of pamphlets. "Here is an itinerary and a map of the facility. You'll catch on. It's not rocket science."

"Do you know if I have a roommate?"

"You did," Jonah smirks and brushes the hair from his forehead. "He died two days ago during his Fear Tactics final. Yep, even Legionaries can drown." When my eyes widen, he snickers and punches my shoulder kiddingly. "Get used to it, pal. People die here every day. It's just how things work."

"Tough place," I say as a group of Legionaries sprint across the training field to my right. They're larger than the other recruits, older and look as if they could kill me with one hit. Cora is among the hodgepodge of stern-faced teenagers. She moves like a shadow. Her legs blur beneath her as she leads the pack in a final lap. I can't help but stare—her dark hair flopping in a ponytail behind her head, the sweat glistening on her arms, and the muscles flexing through her abdomen. There's a ferocious intensity to her persona. I've seen her cry, smile, bleed—but this person is different. She holds herself fearlessly, with unwavering intimidation. I miss the girl who forced me to braid her hair. She was human.

"Don't even think about it! You do not want to mess with the Grads. They will tear you to bits."

"The Grads?"

"They're recruits who've already graduated out of the system—Prime Way's top dogs. They are sent on missions, instruct different courses, and basically do whatever they want. Deven Lukes, that freakish guy with the fire tattoo, is the worse! He instructs my Fear Tactics course. Do something wrong and he'll snap your neck in half! Cora Kingston, that hot chick with the grimace, is another person you do not want to mess with. Unlike Deven, if you do something bad to her, she'll wait to have her revenge until you let your guard drop. Then one day you'll wake up underwater. Believe me. It's happened. So if you want to survive, avoid them like the plague!"

"Have you ever talked to her?"

"Not really. She graduated as a Combat Major before I

arrived and usually hangs out with that communications guru, Matthew Way. Everyone calls her Blue-Jay. Why are you so interested, Kyle?" He tilts his head and musters a giddy smile. "Wait a second. Are you the guy she brought back from her mission? You are, aren't you?! That's insane! Everyone's been talking about you. How'd it happen?"

"Long story," I shrug. My body aches and my head pounds. Bruises scatter my limbs from the many injections. Even my clothes are beginning to feel constricting. I want to tear them all off and sleep until the pain subsides. Was my shirt this tight when I put it on? Did veins bulge on my forearms before the programming procedure? Already my cheeks are covered in stubble. It's puberty all over again!

"We better hurry to the Ground Sector. Your evaluation is in a few minutes and I have to get to combat training before Yuzek kills me." Jonah glances at his watch and motions for me to follow him. "You'll get used to the schedule. It took me several days to settle into Legionary-life."

"How do they…evaluate me? I haven't adhered to my alteration yet."

"It's all about testing your human strength. You'll be forced to fight another soldier. Yuzek, our instructor, will watch and judge you based on your technique and effort. He'll place you in a division. Don't worry about trying to impress him. When the fight starts, lie down and play dead."

"Won't that hurt my score?"

"It doesn't matter! Rankings aren't tallied until you start training tomorrow. Yuzek will still assign you to a division and tonight when you go to bed, you'll have fewer bruises. Believe me. I tried to fight on my first day and came out with a fractured wrist. Winning is impossible for new recruits."

Impossible. The word is a challenge, more luring than a beacon of light in darkness. I've always had a knack for facing contradiction. They told me I wasn't good enough. They told me I couldn't run away. They tell me I can't fight, that I'm not strong enough. People may doubt, but I'll prove them wrong. It's my flaw, that twinge of rebellion festering inside my chest. I decide who I am.

Jonah retraces our steps to the center of Prime Way. He babbles about protocol and activities on the waterfront. His stout, muscular frame moves unnaturally swift. I follow in silence, trying my hardest to match his focused pace. My body is weak. How am I going to survive a fight without submitting? I must impress Yuzek. Lying down isn't an option.

"You're very quiet, Kyle. It's unusual. Most of the new recruits act like chattering teeth, talking until my ears bleed! You don't even seem excited to be here."

"I don't have much to say." I force a grin and casually run my fingers through my hair. "This place is very new to me. It'll take some getting used to. My life in Dallas didn't exactly revolve around near death experiences and fights with superhuman teenagers. Then again, I wasn't...superhuman."

"Sounds like a line from a tacky Sci-Fi movie," Jonah laughs. "You're going to fit in here great! Just promise not to kill me if we're ever together in the Arena. I have a feeling that you're going to grow twice my size. The proof is evident."

I try to laugh, but it sounds forced and fake. Guilt stifles the happiness I want to feel. It doesn't matter what I say to persuade myself that what I did was right. Mourning continues to pulse through my growing body. I've sacrificed my humanity to adhere to this new life. I gave away my family, Mikey, everyone. "This is what I want!" I shout silently. "I have no regret, no feeling, and no guilt! This is my life and I can make my own choices. My past doesn't claim me!"

The Ground Sector is unlike any building I've ever seen before. It sits on the rocky slopes overlooking the ocean—tall, windowless, and constructed entirely of concrete blocks. When I first see the structure, I want to turn and sprint back towards the sea of dormitories. It has a menacing appearance, maybe to remind the recruits that possible death waits inside.

Jonah leads me into a crowd of energetic Legionaries waiting by the building's entrance. Their boisterous voices fill the air with chaos. Someone throws a handful of dirt, spraying the division with a mixture of sand and debris. Young girls giggle and stare at me with eyelashes fluttering. I suddenly feel very out-of-place. In a few moments, I'll be forced to fight for my life. This isn't a wrestling match with Ron and his entourage of football players. I will be fighting someone with genetically-altered strength. The odds of escaping evaluation unscathed are slim.

As the masses file into the Ground Sector, I attempt to piece together a strategy. Over the past few weeks of traveling with Cora, I've learned one thing. Lack of strength can be overlooked. All it takes to win a battle is keen observation and quick thinking. If I can somehow manage to pinpoint my opponent's weakness, I might have a chance.

I scan my tattoo on a barcode-reader and walk into the facility's narrow lobby. It's empty. Two elevators are positioned on the opposite wall. They open and close, transporting Legionaries to the training center below. I bite my lip as the line moves. Soon I'll be sucked into the one-way deathtrap.

"Remember. Lie down and play dead," Jonah repeats as we step into the elevator. "This isn't the time to show off. You'll have another chance once your alterations adhere."

"What if I want to fight?" I ask. Sweat discolors the fabric of my uniform. My armpits are starting to smell. It's too late to reapply deodorant. "Do you have any combat advice?"

"Watch your opponent and see how they move. Everyone has a fighting pattern, a rhythm. Harness that pattern to their disadvantage. Most Legionaries have a tendency to be defensive and never offensive. Look for their weak point. Some recruits hold their fists in front of their face. In that situation, aim for their stomach. Understand?"

The moment I nod, the elevator stops and the doors open. I move with the crowd into a gym with high vaulted ceilings and padded floor. Florescent lighting flickers above. Exercise equipment and a variety of bars and beams clutter the space; the metal walls covered in artillery. A boxing ring is built in the center of the room. I watch soldiers train. They swing from ropes, roll through spiked simulators, sprint the track, and whap each other with wooden poles. A foul stench fills the air—sweat, body odor, and the metallic smell of blood. How far am I beneath the earth's surface?

"Try not to tremble. Yuzek smells fear," Jonah jokes. "All this looks like fun, doesn't it? Well it's not. Those twirling, spiked things will kill you if you're not careful. The treadmills only have one speed, sixty-miles-per-hour. I'm surprised there aren't sharks in our swimming pool."

We approach the boxing ring. A man with fiery, orange hair is waiting for us. He's extremely built with squinty eyes and sunken cheeks. The moment his pupils find me, his thin lips lift into a coolly amused smile. His demeanor isn't as terrifying as Ramsey's, but still radiates with superiority and stark emotions. One word from him could end my life.

"Looks like we have a new recruit to evaluate," he speaks with a heavy Russian accent.

Everyone cheers and glances skeptically in my direction. They prod each other and snicker. "He won't last long," a boy whispers. "I give him two minutes at the most," an older girl mutters. Their doubt sends anger stampeding through my bloodstream. Back in Dallas I was considered to be athletic, but not here. I am weak compared to the abnormal build of Prime Way's Legionaries.

"Climb into the ring," Yuzek instructs. Once I follow orders, he paces around me. "Your name was Kyle Chase. I observed your programming procedure this morning. What is your number?"

"1026," I answer surely. Maybe if I hide my fear, I can deceive him into thinking that I have none. It's what this program is all about; creating a mask to camouflage our own insecurities.

The man steps away from me. He looks at the elevators as a group of Grads stride into the Ground Sector. His smirk transforms into a devious smile. "237, would you be willing to evaluate our newest recruit?" The moment the words leave his mouth, I get a sinking feeling in my stomach and turn to confront the girl I risked my life to save.

Cora saunters towards the division with a blank expression on her usually stern face. She tosses Matthew her bottle of water and dabs the sweat from her brow. The crowd parts as she slides into the ring. The muscles in her legs quiver as she finds her place in the corner across from me. I stare at her. The color drains from my cheeks when Yuzek tosses us each a metal pole. He wants me to fight her?

"This won't take long, will it? I'm instructing a strategy course in a few minutes and want to lift some weights before teaching." She flips her head forward and twists her hair into a loose bun. We are the same age and yet she has authority over me, dominance. I don't like the feeling of being inferior, especially to the girl I rescued from torture.

"Let's get this over with." I grip the pole firmly and settle into a comfortable fighting stance. I've come to the conclusion that hitting Cora doesn't violate the 'no hitting girls' rule. She doesn't qualify as a normal girl, more like a vicious, man slaughtering siren on steroids. But I won't hurt her. Deep down and in some strange way, I think I have feelings for her.

"Don't worry. I'll take it easy on you, Kyle." She twirls her pole and moves forward. "I'd hate to give that pretty face of yours a black eye."

"Don't do me any favors, Sweetheart."

My remark causes her to snap. She slams the shaft of her weapon into my stomach and sweeps me off my feet. I land hard on my back and emit a groan. She steps over me and slides her pole behind my neck, yanking my head upward until our eyes are inches apart. "Don't ever call me that again."

I nod before rising cautiously to a standing position. Everyone in the room laughs at my pain. Yuzek snickers tauntingly and motions for me to hit her. I must strike back. I must prove that I'm worthy of being noticed, that I have potential. My future here is dependent on the outcome of this match.

When Cora turns to speak with Yuzek, I swing my pole like a baseball bat, aiming for the small of her back. It happens in slow motion. She spins around and catches my weapon in midair, wrenching it from my grasp. I stumble backwards, ducking as metal slices the air above me.

With a bar in each hand, she attacks. I can't defend myself. She whacks me in the gut and smashes my skull against her knee. I lift my hands and grab at the striking poles, only to be punched in the face. Cora lunges towards me with unnatural agility, gripping my wrist and flipping me over her shoulder. I hit the floor and roll to avoid her lashes. Pain shoots through my body. Blood gushes from my nostrils. Malaise aches through my bones.

"Play dead!" Jonah shouts frantically from the complacent audience. I see his face out of my peripheral vision. His arms are crossed over his chest in a salute, maybe to send me good luck.

I won't be defeated.

Adrenaline surges through my veins. It emits enough energy to bring me to my feet. Weight and size is my advantage. Cora is strong and fast, but several inches smaller than me. Simplicity should be my weapon. She's expecting Legionary combat techniques, not a schoolboy's tricks. My fistfights with Ron may be useful after all.

I slam my body against her, tackling my opponent to the padded ground. It's the one move she's not anticipating. The poles fly from her hands as I attempt to pin her down with my thighs. She wriggles and claws at my flesh. The moment I smile, her frustration morphs into murderous anger.

She twists and shoves me off her body. One kick sends me flying against the rails of the ring. Every bone in my ribcage cracks. Agonizing discomfort sears through my torso. I groan and stare at Cora pleadingly. She's going to kill me. I see it in her eyes—that thirst for bloodshed I once saw when we were escaping Truman's labs. There is no escape.

The room is silent as she retrieves her weapon. Her eyes narrow and her lips purse together. She moves towards me, dragging the pole by her side. I glance at Yuzek for help, but he stares blankly. "This is all part of your initiation," he seems to say. "You must learn how to endure pain."

Cora pauses and looks down at my battered figure. After a few moments of watching me writhe, she musters a deceptive smile. "Welcome to the Prime Way Program." She lifts the pole over her head and with a single swipe, renders me unconscious.

I'm unaware of my surroundings, the ache pulsing through my body, and the arms heaving me off the floor of the Ground Sector. Muscles twist beneath my skin, cracks fill my bones, and a migraine spreads through my brain—yet I feel nothing. There is peace in forced sleep. It acts as an immediately and temporary pain reliever. I allow the drowsy darkness to consume my thoughts and alter my genetics without discomfort. Maybe when I wake, I'll be changed. I will be strong enough to win a fight, fit in with the intense Legionary lifestyle, and become needed and wanted. As humans, all we want is to be accepted, and we will do whatever it takes to belong.

The chill of an icepack causes me to stir. I breathe heavily, noticing the rough fabric of a blanket beneath me. My eyes sting as they move behind their heavy lids. Pain emits from every nerve. I groan, wishing that the numbness of unconsciousness could last longer. I've only been at Prime Way for a few hours and already feel as if I could fall apart—not the best first impression of my new home.

"That was real stupid," Jonah's voice echoes from the room beyond my eyelids. "Cora is the deadliest fighter on campus. I told you to play dead! Now you look like you've been hit by a truck!"

"I'm horrible at following orders. Ask my parents," I mumble. Heat slashes through my ribcage. The pain brings tears to my dry ducts. I swallow the metallic saliva resting on my tongue and slowly open my eyes. I'm lying in the infirmary on one of the many antique medical beds. Everything is white—the walls, the stiff furniture, even the uniforms of the volunteer Medical Majors.

Jonah is sitting in a chair next to my cot with an issue of Sports Weekly resting in his lap. He looks at me and musters an amused smile. "Don't look in the mirror for a while, man. Your left eye is blacker than my t-shirt. You have a minor concussion. Three of your ribs are cracked. Your spine has been bruised, as well as most of your body. Lucky for you, we heal much faster than normal humans."

"Everything hurts." I grit my teeth and clutch my stomach. Were my abs this defined a few hours ago? I don't remember my forearms being as large. "Have you been sitting here this entire time?"

"Yeah, so? It was either I wait here with you and seem like a concerned friend, or fight body-builder Theo in the ring. I may look like a total stud, but I do not take a punch well."

When I laugh, bile floods my mouth. I cough and spit the acid into a metal bowl. My esophagus stings. "Is every day like this? Should I expect routine pain?"

"Once you adhere to your alterations, all this will come naturally. Pain is a part of our lifestyle. It makes us strong. But with programming, it isn't as crippling. We can bear the burden easier."

"I need easy. My old life was hard enough. Coming here was meant to be a challenge, but also an escape. If I get hurt, I want it to mean something. It shouldn't discourage me."

Jonah removes the icepacks from my legs and passes me a bottle of water. "Not to sound like a little girl or anything, but do you want to be friends? It's easier to ask..."

"Sure. I need a friend."

"Good, because Yuzek assigned you to my division. You're part of our family now, Cowboy. You've been initiated into the Legionary brotherhood." He grins and carefully pats my shoulder. "Sit with us tonight at dinner. I'll introduce you to the gang."

"I won't get beat up, will I?"

"Only if you provoke the Grads," he answers with a smirk. "Everyone else is laidback, especially the soldiers in basic and intermediate training. You'll notice that the newer recruits are a little more personable. The longer you stay here, the colder you get. It's like the Program brainwashes you, makes you like the Grads—harsh and emotionless. They say that it's the only way to be free of weakness."

"Sounds like...bologna."

"Exactly! You catch on quick, Kyle." His energetic personality and childish enthusiasm are refreshing. It lightens

the stress building inside my chest. I'm glad to have him as a friend. He reminds me of Mikey, my best-friend in Dallas—the one I left behind.

I pull myself to a sitting position as a Grad joins Jonah by my side. She looks to be several years younger than us, but her eyes are aged and cold. Without words, she smears salve onto my cuts and forces me to drink a glassful of medicine. Once my wounds have been attended to, she leaves.

Yuzek saunters into the infirmary with a perturb smirk on his lips. His black uniform contrasts against the whitewashed interior like an inkblot. "Alive and well, I see," he says and tosses me a bottle of pain relievers. "Congratulations on your evaluation. I'd like to offer you a spot in my elite combat training course. All of my students are handpicked from the top-ranked recruits. You are one of them."

"How? I lost the fight," I say.

"Failure is imminent. Humans are inferior to the Legionary species. Never in my many years of teaching have I seen a new recruit win their first fight. It's genetically impossible." He grabs a stool and sits at the foot of my cot. His harsh presence makes me uncomfortable. "The evaluation is not focused on the outcome of the match, more how the recruit responds to the intense situation. They are ranked by their natural strength and strategic mentality, whether or not they can spot their opponent's weakness. Once their programming adheres, I have no way of determining which of their instincts are implanted or natural. You pinpointed 237's weakness, concocted and executed a plan of action, all without panicking. She beat you to a pulp, and yet you endured the torture without relenting. You performed well, not perfect, but well. So I'm offering you a chance to climb up the training ladder."

I stutter at a loss for words. Yuzek wants me in a special combat course? That's impossible. He saw what Cora did to me. I hardly kept myself from dying! But instead of denying the offer and possibly ruining my chance at a high status, I accept.

Yuzek nods and turns his stern focus to Jonah. "I heard what you said today, 983. Don't you ever tell another recruit to 'lie down and play dead'. Submission is a form of cowardice and we see cowardice as weakness. If you've forgotten, weak soldiers are deleted from the Program. Understand?"

"Yes, sir. It won't happen again," Jonah answers hastily. The color drains from his face.

"You're dismissed from your post. Go join the others in the cafeteria. I want to speak with 1026 in private." His last sentence startles me. Private? What could he possibly have to say?

Jonah rises and walks towards the infirmary's exit. He glances at me sympathetically before leaving. I don't know how to react, suddenly being alone with the Russian instructor. Yuzek has authority over me, power that can make my life a living hell. Should I trust him? I can't decide who to trust nowadays. Lies and truth coincide. Motives are never pure. Someone is always trying to pin me down.

"I can't stay long. They'll notice," he says in a slurred whisper. His eyes soften and his words gain depth. "Be very careful, Kyle. They're watching you too."

"Excuse me?"

"You're special. That's why you were recruited. It wasn't random or accidental. Everything was done for a reason. Now they're waiting to see how the programming affects your nature."

"I don't understand..."

"You're not meant to. Just watch your back. One wrong move and they'll delete you from the Program...permanently. I'm only telling you this as a warning. Don't be fooled by their deception. Not everything is how it seems." He looks nervously at the security camera bolted into the wall. His expression hardens until it is unreadable. "Do as they tell you, no matter what it is. Follow every instruction. I'll be around if you need help or tutoring."

"Why me? How am I special?"

"Recognizing your differences will only bring more danger. It's better for things to work themselves out on their own. Act ignorant to everything I've just said, as if you know nothing.

They must believe you are who they think, even if you're not. It's the only way to keep you alive."

I sit in shock with the weight of reality crushing my shoulders. There are people here who might kill me because of what I may or may not be? What do they think I am? How could it cost me my life? I've done nothing special.

"Why are you helping me?" I ask quietly. Pain rumbles through my torso. Paranoia settles into my thoughts. I forget to breathe as a Grad saunters past, and find myself wondering whether or not she is planning my demise.

"I don't want you to become who they're hoping for. That is the only reason I am breaking protocol and jeopardizing my job," he answers bluntly. "Do your absolute best in training, play the part of a dutiful soldier, and become one of thousands. Maybe the excitement of Kyle Chase's arrival will fade and the Faculty will forget your purpose." He stands and salutes me. "Try not to be discouraged, my friend. You're safe for the time being. No one will pay you notice until after basic training. Until then, enjoy your new life."

I sigh and rest my head against the bed's backboard. "My life is falling to pieces. How can I become a Legionary while knowing in the back of my head that if I'm not careful, I'll become...?"

"You decide your own identity," he adds. "The Prime Way Program will try to recreate who you are. Don't allow it. Learn and adapt, but never forget. I'll do what I can to help. Trust me."

When I nod, Yuzek turns and exits the infirmary.

Anguish aches through my body. Confusion consumes my thoughts. I stare at the opposite wall in silence, trying desperately to make sense of my situation. What once seemed simple a few hours ago has suddenly become as complex as a hard-drive. I am abnormal and if I don't adapt to fit Prime Way's standards, they will kill me. I've walked into a deathtrap.

"You're free to leave now," the Grad says. She's sitting at a desk across the room and is busy sorting through a stack of files. "Those wounds should heal within the next few days. Ask for an

extra vitamin at dinner. It'll help hurry the process."

I thank her and hastily climb to my feet. My head pounds. The muscles in my torso twist uncontrollably. I need to get out of here, find some sort of normality among the foreign chaos. I've sacrificed everything and to gain what, a black eye and a looming death sentence?

"Play the part...you're safe...enjoy life," Yuzek's voice repeats. He believes I can blend in. He believes this threat will pass. Should I still worry? It's easy to shrug off my fear and replace it with smiles and rowdy behavior, but will that really dissolve my problems? Fitting in is no longer just a desire. It is mandatory for my survival.

I leave the infirmary and make my way towards the cafeteria. The sun is beginning to set, casting magenta hues across the horizon. Ice frosts the pavement. The roar of tumbling surf echoes in the distance. I move swiftly through the vacant streets, noticing the heavy aroma of food in the frigid air. Dinner is being served.

"1026, may I talk with you for a moment?" Director Ramsey emerges from the Administration Building. I cringe at the sound of his voice. The same man who observed my creation may be the one to strip it away from me.

I stop and face him with forced respect. My hands tremble with anger. He deceived me, fed me lies that didn't belong in my head. I wasn't recruited to be a normal soldier, training to defend my country. No, I was chosen because my genetics are different. Ramsey and the Faculty believe the Program will morph me into something I'm not.

"Yuzek told me that you aced your evaluation and won a spot in his Elite combat course. That's almost unheard of. Congratulations. You must be proud." His eyes burrow into me like daggers, ready to scrape out my heart and everything else of life substance.

"Pride doesn't associate with defeat," I answer.

"Very true." He adjusts his crimson necktie and fakes a smile. "I'm pleased to have you in this Program. You seem to have a bright future in store for you."

"Well, I hope I live up to your expectations. Goodnight, sir." I slide past him and continue on my trek to the cafeteria. I feel his cold stare on my back as I walk away.

The dining hall resembles a warehouse, long and narrow with doors accessible on every side. It matches the architectural build of the campus—bland and colorless. Legionaries file through the entrances, each stopping at a checkpoint to scan their numbers. I join them, absentmindedly scanning my tattoo and wandering into the crowded cafeteria. The place looks as I imagined it—long tables, heaters on every wall, the thick odor of mashed potatoes and sweat. Muscular teenagers flood the room. Their booming voices fill the space with chaos.

I move with the masses to the food line. I'm handed a tray overflowing with dinner—steak, chicken, vegetables, rice, a pint of water, and a plastic container containing three pills and a syringe. These must be the vitamins the Grad had been referring to.

"Kyle, over here!" Jonah waves from a distant table. "I saved you a seat!"

I join him and sit among the division of Legionaries. They stare at me as I swallow my vitamins and inject my wrist with the syringe. Pain is becoming a natural occurrence.

"Kyle, meet Katrina Reed and Ave Givens," Jonah says and motions to the two teenagers sitting across from us. "They're in our division; level three, Experienced training."

"Yep, the almost Grads. We're the senior recruits in the system," Ave snickers. He's tall with shaggy, dark hair. Unlike Jonah, there is emptiness in his eyes. The Program has left its mark.

"You're the guy Cora brought back from her mission!" Katrina exclaims. She's pretty and petite with short, cherry-red hair and oversized eyes. Her expressions are animated, almost forced. She jumps from her chair and throws her arms around my neck, embracing me. Her uniform is splattered with acrylic paint. "I'm her roommate, number 644. She may have talked about me...maybe not. We're only like sisters. Gosh, when describing how you two met, she forgot to say how attractive you

are!"

"Uh...thanks." Blood rushes to my face. I smile and stuff my mouth with a forkful of rice.

"And he's polite!" Katrina giggles. "Humble, cute Texan accent, blonde, and soon to be ripped. Kyle, you can definitely sit next to me in the Arena tonight."

"I thought I was going to sit next to you?!" Ave fusses.

"Not anymore. I changed my mind when the super-hot, new guy sat at our table."

"Desperate, Trina?" Jonah mumbles. "Give the man a break."

"What's the Arena?" I ask to end the embarrassing conversation.

"It's a fighting exhibition. Once a recruit finishes basic training, they must pass a final in each course. Combat requires them to fight in the Arena. They suit up and usually compete against a Grad, no weapons allowed. Last person still conscious wins. It's interesting to watch. Everyone roots for their favorite participant," Ave explains. "It's my favorite camp-wide activity."

"I heard Cora beat you up during your evaluation...."

"That'd explain his black eye, Tri!" Ave looks at me apologetically. "How's the transformation coming? Are you hurting yet? The worst of the aftermath usually strikes in the middle of the night so be prepared to drink a lot of coffee in the morning. You won't be getting any sleep."

"I feel as if I'm changing into a werewolf or something."

"Minus the furry coat," Jonah laughs. He chews on a piece of steak and high-fives a passing recruit. "So what did Yuzek talk about?"

"Nothing really," I lie. "He discussed details concerning my placement in his combat course. That's all. No conspiracy or top secret plan."

Their attention drifts into separate conversations. I eat slowly and in silence, observing my surroundings carefully. The teenagers are boisterous and yet they preserve conduct and remain in their seats. It's as if the Program has altered their behavior, perfected the disrespectful demeanor of youth. Will I become one of them, controlled and obedient? Or will my genetics take a turn for the worse?

A flock of Graduates move across the back wall. I look for Cora among the entourage, but she's not with them. Emptiness burrows through my chest at her absence. I don't understand why. We hardly know each other. It doesn't matter that I saved her life or sacrificed everything to be around her. She sees me as weakness, and Cora Kingston is not weak.

"Nice shiner," her voice echoes from behind. I look up from my plate as Matthew and Cora sit in the chairs next to me. They've both showered and changed out of their sweaty uniforms.

"This is a first," Jonah whispers and stares at Cora wide-eyed. "The Grads never sit with us."

"Photo moment!" Katrina squeals and pulls a camera from her pocket. "Cora, lean closer to Kyle. You brought him here. It's only fair that you should be in his pre-Legionary picture!"

"My what?" I ask as Cora sighs and leans closer to me.

"Trina takes pictures of the new recruits. It is tradition," she explains and musters a smile. I look at her as the camera flashes. Her eyes sparkle when she smiles.

"Blue-Jay, you must've hit him hard!" Matthew chuckles and inspects my bruised face with amusement. "That's the blackest one I've seen yet!"

"He'll be fine. He takes punches well."

"They still hurt," I scoff. "You sure took it easy on me."

"Get used to it. Pain is a part of the Program," she smirks and leans closer to me. "And just so you know, I don't take it easy on anyone."

A boy bumps against her, dumping the contents of his tray onto her lap. "Oops," he snickers and scatters a stack of napkins over her head. His left forearm is sleeved in yellow and red flames.

"You are such a jerk, Deven!" Cora screams, infuriated. She stands to brush the rice off her torso. Her eyes are ignited with anger. "I'm going to kill you!"

"Go ahead and try, Sweetheart. I need a good laugh."

Cora grabs his tray and whacks him over the head, severing the plastic slat into four broken shards. "Laughing yet?" she whispers before spitting onto his fitted t-shirt.

"You little…" He lunges at her, gripping her waist and knocking her against the table. The sudden violence sends a rush of adrenaline through my body. It brings me to my feet.

I know I shouldn't get involved. Enemies are the last thing I need here, but seeing Cora in pain replaces my selfishness with protectiveness. I slam against Deven's programmed body and punch my fist into his stomach. He recoils from his victim and stares at me with poison tipped daggers spewing from his pupils. I don't have time to react to his attack.

He clutches my throat and throws me to the concrete floor. Pain ruptures my nerves and cells, aching through my head with crippling intensity. I attempt to scramble away from his kicking feet, but to no prevail. His heels ram into my body with the strength of a raging bull, bruising my cracked ribcage and bloodying my face.

"Leave him alone!" Matt rises and shoves Deven away from me. "He hasn't adhered to his programming yet. Pick on someone your own size!"

Deven sneers and rips me up by the collar of my shirt. "You're going to regret that, new guy. I can make your life here a living hell. Just watch me." His words are seaming with threats. "What you see in the Arena tonight is what I'm planning to do to you." He shoves me into my chair and walks away, disappearing into the crowd of Legionaries.

"Are you okay, Kyle?" Katrina reaches across the table and dabs the blood from my mouth. "Why'd you do that?"

"I just don't like bullies," I answer and look at Cora. She's staring at her plate with a scowl on her face. "Did he hurt you?"

She scoffs and glares at me hatefully. "Let's get one thing straight. You embarrass me like that again and I swear I'll kill you too. Understood?"

When I nod, she stands and storms away with Matthew following at her heels. I feel sick, like my entrails are being

ripped in half. I bury my face in my hands and grit my teeth,
praying that the pain will subside. Why can't life be easy? I
always seem to fall into difficulty.

"We better go to the Arena now if we want good seats."
Jonah says to break the tension. "Come on, Kyle. You can moan
as loud as you want once the game starts. No one will hear you."

The flashback subsides, leaving me with faint memories and impenetrable darkness.

I stir, noticing the soft fabric of a blanket over my body. I'm no longer in pain. Fatigue has melted away, leaving my thoughts clear and my body responsive. I moan and open my eyes. I'm lying on a queen-size bed in a small bedroom—rock walls, low ceiling, and modern furniture. The trickle of water can be heard from the adjoining bathroom.

I push off the sheets and glance down at my bare torso. A fresh scar has taken the place of my wound—painless and unnoticeable. The newfound comfort is refreshing. I've been in pain for too long.

"Do you want to hop in the shower? You must feel gross." Cora saunters out of the bathroom with a towel wrapped around her head. She has changed into a clean pair of jeans and an oversized button-up.

"Where are we?" I prop myself against a stack of pillows, watching her wring the water from her hair. She smiles and collapses onto the mattress.

"Outpost-bronze, somewhere in Minnesota. Byron and Callan are sleeping in the bunkroom down the hall, Sarah is taking a bath, James and Scar have disappeared, and Mikey is who-knows-where. Truman is flying in later this afternoon. He wants to discuss what happened in the Titan's City." She leans against my chest. The aroma of lavender wafts from her clean skin. "I've been in this room since we arrived—watched an old movie, ate some food, took a shower. You missed out."

I laugh. Her presence lightens my burden. I don't feel lonely when she smiles. Her blithe attitude drowns the fear and duty corrupting my sanity. "I'm sorry for passing out when I did. It was bad timing."

"You're human, Kyle. It's okay to reveal that every once in a while." Cora toys with the charm around her neck and inspects the tattoo on my left wrist. "I want to get one of these. It's who I am now." Her hand rests on my ribcage where a paragraph has recently been inked. "May I read it now?"

I roll onto my side and motion to the large mark. "You have a right to know what it says."

She tilts her head and reads the words aloud. "We who are strong ought to bear with the failings of the weak and not to please ourselves, Romans 15:1." Inquisition crosses her gaze, mixed with a sudden gleam of understanding. "This is who you are."

"It's who I want to be. Strength is for service, not status."

"More people should think like you," she sighs and traces the blue lines on my wrist. "What are we going to do? Those explosions won't hinder Deven's invasion. He will continue to attack until we're all exterminated. We don't even know if the other squad successfully destroyed the threat. In a few hours, we may all be dead or under mind control."

"This world is a mess. *We* are a mess," I say bitterly. There are many decisions to be made. The future of the world depends of me, an eighteen-year-old-kid. I'm not old enough for this role. Everything I do ends in death of some form. No one is safe with me as their protector.

"Your army will keep the Regiment at bay for the time being. We're safe. We can relax for a few days and heal. There comes a time when everyone must rest. You can't expect to win this war if you enter it defeated. Eat a lot of food, sleep, and *please* take a shower! You do not smell nice."

"They don't have deodorant available in the Dead Zone," I smirk and slide off the bed. My stained camouflage has been stripped from my body, leaving me dressed in only a pair of black gym-shorts. My skin is covered with a film of debris. "I'm glad you're here, Cora. A sword isn't the same without his arrow."

She laughs at my remark and hastily braids her hair. "Go before you break out in song." The moment she tosses me a fresh towel, there is a knock at the door.

"May I come in?" Mikey leans over the threshold. When I nod, he grins and walks into the room. His muddy sneakers, disheveled hair, and geeky demeanor are nostalgic. My best-friend hasn't changed. "Kyle, you look rugged! And what's that smell? Whew, it's making my eyes water…"

"I'm going to the shower now," I rebuff. "It's not like you've been rolling around in gore and charred flesh for the past year, Mikey."

"I *would* if that stupid programming worked on me!" He plops down in an overstuffed chair and flips lazily through a faded magazine. "By the way, Truman is here. I saw his airship in Hangar B."

I moan and snatch a pair of clothes from the apartment's closet. "Why can't he arrive on schedule? I have enough problems. I certainly do not need an early politician."

"Don't worry about Truman," Cora says. "I'll stall him until you are ready to talk." She laces her boots and rises from the bed. "We'll be in the atrium. Take all the time you need." She kisses my cheek before leaving the suite. The public affection sends a shock of anxiety through my body. I cringe at the pain and clutch my head, enduring another wave of aching torment. Panic mixes with images, sudden flashes of battle. I hear screams, feel blood lapping at my ankles, and smell the suffocating odor of decay. It's real. It happened, and I'm forced to relive the events daily.

"I thought the anxiety attacks had ended." Mikey stares at me as I slump against a metal desk.

"Everything triggers a memory. I can't even kiss Cora without reliving the night she almost died." I shake my head and sigh. "This war is killing me, Mikey. I'm losing my mind."

"We've all been through a lot, you and Cora especially. Everyone is suffering. It's difficult to remember what we *stand* for, when everything around us is crumbling." He pauses. "A few years ago, everyone thought you were a lost cause; but not anymore. You completed your mission, Kyle. You became someone worthy of being remembered. The world rallies by your side, and you know I'd be fighting alongside you if I could. We stand for honor and justice, genuine strength amidst an enemy of deception. Like *the sword and the arrow*, we are united. No one wants a *together* leader. We want an *imperfect* you." He stands and punches me kiddingly in the shoulder. "I believe in you, old friend."

His final statement catches me off guard. *Old friend*—it's what Yuzek used to call me. My brain pounds beneath my skull and my vision dilates. I clutch my abdomen and grip the armrest of a chair. Images wash through my blood like waves, a riptide of colors and dialogue.

"Aim for the head," Yuzek instructs. He gazes through the scope of his .50 caliber M2 machinegun, aiming for a target further down the range. Stuffed dummies bob up and down in the

distant simulation, spraying bullets in all directions—Prime Way's most dangerous method of training. One wrong move could end our lives. "Never shoot to injure. You shoot to kill."

I press my chest to the ground and stare through the narrow slats in the barricade. The butt of my AR15 is wedged against my right shoulder-blade. I mimic Yuzek and gaze through the weapon's scope, focusing on my target. "Do we always have to kill?"

"It's what the Program believes."

"What do you believe?" I pull the trigger. My bullet embeds itself in a dummy's forehead.

"You're a sharp shooter, Kyle." He frowns the moment my name slips from his mouth. It's against protocol to recognize any soldier by their pre-Legionary name. "My beliefs are irrelevant, old friend." His thin lips lift into a pleased grimace as he kills three of the simulator's fire squad.

"I've been staying off the Faculty's radar. I think they've forgotten about me."

"No," Yuzek interjects. "You're still an item of interest. Continue to work hard and don't do anything stupid. Your basic training finals are next week, aren't they? You're ranked first in your division as of now. You should pass into Intermediate without any problems. And what is this I hear about you and 237? You both have been skipping curfew to sit on the beach? Don't think Director Ramsey hasn't noticed. We do have security cameras."

"Cora and I are friends. That's all."

"Be careful. You don't want to draw any more attention to yourself."

"What is it they want from me, Yuzek? I've been here for weeks and you've yet to disclose the reasoning behind my recruitment. Who do they think I am?"

"You're nothing yet. It's what you might become that has them excited," he tells me. "The programming procedure was designed to abate weakness. It erases borderline personality and adheres to your dominate mentality. In most cases, this causes the recruit to be resilient and emotionless. They become

obedient, numb, and will kill without a second thought. Levels of severity vary depending on their genetic pliability..."

"And my genetics are the most pliable the Faculty has ever seen," I conclude.

"Exactly. They expect you to transform into a prime soldier, dangerous and loyal to the Program; but it all depends on what lies inside your heart. If your good-nature is dominate, the programming will affect you in a completely different way. Your conscience will become unwavering and that scares the leaders here half to death. Their super-weapon will be...useless."

"You want me to become useless?"

"No, I just don't want the good parts of you to die. There are ways to be strong without merciless cruelty. Remember that. You've already defied all odds getting here. You were accidentally abducted by our enemies, escaped a maximum security facility without enhanced abilities, protected and aided 237 on her mission, and the list continues. You have outsmarted highly trained officers and terrorist groups, chose deception over brute force. Your level of natural quick response and strategy is off the charts. Not once in my decade of service have I met a recruit of your...caliber." He fires five more shots, massacring the remaining dummies and shutting off the simulation. He tilts his head to look at me. "I'm proud of how far you've come. You will do great things here, I know. Strength matched with humility is stronger than any evil. A bad man may win battles, but a good man will win the war."

Yuzek was the only man who has ever cared about my well-being. He believed in genuine, human strength; not what the Program tried to concoct. His memory still haunts me. I want to become someone he'd be proud to call *friend*, honor his sacrifice. He was my mentor and in many ways, more of a father to me than my own dad. I'll never forget the words he said.

I bury my face in hands. Anxiety spreads through my body like a virus. I rub my eyes to wipe away the images. Darkness looms over my head, a constant reminder of the horrors thriving outside. The past year has been purgatory, a living hell. I've tried desperately to help my country, only to watch more people die. I thought I lost Cora. I thought

I'd have to endure the rest of my life alone. The pain of responsibility has ravaged whatever life still remained in my chest.

"You're going to be okay, man." Mikey moves towards the door. "I'll be with Cora and Truman in the atrium if you need me." He disappears down the corridor, leaving me alone to battle my own fears.

I shower, change, and eat everything in the apartment's mini-fridge. Once I've managed to repair my appearance, I leave the safety of my room and follow the winding hallway towards the outpost's atrium. I designed this place—the underground passages, modern architecture, and accommodating living space. Thousands of civilians now occupy the stronghold.

"Legion!" A group of children rush to my side. They laugh and tug on my arms, beaming with excitement. I smile and toss one of the boys over my shoulder. A little girl clings to my leg. The sight of her reminds me of Lucy.

I waddle into the atrium and gently pry the small bodies from my limbs. "I have to talk with Truman and Blue-Jay right now, but maybe we can play later." My words take effect immediately. The children release their grasp and watch me leave with awful eyes.

Adults crowd the stadium-size space—some cleaning weapons, others eating lunch. A few elderly men are seated in the far corner playing a game of cards. The commotion is peaceful. People have lives beneath the earth's surface. They have families, jobs, and safety. They don't worry. They have hope that I'll restore their homes and restart civilization.

I weave between the lines of tables to where Cora is standing with Truman and Mikey. They pause and look at me, waiting until I reach their circle before continuing the conversation.

"We did all that we could," Cora tells Truman. "Our objective was to rescue my brother without alerting the Titan of our presence. We wanted to sneak into the City off-grid. The second squad's mission was an addition. They were meant to discover and destroy whatever danger the Titan had concocted, and they gave their lives to ensure that the threat was annihilated."

"President Marner wants proof," the man answers. He straightens his gray necktie and runs his fingers through his gelled hair. I notice blots of smut on his usually pristine suit. Even the clean order of Charles Truman has been smite by Deven's invasion. "I'm sorry for your loss, but

Dimidium's congress needs surety of the nation's safety. We can't turn a blind-eye to what may be brewing on our borders."

"How do we get that information? None of us are willing to stomp back into the Regiment's stronghold to make sure our bombs exploded what needed to be exploded," Mikey adds. "Tell the president that Legion's division is done taking orders! This is our war, not his. We will fight and protect what we feel is important. He doesn't tell us what to do!"

"I'll pretend I didn't hear that, Mr. Stevens." Truman turns his focus to me. He smiles and shakes my hand enthusiastically. "It's good to see you alive, Kyle. Everyone was beginning to worry."

"Didn't you hear? I'm indestructible now."

"It wouldn't surprise me," he laughs. "How are you holding up?"

"I'm alive and still somewhat sane," I answer.

Truman and I have developed a friendship over the past year. He let me stay at his apartment when I was in Dimidium, since the housing-complexes were filled. I've learned a lot about him, gained a respect for his loyalty to Marner. He was once married and had a little girl. Both his wife and daughter were killed in a fire a few years ago. After that, he spent all of his time working to fill the void losing his family caused. He's no different from Cora and me. We've all lost people we love.

"I won't ask anything more of your troops. You know what has to be done to win this war," he speaks. "I'll tell Marner that you have everything under control."

I nod. "My division will stay here for a few days to recuperate and plan our next move. I'll put the rest of my army on high alert. Deven won't be able to move without me knowing."

Truman relaxes and crosses his arms over his chest. "I believe in the impossible odds." The moment he says those words, I notice a tattoo on his wrist—*the sword and the arrow*. He has joined the movement, united with people of a different species. He has believed in our potential since the dawn of the Program—creating good from corruption. We decide our own identity.

"Truman, the cargo has been unloaded. Do you want me to move the airship into Hangar C?" Matthew strolls into the atrium. He stops and stares at us wide-eyed, the blood draining from his face. There is a sense of surprise in his shifty eyes, as if he wasn't expecting to see us alive.

"It's…good to see you all again. Truman didn't tell me you'd be here."
His behavior is baffling, uneasy. It unearths a sense of distrust in the
depths of my mind. Matthew betrayed me once. Why wouldn't he do it
again?

I bite my lip, trying to dull my anger with the feeling of pain. He
kissed Cora. He lied to me. While I was away trying to stop Deven's
invasion, he was attempting to steal the only girl I've ever loved. I will
never be able to trust him. He only cares about himself.

"I'm glad you're alive, Cora. I was worried," Matthew stutters.

"You shouldn't have been," she answers coolly. "Now if you would
all excuse me, I'm meeting Sarah and Callan in the gym." Cora backs
away from the circle and gently touches my arm. "See you at dinner,
Kyle." She casts Matt a stern glance before leaving.

"I think Kyle and I have plans too," Mikey states awkwardly. "We
have to…talk with James about his super-suit. Come on, Kyle. We don't
want to keep him waiting."

I'm grateful for the escape and follow my friend out of the atrium.
We saunter down narrow hallways and across stone bridges, heading into
the lower tunnels. Mikey has no intention of fulfilling his plans.
Stonecipher's room is in the opposite direction. This is his way of giving
me time alone, away from the adoring crowds and demanding officials.
He and Cora are the only people on this planet who can read my
emotions. They are my best-friends, my family.

We walk through stretches of darkness, coming to a stop at the edge
of a deep ravine. This part of the outpost is deserted. Shadows blanket
the cavern. Stalagmites and stalactites gleam like sharp teeth all around
us. The faint rush of water echoes below. I glance over the edge of the
chasm and stare into the black abyss. If I jumped, would I survive the
fall?

"Callan and Sarah seem happy," Mikey speaks after several minutes
of silence have passed. "They're grateful to be together again. And did
you know that Stonecipher and Scar were engaged a decade ago? Yeah,
they've been talking nonstop. That must make you feel good." He tosses
a rock into the ravine and waits for me to respond. When I don't, he
continues. "And what about you and Cora? Aren't you happy to be with
her again? She loves you a ton…"

"I love her too," I say. "She's the one, Mikey. I'll never be able to love anyone else. So yes, I am glad she's alive and here with me; but I can't be *happy*. Six of my soldiers died and I can't help but wonder if I could've saved them."

My head aches. Sweat beads on my forehead. Panic erupts inside my chest as I remember the explosions. My programming is suffocating my sanity.

CHAPTER 13

I am standing in my bedroom. Heaps of clothing lay on the carpeted floor. The air is warm and smells musty. Darkness envelops the familiar space, swallowing me into its nostalgic shadows. I am alone. Both beds are empty.

Like a ghost, I move silently through the empty house. Each step draws me deeper into the memories I've long since forgotten, exhuming details and resurrecting events. I pass my sisters' room. Lucy's favorite teddy-bear is lying in the threshold. Its fur is damp and infested with mildew, slowly decaying on the aged floorboard. The sight sends a shiver through my body, unearthing a crippling sense of panic. Something isn't right. My family should be here. I need to get out of the house.

My legs propel me down the hallway. My heart pounds like a drum. Breath catches inside my throat as I leap over the banister and fall to the main floor. I land in the center of the living-room, crouching down to survey my surroundings. The silence is unearthly. Even at night, my house never felt this quiet—as if someone is lurking in the darkness, ready to prey on my weakness.

I hear a clatter in the kitchen and move cautiously towards the sound. My fists wrap around a bookend perched on a shelf. Without hesitation, I enter the adjoining room, prepared to combat whatever enemy may be waiting. Nothing could prepare me for what I see next.

The bookend tumbles from my grasp. I can't breathe. I can't move. My feet are glued to the rotting linoleum floor. My eyes widen in shock as I gaze at the horrific scene. In the center of the kitchen, bound to a wooden post, is my family. They stare at me with desperation—Mom, Dad, Harry, Julia, Benji, and Lucy. Tape covers their mouths. Their clothing is drenched with gasoline.

I am paralyzed.

"You weren't expecting this, were you?" Deven's voice echoes from the shadows with malicious venom. His frigid eyes glint in the dark, striking at me like daggers. "You thought your family was exempt from our little game. You thought I'd spare them. Why? Did you think I'd reserve my genius by only targeting your undead girlfriend? She is but one of your many weaknesses, Kyle." He grins and steps into the dim light. "Let's list all of them, shall we? Number one, you love Cora Kingston a bit too much. Those feelings will be the death of you. Two, deep down you're still dedicated to your rotten family. You've never been able to forget them. Three, you can't let people die. It suffocates you, little by little. Your bravery does not ease your pain. All this death is finally sucking the life out of you..."

Obscenities fly from my mouth but with a single flash of his eyes, I am silenced.

"You won't be able to function after my next attack." He laughs and circles my family. "I shall kill everyone you love. They'll drop like flies and the trauma of their deaths with strip your sanity. Then without a leader to rally an opposing army, this war will end. I'll complete my invasion and the world will recreate, a place filled only with our species. So buckle up, Kyle. Your end is nearing."

With a brush of his hand, the room ignites. Fire spreads across the floor and up the walls, consuming my family in a fiery inferno. I yell and scream, trying desperately to break paralysis. Julia and Lucy squeal. Harry yanks at his restraints. Benji sobs. My parents writhe in pain. Their bodies become torches and all I

235

can do is watch in terror, weeping as my own flesh-and-blood is killed.

"You're next," Deven sneers. He smiles as the flames race towards my feet. They lap at my ankles and up the fabric of my jeans. Then with a final gust, I am enveloped in certain death.

My torso lurches forward, yanking my body into a sitting position. I gasp and glance around the dark apartment. The glow of a nightlight illuminates the modern furniture and rock walls. I clutch my chest and breathe, wiping the sweat from my face. It was just a dream. My family is still alive.

I rise from my pallet on the floor, beside Cora's bed, and rush to the bathroom. White light divides the room's darkness. I lean over the toilet and vomit. Acid and angst stings my throat. Panic is crippling. What if Deven targets my family next? They're not safe in Dallas.

"Are you okay?" Cora's sleepy face watches me quizzically from the doorway. She rubs her eyes and kneels by my side. Her hands press against my back as I cough the remaining fear from my body. "Shhh, everything's alright." She brushes the damp hair from my forehead and forces my eyes to meet hers. "You had a nightmare, didn't you?"

I pull her against my chest, trying to find peace in reality. Deven may have stolen a year of her life, but she is still alive. We're together—unbound by time, unbound by death. I can cope with the darkness now that she's here. Together, we are strong. We can win Deven's game.

"Whatever happened…wasn't real. It is *never* real," she whispers. "Our programming conjures those images to deceive us, like the simulations at Prime Way. They're designed to expose our fears." Her braid touches my cheek. It sends a pulse of hope through my aching chest.

"He killed my family, Cora. He burned them to the ground…" I trail off, choking on the dream's memories. I heard my sisters' scream. I felt the fire, the smoke charring my lungs. "He's planning to strike them next. They are my only weakness he hasn't already targeted."

"You think Deven's going after your family?"

"He's already tried to kill you, my soldiers, strip away my health and sanity. What else is there for him to attack? He knows that once I've been destroyed, the invasion will be final; and he will do whatever it takes to ensure that his plan isn't compromised. *We* are the only barrier separating him from victory," I tell her. Truthful intensity projects from my voice. "I'm not the only target in his scope. He wants us all dead. We are the final game, Cora. Deven's next attack will not be on Dimidium or humankind. He's coming for us…"

A stern grimace replaces her smile. She sits across from me, staring at the tile floor in silence. After pondering the dangerous possibility, she speaks. "How much time do you think we have?"

"A few weeks."

She nods. "Then you should probably leave tonight. I'll need you back in a few days to help with war preparations. That doesn't give you very long."

"I don't understand…"

"Go and fix your family, Kyle. The Blue-Jay can handle things here until you return. We're a team. Let's prove it." She sandwiches my hand between hers. "I will send notifications to all divisions, telling them to regroup at the old Prime Way facility. We'll be waiting for you there. But until then, ensure that your family will remain safe throughout the coming war. You can't be an effective leader if you're worried about Deven harming them. Trust me. The world won't explode in the next few days."

"Are you sure?"

Cora's smile returns. "Just promise me that you'll come back."

"I'll *always* come back."

After I kiss her goodbye, I change into a set of clean armor, pack my few belongings, and walk into the vacant hallway. I pass guards and video cameras as I move towards the hangars located in the North Wing. Security thickens the higher I travel, but no one questions my motives or stops me from climbing. I have clearance to use any vehicle or weapon, travel through restricted areas, and access confidential information. Legion has power and influence—the persona Yuzek believed would adhere to my humanity. He understood what I'd become, knew of the approaching darkness and what fate would befall earth if someone didn't rise against the enemy. Everything I am stems from his inclination.

"We who are strong ought to bear with the failings of the weak and not to please ourselves," I repeat in my head. Cora is right to tell me to leave. My family is in danger. They are weak and I am strong. I must protect the people I sacrificed.

The clock on my wrist strikes two o' clock as I enter the outpost's armory. I snatch a nuclear-powered rifle off a rack, fasten knives and handguns to my belt, and toss a handful of grenades into my backpack. Once I've armed myself, I continue towards my destination.

Florescent lights illuminate the desolate hangar. Airships crowd the space, all varying in size and capacity—some large and shaped like flying saucers, others single-passenger jets. I've piloted each of them over the past year, my favorite being the fastest and most high-tech of the assortment. It resembles a spindly helicopter—rounded cockpit, white plating, and rotating turbines. If I reach the proper altitude, I can arrive in Dallas within a couple of hours.

I grip the handlebars of my motorcycle, which Stonecipher parked in the far corner of the hangar, and walk it to the back of my designated plane. Carefully I secure my bike to the aircraft with a wad of cords. Once I land in Texas, I will need another form of transportation.

"You're relentless!" Mikey strolls from the hangar's wide entrance with a set of armor fastened over his jeans and t-shirt. A burlap bag and a machinegun are slung across his right shoulder.

"How'd you know I was here?"

"I can't sleep nowadays so I volunteered to take the night shift in the control room, watching security feed from the East Wing. I saw you leave your room and figured this is where you were headed. Not many people wake up in the middle of the night and put on armor to just take a walk." He tosses his bag into my airship's cockpit. "I'm coming too."

"You don't even know where I'm going," I say as I finish roping off my motorcycle. "I could be headed into the Kill Zone to complete a suicide mission…"

"Or going home," he adds. "You haven't seen your family in two years. After losing a squad of soldiers and coping with more of Deven's threats, you must be worried about their safety. I get it."

"You gathered all that from a security feed?"

Mikey snickers. "Nah, it was a hunch that *you* just confirmed. Now let's go before someone realizes what we're doing." He climbs into the plane's passenger seat and fastens his safety restraints. "Come on, grandpa. We don't have all day!"

"I'm going to regret this," I mumble as I slide into the cockpit. Switches are flipped. Icons flicker across the dashboard, glowing with numbers and abbreviations. I disarm the helicopter's tracking beacon and activate its turbines. After adjusting my headset's frequency and inspecting the craft's power source, I prepare for takeoff.

The hangar's hatch opens, sliding apart to reveal the night sky. I wipe my hands across the control panel to launch the airship into flight mode. Slowly we lift off the ground, hovering silently in midair. I push the throttle forward and with one hand on the joystick, navigate my plane out of the outpost and into dangerous territory.

Night swallows us whole. Stars replace the banal glow of florescent lighting. Rudimentary terrain stretches in all directions, a vast canvas of dilapidated buildings and sycophants—empty and desolate. I stare ahead at the hazy horizon to block out the morbid scenery. It's easier to live in ignorance among evil than choose to stare it in the face. No one wants to admit that their livelihood has been destroyed; but for me, that *realization* has become my life.

Once we've reached our designated altitude, I switch the aircraft to cruise control and reach for my backpack. I unzip the front pocket, remove a photograph of Cora and me, and wedge it against the dashboard. Nowadays I need a constant reminder of what I'm fighting for—justice, hope, and my family; conclusive of Cora, Mikey, and every teenager with Legionary blood rushing through their veins. Maybe that's my problem, why I'm slowly losing my strength to anxiety. I consider now a fourth of the nation's population my family. I've opened my arms too wide.

"Kyle, I need another favor." Mikey picks at his fingernails nervously. He glances in my direction with begging eyes. "Would you issue me clearance for another programming procedure?"

"You've been through the process twice already."

"Third time's a charm?" He musters a pleading smile and motions to his scrawny torso. "Come on, man. You're a superhero and I'm *below* average! I can't even help unload cargo from our transport vehicles. What's the worst thing another brain shock could do to me?"

"I don't know, Mikey…"

"Please. I'm tired of being useless. This is what I want, Kyle. I want to be a Legionary like you!"

I sigh and stare into oblivion. "Fine, but this is the last time I'll clear you for the procedure. You're great the way you are, Mikey. You don't need muscles or enhanced abilities to prove you're something of worth."

"Save the motivational lecture for someone else," he smirks. "Mom made me listen to plenty of that mumbo-jumbo in high school." He leans his head against the window and gazes out at the sea of clouds. "This is all so...surreal. We used to dream about this kind of stuff when we were kids, remember? All the talk about superpowers and laser guns..."

"That was before we grew up."

"Before *you* grew up," he rephrases. "Even in high school, I was considered the freaky tech guy. You were able to break your image— bought a motorcycle, started fights at lunch, and became a self-absorbed loner. Girls drooled over you, but every day was hell for me. While you were off crashing parties, wrestling Ron in the parking lot, and getting yourself thrown in jail, I was doing my best to stay alive! I tried to change, you know, be cool like the other kids. No one liked me. They thought I was weird." He shrugs to shake off the memories. "You were always my best-friend. I might have been a little jealous, but I never hated you. I guess deep down...I knew this day would come and you'd need me. So don't bother to apologize. All that is in the past. We've both changed."

"There are many things I haven't told you," I say. "You've heard about my experience in the Prime Way Program but...you don't know how I got there. I want to tell you now. We have time." I pause to formulate my story. "It was after a fight with my parents. I walked to your house. You drove me to the airport, lectured me on the consequences of leaving, and dropped me off. I was planning to fly to Atlanta to work for my great-uncle at his car dealership in return for food and housing. This much you already know.

"I remember waiting for my flight at the Dallas airport when a surge of passengers flooded the main terminal. Most hurried to baggage claim. Others walked directly to the building's exit. I had pressed myself against a wall to avoid being swept away by the frenzy, when a girl bumped into me. She made brief eye-contact, gripped my wrist, and continued in the direction of the main door. It was at this moment when a pair of men, tall and built, grabbed her by the arms and subtly injected her neck with a syringe. I watched her pace falter and her muscles stiffen. The abductors then lifted her off the ground and dragged her out of the airport.

"I don't know what compelled me to follow them. But I did. I walked outside and searched for the girl. She was nowhere to be found. After a few minutes of wandering the parking lot aimlessly, I gave up and headed back towards my terminal. That's when things took a disastrous turn.

"I was taken. Why it happened, I have no idea. Fate has an odd way of working itself out. One minute I was on the sidewalk. The next, I was laying in the back of a van with a needle protruding from my neck. It was a mistake. They didn't want me. They wanted Matthew. And the girl they abducted was no other than Cora Kingston. She'd stolen plans for a nuclear-bomb from a US military outpost, thinking she had retrieved them from a band of terrorist, and was tracked to Dallas where she had a connecting flight. Prime Way had been lying to all of us from the beginning. They told us we were the good guys. We were not good.

"I'd experienced too much of Charles Truman's operation to be released. They took me, locked me inside a top secret facility, and waited for orders from Benjamin Marner. I didn't know who they were. I became susceptible to lies, and they were tossed at me from all directions.

"Long story short, Cora and I escaped but I couldn't go to Atlanta as planned. Truman would track me down. I couldn't go home. I'd put my family in danger. So there was only one option left. I would travel with Cora in hopes of being recruited by the Program. It was the prospect of an exciting life, a world beyond Dallas. I'd become a Legionary with superhuman strength and abilities, train into something of worth and value, and protect my country. It's what I wanted most.

"We were met in Virginia by the program's recruiter, Vince Armstrong, and Matthew. They had come to deliver the news of my recruitment. I had been chosen. The Prime Way Program wanted me. They said I was special. No one had ever wanted me.

"Once I signed a contract and gave them a sample of my blood, I was enlisted. Everything after that was a blur. They faked my death to wipe me off the public database, loaded me in a train-car, and sent me to the Prime Way facility located a few miles north of Portland, Maine. This was how I was sucked into the world of the Prime Way Program—a single mistake, convincing lies, and the urge to restart my life.

"I trained for months, ranked first in my division, and passed into intermediate training with honors. Life was…good. I had friends and for the first time in my life, I felt like I had a purpose. It wasn't until you tracked me using the hidden beacon in my phone-case that things got rough. The facility went into lockdown. Curfew was raised, security heightened. Our every move was monitored. Then one of my friends, Jonah, died in an accidental fire. I knew something wasn't right so I investigated. What I found completely rewrote my future and the future of my species. Ramsey and the Faculty had been lying to all of us. We weren't training to protect our country. We were experiments, superhuman soldiers unlawfully created to overtake the country—the bad guys.

"Labeled a criminal and potential threat, I was forced to hide from my friends until I could gather them and relay the information. After that, we ran to the opposing force—Charles Truman and Benjamin Marner of the CIA. You know the remainder of the story. We stopped a lethal attack on the United States. I was shot in the chest, and the Program closed. All Legionaries were locked away in a maximum security facility…except five. Cora and I were among those who escaped.

"Now you know exactly what changed me, Mikey. All that I am now is defined by those events," I tell him. "It took risking everything to conquer the unconquerable."

"I'm glad all this has happened," he says with a smile. "If not, my best-friend wouldn't be as cool as he is now. Normality is so overrated."

"Your heart is better than mine, old friend."

A crescent moon hangs suspended in the dark sky. Clouds part, revealing snowcapped mountains and dark cities. An alert flashes across the dashboard, warning us of an approaching Kill Zone. I slide my hands across the control panel to see a holographic map of the plane's route. We have entered into Sector 8.

"Outpost-bronze contacting 1026," a familiar voice speaks through my headset's frequency. "Do you copy, 1026? This is the Blue-Jay speaking."

"Couldn't go back to sleep, Cora?" I grin and reactivate the aircraft's tracking beacon. "I've only been gone for a few hours. Do you miss me already?"

"Of course," she answers. "How are things from where you are?"

"Quiet. I haven't seen a trace of enemy presence since departure. This flight may be uneventful." I uncap a bottle of water and quickly guzzle the contents. "Will you be in the control center until I arrive at destination? It'll be nice to talk with someone. It's very lonely up here."

"I know Mikey is with you, Kyle."

"Sneaking around is not an option anymore, is it?" I snicker and glance over at my friend who is busy drawing diagrams in the window's condensation. "He wanted to go home and I didn't see the harm in letting him tagalong."

"Hey, you practically begged me to come!" Mikey rebuffs sarcastically.

I smirk and stare at the picture of Cora taped to the dashboard. "Stay safe and keep a weapon on you at all times. In case something happens to me, I need to know that you'll be okay. We may not be able to contact one another until I pass back into government owned territory. Deven has blocked all communications from Sectors 6, 9, 11, and the Dead Zone. Mikey and I will enter Sector 6 in exactly five-minutes."

"The control center will be under high alert. I'll be monitoring your progress until you arrive in Dallas." She pauses. Her voice lowers to a whisper. "Please, don't do anything reckless. I need you to come back in one piece."

"Why?"

"Because I love you, Stupid!" she replies with a laugh. "Everyone needs you. I'll never be Legion in their eyes. So if not for me, hurry back for them."

"You're enough. Mikey and I will stay out of trouble…at least for now," I say. "We're about to pass into Sector 6. I need to shut off my headset's frequency so it can't be tracked. We will make contact once it's safe. Talk to you soon, Cora. I love you." I remove my headset and disarm the transmitter. Emptiness forms a devoid inside my chest. A shiver quakes down my spine. We are officially alone above this no-man's-land.

Turbulence shakes the aircraft. I grip the joystick and override cruise control, manually piloting the plane. Unease pricks my surety. Something doesn't feel right. The earth below is too quiet, too uninhabited. I've studied the Regiment's tactics. They rarely make their presence known before an attack—hiding and camouflaging their camps in the ruins of bombed Sectors. If an enemy squadron spots us, it'll only be a matter of minutes before we're blown from the sky.

"You sense it too," Mikey mumbles. He tightens his safety restraints and clutches his glowing rifle. "They're watching us, aren't they? I have a strange feeling that..."

A ball of energy explodes across the windshield. Warning sensors flash red. Sirens wail. The sudden attack catches me by surprise. I struggle to control the helicopter as shots are fired at us from below. We've been recognized.

"Brace yourself!" I shout and force the craft into a spiral. Sky and earth form a single void as we spin, corkscrewing into a freefall. I shove the throttle forward. A gust of power emits from the plane's turbines, guiding us into a stable altitude. My eyes are glued to the dashboard. My hands navigate the controls, weaving between blasts of energy and away from the Kill Zone.

"I think I'm going to be sick!" Mikey gags and presses his skull against the headrest. His face turns green as I yank back the joystick, shooting us into a cluster of clouds. "I've always hated roller coasters." His eyes droop as the plane swings side-to-side, dodging fatal charges.

I activate the gun system and fasten a pair of scopes to my eyes. My vision enhances to match the technology, revealing the concealed enemy. With a press of my thumb, missiles eject from beneath the aircraft. They slam into the earth like daggers, setting electric fire to the war-camp.

Laser bullets ricochet off the steel plating. Energy ignites the surrounding air. I hold my breath as the plane's turbines deaden, shuttering to an unfortunate halt. The cockpit dips downward, diving into the shadowed abyss. I slide my hands across the dark dashboard. All circuits have been shocked, electrically fried. I tug at the joystick but all I can do is maneuver the smoking craft in a descending glide.

"Kyle, what's happening?!" Mikey gazes at me in a panic as I crack open the control panel and begin tampering with the tangles of wires. "We're going to die! Fix this thing!"

"The thought may have crossed my mind," I snap and fit a pair of wires to a disconnected circuit. Gravity tosses my body against the ceiling. I grit my teeth and reach desperately towards the panel. "Do you have a piece of string or something sticky?"

"No!" Mikey's eyes are glued to the approaching earth. His fingernails dig into the leather of his armrests. "You might want to hurry…"

I rub my neck out of anxiety, feeling the cord of leather beneath my armor. I grin and rip off the necklace. "Cora, you've saved us again." I lunge forward, securing the wires to the circuit with the strand of rabbit hide. A rumble of power shakes the aircraft.

With a sigh of relief, I refasten my restraints and grab the machine's controls. The ground is less than a hundred-feet away. "Work!" I beat my fist against the keypad. Screens flicker to life. Illuminated icons shimmer across the dashboard. The helicopter creaks as its nuclear-energy stabilizes.

"And this is why I hate airplanes!" I laugh, gasping as the turbines regain power. The faster they rotate, the brighter they glow. Adrenaline surges through my bloodstream. A relieved shout projects from my lungs. I pull the joystick, guiding Mikey and me away from certain death. We shoot into the sky, both of us high-fiving and boisterously expressing our relief. Today is not our day to die.

"1026, back online." I trigger the tracking beacon and resume cruise control. My lips part into a smile as I glance down at the wooden charm dangling inside the control panel—*the sword and the arrow*. The simple emblem has transformed my life. It's become my identity.

"That was intense!" Mikey snickers and heaves a dramatic sigh. "I guess the worst is over. In a few hours, we'll be home."

"It's been two years. What if my family doesn't want to see me? They haven't answered my phone calls, responded to any of my letters. I haven't considered the chances that…they might not want me to come back. I'm going now because I need to keep them safe. It's my duty to protect them, but what if they've decided that I'm no longer good enough to be their son or brother?"

"Don't think such nonsense! Put on your big-boy boxers and let's do this!"

The next few hours pass without incident. We arrive in Dallas as morning paints the horizon. After I land the plane in a deserted parking lot and unhook my motorcycle, Mikey and I begin our drive homeward. It's hard to be back. Sixteen-years of my life were spent in these streets, in those buildings, under that awning. I feel as if I'm riding through a nightmare, a scene where my memories have morphed into the emotions they once emitted. This isn't a happy place. All I remember of Dallas is anger, pain, and unquenchable loneliness that drove me to recklessness. We always want what we don't have. I just wanted to belong somewhere, feel accepted. Sometimes I wonder what life would've been like if I hadn't run away. Maybe I'd be dead, committed suicide after another fight with my parents. Maybe I'd be working in an auto-repair-shop, angry at myself and the world. I could spend hours concocting possible scenarios, but none of it matters anymore. I didn't stay. I ran away. That one choice transformed my life for the better. Some may disagree, thinking a bad home is less twisted than a war between superhuman teenagers, but they'd be wrong. War can be many things. It can be fought with bombs and swords, but the most painful and destructing attacks come from our mouths. I've spent my entire life in a battlefield. Except now, the scars I receive are more visible.

Sunlight burns through my old neighborhood, adding a dose of warmth to the vacated buildings and cracked streets. My house looks the same—peeling paint, dilapidated roof, and an overgrown yard. Instead of the eyesore it was once considered, my old home blends with apocalyptic suburbia. I'm almost glad it hasn't been repaired. At least something has remained the same throughout Deven's invasion, allowed me to indulge in bittersweet nostalgia.

I park my bike at the mailbox and hesitantly step onto the curb. Quickly I remove my armor and weapons, stashing the load beneath a cluster of shrubs. Maybe if I look normal, they'll forget what I've become. "Let's do this."

Mikey pats my shoulder and moves swiftly up the driveway. I follow him at a distance, unable to take my eyes off the house. Reminiscing is unavoidable. With every step, I relive my childhood. It's painful. My wounded heart aches with every flashback. I don't want to remember, but I know I can't forget. I'm stuck between two obstacles that threaten to crush my sanity.

The front door slings open. Two small bodies rush out to meet me, sprinting across the lawn as fast as their legs will carry them. I'm paralyzed as Benji and Lucy wrap themselves around my waist. Tears form in my eyes and a smile stretches across my face. I sink to my knees, squeezing my brother and sister tight against my chest. I've missed them so much.

"Kyle, where've you been?!" Benji sobs and clings to my neck. He's grown a foot in height over the past two-years. His childish features are fading. "You *promised* you'd come back. You didn't come back. I thought you had forgotten about us."

"I'm sorry. It wasn't safe for me to come home. I had to keep you safe," I tell him. "Not a day passes without me thinking of you. We're family, Benji. I could *never* forget." I squeeze his shoulder in confirmation. "You've gotten so tall."

"You too," he sniffles and wipes his eyes. When I laugh, his thin lips lift into a beaming smile.

"Do you remember me?" Lucy tugs at the hem of my shirt. She tilts her small head and looks at me with an inquisitive gleam in her oversized eyes. Her curly, blonde hair is tangled.

"Let me think…" I furrow my brow kiddingly and lift her into my arms. "Are you my grandma?"

She giggles. "No, I'm your sissy! My name is Lucy."

"That's right! You've gotten so big since I last saw you. How old are you now, twenty-five?" I twirl her around and set her on my shoulders. Her laughter sends a gust of joy through my heart. "Do you know who I am, Lu?"

"You're Kyle," she answers with a grin. "I've seen you and Birdy on TV! You're superheroes."

"Did you bring your sword?" Benji inspects my empty belt eagerly. "I'd like to hold it."

"Maybe later. I left everything by my motorcycle." I reach into my pocket and remove a radioactive switchblade. "This is for you. Be careful and only use it to protect people, never to harm. You're a man now, Benji." I place the small knife in the palm of his hand and marvel at the awe in his eyes. Maybe he'll forgive me. Maybe he wants me back in his life.

With Lucy on my shoulders and Benji tucked beneath my right arm, I move towards the front door. My parents, Julia, and Ms. Leslie Stevens are waiting in the battered threshold wearing their pajamas. They stare at me in shock as I climb the porch steps. Julia is the first to break the awkward tension. She embraces me. Her expression loses its skepticism. Tears spill from her usually judgmental eyes as I return the hug. The past is irrelevant. She's my sister and I love her.

"I knew you'd come back," Leslie Stevens says and touches my face with her slender hands. She's frailer than I remember. "Kyle, I'm so proud of you." Her voice is sweet and soft. She has always been like a mother to me. "Thanks for bringing Mikey home."

I smile, unable to find the right words to say. These are the people I left behind. This is my family. Before the Prime Way Program and Legion, my purpose was to be a good brother and son. It's a mission I failed to complete.

"Hi, Mom and Dad."

My parents gaze at me, dumbstruck. I reach out to hug my mother, afraid of rejection, but she grips my forearm and sobs. Tears gust from her eyes as she turns and saunters back into the house, forgetting my presence as if I'm nothing but a pesky salesman. The gesture feels like a punch to the stomach. Nausea stabs through my torso. I know what I did was wrong, but it had to be done! I had to leave this godforsaken place. I had to become what I am today. My mistake is saving the world!

"So you're military now…General Kyle Chase," my dad stutters. His blonde hair has grayed and more wrinkles have formed around his mouth. "Probably the youngest General ever enlisted."

"That's only my government title. I'm called many other things," I say nervously.

He nods. "You hungry?"

CHAPTER 14

I feel as if I'm standing in a simulation, a conjured setting based on the details of my memories. Nothing has changed—the dust at the foot of the stairs, Lucy's dolls beneath the couch, the heavy aroma of mold and coffee. My older brother's Leatherman jacket still lies in a heap by the fireplace. No one's even bothered to patch up the hole I punched in the wall during a previous argument. With every step, I doubt reality more. I spent sixteen-years beneath this roof, sitting in that cluttered living-room and stomping up those stairs. This was my home.

Benji and Lucy lead me into the kitchen. Their garrulous voices drown my worries. I carry my little sister and wrestle with my younger brother. Their fingers slide between mine; desperate for my attention, desperate for me. They make me feel wanted.

"I shall kill everyone you love. They'll drop like flies and the trauma of their deaths will strip your sanity," Deven's voice echoes. It unleashes recollections of my dream. I remember his smile as he set fire to my family. I remember their screams. Deven will no longer hurt the people I love. He'll die first.

I sit in my chair at the kitchen table.

Julia passes me a bowl of oatmeal and a cup of coffee. She smiles. "I'm glad you're home, little brother." Her sincerity is startling. I've always known her to be harsh and reckless—a partier on the weekends, part of Scrub High School's popular crowd, anorexic, the girl who had a different boyfriend every week. Now when she looks at me, I see

249

something genuine beneath her layers of masks.

Mikey nudges me as my parents take their seats. "Don't let them get to you. Remember why we came. You're not here to win their approval."

"I don't need approval. I need peace," I whisper in response before gulping a mouthful of coffee.

Tension fogs the air as the eight of us eat breakfast. My dad talks gibberish. My mom fiddles with her napkin nervously. Then after fifteen-minutes of uncomfortable silence, Mikey intervenes and tells my family about our journey here.

"You have tattoos, Kyle?" Benji interrupts and grabs my inked wrist. I glance around the table, noticing the abhorrence riddled across my mother's face. She hated when Harry came home with an ear-piercing. I can't imagine what she must be thinking now.

"I have three," I answer proudly. There's no use denying it. I'm not ashamed of what I've drawn on my body. These markings remind me who I am, why I'm fighting.

"How is your girlfriend?" Julia asks. "She seems…like an interesting person."

"Cora's great. She is rallying our troops together at the old Prime Way facility. I'm glad you got to meet her. She means a lot to me."

"At least he cares for *someone*," my mother mutters. She bites her tongue and looks into my eyes apologetically.

"Kyle has been leading the Legionaries for the past year," Mikey adds to replace the hateful jab. "He has stifled the spread of radiation into our western Sectors, barricaded the Regiment from advancing into government territories, and stopped various attacks on our remaining strongholds. He's saving all of our lives. You should be proud of him."

"I've seen you fight the Regiment on television!" Benji tells me. "We all watched a broadcast at outpost-silver last week. You had your sword and you charged into a pack of Centurions!" He stands on his chair and theatrically stabs the air with his invisible weapon. "You jumped over a building and ran as fast as a racecar!" He makes sound effects as he reenacts the news feed. "Three-hundred people were rescued from the Titan's captivity…"

"Benji, sit down!" my dad commands in an irritated tone. He sips his tea with prejudice. My family's dynamics haven't changed.

"Mommy, is Kyle a superhero?" Lucy questions.

My mother hesitates. She stares at me sorrowfully and shrugs her shoulders. "Kyle can be your superhero, Lucy, but he's not mine. He is my son. He'll *always* be my son."

In some small way, her response emits clemency.

"Our last neighbor vacated Dallas yesterday. The suburbs are officially abandoned. Everyone has either fled to the outpost downtown or headed west," my mom says. "Rations are scarce. Batteries are impossible to find nowadays. I've even heard rumors that Dimidium is planning to shut off our power. How are we going to live in the dark? We'll all die!"

"Alice, don't say such things in front of the children. You'll scare them," my father snaps harshly.

"Nothing could scare them now! They've seen our friends lying dead in the gutter, slept through bombings. It's a miracle that we haven't been killed! It's as if someone has been watching us, placed an invisible force-field around this house. Why should we lie and tell them everything's going to be okay?! It's not!" She buries her face in her hands and weeps.

"My soldiers and I are doing what we can to restore peace. I'm trying," I tell her. "No one's going to hurt any of you. I promise. I'll keep you all safe."

"Why did you leave, Kyle?"

"It doesn't matter anymore."

"I can't imagine what you've been through. The past two years must've been hell," Ms. Leslie adds. "Cora told us tidbits of your story. We heard the rest from Dimidium's news broadcasts…"

"It's not like *our* lives have been perfect," Julia mumbles between bites of oatmeal.

"No, we've hit some rough spots too. Before the war started, things were finally starting to get better. We learned you weren't dead, your parents received financial aid and became overnight celebrities, and we all attended Harry's wedding that you so graciously paid for. Weeks later, half of the nation was wiped off the map. We didn't know how to react. Life just…stopped." She motions to her torso. "I started passing kidney stones a few months into the invasion. They haven't stopped since. That's why I'm not exactly the pinnacle of health at the moment."

"Why *have* you come back, son?" my father questions. His brow furrows and his lips form a straight line. "It's been two years. Why choose to return home now?"

I take another gulp of coffee before answering. "You're not safe here and I can't stay to protect you. I'm afraid the Titan will strike at you to hurt me and I can't continue to fight if I know you're in danger. So I came to ensure that you all stay safe throughout the coming battles. This war is worsening by the day. It's a matter of time before Dallas is invaded. The only place you'll be safe is at an outpost. My soldiers will take care of you." I pause and search each of their faces for a sign of trust. They gaze at me blankly. "I'm sorry for hurting you. It wasn't intentional, and I don't expect you to ever accept me back into the family. I chose to leave Dallas, trick you into believing I was dead, and become a Legionary. You have every right to shun me. It's okay. After the war, you never have to see me again; but right now, I need to keep you safe. Let me do what I should've done two years ago. Let me take care of my family."

"Kyle, I don't doubt your intentions but we're not leaving our home. Harry and his wife are still missing. They were living in Oklahoma City before the invasion. After the Titan's attack, we lost all communication. What if they're trying to get here? If we leave now, we may never see them again. Until they're found, we stay. This is my decision. I'm still head of the family, remember?" He switches topics, ending the conversation. My request has been denied.

After I finish eating, Benji and Lucy drag me into the living-room. We sit on the floor and sort through a stack of board games. It's nostalgic. I've sat in this spot so many times, playing with my younger siblings. I used to wrestle with my brother, toss him onto the couch, and teach him how to play poker. Lucy would make me brush her dolls' hair and play hide-and-go-seek. At the time, their immaturity annoyed me. Now I realize that the time I spent laughing with them was probably the best hours of my past, the only memories I force myself to constantly remember.

Mikey strolls from the kitchen and plops onto the couch. "You okay?"

I nod and shuffle a deck of cards. "That didn't go as I had hoped."

"Does it ever?"

Benji yells and leaps onto my back. He and Lucy tackle me to the ground, both lying in a heap on my stomach. I grin and lift them above me with one hand, snickering at the astonishment on their faces. They laugh as I throw them into the air and onto the sofa.

"Kyle…" Julia enters the room but stops to stare at the laughing children. "Your clothes are where you left them, if you want to change and clean up. The upstairs shower still works."

"Thanks, Jules." I smile and rise to my feet. Benji runs after me as I climb the flight of stairs to the second floor. We walk down the dimly lit corridor to our old bedroom.

A bare bulb illuminates the cluttered space—piles of laundry, two unmade beds, and desks covered with trinkets and ancient homework. I forget to breathe the moment my feet cross the room's threshold. This must be a dream. I didn't think I'd ever come back.

I finger a keychain and pull my cowboy-hat from a peg on the wall. These were my things—the muddy sneakers, childhood action-figures, and the Harley Davidson catalogues. Nothing has been changed, not even the sheets on my mattress. It's as if I never left.

Benji jumps on his bed, bouncing giddily as I sort through a stack of travel pamphlets. He watches me, observing my actions intently. "I don't care what mom and dad say. You're cooler now that you have super-powers," he says. "My best-friend had action-figures of you and Blue-Jay, but he's dead now. Lots of people are dead. I was scared that I'd die too but I'm not anymore. You're going to stay here and protect us, aren't you?"

I lean against the wall, saddened by the desperation in his voice. "You know I can't stay. There are people who need my help. They need me to save them. It's my job."

His glee melts away. He searches through the drawer of his nightstand, removing a chunk of metal. "Do you know what this is? It's a piece of your crashed motorcycle; the one we all thought killed you! I thought you were dead, Kyle. I didn't think I'd ever see you again…"

"Benji, I'm sorry. This isn't what I wanted for you. Please know that. You were supposed to finish school, grow up and be happy." I kneel beside him and press my hands against his shoulders. He gazes at me with tears in his eyes. "Try to understand that if it weren't for the mistakes I've made, we'd all be dead right now. Somehow my bad decisions have turned into something useful. Even though there are times I wish I could've done things differently, I don't dwell on my past choices. They've given me…so much hope, even in darkness as thick as this. I'm not angry anymore. I have purpose, a reason to live. I don't know why I've been chosen for this role. It's never what I intended to become, but it is *who I am*."

"I wish I could be like you," he mumbles. "Dad says I'm too young to be a hero, not strong or good enough. I guess it's true. I don't really know what's right anymore. The rules seem to change with every passing day."

"It doesn't matter what people tell you is right or wrong. You must stand up for what you believe in, no matter the odds or consequences," I tell him. "Genuine courage and heroism are not doing what the world thinks is good, but sacrificing your own well-being for what you know is important. Courage *is* sacrifice. Heroism *is* honor. It's our duty to defend the weak, to protect those we love. Chivalry is not dead, Benji. This world needs leaders who stand on the foundation of integrity. This world needs heroes like you."

"What can I do? I'm still a kid," he responds.

"A few years ago, do you think people looked at me and thought to themselves, *'Yes, that boy's going to be a hero one day'*? Of course not. They hardly paid a second glance when passing me on the street. I was nobody…"

"You're like David who fought Goliath! Ms. Leslie read us the story from her Bible last night. She said heroes are made from unlikely characters."

"She's right. It doesn't matter how old or strong you are. All that matters is what lies inside your heart. A bad man may win battles, but a good man will win the war. Even though you might not be able to fight with me on the battlefield, you're still a soldier. Your mission is to protect our family. *We who are strong ought to bear with the failings of the weak and not to please ourselves*. It is Legion's creed," I say and salute him. "You're a man now, Benji."

He wraps his arms around my neck and hugs me. "I love you, Kyle."

"I love you too. Right now I need to find a way to keep you all safe. Harry is missing and Mom and Dad won't leave this place until he's found."

"Then find him."

The answer to my problem is simple. If I find Harry and bring him home, my family will move to the outpost and they'll be safe. I might earn forgiveness from my parents, create a catharsis. This is a task that *can* be completed. A rescue mission fits my knowledge and expertise.

"Benji, you're a genius!" I pat him on the back and rush out the door. My legs propel me down the hallway. My heart pounds like a drum. Breath catches inside my throat as I leap over the banister and fall to the main floor. I land in the center of the living-room, crouching down to regain my balance.

Mikey and his mom rise from the couch and stare at me wide-eyed. My parents emerge from the kitchen, waiting for an explanation. I stand with my head held high. Today, I right the wrong committed two years ago. I'm piecing my family back together.

"You said that if Harry and his wife were found, you'd move to outpost-silver. They're my family too," I say with inexorable confidence. "I'm going after them. If I leave now, I should be back by tomorrow morning."

"We don't even know where they are," Ms. Leslie adds. "It could take weeks of searching…"

"Not exactly. I passed through Oklahoma a few months ago. It's been overrun with the Titan's soldiers, marked a potential Kill Zone. The sector's occupants have either fled or been imprisoned in a mass concentration camp. I know the place. It's a minimum security facility. I can get in and out with as little as a few grenades and my sword. Mikey, I could use your help."

"You already know my answer, pal."

"I want to come too," my father speaks. He steps forward and looks at me with a sudden sense of determination. "Harry is my son. I want to help rescue him. Besides, this will be a great opportunity for me to see you in action, maybe make up for lost time."

"This isn't a game, Dad. The people we are fighting will kill you. They aren't normal soldiers."

"I'll stay out of your way and follow every command, I swear. Now do I get one of those laser guns or something that shoots fire?" He laughs at his own remark. His vapid eyes suddenly gain a childish sparkle. "Alice, keep the doors locked and the gun loaded. I'll be back soon."

"Daniel, it's dangerous out there! I can't afford to lose you too."

"Don't worry. General Kyle Chase will take care of me."

Without tension or argument, my mother agrees and preparations begin for our departure. Julia packs rations. Benji and Lucy gather basic supplies. Ms. Leslie bundles us in old jackets and scarves. They rush around the house in a frantic tizzy, but to me the chaos feels warm and wanting. In this moment, I don't feel alienated. Acceptance is not my mission. I already have a family who knows everything about me, a family who fights for me and what I stand for. When this war is over, do I really want to live in Dallas with the people who raised me, or do I want to be with the thousands of Legionaries who were responsible for what I've become? I'll never leave Cora. She's my forever and always, my family. Even if I were forced to choose between her and saving the world, I wouldn't be able to give her up, not to save a billion lives.

Keep your eyes looking ahead but never forget what lies behind you.

"Bring them home," my mom instructs. She touches my arm timidly. "Protect my family. I can't face this world without them. They're all I have left."

"No harm will come to Dad or Harry. I'll bring them back," I tell her. "This is what I do. I find and protect people. You don't have to be scared because I will keep you safe, Mom. I'm sorry for how I hurt you in the past. Running away was just…a coward's escape. I was a coward."

A tear slips down her cheek as she embraces me. "You're a brave man, Kyle. It doesn't matter what you are. I still love you." Her hands cup my face. "You'll save us all."

The sincere belief in her voice emits a rupture of emotions in the shattered depths of my chest. I've never received anything but slander from my mother. Her judgmental remarks and skepticism have always been contributed to her personality, her annoyance of me. This is the first time she's ever admitted motherly love and pride to her son.

"See you soon," Benji says and salutes me. "I believe in the impossible odds." His statement catches me by surprise. It is my slogan, a sliver of verbiage hope.

I smile and lift Lucy into my arms. She grips my neck and runs her small hands through my hair, fingering my nose and giggling when I kiss her cheek.

"Where you going, Kyle?" she mumbles. "You leaving?"

"I will be back, Lu." I hug her tiny figure and set her on the ground. "Maybe next time I come to visit, I'll bring Birdy with me. Would you like that?"

When she nods, I turn and open the front door. Mikey and my father walk outside. We move down the debris-strewn driveway to our transportation. It doesn't matter what I have to do. I will bring my brother home.

Fog drifts aimlessly across the deserted parking lot. Weeds sprout from cracks in the pavement. The once manicured flowerbeds of the shopping center have been converted into gravesites, all filled with corpses. This was my hometown. I used to buy food from the grocer down the street, take Benji to this complex to purchase his school clothes. Everything has conformed to the brutality of this world, morphed into a dark and deadly place. Civilization has crumbled all because one man had the desire to perfect humankind, strip away our weakness and create beings without inadequacies. Without weakness, we are susceptible to the worst disease—arrogance.

I strap my motorcycle to the back of the helicopter, inspecting the turbines and fuel capsules. Mikey sits in the cockpit, encoding a flight plan into the navigation system and hacking the concentration camp's database. My father paces around us with a rifle clutched to his torso. He scans our surroundings warily, flinching at the slightest sound.

"We're safe." I smirk when he aims his gun at a squawking Blue-Jay. "Though it may come as a surprise, this area is considered a Safe Zone."

"I'm sorry. I haven't been out of the house in weeks," he admits. An inexperienced, tagalong adult is the last person I'd want joining this endeavor; but he's my dad. How could I have said no?

I sigh and fasten my suit of armor over my clothing, tying my sword to my belt. "Climb into the backseat. We should be able to fit Harry and his wife in the cargo hold."

"I found them!" Mikey shouts. "They are in the camp, barracks four and nine."

"We have a destination."

A frigid breeze blows from the east, lifting the complex's inert American flag into motion. I watch it sway at the top of its post, a tattered banner of red, white, and blue. The sight causes a nuance of doubt to creep into my thoughts. This country will never be the same. It's been reconfigured, forced to adapt to its alien invaders. In a way, I find the irony humorous. What was originally created to protect this nation has taken on its secondary purpose, become the virus Prime Way developed. It seems that even though my army split from the enemy, we continue to be our home's downfall.

"You're in restricted area!" a voice shouts from behind me. "What is your identification number?! Who gave you clearance to park your aircraft in my Sector?!"

"Number 1026. I have been issued high level clearance by President Marner." I glance over my shoulder at a squad of Legionaries—Dallas' home-troops. When they see my face, their eyes widen and they hastily lower their guns.

"Legion…" The division's leader fumbles for words. He quickly removes his helmet and stares at me with panic. I recognize his face immediately—black hair, beady eyes. He's the bully who terrorized me throughout high school —quarterback, Ron Thatcher.

"My apologies. Your plane's serial number wasn't registered in our database," he says without pausing for a breath. "We've been doing our absolute best to keep the perimeter secured. I have soldiers guarding your old house every day and night."

I nod, trying to muster enough courage to show forgiveness to my old enemy. Ron has become a Legionary. He is part of my family. The past is gone, erased. A good leader recognizes the abilities of others, demonstrates grace. It's what I must do.

"I'm in need of more soldiers. Contact outpost-bronze and tell them I wish to have your division promoted from home-troops to active-officers. Report to the Prime Way facility in two days if you want the position. You're doing a great job, Ron. Keep up the good work."

His jaw drops in shock as I finish inspecting my helicopter. "Uh…thank you."

I climb behind the plane's controls and prepare for flight. My hands slide across the dashboard, powering the craft. Moments later, the three of us are soaring above Texas.

Sunlight burns away the dark setting, replacing the morbid decay of my hometown with golden rays and cumulous clouds. I sit back in my chair and gaze at the scene, finally able to breathe. For so long I've been consumed with death. It thrives around me, growing and spreading until it suffocated every ounce of existing life, including mine. Up here, there is no death or darkness. Maybe it's because men can't touch these heights. It seems that God himself has set limits to our destructive power.

I adjust my headset and activate the transmitter. "Legion contacting outpost-bronze. Is the Blue-Jay on this frequency?"

Her voice answers quicker than I'm expecting. "Took you long enough, Kyle. I was beginning to worry. Is something wrong? You're not in Dallas anymore, are you?"

"No, I'm headed to Oklahoma to find my older brother. He went missing when the war started. Don't worry. Mikey and I will be careful," I tell her with a hint of sarcasm. "Are you tracking me?"

"It's my job, remember? Besides rallying our troops for battle, I am currently working in the control center to monitor your flight, make sure you stay safe. Believe me. I'm not one of those protective, OCD girlfriends who tracks their boyfriend to keep tabs on him. Don't take this the wrong way but…I'm not exactly worried about you cheating."

"Fair enough," I laugh. "Maybe I should be keeping tabs on you."

"That was hurtful," she scoffs. "Know one thing, Kyle Chase. I could *never* love anyone as much as I love you. Remember that when you're surrounded by beautiful, weeping women in need of assistance. I'll be here waiting…also in need of assistance. This Legion-stuff is definitely harder than it looks! I've been contacting divisions all morning, video chatting with President Marner and taking inventory of our supplies. I want you to come *home*!"

"Are you talking to Cora?" my father asks from the backseat.

"That didn't sound like Mikey. Who's with you?"

"My dad," I answer. "He wanted to tagalong."

"That's great. He needs to see how amazing you are." She grows quiet. "…I better go. Byron wants to discuss travel preparations. I'll talk to you later, Kyle."

"Goodbye," I whisper as the call ends. My eyes focus on the photograph attached to the windshield, then sinks down to where my necklace hangs inside the dashboard. I smile. "We'll be in Oklahoma within the hour. Tighten your restraints. This might be a bumpy ride."

The silence permits my thoughts to wander. I think of Cora, Prime Way, life before responsibilities and my role as Legion. Memories swarm my brain.

> *I kneel beside my dying trainer, staring aghast at the puddle of blood beneath his body. He saved my life. He chose courage*

over bravery, honor instead of selfishness. No one has ever cared for me enough to pay such a price for my survival. "I'm sorry, Yuzek."

"Don't be, old friend." He shakes his head slowly. "In life, there are many paths which we can take. Some lead to death and destruction, while others lead to a better future. Have courage to take the right path. You have a lot in store for you." His breathing grows shallow. His chest rises and falls at an unnatural pace. "Promise me that you'll make a difference. We only have one life to be something worth remembering." He places his hand on my chest. "You have a good heart. I'm proud of you."

"I promise."

The man smiles. His eyes begin to close. "None of this happened by accident. Prime Way was meant to prepare you for the coming darkness. What lies ahead will not be pleasant. You'll be forced to do hard things, face death and sacrifice. I believe in the impossible odds. I believe in you..."

Before another word can be said, his heart stops. On the deck of the Destroyer, beneath torrents of freezing rain, my mentor dies.

Mikey babbles repetitively. My father points to different icons on the aircraft's dashboard, asking questions and prodding futuristic devices. I block their voices from my thoughts. My fingers ease against the plating of my armor, touching the indention in my chest. Yuzek's last words repeat in my head. Somehow he knew this war was approaching. He knew what I'd become. How could a man bear knowledge of the future? What secrets did he keep from me?

I adjust the helicopter's speed and deactivate cruise control. My right hand grips the joystick, shifting the plane a few degrees to the east. Pain pierces through my sternum. The discomfort unearths traumatic memories of the past, reminds me of my possible death.

Programming sears through my veins. Buzzing trembles through my ear-canals. I attack, slamming my fist into Deven's stomach with so much force, the impact throws him backwards. He lunges, gripping my neck. I gasp for breath and knee him in the stomach. Stumbling across the deck, I grab the knife protruding from Yuzek's torso and slice Deven's cheeks. Before I can kill him, he pops my wrists out of socket and knocks me to the ground. I drop the knife.

Deven removes his gun. "Keep your eyes open, Kyle. I'd hate for you to miss the sight of blood gushing from Cora's chest, her agonizing scream as I suck the life from her body." He laughs and aims his weapon at the girl with the braid. "Goodbye, Sweetheart..."

Panic and adrenaline numbs my discomfort. I leap from the ground and shield Cora as Deven pulls the trigger. I feel the impact immediately, a sharp and intense pain slicing through my chest. Cora screams, gazing in shock at the hole in my heart. I stare at her and fall to my knees.

"A little out of order, but I'm flexible." Deven shrugs, preparing to shoot the girl I've grown to love. No, he can't have her. I'll kill him before I allow lead to enter Cora's body.

I rise and attack my enemy with newfound intensity. He looks at me with terror as I rip the pistol from his grasp and fling it over the ship's rail. Without hesitance, I batter him with punches. A blow to the head causes Deven to lose his balance. He tumbles over the edge of the boat and into the tumultuous waves. I watch him vanish, feeling a mixture of relief and regret. Deven Lukes is dead.

I inch backwards and collapse onto the steel floor. I clutch my wound. Blood soaks my clothing, dripping off my skin and onto the ground. Cora leans over my dying body with tears spilling from her eyes. She combs her hands through my wet hair.

"Why'd you do that?!" She sobs, shielding me from the rain. "That bullet was meant for me! We're both going to die anyways. Why would you want that extra pain?"

"You're someone worth dying for," I answer. It's a struggle to breathe. My body shakes uncontrollably. "It won't matter in a few moments whether I'm dead or alive. Go! Get out of here. You're a strong swimmer. You can live."

"I'm not leaving you." She removes her shirt and gently presses the fabric to my chest. "Stay with me, Kyle. Everything's

going to be alright." Her head rests on my chest. "Don't leave
me. Please. I need you. I can't face this alone."

The Destroyer shutters. A blast erupts from below. Our time
has run out. We're going to die.

"I love you," she whispers as an orange cloud explodes from
behind. Flames lap at the air above us. The heat singes our flesh.
She places her hands on my cheeks and leans close to me. The
last thing I remember is the brush of Cora's lips against mine as
we are sucked into the inferno.

Mikey shakes my shoulder, drawing me from my reverie. "What's
wrong with you, Kyle? You blanked out for a moment. Is everything
okay?"

I nod and force a smile. "Yeah, I was just thinking."

"Make sure you keep your eyes on the horizon." He sinks back into
his seat and continues a conversation with my dad.

I'm done with talking, wasting my time behind computer screens and
memories. The heat of battle is approaching and my family must remain
safe. The Titan has countless tricks up his sleeve. He'll be coming to kill
me and my soldiers. I refuse to be unprepared.

"Dad, rescuing Harry might get a bit messy. I want you and Mikey to
stay at the portable command center, which we'll set up in the ruins
surrounding the city. You'll be safe."

"I don't want to be safe, Kyle. I want to fight the people who took my
son. I want to watch their prison blow to pieces!"

"Kyle will wear a video camera," Mikey adds. "You can watch him in
action. Everything he sees, you'll see. That way, you will stay safe and
still experience the mission. We can help rescue Harry from a distance,
Mr. Chase."

"Are you sure you can do this alone?" my father asks me. His brow
furrows and his lips form a straight line. He doesn't know what I'm
capable of doing.

"Yes. This has been my job for the past year-and-a-half. It's what I've
been trained to do," I tell him. "We'll piece our family back together. I
promise."

The flight passes without incident. I land the aircraft in a field a few
miles north of the concentration camp, help Mikey set up a command
center in an old farmhouse, and prepare for infiltration. The landscape is

overgrown. Grass and vines consume buildings. Civilization lies in ruins, demolished as if multiple tornados swept through Oklahoma. Sometimes I forget that the world didn't always appear this way, that cities were once filled with people and bustle. If we're surrounded by darkness long enough, we become blinded to the light.

I inhale deeply as Mikey fastens a small video camera to my chest plate. Gloves are strapped. Armor is secured. Motorcycle is refueled. I exhale and fit a pair of earbuds beneath the thick exterior of my helmet, blasting rock music. Preparations have begun.

"Your backpack is full of explosives. Blow them to smithereens," Mikey instructs.

My dad embraces me awkwardly and pats my oversized shoulder. He musters a grateful smile and says four words I'll never forget. "I forgive you, son." His clemency lightens the burdens weighing on my thoughts. It's the only thing I need to keep fighting.

I nod and walk onto the rickety front porch, shaking the emotion and personal worries from my brain. Doubt is immediately drowned in adrenaline. I unsheathe my sword and move with long strides to the parked motorcycle. Engine cranks. Exhaust rumbles from the tailpipe. I climb onto my bike, turn up the music blasting through my ear-canals, and clutch the gas. Time to fight.

Hollow high rises surround me. The effervescence of lost life radiates from derelict structures and ivy curtained newsstands. All that remains is a grisly visage, a vestigial knowledge of a civilization long gone. The world has been distilled, transformed into an absolute maw of mangled memories. Wind whistles through the skeletal ruins, a voice on the verge of breaking. Abandoned cars scatter the roadside. This wasn't the future anyone expected, to be destroyed by their own creations. They wanted perfection. They wanted safety; that sugary dream of all of our childhoods, now a tasteless joke. The irony is almost laughable!

As I crest the summit of a dilapidated overpass, I lift my head and allow the scorching sunlight to blaze red through my eyelids, saturating my brain. When I was a kid, I used to stare at the sun out of curiosity. But now I'm older, wiser, gunning a motorcycle down a forgotten boulevard.

"I'll be home soon, Cora." Her name rolls off my tongue like honey. I feel good just saying it. She is so unbearably beautiful and sometimes I see a future with her in my head—a happy life spent together in a fixed world. She's my family and I love her, *forever and always*.

The next half-hour comes as a montage—explosions, wind beating against my armored chest, sirens and shouts. It's all déjà vu, a routine activity like attending school or eating cereal for breakfast. I can almost say that I'm getting bored with easy battles. The Centurions don't even seem to put up a fight anymore. By the time I burst through the gates of the concentration camp, I've killed half of the guards. My glitches have become reflexes, untamed and precise. It's all beginning to annoy me.

An enticing beat echoes through my helmet, the clang of symbols and pounding of drums. Electric guitars squeal as I swerve my bike to a rapid halt. Dust forms a smoke shield as I clutch my rifle to my chest, slide off the motorcycle with poignant confidence, and throw grenades into the approaching masses of soldiers. Blue fire ignites the frigid air. Energy slashes through the camp, emitting a discharge that shatters every glass window. I shoot my nuclear-powered gun and slay the enemy with my radioactive sword. Ash and gore shower my armor. It's all routine.

Lyrics scream into my ears. An instrumental solo plays through my movements like theme music, fueling unmatchable strength and motivation. I leap off buildings; twisting and rolling, stabbing and snapping. My limbs strike in slow motion. I grab the Titan's troops and throw them into the electric, barbwire fence encircling the perimeter, twenty-feet off the ground.

Charges detonate, blowing apart the barrier separating freedom from captivity. Flames billow out of watchtowers and soldier housing, the smoke severing daylight. I kick in the doors of prisoner barracks and free the starving men and women locked in torture chambers.

"Get out!" I yell harshly at the hesitant captives. They gather their families and rush out of the camp, setting rebellious fire to the Titan's facility.

Sweat soaks my underclothes. Pain aches through my torso. I fight relentlessly towards my brother's confines, spearing Elite and catapulting young recruits. Gaunt people sprint past me. Some stop and weep with gratitude. Others cast me appreciative glances. Their reactions are predicted. I can almost mimic each overjoyed whimper and sincere "thank you". Saving lives doesn't make me a hero, does it? I don't feel like a hero, more like an abnormal teenage boy pretending to be an adult.

Music continues to block the chaos from reaching my ears. I dart down a smoky alleyway and squeeze myself through a stampeding crowd of prisoners. The breeze is fetid. I grimace at the smell of decaying flesh and dysentery, remembering what I had been taught in high school about concentration camps. We've allowed history to repeat itself. By forgetting our past, we've tumbled into a relapse.

"Harry!" I shout franticly, ducking in and out of barracks and strategically placing explosives throughout the facility. Soldiers lunge at me but I force them to their knees.

As I round a corner, I catch sight of him slipping out of his confine— tall and tattooed with brown hair and my mother's green eyes. He looks at me in shock, pale-faced and immovable; his body underweight and cheeks sunken. A woman clings fearfully to his left arm. She's in her early twenties, blonde and petite—my sister-in-law.

"You're huge," he scoffs coyly as I jog towards him. "I didn't think I'd ever see you again. So much has happened..." He hesitates before embracing me.

"I'm glad you're okay. Dad and Mom are worried sick."

"I bet they are." He musters a nervous smile and motions to his wife. "Kyle, this is Beatrice. We were married last year. Thanks for...paying for our wedding."

"We owe you," she adds with sincerity. Her weary eyes gaze at me with awe.

"How long have you been here?"

"A few months," my brother answers. "We were living in the suburbs when the Regiment invaded."

"Do they know you're my brother?"

"They have no idea. When Beatrice and I were married, Charles Truman encouraged me to take on her last name to ensure both your and our safety."

Explosions shake the earth. Fire spreads through the camp, burning away all traces of hell. Soldiers scramble through the ruins, desperately trying to salvage supplies from the raging inferno. I glance at my wristwatch. It's time to go.

"Help me gather the remaining survivors. We're leaving," I say and hand Harry my rifle. "Meet me at the main gate in exactly five-minutes. I'll be waiting."

Smoke and dust stings my lungs as I sprint away from my brother and into the fiery tangle of streets. I slam my body against a barred doorway, stumbling into the burning building. Soot blinds me as I search the space for innocent captives. Embers rain onto my back, singing my neck with searing heat. I shout and stumble wearily through the charred corridors, glancing beneath rotting bunks and behind wall panels. Panic pours into my kaleidoscope of emotions, mixing with my anxiety and adrenaline. I can't let any more people die. I must protect them!

As if on cue, a set of arms wrap around my waist and a head presses against my spine. I turn to face three young children, all bony and covered with radiation-boils. They sob as the ceiling gives way, curtaining us with glowing coals. If we don't escape now, we will all die.

"Hold onto me!" I yell over the roar of flames and lift the minors into my arms. A boy hangs off my back. One girl clings to my shoulder and the other sits limply against my chest. "We're going to be okay!" I kick my way through the hellish ruins, remembering the day I carried Jonah out of a fire. He died and there was nothing I could've done to save him. I won't allow that to happen again.

With a final shove, the four of us burst out of the barracks and into blinding sunlight. I cough the ashen debris from my body and set the children on their feet. Immediately they join the mob of escaping prisoners, rushing towards the tear in the electric fence. It doesn't matter how many times I tell myself that quitting my role as Legion is cowardice and will emit little comfort, the deceiving cogs of cogency still spin. I'll never be courageous enough to be truly selfless.

"Run! Go! Get out of here!" I shout as I move towards my parked motorcycle. Masses swarm past me like a flock of fleeing birds, soaring out of their cage. In a matter of minutes, the concentration camp's occupants have been evacuated. All that remains are the Titan's brainwashed servants, and I care little for their well-being.

I kill a guard preparing to open fire and climb onto my bike. With a flick of my wrist, the engine rumbles to life. I spot my brother and his wife at the gate's threshold. They look at me gratefully before exiting the facility. After the last civilian has crossed the perimeter, I lurch my motorcycle into motion.

Countdown begins and everything slows. I'm racing towards the fence with blood and sweat oozing from my pores. I am weightless, focused, my programming intensified. Buzzing fills my ears. Testosterone vibrates through my veins, bulking every muscle. The gust of inhuman strength works like a drug, stifling my doubts with genetically-altered confidence. My blood has been transformed into a weapon. It's a gift, and like all gifts, mine comes with a choice. I can either use these abilities for evil, to satisfy my own selfish cravings, or I can harness them to help others. I've made my decision.

All at once the nuclear-explosives detonate and I am no longer racing—I am flying.

The blast demolishes every structure and living being within the camp, wiping away Deven's sin in a single cloud of swirling heat and bumbling fire. I feel the impact wash across the earth and look ahead at the teary-eyed survivors. They stop running and turn to stare at the growing pillar of flaming wrath. No more torture, fear, or starvation. They're safe.

I slow my motorcycle to a stop, facing the crowd with calm authority. "It's over. You're free," I state with empathetic charisma. "I understand that many of you are confused, lost. You've been in that camp since the war began and have no idea where to go next. Your families are missing, your homes are gone, and everything you once knew as reality has been…destroyed. I *understand* and I *want* to help. There's an outpost not too far from here where you will be safe; but if you'd rather stay in Oklahoma City and brave the current situation on your own, I won't protest. Form caravans if you wish to travel or colonies if you're set on staying in an unprotected region. Safety is in numbers. The Titan may have stolen a year of your life, killed and tortured your family and friends, but you're alive. Survival is of dire *importance*. After this war has ended, we'll need to rebuild and start over. The blackboard has been erased. It'll be up to us to rewrite the equation. So take care of each other, be kind and neighborly, and never forget that you are our nation's future. I believe in the impossible odds."

The masses disperse slowly, overwhelming me with unneeded words of praise and pats on the back. I've never liked attention. Can't I do something good without receiving notice? I prefer invisibility, flying under the radar. It's who I am, who I was created to be. Is it possible to be an invisible leader?

"That was impressive, little brother. You've certainly…changed,"

Harry tells me. He and Beatrice emerge from the mob of refugees. Their presence is foreign, like a pair of strangers. I don't know my family anymore. I've become someone new, different, a Legionary lookalike of the old Kyle Chase. It's okay that I'll never belong in Dallas. I know where I belong. That single nuance of understanding is enough to satisfy my longing.

"Let's get you home," I say with a sincere half-smile.

Moments later, the five of us are soaring above the tumultuous west, drifting among silver clouds in a machine that exceeds its age in time. My dad, brother, and sister-in-law are crammed in the cargo hold, all laughing and clinging gratefully to one another. I fixed what I destroyed—I pieced my family back together. The simple deed emits more peace than I've experienced in the past two-years, finally giving me closure. I can move on with my life. For the first time in months, my focus has a single target.

"You did a good thing," Mikey whispers as I move illuminated icons across the holographic dashboard. "Your father is actually *proud* of who you are."

"I'm just glad they're all safe."

The plane's transmitter flashes with an incoming call. I activate cruise control and adjust my headset, flipping multiple switches to gain access to the military frequency. Cora's voice meets my ears like classical music, a harmonic chorus of antonyms and an illustrious orchestra of syllables.

I grin out of habit. "Cora, you called at a perfect time! Harry and his wife have been rescued, Deven's concentration camp is destroyed, and its prisoners are free. We're headed to Dallas now…"

"Kyle."

"My family will be transferred to the outpost by nightfall. I'll help them unpack and…"

"Kyle."

"They'll be happy there, I know. Our soldiers will keep them safe…"

"Kyle, shut up for one moment and listen to me!" she snaps harshly. Her voice is tense and strained, like a guitar string on the verge of snapping. She inhales deeply to regain her composure. "We have a problem and…I need you to come home now."

"What's happened?"

"Callan is sick. His brainstem is shutting down. He's dying and…I know Deven is causing it to happen, even though we all thought Cal was immune to the technology. We're being attacked like you predicted. In a few days, we could all be thoughtless or dead."

I can't breathe or speak. My heart stops. The Titan's mind control technology wasn't destroyed in the explosions. We are still targets, his soon to be puppets. The realization is suffocating. I fumble for a response. "Cora, are *you* okay? Have you had Sarah check your vitals?"

"Everyone, including me, is fine at the moment. James is working to find a way to alter our genetic-codes to make it more difficult for the Regiment to hack into our brains. The strike at Callan was just a warning. Deven said…"

"Wait, you've already talked with him!"

"He requested a video conference a few hours ago. We talked inside Prime Way's simulation-chamber. Somehow he was able to hack into the computer system and simulate an actual meeting…"

"What does he want?"

She pauses. "He wants to play a game."

ABOUT THE AUTHOR

Caroline George's life-long love of literature and science-fiction inspired her to write her debut series, *The Prime Way Program*. With the overwhelming support of her family and Literature professor, she began pursuing her goal of becoming a bestselling author.

Caroline lives in Georgia, where the diverse terrain and city-life feed her visions for *The Prime Way Trilogy*. She spends most of her time writing novels, playing guitar, and spreading her passion for young-authors throughout her community.

"Age shouldn't limit a person from pursuing their dreams. If they're willing to fight for what they love, the opportunities are endless".

You can find out more about Caroline and *The Prime Way Trilogy* at www.theprimewayprogram.com.

19166614R00170